MW00508868

Anthony Trollope

Framley Parsonage

Vol. II

Anthony Trollope

Framley Parsonage

Vol. II

Reprint of the original, first published in 1861.

1st Edition 2022 | ISBN: 978-3-37505-437-3

Verlag (Publisher): Salzwasser Verlag GmbH, Zeilweg 44, 60439 Frankfurt, Deutschland
Vertretungsberechtigt (Authorized to represent): E. Roepke, Zeilweg 44, 60439 Frankfurt, Deutschland
Druck (Print): Books on Demand GmbH, In de Tarpen 42, 22848 Norderstedt, Deutschland

FRAMLEY PARSONAGE.

BY

ANTHONY TROLLOPE,

AUTHOR OF "BARCHESTER TOWERS," ETC. ETC.

COPYRIGHT EDITION.

IN TWO VOLUMES.

VOL. II.

LEIPZIG

BERNHARD TAUCHNITZ

1861.

CONTENTS

OF VOLUME II.

FRAMLEY PARSONAGE.

CHAPTER I.

Non-Impulsive.

It cannot be held as astonishing, that that last decision on the part of the giants in the matter of the two bishoprics should have disgusted Archdeacon Grantly. He was a politician, but not a politician as they were. As is the case with all exoteric men, his political eyes saw a short way only, and his political aspirations were as limited. When his friends came into office, that bishop bill, which as the original product of his enemies had been regarded by him as being so pernicious — for was it not about to be made law in order that other Proudies and such like might be hoisted up into high places and large incomes, to the terrible detriment of the Church? — that bishop bill, I say, in the hands of his friends, had appeared to him to be a means of almost national salvation. And then, how great had been the good fortune of the giants in this matter! Had they been the originators of such a measure they would not have had a chance of success; but now — now that the two bishops were falling into their mouths out of the weak hands of the gods, was not their success ensured? So Dr. Grantly had girded up his loins and marched up to the fight, almost regretting that the triumph would be so easy. The subsequent failure was very trying to his temper as a party man.

It always strikes me that the supporters of the Titans are in this respect much to be pitied. The giants themselves, those who are actually handling Pelion and breaking their shins over the lower rocks of Ossa, are always advancing in some sort towards the councils of Olympus. Their highest policy is to snatch some ray from heaven. Why else put Pelion on Ossa, unless it be that a furtive hand, making its way through Jove's windows, may pluck forth a thunder bolt or two, or some article less destructive, but of manufacture equally divine? And in this consists the wisdom of the higher giants — that, in spite of their mundane antecedents, theories, and predilections, they can see that articles of divine manufacture are necessary. But then they never carry their supporters with them. Their whole army is an army of martyrs. "For twenty years I have stuck to them, and see how they have treated me!" Is not that always the plaint of an old giant-slave? "I have been true to my party all my life, and where am I now?" he says. Where, indeed, my friend? Looking about you, you begin to learn that you cannot describe your whereabouts. I do not marvel at that. No one finds himself planted at last in so terribly foul a morass, as he would fain stand still for ever on dry ground.

Dr. Grantly was disgusted; and although he was himself too true and thorough in all his feelings, to be able to say aloud that any giant was wrong, still he had a sad feeling within his heart that the world was sinking from under him. He was still sufficiently exoteric to think that a good stand-up fight in a good cause was a good thing. No doubt he did wish to be

Bishop of Westminster, and was anxious to compass that preferment by any means that might appear to him to be fair. And why not? But this was not the end of his aspirations. He wished that the giants might prevail in everything, in bishoprics as in all other matters; and he could not understand that they should give way on the very first appearance of a skirmish. In his open talk he was loud against many a god; but in his heart of hearts he was bitter enough against both Porphyrion and Orion.

"My dear doctor, it would not do; — not in this session; it would not indeed." So had spoken to him a half-fledged, but especially esoteric young monster-cub at the Treasury, who considered himself as up to all the dodges of his party, and regarded the army of martyrs who supported it as a rather heavy, but very useful collection of fogeys. Dr. Grantly had not cared to discuss the matter with the half-fledged monster-cub. The best licked of all the monsters, the giant most like a god of them all, had said a word or two to him; and he also had said a word or two to that giant. Porphyrion had told him that the bishop bill would not do; and he, in return, speaking with warm face, and blood in his cheeks, had told Porphyrion, that he saw no reason why the bill should not do. The courteous giant had smiled as he shook his ponderous head, and then the archdeacon had left him, unconsciously shaking some dust from his shoes, as he paced the passages of the Treasury chambers for the last time. As he walked back to his lodgings in Mount Street, many thoughts, not altogether bad in their nature, passed through his mind. Why should he trouble himself about a bishopric? Was he not well as he was, in his rectory down at Plumstead? Might it not be ill for him at his age to transplant himself into new soil, to engage in new duties, and live among new people? Was he not useful at Barchester, and respected also; and might it not be possible, that up there at Westminster, he might be regarded merely as a tool with which other men could work? He had not quite liked the tone of that specially esoteric young monster-cub, who had clearly regarded him as a distinguished fogey from the army of martyrs. He would take his wife back to Barsetshire, and there live contented with the good things which Providence had given him.

Those high political grapes had become sour, my sneering friends will say. Well? Is it not a good thing that grapes should become sour which hang out of reach? Is he not wise who can regard all grapes as sour which are manifestly too high for his hand? Those grapes of the Treasury bench, for which gods and giants fight, suffering so much when they are forced to abstain from eating, and so much more when they do eat, — those grapes are very sour to me. I am sure that they are indigestible, and that those who eat them undergo all the ills which the Revalenta Arabica is prepared to cure. And so it was now with the archdeacon. He thought of the strain which would have been put on his conscience had he come up there to sit in London as Bishop of Westminster; and in this frame of mind he walked home to his wife.

During the first few moments of his interview with her all his regrets had come back upon him. Indeed, it would have hardly suited for him then to have preached this new doctrine of rural contentment. The wife of his bosom, whom he so fully trusted — had so fully loved — wished for grapes that hung high upon the wall, and he knew that it was past his power to teach her at the moment to drop her ambition. Any teaching that he might effect in that way, must come by degrees. But before many minutes were over he had told her of her fate and of his own decision. "So we had better go back to Plumstead," he said; and she had not dissented.

"I am sorry for poor Griselda's sake," Mrs. Grantly had remarked later in the evening, when they were again together.

"But I thought she was to remain with Lady Lufton."

"Well; so she will, for a little time. There is no one with whom I would so soon trust her out of my own care as with Lady Lufton. She is all that one can desire."

"Exactly; and as far as Griselda is concerned I cannot say that I think she is to be pitied."

"Not to be pitied, perhaps," said Mrs. Grantly. "But, you see, archdeacon, Lady Lufton, of course, has her own views."

"Her own views?"

"It is hardly any secret that she is very anxious to make a match between Lord Lufton and Griselda. And though that might be a very proper arrangement if it were fixed—"

"Lord Lufton marry Griselda!" said the archdeacon, speaking quick and raising his eyebrows. His mind had as yet been troubled by but few thoughts respecting his child's future establishment. "I had never dreamt of such a thing."

"But other people have done more than dream of

it, archdeacon. As regards the match itself, it would, I think, be unobjectionable. Lord Lufton will not be a very rich man, but his property is respectable, and as far as I can learn his character is on the whole good. If they like each other, I should be contented with such a marriage. But, I must own, I am not quite satisfied at the idea of leaving her all alone with Lady Lufton. People will look on it as a settled thing, when it is not settled — and very probably may not be settled; and that will do the poor girl harm. She is very much admired; there can be no doubt of that; and Lord Dumbello—"

The archdeacon opened his eyes still wider. He had had no idea that such a choice of sons-in-law was being prepared for him; and, to tell the truth, was almost bewildered by the height of his wife's ambition. Lord Lufton, with his barony and twenty thousand a year, might be accepted as just good enough; but failing him there was an embryo marquis, whose fortune would be more than ten times as great, all ready to accept his child! And then he thought, as husbands sometimes will think, of Susan Harding as she was when he had gone a-courting to her under the elms before the house in the warden's garden at Barchester, and of dear old Mr. Harding, his wife's father, who still lived in humble lodgings in that city; and as he thought, he wondered at and admired the greatness of that lady's mind.

"I never can forgive Lord De Terrier," said the lady, connecting various points together in her own mind.

"That's nonsense," said the archdeacon. "You must forgive him."

"And I must confess that it annoys me to leave London at present."

"It can't be helped," said the archdeacon, somewhat gruffly; for he was a man who, on certain points, chose to have his own way — and had it.

"Oh, no; I know it can't be helped," said Mrs. Grantly, in a tone which implied a deep injury. "I know it can't be helped. Poor Griselda!" And then they went to bed.

On the next morning Griselda came to her, and in an interview that was strictly private, her mother said more to her than she had ever yet spoken, as to the prospects of her future life. Hitherto, on this subject, Mrs. Grantly had said little or nothing. She would have been well pleased that her daughter should have received the incense of Lord Lufton's vows — or, perhaps, as well pleased had it been the incense of Lord Dumbello's vows — without any interference on her part. In such case her child, she knew, would have told her with quite sufficient eagerness, and the matter in either case would have been arranged as a very pretty love match. She had no fear of any impropriety or of any rashness on Griselda's part. She had thoroughly known her daughter when she boasted that Griselda would never indulge in an unauthorized passion. But as matters now stood, with those two strings to her bow, and with that Lufton-Grantly alliance treaty in existence — of which she, Griselda herself, knew nothing — might it not be possible that the poor child should stumble through want of adequate direction? Guided by these thoughts, Mrs. Grantly had resolved to say a few words before she left London. So she wrote a line to her daughter, and Griselda reached Mount Street at two o'clock in Lady Lufton's carriage, which, during the interview, waited for her at the beer-shop round the corner.

"And papa won't be Bishop of Westminster?" said the young lady, when the doings of the giants had been sufficiently explained to make her understand that all those hopes were over.

"No, my dear; at any rate not now."

"What a shame! I thought it was all settled. What's the good, mamma, of Lord De Terrier being prime minister, if he can't make whom he likes a bishop?"

"I don't think that Lord De Terrier has behaved at all well to your father. However that's a long question, and we can't go into it now."

"How glad those Proudies will be!"

Griselda would have talked by the hour on this subject had her mother allowed her, but it was necessary that Mrs. Grantly should go to other matters. She began about Lady Lufton, saying what a dear woman her ladyship was; and then went on to say that Griselda was to remain in London as long as it suited her friend and hostess to stay there with her; but added, that this might probably not be very long, as it was notorious that Lady Lufton, when in London, was always in a hurry to get back to Framley.

"But I don't think she is in such a hurry this year, mamma," said Griselda, who in the month of May preferred Bruton Street to Plumstead, and had no objection whatever to the coronet on the panels of Lady Lufton's coach.

And then Mrs. Grantly commenced her explanation — very cautiously. "No, my dear, I daresay she is not in such a hurry this year, — that is, as long as you remain with her."

"I am sure she is very kind."

"She is very kind, and you ought to love her very much. I know I do. I have no friend in the world for whom I have a greater regard than for Lady Lufton. It is that which makes me so happy to leave you with her."

"All the same I wish that you and papa had remained up; that is, if they had made papa a bishop."

"It's no good thinking of that now, my dear. What I particularly wanted to say to you was this: I think you should know what are the ideas which Lady Lufton entertains."

"Her ideas!" said Griselda, who had never troubled herself much in thinking about other people's thoughts.

"Yes, Griselda. While you were staying down at Framley Court, and also, I suppose, since you have been up here in Bruton Street, you must have seen a good deal of — Lord Lufton."

"He doesn't come very often to Bruton Street, — that is to say, not *very* often."

"H-m," ejaculated Mrs. Grantly, very gently. She would willingly have repressed the sound altogether, but it had been too much for her. If she found reason to think that Lady Lufton was playing her false, she would immediately take her daughter away, break up the treaty, and prepare for the Hartletop alliance. Such were the thoughts that ran through her mind. But she knew all the while that Lady Lufton was not false. The fault was not with Lady Lufton; nor perhaps, altogether with Lord Lufton. Mrs. Grantly had understood the full force of the complaint which Lady

Lufton had made against her daughter; and though she had of course defended her child, and on the whole had defended her successfully, yet she confessed to herself that Griselda's chance of a first-rate establishment would be better if she were a little more impulsive. A man does not wish to marry a statue, let the statue be ever so statuesque. She could not teach her daughter to be impulsive, any more than she could teach her to be six feet high; but might it not be possible to teach her to seem so? The task was a very delicate one, even for a mother's hand.

"Of course he cannot be at home now as much as he was down in the country, when he was living in the same house," said Mrs. Grantly, whose business it was to take Lord Lufton's part at the present moment. "He must be at his club, and at the House of Lords, and in twenty places."

"He is very fond of going to parties, and he dances beautifully."

"I am sure he does. I have seen as much as that myself, and I think I know some one with whom he likes to dance." And the mother gave her daughter a loving little squeeze.

"Do you mean me, mamma?"

"Yes, I do mean you, my dear. And is it not true? Lady Lufton says that he likes dancing with you better than with any one else in London."

"I don't know," said Griselda, looking down upon the ground.

Mrs. Grantly thought that this upon the whole was rather a good opening. It might have been better. Some point of interest more serious in its nature than that of a waltz might have been found on which to connect her daughter's sympathies with those of her future husband. But any point of interest was better than none; and it is so difficult to find points of interest in persons who by their nature are not impulsive.

"Lady Lufton says so, at any rate," continued Mrs. Grantly, ever so cautiously. "She thinks that Lord Lufton likes no partner better. What do you think yourself, Griselda?"

"I don't know, mamma."

"But young ladies must think of such things, must they not?"

"Must they, mamma?"

"I suppose they do, don't they? The truth is, Griselda, that Lady Lufton thinks that if — Can you guess what it is she thinks?"

"No, mamma." But that was a fib on Griselda's part.

"She thinks that my Griselda would make the best possible wife in the world for her son; and I think so too. I think that her son will be a very fortunate man if he can get such a wife. And now what do you think, Griselda?"

"I don't think anything, mamma."

But that would not do. It was absolutely necessary that she should think, and absolutely necessary that her mother should tell her so. Such a degree of unimpulsiveness as this would lead to — heaven knows what results! Lufton-Grantly treaties and Hartletop interests would be all thrown away upon a young lady who would not think anything of a noble suitor sighing for her smiles. Besides, it was not natural. Griselda, as her mother knew, had never been a girl of headlong feeling; but still she had had her likes and her dislikes. In that matter of the bishopric she was keen enough; and no one could evince a deeper interest in the subject of a well-made new dress than Griselda Grantly. It was not possible that she should be indifferent as to her future prospects, and she must know that those prospects depended mainly on her marriage. Her mother was almost angry with her, but nevertheless she went on very gently:

"You don't think anything! But, my darling, you must think. You must make up your mind what would be your answer if Lord Lufton were to propose to you. That is what Lady Lufton wishes him to do."

"But he never will, mamma."

"And if he did?"

"But I'm sure he never will. He doesn't think of such a thing at all — and — and —"

"And what, my dear?"

"I don't know, mamma."

"Surely you can speak out to me, dearest! All I care about is your happiness. Both Lady Lufton and I think that it would be a happy marriage if you both cared for each other enough. She thinks that he is fond of you. But if he were ten times Lord Lufton I would not tease you about it if I thought that you could not learn to care about him. What was it you were going to say, my dear?"

"Lord Lufton thinks a great deal more of Lucy Robarts than he does of — of — of any one else, I believe," said Griselda, showing now some little animation by her manner, "dumpy little black thing that she is."

"Lucy Robarts!" said Mrs. Grantly, taken by surprise at finding that her daughter was moved by such a passion as jealousy, and feeling also perfectly assured that there could not be any possible ground for jealousy in such a direction as that. "Lucy Robarts, my dear! I don't suppose Lord Lufton ever thought of speaking to her, except in the way of civility."

"Yes, he did, mamma! Don't you remember at Framley?"

Mrs. Grantly began to look back in her mind, and she thought she did remember having once observed Lord Lufton talking in rather a confidential manner with the parson's sister. But she was sure that there was nothing in it. If that was the reason why Griselda was so cold to her proposed lover, it would be a thousand pities that it should not be removed.

"Now you mention her, I do remember the young lady," said Mrs. Grantly, "a dark girl, very low, and without much figure. She seemed to me to keep very much in the background."

"I don't know much about that, mamma."

"As far as I saw her, she did. But, my dear Griselda, you should not allow yourself to think of such a thing. Lord Lufton, of course, is bound to be civil to any young lady in his mother's house, and I am quite sure that he has no other idea whatever with regard to Miss Robarts. I certainly cannot speak as to her intellect, for I do not think she opened her mouth in my presence; but —"

"Oh! she has plenty to say for herself, when she pleases. She's a sly little thing."

"But, at any rate, my dear, she has no personal attractions whatever, and I do not at all think that Lord Lufton is a man to be taken by — by — by anything that Miss Robarts might do or say."

As those words "personal attractions" were uttered, Griselda managed so to turn her neck as to catch a side view of herself in one of the mirrors on the wall, and then she bridled herself up, and made a little play with her eyes, and looked, as her mother thought, very well. "It is all nothing to me, mamma, of course," she said.

"Well, my dear, perhaps not. I don't say that it is. I do not wish to put the slightest constraint upon your feelings. If I did not have the most thorough dependence on your good sense and high principles, I should not speak to you in this way. But as I have, I thought it best to tell you that both Lady Lufton and I should be well pleased if we thought that you and Lord Lufton were fond of each other."

"I am sure he never thinks of such a thing, mamma."

"And as for Lucy Robarts, pray get that idea out of your head; if not for your sake, then for his. You should give him credit for better taste."

But it was not so easy to take anything out of Griselda's head that she had once taken into it. "As for tastes, mamma, there is no accounting for them," she said; and then the colloquy on that subject was over. The result of it on Mrs. Grantly's mind was a feeling amounting almost to a conviction in favour of the Dumbello interest.

CHAPTER II.

Impulsive.

I TRUST my readers will all remember how Puck the pony was beaten during that drive to Hogglestock. It may be presumed that Puck himself on that occasion did not suffer much. His skin was not so soft as Mrs. Robarts' heart. The little beast was full of oats and all the good things of this world, and therefore, when the whip touched him, he would dance about and shake his little ears, and run on at a tremendous pace for twenty yards, making his mistress think that he had endured terrible things. But, in truth, during those whippings Puck was not the chief sufferer.

Lucy had been forced to declare — forced by the strength of her own feelings, and by the impossibility of assenting to the propriety of a marriage between Lord Lufton and Miss Grantly —, she had been forced to declare that she did care about Lord Lufton as much as though he were her brother. She had said all this to herself — nay, much more than this — very often. But now she had said it out loud to her sister-in-law; and she knew that what she had said was remembered, considered, and had, to a certain extent, become the cause of altered conduct. Fanny alluded very seldom to the Luftons in casual conversation, and never spoke about Lord Lufton, unless when her husband made it impossible that she should not speak of him. Lucy had attempted on more than one occasion to remedy this, by talking about the young lord in a laughing and, perhaps, half-jeering way; she had been sarcastic as to his hunting and shooting, and had boldly attempted to say a word in joke about his love for Griselda. But she felt that she had failed; that she had failed altogether as regarded Fanny; and that as to her brother, she would more probably be the means of opening his eyes, than have any effect in keeping them closed. So she gave up her efforts and spoke no further word about Lord Lufton. Her secret had been told, and she knew that it had been told.

At this time the two ladies were left a great deal alone together in the drawing-room at the parsonage; more, perhaps, than had ever yet been the case since Lucy had been there. Lady Lufton was away, and therefore the almost daily visit to Framley Court was not made; and Mark in these days was a great deal at Barchester, having, no doubt, very onerous duties to perform before he could be admitted as one of that chapter. He went into, what he was pleased to call residence, almost at once. That is, he took his month of preaching, aiding also in some slight and very dignified way, in the general Sunday morning services. He did not exactly live at Barchester, because the house was not ready. That at least was the assumed reason. The chattels of Dr. Stanhope, the late prebendary, had not been as yet removed, and there was likely to be some little delay, creditors asserting their right to them. This might have been very inconvenient to a gentleman anxiously expecting the excellent house which the liberality of past ages had provided for his use; but it was not so felt by Mr. Robarts. If Dr. Stanhope's family or creditors would keep the house for the next twelve months, he would be well pleased. And by this arrangement he was enabled to get through his first month of absence from the Church of Framley without any notice from Lady Lufton, seeing that Lady Lufton was in London all the time. This also was convenient, and taught our young prebendary to look on his new preferment more favourably than he had hitherto done.

Fanny and Lucy were thus left much alone: and as out of the full head the mouth speaks, so is the full heart more prone to speak at such periods of confidence as these. Lucy, when she first thought of her own state, determined to endow herself with a powerful gift of reticence. She would never tell her love, certainly; but neither would she let concealment feed on her damask cheek, nor would she ever be found for a moment sitting like Patience on a monument. She would fight her own fight bravely within her own bosom, and conquer her enemy altogether. She would either preach, or starve, or weary her love into subjection, and no one should be a bit the wiser. She would teach herself to shake hands with Lord Lufton without a quiver, and would be prepared to like his wife amazingly — unless indeed that wife should be Griselda Grantly. Such were her resolutions; but at the end of the first week they were broken into shivers and scattered to the winds.

They had been sitting in the house together the whole of one wet day; and as Mark was to dine in Barchester with the dean, they had had dinner early, eating with the children almost in their laps. It is so that ladies do, when their husbands leave them to themselves. It was getting dusk towards evening, and they were still sitting in the drawing-room, the children now having retired, when Mrs. Robarts for the fifth time since her visit to Hogglestock began to express her wish that she could do some good to the Crawleys, — to Grace Crawley in particular, who, standing up there at her father's elbow, learning Greek irregular verbs, had appeared to Mrs. Robarts to be an especial object of pity.

"I don't know how to set about it," said Mrs. Robarts.

Now any allusion to that visit to Hogglestock always drove Lucy's mind back to the consideration of the subject which had most occupied it at the time. She at such moments remembered how she had beaten Puck, and how in her half-bantering but still too serious manner she had apologized for doing so, and had explained the reason. And therefore she did not interest herself about Grace Crawley as vividly as she should have done.

"No; one never does," she said.

"I was thinking about it all that day as I drove home," said Fanny. "The difficulty is this: What can we do with her?"

"Exactly," said Lucy, remembering the very point of the road at which she had declared that she did like Lord Lufton very much.

"If we could have her here for a month or so and then send her to school; — but I know Mr. Crawley would not allow us to pay for her schooling."

"I don't think he would," said Lucy, with her thoughts far removed from Mr. Crawley and his daughter Grace.

"And then we should not know what to do with her; should we?"

"No; you would not."

"It would never do to have the poor girl about the house here, with no one to teach her anything. Mark would not teach her Greek verbs, you know."

"I suppose not."

"Lucy, you are not attending to a word I say to you, and I don't think you have for the last hour. I don't believe you know what I am talking about."

"Oh, yes, I do — Grace Crawley; I'll try and teach her if you like, only I don't know anything myself."

"That's not what I mean at all, and you know I would not ask you to take such a task as that on yourself. But I do think you might talk it over with me."

"Might I? very well; I will. What is it? oh, Grace Crawley — you want to know who is to teach her the irregular Greek verbs. Oh dear, Fanny, my head does ache so: pray don't be angry with me." And then Lucy throwing herself back on the sofa, put one hand up painfully to her forehead, and altogether gave up the battle.

Mrs. Robarts was by her side in a moment. "Dearest Lucy, what is it makes your head ache so often now? you used not to have those headaches."

"It's because I'm growing stupid: never mind. We will go on about poor Grace. It would not do to have a governess, would it?"

"I can see that you are not well, Lucy," said Mrs. Robarts, with a look of deep concern. "What is it, dearest? I can see that something is the matter."

"Something the matter! No, there's not; nothing

worth talking of. Sometimes I think I'll go back to Devonshire and live there. I could stay with Blanche for a time, and then get a lodging in Exeter."

"Go back to Devonshire!" and Mrs. Robarts looked as though she thought that her sister-in-law was going mad. "Why do you want to go away from us? This is to be your own, own home, always now."

"Is it? Then I am in a bad way. Oh dear, oh dear, what a fool I am! What an idiot I've been! Fanny, I don't think I can stay here; and I do so wish I'd never come. I do — I do — I do, though you look at me so horribly," and jumping up she threw herself into her sister-in-law's arms and began kissing her violently. "Don't pretend to be wounded, for you know that I love you. You know that I could live with you all my life, and think you were perfect — as you are; but —"

"Has Mark said anything?"

"Not a word, — not a ghost of a syllable. It is not Mark; oh, Fanny!"

"I am afraid I know what you mean," said Mrs. Robarts in a low tremulous voice, and with deep sorrow painted on her face.

"Of course you do; of course you know; you have known it all along; since that day in the pony carriage. I knew that you knew it. You do not dare to mention his name; would not that tell me that you know it? And I, I am hypocrite enough for Mark; but my hypocrisy won't pass muster before you. And, now, had I not better go to Devonshire?"

"Dearest, dearest Lucy."

"Was I not right about that labelling? O heavens! what idiots we girls are! That a dozen soft words should have bowled me over like a ninepin, and left me without an inch of ground to call my own. And I was so proud of my own strength; so sure that I should never be missish, and spoony, and sentimental! I was so determined to like him as Mark does, or you —"

"I shall not like him at all if he has spoken words to you that he should not have spoken."

"But he has not." And then she stopped a moment to consider. "No, he has not. He never said a word to me that would make you angry with him if you knew of it. Except, perhaps, that he called me Lucy; and that was my fault, not his."

"Because you talked of soft words."

"Fanny, you have no idea what an absolute fool I am, what an unutterable ass. The soft words of which I tell you were of the kind which he speaks to you when he asks you how the cow gets on which he sent you from Ireland, or to Mark about Ponto's shoulder. He told me that he knew papa, and that he was at school with Mark, and that as he was such good friends with you here at the parsonage, he must be good friends with me too. No; it has not been his fault. The soft words which did the mischief were such as those. But how well his mother understood the world! In order to have been safe, I should not have dared to look at him."

"But, dearest Lucy —"

"I know what you are going to say, and I admit it all. He is no hero. There is nothing on earth wonderful about him. I never heard him say a single word of wisdom, or utter a thought that was akin to poetry. He devotes all his energies to riding after a fox or killing poor birds, and I never heard of his doing a single great action in my life. And yet —"

Fanny was so astounded by the way her sister-in-law went on, that she hardly knew how to speak. "He is an excellent son, I believe," at last she said, —

"Except when he goes to Gatherum Castle. I'll tell you what he has: he has fine straight legs, and a smooth forehead, and a good-humoured eye, and white teeth. Was it possible to see such a catalogue of perfections, and not fall down, stricken to the very bone? But it was not that that did it all, Fanny. I could have stood against that. I think I could at least. It was his title that killed me. I had never spoken to a lord before. O me! what a fool, what a beast I have been!" And then she burst out into tears.

Mr. Robarts, to tell the truth, could hardly understand poor Lucy's ailment. It was evident enough that her misery was real; but yet she spoke of herself and her sufferings with so much irony, with so near an approach to joking, that it was very hard to tell how far she was in earnest. Lucy, too, was so much given to a species of badinage which Mrs. Robarts did not always quite understand, that the latter was afraid sometimes to speak out what came uppermost to her tongue. But now that Lucy was absolutely in tears, and was almost breathless with excitement, she could not remain silent any longer. "Dearest Lucy, pray do not speak in that way; it will all come right.

Things always do come right when no one has acted wrongly."

"Yes, when nobody has done wrongly. That's what papa used to call, begging the question. But I'll tell you what, Fanny; I will not be beaten. I will either kill myself or get through it. I am so heartily self-ashamed that I owe it to myself to fight the battle out."

"To fight what battle, dearest?"

"This battle. Here, now, at the present moment, I could not meet Lord Lufton. I should have to run like a scared fowl if he were to show himself within the gate; and I should not dare to go out of the house, if I knew that he was in the parish."

"I don't see that, for I am sure you have not betrayed yourself."

"Well, no; as for myself, I believe I have done the lying and the hypocrisy pretty well. But, dearest Fanny, you don't know half; and you cannot and must not know."

"But I thought you said there had been nothing whatever between you."

"Did I? Well, to you I have not said a word that was not true. I said that he had spoken nothing that it was wrong for him to say. It could not be wrong ——. But never mind. I'll tell you what I mean to do. I have been thinking of it for the last week — only I shall have to tell Mark."

"If I were you I would tell him all."

"What, Mark! If you do, Fanny, I'll never, never, never speak to you again. Would you — when I have given you all my heart in true sisterly love?"

Mrs. Robarts had to explain that she had not proposed to tell anything to Mark herself, and was persuaded, moreover, to give a solemn promise that she would not tell anything to him unless specially authorized to do so.

"I'll go into a home, I think," continued Lucy. "You know what these homes are?" Mrs. Robarts assured her that she knew very well, and then Lucy went on: "A year ago I should have said that I was the last girl in England to think of such a life, but I do believe now that it would be the best thing for me. And then I'll starve myself, and flog myself, and in that way I'll get back my own mind and my own soul."

"Your own soul, Lucy!" said Mrs. Robarts, in a tone of horror.

"Well, my own heart, if you like it better; but I hate to hear myself talking about hearts. I don't care for my heart. I'd let it go — with this young popinjay lord or any one else, so that I could read, and talk, and walk, and sleep, and eat, without always feeling that I was wrong here — here — here," and she pressed her hand vehemently against her side. "What is it that I feel, Fanny? Why am I so weak in body that I cannot take exercise? Why cannot I keep my mind on a book for one moment? Why can I not write two sentences together? Why should every mouthful that I eat stick in my throat? Oh, Fanny, is it his legs, think you, or is it his title?"

Through all her sorrow, — and she was very sorrowful, — Mrs. Robarts could not help smiling. And, indeed, there was every now and then something even in Lucy's look that was almost comic. She acted the irony so well with which she strove to throw ridicule on herself! "Do laugh at me," she said. "Nothing on earth will do me so much good as that; nothing, unless it be starvation and a whip. If you would only tell me that I must be a sneak and an idiot to care for a man because he is good-looking and a lord!"

"But that has not been the reason. There is a great deal more in Lord Lufton than that; and since I must speak, dear Lucy, I cannot but say that I should not wonder at your being in love with him, only — only that ——"

"Only what? Come, out with it. Do not mince matters, or think that I shall be angry with you because you scold me."

"Only that I should have thought that you would have been too guarded to have — have cared for any gentleman till — till he had shown that he cared for you."

"Guarded! Yes, that's it; that's just the word. But it's he that should have been guarded. He should have had a fire-guard hung before him — or a love-guard, if you will. Guarded! Was I not guarded, till you all would drag me out? Did I want to go there? And when I was there, did I not make a fool of myself, sitting in a corner, and thinking how much better placed I should have been down in the servants' hall. Lady Lufton — she dragged me out, and then cautioned me, and then, then — Why is Lady Lufton to have it all her own way? Why am I to be sacrificed for her? I did not want to know Lady Lufton, or any one belonging to her."

"I cannot think that you have any cause to blame

Lady Lufton, nor, perhaps, to blame anybody very much."

"Well, no, it has been all my own fault; though, for the life of me, Fanny, going back and back, I cannot see where I took the first false step. I do not know where I went wrong. One wrong thing I did, and it is the only thing that I do not regret."

"What was that, Lucy?"

"I told him a lie."

Mrs. Robarts was altogether in the dark, and feeling that she was so, she knew that she could not give counsel as a friend or a sister. Lucy had begun by declaring — so Mrs. Robarts thought — that nothing had passed between her and Lord Lufton but words of most trivial import, and yet she now accused herself of falsehood, and declared that that falsehood was the only thing which she did not regret!

"I hope not," said Mrs. Robarts. "If you did, you were very unlike yourself."

"But I did, and were he here again, speaking to me in the same way, I should repeat it. I know I should. If I did not, I should have all the world on me. You would frown on me, and be cold. My darling Fanny, how would you look if I really displeasured you?"

"I don't think you will do that, Lucy."

"But if I told him the truth I should, should I not? Speak now. But no, Fanny, you need not speak. It was not the fear of you: no, nor even of her: though Heaven knows that her terrible glumness would be quite unendurable."

"I cannot understand you, Lucy. What truth or what untruth can you have told him if, as you say, there has been nothing between you but ordinary conversation?"

Lucy then got up from the sofa, and walked twice the length of the room before she spoke. Mrs. Robarts had all the ordinary curiosity — I was going to say, of a woman, but I mean to say, of humanity; and she had, moreover, all the love of a sister. She was both curious and anxious, and remained sitting where she was, silent, and with her eyes fixed on her companion.

"Did I say so?" Lucy said at last. "No, Fanny; you have mistaken me: I did not say that. Ah, yes, about the cow and the dog. All that was true. I was telling you of what his soft words had been while I was becoming such a fool. Since that he has said more."

"What more has he said, Lucy?"

"I yearn to tell you, if only I can trust you;" and Lucy knelt down at the feet of Mrs. Robarts, looking up into her face and smiling through the remaining drops of her tears. "I would fain tell you, but I do not know you yet, — whether you are quite true. I could be true, — true against all the world, if my friend told me. I will tell you, Fanny, if you say that you can be true. But if you doubt yourself, if you must whisper all to Mark — then let us be silent."

There was something almost awful in this to Mrs. Robarts. Hitherto, since their marriage, hardly a thought had passed through her mind which she had not shared with her husband. But now all this had come upon her so suddenly, that she was unable to think whether it would be well that she should become the depositary of such a secret, — not to be mentioned to Lucy's brother, not to be mentioned to her own husband. But who ever yet was offered a secret and declined it? Who at least ever declined a love secret? What sister could do so? Mrs. Robarts therefore gave the promise, smoothing Lucy's hair as she did so, and kissing her forehead and looking into her eyes, which, like a rainbow, were the brighter for her tears. "And what has he said to you, Lucy?"

"What? Only this, that he asked me to be his wife."

"Lord Lufton proposed to you?"

"Yes; proposed to me? It is not credible; is it? You cannot bring yourself to believe that such a thing happened; can you?" And Lucy rose again to her feet, as the idea of the scorn with which she felt that others would treat her — with which she herself treated herself — made the blood rise to her cheek. "And yet it is not a dream. I think that it is not a dream. I think that he really did."

"Think, Lucy!"

"Well; I may say that I am sure."

"A gentleman would not make you a formal proposal, and leave you in doubt as to what he meant."

"Oh dear, no. There was no doubt at all of that kind; none in the least. Mr. Smith in asking Miss Jones to do him the honour of becoming Mrs. Smith never spoke more plainly. I was alluding to the possibility of having dreamt it all."

"Lucy!"

"Well; it was not a dream. Here, standing here, on this very spot, on that flower of the carpet, he begged me a dozen times to be his wife. I wonder whether you and Mark would let me cut it out and keep it."

"And what answer did you make to him?"

"I lied to him, and told him that I did not love him."

"You refused him?"

"Yes; I refused a live lord. There is some satisfaction in having that to think of; is there not? Fanny, was I wicked to tell that falsehood?"

"And why did you refuse him?"

"Why? Can you ask? Think what it would have been to go down to Framley Court, and to tell her ladyship in the course of conversation that I was engaged to her son. Think of Lady Lufton. But yet it was not that, Fanny. Had I thought that it was good for him, that he would not have repented, I would have braved anything — for his sake. Even your frown, for you would have frowned. You would have thought it sacrilege for me to marry Lord Lufton! You know you would."

Mrs. Robarts hardly knew how to say what she thought, or indeed what she ought to think. It was a matter on which much meditation would be required before she could give advice, and there was Lucy expecting counsel from her at that very moment. If Lord Lufton really loved Lucy Robarts, and was loved by Lucy Robarts, why should not they two become man and wife? And yet she did feel that it would be — perhaps, not sacrilege, as Lucy had said, but something almost as troublesome. What would Lady Lufton say, or think, or feel? What would she say, and think, and feel as to that parsonage from which so deadly a blow would fall upon her? Would she not accuse the vicar and the vicar's wife of the blackest ingratitude? Would life be endurable at Framley under such circumstances as those?

"What you tell me so surprises me, that I hardly as yet know how to speak about it," said Mrs. Robarts.

"It was amazing; was it not? He must have been insane at the time; there can be no other excuse made for him. I wonder whether there is anything of that sort in the family."

"What; madness?" said Mrs. Robarts, quite in earnest.

"Well; don't you think he must have been mad when such an idea as that came into his head? But you don't believe it; I can see that. And yet it is as true as heaven. Standing exactly here, on this spot, he said that he would persevere till I accepted his love. I wonder what made me specially observe that both his feet were within the lines of that division."

"And you would not accept his love?"

"No; I would have nothing to say to it. Look you, I stood here, and putting my hand upon my heart, — for he bade me to do that, — I said that I could not love him."

"And what then?"

"He went away, — with a look as though he were heart-broken. He crept away slowly, saying that he was the most wretched soul alive. For a minute I believed him and could almost have called him back. But, no, Fanny; do not think that I am over proud, or conceited about my conquest. He had not reached the gate before he was thanking God for his escape."

"That I do not believe."

"But I do; and I thought of Lady Lufton too.

How could I bear that she should scorn me, and accuse me of stealing her son's heart? I know that it is better as it is; but tell me; is a falsehood always wrong, or can it be possible that the end should justify the means? Ought I to have told him the truth, and to have let him know that I could almost kiss the ground on which he stood?"

This was a question for the doctors which Mrs. Robarts would not take upon herself to answer. She would not make that falsehood matter of accusation, but neither would she pronounce for it any absolution. In that matter Lucy must regulate her own conscience.

"And what shall I do next?" said Lucy, still speaking in a tone that was half tragic and half jeering.

"Do?" said Mrs. Robarts.

"Yes, something must be done. If I were a man I should go to Switzerland, of course; or, as the case is a bad one, perhaps as far as Hungary. What is it that girls do? they don't die now-a-days, I believe."

"Lucy, I do not believe that you care for him one jot. If you were in love you would not speak of it like that."

"There, there. That's my only hope. If I could laugh at myself till it had become incredible to you, I also, by degrees, should cease to believe that I had cared for him. But, Fanny, it is very hard. If I were to starve, and rise before daybreak, and pinch myself, or do some nasty work, — clean the pots and pans and the candlesticks; that I think would do the most good. I have got a piece of sack-cloth, and I mean to wear that, when I have made it up."

"You are joking now, Lucy, I know."

"No, by my word; not in the spirit of what I am

saying. How shall I act upon my heart, if I do not do it through the blood and the flesh?"

"Do you not pray that God will give you strength to bear these troubles?"

"But how is one to word one's prayer, or how even to word one's wishes? I do not know what is the wrong that I have done. I say it boldly; in this matter I cannot see my own fault. I have simply found that I have been a fool."

It was now quite dark in the room, or would have been so to any one entering it afresh. They had remained there talking till their eyes had become accustomed to the gloom, and would still have remained, had they not suddenly been disturbed by the sound of a horse's feet.

"There is Mark," said Fanny, jumping up and running to the bell, that lights might be ready when he should enter.

"I thought he remained in Barchester to-night."

"And so did I; but he said it might be doubtful. What shall we do if he has not dined?"

That, I believe, is always the first thought in the mind of a good wife when her husband returns home. Has he had his dinner? What can I give him for dinner? Will he like his dinner? Oh dear, oh dear! there's nothing in the house but cold mutton. But on this occasion the lord of the mansion had dined, and came home radiant with good-humour, and owing, perhaps, a little of his radiance to the dean's claret.

"I have told them," said he, "that they may keep possession of the house for the next two months, and they have agreed to that arrangement."

"That is very pleasant," said Mrs. Robarts.

"And I don't think we shall have so much trouble about the dilapidations after all."

"I am very glad of that," said Mrs. Robarts. But nevertheless she was thinking much more of Lucy than of the house in Barchester Close.

"You won't betray me," said Lucy, as she gave her sister-in-law a parting kiss at night.

"No; not unless you give me permission."

"Ah; I shall never do that."

CHAPTER III.

South Audley Street.

THE Duke of Omnium had notified to Mr. Fothergill his wish that some arrangement should be made about the Chaldicotes mortgages, and Mr. Fothergill had understood what the duke meant as well as though his instructions had been written down with all a lawyer's verbosity. The duke's meaning was this, that Chaldicotes was to be swept up and garnered, and made part and parcel of the Gatherum property. It had seemed to the duke that that affair between his friend and Miss Dunstable was hanging fire, and, therefore, it would be well that Chaldicotes should be swept up and garnered. And, moreover, tidings had come into the western division of the county that young Frank Gresham of Boxall Hill was in treaty with the Government for the purchase of all that Crown property called the Chace of Chaldicotes. It had been offered to the duke, but the duke had given no definite answer. Had he got his money back from Mr. Sowerby he could have forestalled Mr. Gresham; but now that did not seem to be probable, and his grace was resolved that either the one property or the other should be duly garnered. Therefore Mr. Fothergill went up to town, and, therefore, Mr. Sowerby was, most unwillingly, compelled to have a business interview with Mr. Fothergill. In the meantime, since last we saw him, Mr. Sowerby had learned from his sister the answer which Miss Dunstable had given to his proposition, and knew that he had no further hope in that direction.

There was no further hope thence of absolute deliverance, but there had been a tender of money services. To give Mr. Sowerby his due, he had at once declared that it would be quite out of the question that he should now receive any assistance of that sort from Miss Dunstable; but his sister had explained to him that it would be a mere business transaction; that Miss Dunstable would receive her interest; and that, if she would be content with four per cent., whereas the duke received five, and other creditors six, seven, eight, ten, and heaven only knows how much more, it might be well for all parties. He, himself, understood, as well as Fothergill had done, what was the meaning of the duke's message. Chaldicotes was to be gathered up and garnered, as had been done with so many another fair property lying in those regions. It was to be swallowed whole, and the master was to walk out from his old family hall, to leave the old woods that he loved, to give up utterly to another the parks and paddocks and pleasant places which he had known from his earliest infancy, and owned from his earliest manhood.

There can be nothing more bitter to a man than

such a surrender. What, compared to this, can be the loss of wealth to one who has himself made it, and brought it together, but has never actually seen it with his bodily eyes? Such wealth has come by one chance, and goes by another: the loss of it is part of the game which the man is playing; and if he cannot lose as well as win, he is a poor, weak, cowardly creature. Such men, as a rule, do know how to bear a mind fairly equal to adversity. But to have squandered the acres which have descended from generation to generation; to be the member of one's family that has ruined that family; to have swallowed up in one's own maw all that should have graced one's children, and one's grand-children! It seems to me that the misfortunes of this world can hardly go beyond that!

Mr. Sowerby, in spite of his recklessness and that dare-devil gaiety which he knew so well how to wear and use, felt all this as keenly as any man could feel it. It had been absolutely his own fault. The acres had come to him all his own, and now, before his death, every one of them would have gone bodily into that greedy maw. The duke had bought up nearly all the debts which had been secured upon the property, and now could make a clean sweep of it. Sowerby, when he received that message from Mr. Fothergill, knew well that this was intended; and he knew well also, that when once he should cease to be Mr. Sowerby of Chaldicotes, he need never again hope to be returned as member for West Barsetshire. This world would for him be all over. And what must such a man feel when he reflects that this world is for him all over?

On the morning in question he went to his appointment, still bearing a cheerful countenance. Mr. Fothergill, when in town on such business as this, always had a room at his service in the house of Messrs. Gumption and Gagebee, the duke's London law agents, and it was thither that Mr. Sowerby had been summoned. The house of business of Messrs. Gumption and Gagebee was in South Audley Street; and it may be said that there was no spot on the whole earth which Mr. Sowerby so hated as he did the gloomy, dingy back sitting-room upstairs in that house. He had been there very often, but had never been there without annoyance. It was a horrid torture-chamber, kept for such dread purposes as these, and no doubt had been furnished, and papered, and curtained with the express object of finally breaking down the spirits of such poor country gentlemen as chanced to be involved. Everything was of a brown crimson, — of a crimson that had become brown. Sunlight, real genial light of the sun, never made its way there, and no amount of candles could illumine the gloom of that brownness. The windows were never washed; the ceiling was of a dark brown; the old Turkey carpet was thick with dust, and brown withal. The ungainly office-table, in the middle of the room, had been covered with black leather, but that was now brown. There was a bookcase full of dingy brown law books in a recess on one side of the fireplace, but no one had touched them for years, and over the chimney-piece hung some old legal pedigree table, black with soot. Such was the room which Mr. Fothergill always used in the business house of Messrs. Gumption and Gagebee, in South Audley Street, near to Park Lane.

I once heard this room spoken of by an old friend of mine, one Mr. Gresham of Greshamsbury, the father of Frank Gresham, who was now about to purchase that part of the Chace of Chaldicotes which belonged to the Crown. He also had had evil days, though now happily they were past and gone; and he, too, had sat in that room, and listened to the voice of men who were powerful over his property, and intended to use that power. The idea which he left on my mind was much the same as that which I had entertained, when a boy, of a certain room in the castle of Udolpho. There was a chair in that Udolpho room in which those who sat were dragged out limb by limb, the head one way and the legs another; the fingers were dragged off from the hands, and the teeth out from the jaws, and the hair off the head, and the flesh from the bones, and the joints from their sockets, till there was nothing left but a lifeless trunk seated in the chair. Mr. Gresham, as he told me, always sat in the same seat, and the tortures he suffered when so seated, the dislocations of his property which he was forced to discuss, the operations on his very self which he was forced to witness, made me regard that room as worse than the chamber of Udolpho. He, luckily — a rare instance of good fortune — had lived to see all his bones and joints put together again, and flourishing soundly; but he never could speak of the room without horror.

"No consideration on earth," he once said to me, very solemnly, — "I say none, should make me again enter that room." And indeed this feeling was so strong with him, that from the day when his affairs took a turn he would never even walk down South Audley Street. On the morning in question into this torture-chamber Mr. Sowerby went, and there, after some two or three minutes, he was joined by Mr. Fothergill.

Mr. Fothergill was, in one respect, like to his friend

Sowerby. He enacted two altogether different persons on occasions which were altogether different. Generally speaking, with the world at large, he was a jolly, rollicking, popular man, fond of eating and drinking, known to be devoted to the duke's interests, and supposed to be somewhat unscrupulous, or at any rate hard, when they were concerned; but in other respects a good-natured fellow; and there was a report about that he had once lent somebody money, without charging him interest or taking security. On the present occasion Sowerby saw at a glance that he had come thither with all the aptitudes and appurtenances of his business about him. He walked into the room with a short, quick step; there was no smile on his face as he shook hands with his old friend; he brought with him a box laden with papers and parchments, and he had not been a minute in the room before he was seated in one of the old dingy chairs.

"How long have you been in town, Fothergill?" said Sowerby, still standing with his back against the chimney. He had resolved on only one thing — that nothing should induce him to touch, look at, or listen to any of those papers. He knew well enough that no good would come of that. He also had his own lawyer, to see that he was pilfered according to rule.

"How long? Since the day before yesterday. I never was so busy in my life. The duke, as usual, wants to have everything done at once."

"If he wants to have all that I owe him paid at once, he is like to be out in his reckoning."

"Ah, well; I'm glad you are ready to come quickly to business, because it's always best. Won't you come and sit down here?"

"No, thank you; I'll stand."

"But we shall have to go through these figures, you know."

"Not a figure, Fothergill. What good would it do? None to me, and none to you either, as I take it; if there is anything wrong, Potter's fellows will find it out. What is it the duke wants?"

"Well; to tell the truth, he wants his money."

"In one sense, and that the main sense, he has got it. He gets his interest regularly, does not he?"

"Pretty well for that, seeing how times are. But, Sowerby, that's nonsense. You understand the duke as well as I do, and you know very well what he wants. He has given you time, and if you had taken any steps towards getting the money, you might have saved the property."

"A hundred and eighty thousand pounds! What steps could I take to get that? Fly a bill, and let Tozer have it to get cash on it in the city!"

"We hoped you were going to marry."

"That's all off."

"Then I don't think you can blame the duke for looking for his own. It does not suit him to have so large a sum standing out any longer. You see, he wants land, and will have it. Had you paid off what you owed him, he would have purchased the Crown property; and now, it seems, young Gresham has bid against him, and is to have it. This has riled him, and I may as well tell you fairly, that he is determined to have either money or marbles."

"You mean that I am to be dispossessed."

"Well, yes; if you choose to call it so. My instructions are to foreclose at once."

"Then I must say the duke is treating me most uncommonly ill."

"Well, Sowerby, I can't see it."

"I can, though. He has his money like clockwork; and he has bought up these debts from persons who would have never disturbed me as long as they got their interest."

"Haven't you had the seat?"

"The seat! and is it expected that I am to pay for that?"

"I don't see that any one is asking you to pay for it. You are like a great many other people that I know. You want to eat your cake and have it. You have been eating it for the last twenty years, and now you think yourself very ill-used because the duke wants to have his turn."

"I shall think myself very ill-used if he sells me out — worse than ill-used. I do not want to use strong language, but it will be more than ill-usage. I can hardly believe that he really means to treat me in that way."

"It is very hard that he should want his own money!"

"It is not his money that he wants. It is my property."

"And has he not paid for it? Have you not had the price of your property? Now, Sowerby, it is of no use for you to be angry; you have known for the last three years what was coming on you as well as I did. Why should the duke lend you money without an object? Of course he has his own views. But I do say this; he has not hurried you; and had you been able to do anything to save the place you might have done it. You have had time enough to look about you."

Sowerby still stood in the place in which he had first fixed himself, and now for awhile he remained silent. His face was very stern, and there was in his countenance none of those winning looks which often told so powerfully with his young friends, — which had caught Lord Lufton and had charmed Mark Robarts. The world was going against him, and things around him were coming to an end. He was beginning to perceive that he had in truth eaten his cake, and that there was now little left for him to do, — unless he chose to blow out his brains. He had said to Lord Lufton that a man's back should be broad enough for any burden with which he himself might load it. Could he now boast that his back was broad enough and strong enough for this burden? But he had even then, at that bitter moment, a strong remembrance that it behoved him still to be a man. His final ruin was coming on him, and he would soon be swept away out of the knowledge and memory of those with whom he had lived. But, nevertheless, he would bear himself well to the last. It was true that he had made his own bed, and he understood the justice which required him to lie upon it.

During all this time Fothergill occupied himself with the papers. He continued to turn over one sheet after another, as though he were deeply engaged in money considerations and calculations. But, in truth, during all that time he did not read a word. There was nothing there for him to read. The reading and the writing, and the arithmetic in such matters, are done by underlings — not by such big men as Mr. Fothergill. His business was to tell Sowerby that he was to go. All those records there were of very little use.

The duke had the power; Sowerby knew that the duke had the power; and Fothergill's business was to explain that the duke meant to exercise his power. He was used to the work, and went on turning over the papers, and pretending to read them, as though his doing so were of the greatest moment.

"I shall see the duke myself," Mr. Sowerby said at last, and there was something almost dreadful in the sound of his voice.

"You know that the duke won't see you on a matter of this kind. He never speaks to any one about money; you know that as well as I do."

"By —, but he shall speak to me. Never speak to any one about money! Why is he ashamed to speak of it when he loves it so dearly? He shall see me."

"I have nothing further to say, Sowerby. Of course I shan't ask his grace to see you; and if you force your way in on him you know what will happen. It won't be my doing if he is set against you. Nothing that you say to me in that way, — nothing that anybody ever says, — goes beyond myself."

"I shall manage the matter through my own lawyer," said Sowerby; and then he took his hat, and, without uttering another word, left the room.

We know not what may be the nature of that eternal punishment to which those will be doomed who shall be judged to have been evil at the last; but methinks that no more terrible torment can be devised than the memory of self-imposed ruin. What wretchedness can exceed that of remembering from day to day that the race has been all run, and has been altogether lost; that the last chance has gone, and has gone in vain; that the end has come, and with it disgrace, contempt, and self-scorn — disgrace that never can be redeemed, contempt that never can be removed, and self-scorn that will eat into one's vitals for ever?

Mr. Sowerby was now fifty; he had enjoyed his chances in life; and as he walked back, up South Audley Street, he could not but think of the uses he had made of them. He had fallen into the possession of a fine property on the attainment of his manhood; he had been endowed with more than average gifts of intellect; never-failing health had been given to him, and a vision fairly clear in discerning good from evil; and now to what a pass had he brought himself!

And that man Fothergill had put all this before him in so terribly clear a light! Now that the day for his final demolishment had arrived, the necessity that he should be demolished — finished away at once, out of sight and out of mind — had not been softened, or, as it were, half hidden, by any ambiguous phrase. "You have had your cake, and eaten it — eaten it greedily. Is not that sufficient for you? Would you eat your cake twice? Would you have a succession of cakes? No, my friend; there is no succession of these cakes for those who eat them greedily. Your proposition is not a fair one, and we who have the whip-hand of you will not listen to it. Be good enough to vanish. Permit yourself to be swept quietly into the dunghill. All that there was about you of value has departed from you; and allow me to say that you are now rubbish." And then the ruthless besom comes with irresistible rush, and the rubbish is swept into the pit, there to be hidden for ever from the sight.

And the pity of it is this — that a man, if he will

only restrain his greed, may eat his cake and yet have it; ay, and in so doing will have twice more the flavour of the cake than he who with gourmandizing maw will devour his dainty all at once. Cakes in this world will grow by being fed on, if only the feeder be not too insatiate. On all which wisdom Mr. Sowerby pondered with sad heart and very melancholy mind as he walked away from the premises of Messrs. Gumption and Gagebee.

His intention had been to go down to the House after leaving Mr. Fothergill, but the prospect of immediate ruin had been too much for him, and he knew that he was not fit to be seen at once among the haunts of men. And he had intended also to go down to Barchester early on the following morning — only for a few hours, that he might make further arrangements respecting that bill which Robarts had accepted for him. That bill — the second one — had now become due, and Mr. Tozer had been with him.

"Now it ain't no use in life, Mr. Sowerby," Tozer had said. "I ain't got the paper myself, nor didn't 'old it, not two hours. It went away through Tom Tozer; you knows that, Mr. Sowerby, as well as I do."

Now, whenever Tozer, Mr. Sowerby's Tozer, spoke of Tom Tozer, Mr. Sowerby knew that seven devils were being evoked, each worse than the first devil. Mr. Sowerby did feel something like sincere regard, or rather love, for that poor parson whom he had inveigled into mischief, and would fain save him, if it were possible, from the Tozer fang. Mr. Forrest, of the Barchester bank, would probably take up that last five hundred pound bill, on behalf of Mr. Robarts, —

only it would be needful that he, Sowerby, should run down and see that this was properly done. As to the other bill — the former and lesser one — as to that, Mr. Tozer would probably be quiet for a while.

Such had been Sowerby's programme for these two days; but now — what further possibility was there now that he should care for Robarts, or any other human being; he that was to be swept at once into the dung-heap?

In this frame of mind he walked up South Audley Street, and crossed one side of Grosvenor Square, and went almost mechanically into Green Street. At the farther end of Green Street, near to Park Lane, lived Mr. and Mrs. Harold Smith.

CHAPTER IV.

Dr. Thorne.

When Miss Dunstable met her friends, the Greshams, — young Frank Gresham and his wife — at Gatherum Castle, she immediately asked after one Dr. Thorne, who was Mrs. Gresham's uncle. Dr. Thorne was an old bachelor, in whom both as a man and a doctor Miss Dunstable was inclined to place much confidence. Not that she had ever entrusted the cure of her bodily ailments to Dr. Thorne — for she kept a doctor of her own, Dr. Easyman, for this purpose — and it may moreover be said that she rarely had bodily ailments requiring the care of any doctor. But she always spoke of Dr. Thorne among her friends as a man of wonderful erudition and judgment; and had once or twice asked and acted on his advice in matters of much moment. Dr. Thorne was not a man accustomed to the London world; he kept no house there, and seldom even visited the metropolis; but Miss Dunstable had known him at Greshamsbury, where he lived, and there had for some months past grown up a considerable intimacy between them. He was now staying at the house of his niece, Mrs. Gresham; but the chief reason of his coming up had been a desire expressed by Miss Dunstable, that he should do so. She had wished for his advice; and at the instigation of his niece he had visited London and given it.

The special piece of business as to which Dr. Thorne had thus been summoned from the bedsides of his country patients, and especially from the bedside of Lady Arabella Gresham, to whose son his niece was married, related to certain large money interests, as to which one might have imagined that Dr. Thorne's advice would not be peculiarly valuable. He had never been much versed in such matters on his own account, and was knowing neither in the ways of the share market, nor in the prices of land. But Miss Dunstable was a lady accustomed to have her own way, and to be indulged in her own wishes without being called on to give adequate reasons for them.

"My dear," she had said to young Mrs. Gresham, "if your uncle don't come up to London now, when I make such a point of it, I shall think that he is a bear and a savage; and I certainly will never speak to him again, — or to Frank — or to you; so you had better see to it." Mrs. Gresham had not probably taken her friend's threat as meaning quite all that it threatened. Miss Dunstable habitually used strong language; and those who knew her well, generally understood when she was to be taken as expressing her thoughts by figures of speech. In this instance she had not meant it all; but, nevertheless, Mrs. Gresham had used violent influence in bringing the poor doctor up to London.

"Besides," said Miss Dunstable, "I have resolved on having the doctor at my conversazione, and if he won't come of himself, I shall go down and fetch him. I have set my heart on trumping my dear friend Mrs. Proudie's best card; so I mean to get everybody!"

The upshot of all this was, that the doctor did come up to town, and remained the best part of a week at his niece's house in Portman Square — to the great disgust of the Lady Arabella, who conceived that she must die if neglected for three days. As to the matter of business, I have no doubt but that he was of great use. He was possessed of common sense and an honest purpose; and I am inclined to think that they are often a sufficient counterpoise to a considerable amount of worldly experience. If one could have the worldly experience also —! True! but then it is so difficult to get everything. But with that special matter of business we need not have any further concern. We will presume it to have been discussed and completed, and will now dress ourselves for Miss Dunstable's conversazione.

But it must not be supposed that she was so poor in genius as to call her party openly by a name borrowed for the nonce from Mrs. Proudie. It was only among her specially intimate friends, Mrs. Harold Smith and some few dozen others, that she indulged in this little joke. There had been nothing in the least pretentious about the card with which she summoned her friends to her house on this occasion. She had merely signified in some ordinary way, that she would be glad to see them as soon after nine o'clock on Thursday evening, the — instant, as might be convenient. But all the world understood that all the world was to be gathered together at Miss Dunstable's house on the night in question — that an effort was to be made to bring together people of all classes, gods and giants, saints and sinners, those rabid through the strength of their morality, such as our dear friend Lady Lufton, and those who were rabid in the opposite direction, such as Lady Hartletop, the Duke of Omnium, and Mr. Sowerby. An orthodox martyr had been caught from the East, and an oily latter-day St. Paul, from the other side of the water — to the horror and amazement of Archdeacon Grantly who had come up all the way from Plumstead to be present on the occasion. Mrs. Grantly also had hankered to be there; but when she heard of the presence of the latter-day St. Paul, she triumphed loudly over her husband, who had made no offer to take her. That Lords Brock and De Terrier were to be at the gathering was nothing. The pleasant king of the gods, and the courtly chief of the giants could shake hands with each other in any house with the greatest pleasure; but men were to meet who, in reference to each other, could shake nothing but their heads or their fists. Supplehouse was to be there, and Harold Smith, who now hated his enemy with a hatred surpassing that of women — or even of politicians. The minor gods, it was thought, would congregate together in one room, very bitter in their present state of banishment; and the minor giants in another, terribly loud in their triumph. That is the fault of the giants, who, otherwise, are not bad fellows; they are unable to endure the weight of any temporary success. When attempting Olympus — and this work of attempting is doubtless their natural condition — they scratch and scramble, diligently using both toes and fingers, with a mixture of good-humoured virulence and self-satisfied industry that is gratifying to all parties. But whenever their efforts are unexpectedly, and for themselves unfortunately successful, they are so taken aback that they lose the power of behaving themselves with even gigantesque propriety.

Such, so great and so various, was to be the intended gathering at Miss Dunstable's house. She herself laughed, and quizzed herself — speaking of the affair to Mrs. Harold Smith as though it were an excellent joke, and to Mrs. Proudie as though she were simply emulous of rivalling those world-famous assemblies in Gloucester Place; but the town at large knew that an effort was being made, and it was supposed that even Miss Dunstable was somewhat nervous. In spite of her excellent joking it was presumed that she would be unhappy if she failed.

To Mrs. Frank Gresham she did speak with some little seriousness. "But why on earth should you give yourself all this trouble?" that lady had said, when Miss Dunstable owned that she was doubtful, and unhappy in her doubts, as to the coming of one of the great colleagues of Mr. Supplehouse. "When such hundreds are coming, big wigs and little wigs of all shades, what can it matter whether Mr. Towers be there or not?"

But Miss Dunstable had answered almost with a screech, —

"My dear, it will be nothing without him. You don't understand; but the fact is that Tom Towers is everybody and everything at present."

And then, by no means for the first time, Mrs. Gresham began to lecture her friend as to her vanity; in answer to which lecture Miss Dunstable mysteriously hinted, that if she were only allowed her full swing on this occasion, — if all the world would now indulge her, she would — She did not quite say what she would do, but the inference drawn by Mrs. Gresham was this: that if the incense now offered on the altar of Fashion were accepted, Miss Dunstable would at once abandon the pomps and vanities of this wicked world, and all the sinful lusts of the flesh.

"But the doctor will stay, my dear? I hope I may look on that as fixed."

Miss Dunstable, in making this demand on the doctor's time, showed an energy quite equal to that with which she invoked the gods that Tom Towers might not be absent. Now, to tell the truth, Dr. Thorne had at first thought it very unreasonable that he should be asked to remain up in London in order that he might be present at an evening party, and had for a while pertinaciously refused; but when he learned that three or four prime ministers were expected, and that it was possible that even Tom Towers might be there in the flesh, his philosophy also had become weak, and he had written to Lady Arabella to say that his prolonged absence for two days further must be endured, and that the mild tonics, morning and evening, might be continued.

But why should Miss Dunstable be so anxious that Dr. Thorne should be present on this grand occasion? Why, indeed, should she be so frequently inclined to summon him away from his country practice, his compounding board, and his useful ministrations to rural ailments? The doctor was connected with her by no ties of blood. Their friendship, intimate as it was, had as yet been but of short date. She was a very rich woman, capable of purchasing all manner of advice and good counsel, whereas, he was so far from being rich, that any continued disturbance to his practice might be inconvenient to him. Nevertheless, Miss Dunstable seemed to have no more compunction in making calls upon his time, than she might have felt had he been her brother. No ideas on this matter suggested themselves to the doctor himself. He was a simple-minded man, taking things as they came, and especially so taking things that came pleasantly. He liked Miss Dunstable, and was gratified by her friendship, and did not think of asking himself whether she had a right to put him to trouble and inconvenience. But such ideas did occur to Mrs. Gresham, the doctor's niece. Had Miss Dunstable any object, and if so, what object? Was it simply veneration for the doctor, or was it caprice? Was it eccentricity — or could it possibly be love?

In speaking of the ages of these two friends it may be said in round terms that the lady was well past forty, and that the gentleman was well past fifty. Under such circumstances could it be love? The lady, too, was one who had had offers almost by the dozen, — offers from men of rank, from men of fashion, and from men of power; from men endowed with personal attractions, with pleasant manners, with cultivated tastes, and with eloquent tongues. Not only had she loved none such, but by none such had she been cajoled into an idea that it was possible that she could love them. That Dr. Thorne's tastes were cultivated, and his manners pleasant, might probably be admitted by three or four old friends in the country who valued him; but the world in London, that world to which Miss Dunstable was accustomed, and which was apparently becoming dearer to her day by day, would not have regarded the doctor as a man likely to become the object of a lady's passion.

But nevertheless the idea did occur to Mrs. Gresham. She had been brought up at the elbow of this country practitioner: she had lived with him as though she had been his daughter; she had been for years the ministering angel of his household; and, till her heart had opened to the natural love of womanhood, all her closest sympathies had been with him. In her eyes the doctor was all but perfect; and it did not seem to her to be out of the question that Miss Dunstable should have fallen in love with her uncle.

Miss Dunstable once said to Mrs. Harold Smith that it was possible that she might marry, the only condition then expressed being this, that the man elected should be one who was quite indifferent as to money. Mrs. Harold Smith, who, by her friends, was presumed to know the world with tolerable accuracy, had replied that such a man Miss Dunstable would never find in this world. All this had passed in that half comic vein of banter which Miss Dunstable so commonly used when conversing with such friends as Mrs. Harold Smith; but she had spoken words of the same import more than once to Mrs. Gresham; and Mrs. Gresham, putting two and two together as women do, had made four of the little sum; and, as the final result of the calculation, determined that Miss Dunstable would marry Dr. Thorne if Dr. Thorne would ask her.

And then Mrs. Gresham began to bethink herself of two other questions. Would it be well that her uncle should marry Miss Dunstable? and if so, would it be possible to induce him to make such a proposition? After the consideration of many pros and cons, and the balancing of very various arguments, Mrs. Gresham thought that the arrangement on the whole might not be a bad one. For Miss Dunstable she herself had a sincere affection, which was shared by her husband. She had often grieved at the sacrifices Miss Dunstable made to the world, thinking that her friend was falling into vanity, indifference, and an ill mode of life; but such a marriage as this would probably cure all that. And then as to Dr. Thorne himself, to whose benefit were of course applied Mrs. Gresham's most earnest thoughts in this matter, she could not but think that he would be happier married than he was single. In point of temper, no woman could stand higher than Miss Dunstable; no one had ever heard of her being in an ill humour; and then though Mrs. Gresham was gifted with a mind which was far removed from being mercenary, it was impossible not to feel that some benefit must accrue from the bride's wealth. Mary Thorne, the present Mrs. Frank Gresham, had herself been a great heiress. Circumstances had weighted her hand with enormous possessions, and hitherto she had not realized the truth of that lesson which would teach us to believe that happiness and riches are incompatible. Therefore she resolved that it might be well if the doctor and Miss Dunstable were brought together.

But could the doctor be induced to make such an offer? Mrs. Gresham acknowledged a terrible difficulty in looking at the matter from that point of view. Her uncle was fond of Miss Dunstable; but she was sure that an idea of such a marriage had never entered his head; that it would be very difficult — almost impossible — to create such an idea; and that if the idea were there, the doctor could hardly be instigated to make the proposition. Looking at the matter as a whole, she feared that the match was not practicable.

On the day of Miss Dunstable's party, Mrs. Gresham and her uncle dined together alone in Portman Square. Mr. Gresham was not yet in parliament, but an almost immediate vacancy was expected in his division of the county, and it was known that no one could stand against him with any chance of success. This threw him much among the politicians of his party, those giants, namely, whom it would be his business to support, and on this account he was a good deal away from his own house at the present moment.

"Politics make a terrible demand on a man's time," he said to his wife; and then went down to dine at his club in Pall Mall with sundry other young philogeants. On men of that class politics do make a great demand — at the hour of dinner and thereabouts.

"What do you think of Miss Dunstable?" said Mrs. Gresham to her uncle, as they sat together over their coffee. She added nothing to the question; but asked it in all its baldness.

"Think about her!" said the doctor. "Well, Mary; what do you think about her? I dare say we think the same."

"But that's not the question. What do you think about her? Do you think she's honest?"

"Honest? Oh, yes, certainly — very honest, I should say."

"And good-tempered?"

"Uncommonly good-tempered."

"And affectionate?"

"Well; yes, — and affectionate. I should certainly say that she is affectionate."

"I'm sure she's clever."

"Yes, I think she's clever."

"And, and — and womanly in her feelings," Mrs. Gresham felt that she could not quite say lady-like, though she would fain have done so had she dared.

"Oh, certainly," said the doctor. "But, Mary, why are you dissecting Miss Dunstable's character with so much ingenuity?"

"Well, uncle, I will tell you why; because —" and Mrs. Gresham, while she was speaking, got up from her chair, and going round the table to her uncle's side, put her arm round his neck till her face was close to his, and then continued speaking as she stood behind him out of his sight — "because — I think that Miss Dunstable is — is very fond of you; and that it would make her happy if you would — ask her to be your wife."

"Mary!" said the doctor, turning round with an endeavour to look his niece in the face.

"I am quite in earnest, uncle — quite in earnest.

From little things that she has said, and little things that I have seen, I do believe what I now tell you."

"And you want me to —"

"Dear uncle; my own one darling uncle, I want you only to do that which will make you — make you happy. What is Miss Dunstable to me compared to you?" And then she stooped down and kissed him.

The doctor was apparently too much astounded by the intimation given him to make any further immediate reply. His niece, seeing this, left him that she might go and dress; and when they met again in the drawing-room Frank Gresham was with them.

CHAPTER V.

Miss Dunstable at Home.

Miss Dunstable did not look like a love-lorn maiden, as she stood in a small ante-chamber at the top of her drawing-room stairs receiving her guests. Her house was one of those abnormal mansions, which are to be seen here and there in London, built in compliance rather with the rules of rural architecture, than with those which usually govern the erection of city streets and town terraces. It stood back from its brethren, and alone, so that its owner could walk round it. It was approached by a short carriage-way; the chief door was in the back of the building; and the front of the house looked on to one of the parks. Miss Dunstable in procuring it had had her usual luck. It had been built by an eccentric millionnaire at an enormous cost; and the eccentric millionnaire, after living in it for twelve months, had declared that it did not possess a single comfort, and that it was deficient in most of those details which, in point of house accommodation, are necessary to the very existence of man. Consequently the mansion was sold, and Miss Dunstable was the purchaser. Cranbourn House it had been named, and its present owner had made no change in this respect; but the world at large very generally called it Ointment Hall, and Miss Dunstable herself as frequently used that name for it as any other. It was impossible to quiz Miss Dunstable with any success, because she always joined in the joke herself.

Not a word further had passed between Mrs. Gresham and Dr. Thorne on the subject of their last conversation; but the doctor as he entered the lady's portals amongst a tribe of servants and in a glare of light, and saw the crowd before him and the crowd behind him, felt that it was quite impossible that he should ever be at home there. It might be all right that a Miss Dunstable should live in this way, but it could not be right that the wife of Dr. Thorne should so live. But all this was a matter of the merest speculation, for he was well aware — as he said to himself a dozen times — that his niece had blundered strangely in her reading of Miss Dunstable's character.

When the Gresham party entered the ante-room into which the staircase opened, they found Miss Dunstable standing there surrounded by a few of her most intimate allies. Mrs. Harold Smith was sitting quite close to her; Dr. Easyman was reclining on a sofa against the wall, and the lady who habitually lived with Miss Dunstable was by his side. One or two others were there also, so that a little running conversation was kept up in order to relieve Miss Dunstable of the tedium which might otherwise be engendered by the work she had in hand. As Mrs. Gresham, leaning on her husband's arm, entered the room, she saw the back of Mrs. Proudie, as that lady made her way through the opposite door leaning on the arm of the bishop.

Mrs. Harold Smith had apparently recovered from the annoyance which she must no doubt have felt when Miss Dunstable so utterly rejected her suit on behalf of her brother. If any feeling had existed, even for a day, calculated to put a stop to the intimacy between the two ladies, that feeling had altogether died away, for Mrs. Harold Smith was conversing with her friend, quite in the old way. She made some remark on each of the guests as they passed by, and apparently did so in a manner satisfactory to the owner of the house, for Miss Dunstable answered with her kindest smiles, and in that genial, happy tone of voice which gave its peculiar character to her good humour:

"She is quite convinced that you are a mere plagiarist in what you are doing," said Mrs. Harold Smith, speaking of Mrs. Proudie.

"And so I am. I don't suppose there can be anything very original now-a-days about an evening party."

"But she thinks you are copying her."

"And why not? I copy everybody that I see, more or less. You did not at first begin to wear big petticoats out of your own head? If Mrs. Proudie has any such pride as that, pray don't rob her of it. Here's the doctor and the Greshams. Mary, my darling, how are you?" and in spite of all her grandeur of apparel, Miss Dunstable took hold of Mrs. Gresham and kissed her — to the disgust of the dozen-and-a-half of the distinguished fashionable world who were passing up the stairs behind.

The doctor was somewhat repressed in his mode of address by the communication which had so lately been made to him. Miss Dunstable was now standing on the very top of the pinnacle of wealth, and seemed to him to be not only so much above his reach, but also so far removed from his track in life, that he could not in any way put himself on a level with her. He could neither aspire so high nor descend so low; and thinking of this he spoke to Miss Dunstable as though there were some great distance between them, — as though there had been no hours of intimate friendship down at Greshamsbury. There had been such hours, during which Miss Dunstable and Dr. Thorne had lived as though they belonged to the same world: and this at any rate may be said of Miss Dunstable, that she had no idea of forgetting them.

Dr. Thorne merely gave her his hand, and then prepared to pass on.

"Don't go, doctor," she said; "for heaven's sake, don't go yet. I don't know when I may catch you if you get in there. I shan't be able to follow you for the next two hours. Lady Meredith, I am so much obliged to you for coming — your mother will be here, I hope. Oh, I am so glad! From her you know that is quite a favour. You, Sir George, are half a sinner yourself, so I don't think so much about it."

"Oh, quite so," said Sir George; "perhaps rather the largest half."

"The men divide the world into gods and giants," said Miss Dunstable. "We women have our divisions also. We are saints or sinners according to our party. The worst of it is, that we rat almost as often as you do." Whereupon Sir George laughed and passed on.

"I know, doctor, you don't like this kind of thing," she continued, "but there is no reason why you should indulge yourself altogether in your own way, more than another — is there, Frank?"

"I am not so sure but he does like it," said Mr. Gresham. "There are some of your reputed friends whom he owns that he is anxious to see."

"Are there? Then there is some hope of his ratting too. But he'll never make a good staunch sinner; will he, Mary? You're too old to learn new tricks; eh, doctor?"

"I am afraid I am," said the doctor, with a faint laugh.

"Does Doctor Thorne rank himself among the army of saints?" asked Mrs. Harold Smith.

"Decidedly," said Miss Dunstable. "But you must always remember that there are saints of different orders; are there not, Mary? and nobody supposes that the Franciscans and the Dominicans agree very well together. Dr. Thorne does not belong to the school of St. Proudie, of Barchester; he would prefer the priestess whom I see coming round the corner of the staircase, with a very famous young novice at her elbow."

"From all that I can hear, you will have to reckon Miss Grantly among the sinners," said Mrs. Harold Smith — seeing that Lady Lufton with her young friend was approaching — "unless, indeed, you can make a saint of Lady Hartletop."

And then Lady Lufton entered the room, and Miss

Dunstable came forward to meet her with more quiet respect in her manner than she had as yet shown to many of her guests. "I am much obliged to you for coming, Lady Lufton," she said, "and the more so, for bringing Miss Grantly with you."

Lady Lufton uttered some pretty little speech, during which Dr. Thorne came up and shook hands with her; as did also Frank Gresham and his wife. There was a country acquaintance between the Framley people and the Greshamsbury people, and therefore there was a little general conversation before Lady Lufton passed out of the small room into what Mrs. Proudie would have called the noble suite of apartments. "Papa will be here," said Miss Grantly; "at least so I understand. I have not seen him yet myself."

"Oh, yes, he has promised me," said Miss Dunstable; "and the archdeacon, I know, will keep his word. I should by no means have the proper ecclesiastical balance without him."

"Papa always does keep his word," said Miss Grantly, in a tone that was almost severe. She had not at all understood poor Miss Dunstable's little joke, or at any rate she was too dignified to respond to it.

"I understand that old Sir John is to accept the Chiltern Hundreds at once," said Lady Lufton, in a half whisper to Frank Gresham.

Lady Lufton had always taken a keen interest in the politics of East Barsetshire, and was now desirous of expressing her satisfaction that a Gresham should again sit for the county. The Greshams had been old county members in Barsetshire, time out of mind.

"Oh, yes; I believe so," said Frank, blushing. He

was still young enough to feel almost ashamed of putting himself forward for such high honours.

"There will be no contest, of course," said Lady Lufton, confidentially. "There seldom is in East Barsetshire, I am happy to say. But if there were, every tenant at Framley would vote on the right side; I can assure you of that. Lord Lufton was saying so to me only this morning."

Frank Gresham made a pretty little speech in reply, such as young sucking politicians are expected to make; and this, with sundry other small courteous murmurings, detained the Lufton party for a minute or two in the ante-chamber. In the meantime the world was pressing on and passing through to the four or five large reception-rooms — the noble suite which was already piercing poor Mrs. Proudie's heart with envy to the very core. "These are the sort of rooms," she said to herself unconsciously, "which ought to be provided by the country for the use of its bishops."

"But the people are not brought enough together," she said to her lord.

"No, no; I don't think they are," said the bishop.

"And that is so essential for a conversazione," continued Mrs. Proudie. "Now in Gloucester Place —."

But we will not record all her adverse criticisms, as Lady Lufton is waiting for us in the ante-room.

And now another arrival of moment had taken place; — an arrival indeed of very great moment. To tell the truth, Miss Dunstable's heart had been set upon having two special persons; and though no stone had been left unturned, — no stone which could be turned with discretion, — she was still left in doubt as to both these two wondrous potentates. At the very moments of which we are now speaking, light and airy as she appeared to be — for it was her character to be light and airy — her mind was torn with doubts. If the wished-for two would come, her evening would be thoroughly successful; but if not, all her trouble would have been thrown away, and the thing would have been a failure; and there were circumstances connected with the present assembly which made Miss Dunstable very anxious that she should not fail. That the two great ones of the earth were Tom Towers of the *Jupiter*, and the Duke of Omnium, need hardly be expressed in words.

And now, at this very moment, as Lady Lufton was making her civil speeches to young Gresham, apparently in no hurry to move on, and while Miss Dunstable was endeavouring to whisper something into the doctor's ear, which would make him feel himself at home in this new world, a sound was heard which made that lady know that half her wish had at any rate been granted to her. A sound was heard — but only by her own and one other attentive pair of ears. Mrs. Harold Smith had also caught the name, and knew that the duke was approaching.

There was great glory and triumph in this; but why had his Grace come at so unchancy a moment? Miss Dunstable had been fully aware of the impropriety of bringing Lady Lufton and the Duke of Omnium into the same house at the same time; but when she had asked Lady Lufton, she had been led to believe that there was no hope of obtaining the duke; and then, when that hope had dawned upon her, she had comforted herself with the reflection that the two suns, though they might for some few minutes be in the same hemisphere, could hardly be expected to clash, or come across each other's orbits. Her rooms were large and would be crowded; the duke would probably do little more than walk through them once, and Lady Lufton would certainly be surrounded by persons of her own class. Thus Miss Dunstable had comforted herself. But now all things were going wrong, and Lady Lufton would find herself in close contiguity to the nearest representative of Satanic agency, which, according to her ideas, was allowed to walk this nether English world of ours. Would she scream? or indignantly retreat out of the house? — or would she proudly raise her head, and with outstretched hand and audible voice, boldly defy the devil and all his works? In thinking of these things as the duke approached Miss Dunstable almost lost her presence of mind.

But Mrs. Harold Smith did not lose hers.

"So here at last is the duke," she said, in a tone intended to catch the express attention of Lady Lufton.

Mrs. Smith had calculated that there might still be time for her ladyship to pass on and avoid the interview. But Lady Lufton, if she heard the words, did not completely understand them. At any rate they did not convey to her mind at the moment the meaning they were intended to convey. She paused to whisper a last little speech to Frank Gresham, and then looking round, found that the gentleman who was pressing against her dress was — the Duke of Omnium!

On this great occasion, when the misfortune could no longer be avoided, Miss Dunstable was by no means beneath herself or her character. She deplored the calamity, but she now saw that it was only left to her to make the best of it. The duke had honoured her by coming to her house, and she was bound to welcome him, though in doing so she should bring Lady Lufton to her last gasp.

"Duke," she said, "I am greatly honoured by this kindness on the part of your grace. I hardly expected that you would be so good to me."

"The goodness is all on the other side," said the duke, bowing over her hand.

And then in the usual course of things this would have been all. The duke would have walked on and shown himself, would have said a word or two to Lady Hartletop, to the bishop, to Mr. Gresham, and such like, and would then have left the rooms by another way, and quietly escaped. This was the duty expected from him, and this he would have done, and the value of the party would have been increased thirty per cent. by such doing: but now, as it was, the newsmongers of the West End were likely to get much more out of him.

Circumstances had so turned out that he had absolutely been pressed close against Lady Lufton, and she, when she heard the voice, and was made positively acquainted with the fact of the great man's presence by Miss Dunstable's words, turned round quickly, but still with much feminine dignity, removing her dress from the contact. In doing this she was brought absolutely face to face with the duke, so that each could not but look full at the other. "I beg your pardon," said the duke. They were the only words that had ever passed between them, nor have they spoken to each other since; but simple as they were, accompanied by the little byplay of the speakers, they gave rise to a considerable amount of ferment in the fashionable world. Lady Lufton, as she retreated back on to Dr. Easyman, curtseyed low; she curtseyed low and slowly, and with a haughty arrangement of her drapery that was all her own; but the curtsey, though it was eloquent, did not say half so much, — did not reprobate the habitual iniquities of the duke with a voice nearly as potent, as that which was expressed in the gradual fall of her eye and the gradual pressure of her lips. When she commenced her curtsey she was looking full in her foe's face. By the time that she had completed it her eyes were turned upon the ground, but there was an ineffable amount of scorn expressed in the lines of her mouth. She spoke no word, and retreated, as modest virtue and feminine weakness must ever retreat, before barefaced vice and virile power; but nevertheless she was held by all the world to have had the best of the encounter. The duke, as he begged her pardon, wore in his countenance that expression of modified sorrow which is common to any gentleman who is supposed by himself to have incommoded a lady. But over and above this, — or rather under it, — there was a slight smile of derision, as though it were impossible for him to look upon the bearing of Lady Lufton without some amount of ridicule. All this was legible to eyes so keen as those of Miss Dunstable and Mrs. Harold Smith, and the duke was known to be a master of this silent inward sarcasm; but even by them, — by Miss Dunstable and Mrs. Harold Smith, — it was admitted that Lady Lufton had conquered. When her ladyship again looked up, the duke had passed on; she then resumed the care of Miss Grantly's hand, and followed in among the company.

"That is what I call unfortunate," said Miss Dunstable, as soon as both belligerents had departed from the field of battle. "The fates sometimes will be against one."

"But they have not been at all against you here," said Mrs. Harold Smith. "If you could arrive at her ladyship's private thoughts to-morrow morning, you would find her to be quite happy in having met the duke. It will be years before she has done boasting of her triumph, and it will be talked of by the young ladies of Framley for the next three generations."

The Gresham party, including Dr. Thorne, had remained in the ante-chamber during the battle. The whole combat did not occupy above two minutes, and the three of them were hemmed off from escape by Lady Lufton's retreat into Dr. Easyman's lap; but now they, too, essayed to pass on.

"What, you will desert me," said Miss Dunstable. "Very well; but I shall find you out by-and-by. Frank, there is to be some dancing in one of the rooms, — just to distinguish the affair from Mrs. Proudie's conversazione. It would be stupid, you know, if all conversaziones were alike; wouldn't it? So I hope you will go and dance."

"There will, I presume, be another variation at feeding time," said Mrs. Harold Smith.

"Oh, yes; certainly; I am the most vulgar of all wretches in that respect. I do love to set people eating and drinking. — Mr. Supplehouse, I am delighted to see you; but do tell me —" and then she whispered with great energy into the ear of Mr. Supplehouse, and Mr. Supplehouse again whispered into her ear. "You think he will, then?" said Miss Dunstable.

Mr. Supplehouse assented; he did think so; but he had no warrant for stating the circumstance as a fact. And then he passed on, hardly looking at Mrs. Harold Smith as he passed.

"What a hang-dog countenance he has," said that lady.

"Ah! you're prejudiced, my dear, and no wonder; as for myself I always liked Supplehouse. He means mischief; but then mischief is his trade, and he does not conceal it. If I were a politician I should as soon think of being angry with Mr. Supplehouse for turning against me as I am now with a pin for pricking me. It's my own awkwardness, and I ought to have known how to use the pin more craftily."

"But you must detest a man who professes to stand by his party, and then does his best to ruin it."

"So many have done that, my dear; and with much more success than Mr. Supplehouse! All is fair in love and war, — why not add politics to the list? If we could only agree to do that, it would save us from such a deal of heartburning, and would make none of us a bit the worse."

Miss Dunstable's rooms, large as they were — "a noble suite of rooms certainly, though perhaps a little too — too — too scattered, we will say, eh, bishop?" — were now nearly full, and would have been inconveniently crowded, were it not that many who came only remained for half-an-hour or so. Space, however, had been kept for the dancers — much to Mrs. Proudie's consternation. Not that she disapproved of dancing in London, as a rule; but she was indignant that the laws of a conversazione, as re-established by herself in the fashionable world, should be so violently infringed.

"Conversazione will come to mean nothing," she said to the bishop, putting great stress on the latter word, "nothing at all, if they are to be treated in this way."

"No, they won't; nothing in the least," said the bishop.

"Dancing may be very well in its place," said Mrs. Proudie.

"I have never objected to it myself; that is, for the laity," said the bishop.

"But when people profess to assemble for higher objects," said Mrs. Proudie, "they ought to act up to their professions."

"Otherwise they are no better than hypocrites," said the bishop.

"A spade should be called a spade," said Mrs. Proudie.

"Decidedly," said the bishop, assenting.

"And when I undertook the trouble and expense of introducing conversaziones," continued Mrs. Proudie, with an evident feeling that she had been ill-used, "I had no idea of seeing the word so — so — so misinterpreted;" and then observing certain desirable acquaintances at the other side of the room, she went across, leaving the bishop to fend for himself.

Lady Lufton, having achieved her success, passed on to the dancing, whither it was not probable that her enemy would follow her, and she had not been there very long before she was joined by her son. Her heart at the present moment was not quite satisfied at the state of affairs with reference to Griselda. She had gone so far as to tell her young friend what were her own wishes; she had declared her desire that Griselda should become her daughter-in-law; but in answer to this Griselda herself had declared nothing. It was, to be sure, no more than natural that a young lady so well brought up as Miss Grantly should show no signs of a passion till she was warranted in showing them by the proceedings of the gentleman; but notwithstanding this — fully aware as she was of the propriety of such reticence — Lady Lufton did think that to her Griselda might have spoken some word evincing that the alliance would be satisfactory to her. Griselda, however, had spoken no such word, nor had she uttered a syllable to show that she would accept Lord Lufton if he did offer. Then again she had uttered no syllable to show that she would not accept him; but, nevertheless, although she knew that the world had been talking about her and Lord Dumbello, she stood up to dance with the future marquess on every possible occasion. All this did give annoyance to Lady Lufton, who began to bethink herself that if she could not quickly bring her little plan to a favourable issue, it might be well for her to wash her hands of it. She was still anxious for the match on her son's account. Griselda would, she did not doubt, make a good wife; but Lady Lufton was not so sure as she once had been that she herself would be able to keep up so strong a feeling for her daughter-in-law as she had hitherto hoped to do.

"Ludovic, have you been here long?" she said, smiling as she always did smile when her eyes fell upon her son's face.

"This instant arrived; and I hurried on after you, as Miss Dunstable told me that you were here. What a crowd she has! Did you see Lord Brock?"

"I did not observe him."

"Or Lord De Terrier? I saw them both in the centre room."

"Lord De Terrier did me the honour of shaking hands with me as I passed through."

"I never saw such a mixture of people. There is Mrs. Proudie going out of her mind because you are all going to dance."

"The Miss Proudies dance," said Griselda Grantly.

"But not at conversaziones. You don't see the difference. And I saw Spermoil there, looking as pleased as Punch. He had quite a circle of his own round him, and was chattering away as though he were quite accustomed to the wickednesses of the world."

"There certainly are people here whom one would not have wished to meet, had one thought of it," said Lady Lufton, mindful of her late engagement.

"But it must be all right, for I walked up the stairs with the archdeacon. That is an absolute proof; is it not, Miss Grantly?"

"I have no fears. When I am with your mother I know I must be safe."

"I am not so sure of that," said Lord Lufton, laughing. "Mother, you hardly know the worst of it yet. Who is here, do you think?"

"I know whom you mean; I have seen him," said Lady Lufton, very quietly.

"We came across him just at the top of the stairs,"

said Griselda, with more animation in her face than ever Lord Lufton had seen there before.

"What; the duke?"

"Yes, the duke," said Lady Lufton. "I certainly should not have come had I expected to be brought in contact with that man. But it was an accident, and on such an occasion as this it could not be helped."

Lord Lufton at once perceived, by the tone of his mother's voice and by the shades of her countenance that she had absolutely endured some personal encounter with the duke, and also that she was by no means so indignant at the occurrence as might have been expected. There she was, still in Miss Dunstable's house, and expressing no anger as to Miss Dunstable's conduct. Lord Lufton could hardly have been more surprised had he seen the duke handing his mother down to supper; he said, however, nothing further on the subject.

"Are you going to dance, Ludovic?" said Lady Lufton.

"Well, I am not sure that I do not agree with Mrs. Proudie in thinking that dancing would contaminate a conversazione. What are your ideas, Miss Grantly?"

Griselda was never very good at a joke, and imagined that Lord Lufton wanted to escape the trouble of dancing with her. This angered her. For the only species of love-making, or flirtation, or sociability between herself as a young lady, and any other self as a young gentleman, which recommended itself to her taste, was to be found in the amusement of dancing. She was altogether at variance with Mrs. Proudie on this matter, and gave Miss Dunstable great credit for her innovation. In society Griselda's toes were more serviceable to her than her tongue, and she was to be won by a rapid twirl much more probably than by a soft word. The offer of which she would approve would be conveyed by two all but breathless words during a spasmodic pause in a waltz; and then as she lifted up her arm to receive the accustomed support at her back, she might just find power enough to say, "You — must ask — papa." After that she would not care to have the affair mentioned till everything was properly settled.

"I have not thought about it," said Griselda, turning her face away from Lord Lufton.

It must not, however, be supposed that Miss Grantly had not thought about Lord Lufton, or that she had not considered how great might be the advantage of having Lady Lufton on her side if she made up her mind that she did wish to become Lord Lufton's wife. She knew well that now was her time for a triumph, now in this very first season of her acknowledged beauty; and she knew also that young, good-looking bachelor lords do not grow on hedges like blackberries. Had Lord Lufton offered to her, she would have accepted him at once without any remorse as to the greater glories which might appertain to a future marchioness of Hartletop. In that direction she was not without sufficient wisdom. But then Lord Lufton had not offered to her, nor given any signs that he intended to do so; and to give Griselda Grantly her due, she was not a girl to make a first overture. Neither had Lord Dumbello offered; but he had given signs, — dumb signs, such as birds give to each other, quite as intelligible, as verbal signs to a girl who preferred the use of her toes to that of her tongue.

"I have not thought about it," said Griselda, very coldly, and at that moment a gentleman stood before her and asked her hand for the next dance. It was Lord Dumbello; and Griselda, making no reply except by a slight bow, got up and put her hand within her partner's arm.

"Shall I find you here, Lady Lufton, when we have done?" she said; and then started off among the dancers.

When the work before one is dancing the proper thing for a gentleman to do is, at any rate, to ask a lady; this proper thing Lord Lufton had omitted, and now the prize was taken away from under his very nose.

There was clearly an air of triumph about Lord Dumbello as he walked away with the beauty. The world had been saying that Lord Lufton was to marry her, and the world had also been saying that Lord Dumbello admired her. Now this had angered Lord Dumbello, and made him feel as though he walked about, a mark of scorn, as a disappointed suitor. Had it not been for Lord Lufton, perhaps he would not have cared so much for Griselda Grantly; but circumstances had so turned out that he did care for her, and felt it to be incumbent upon him as the heir to a marquisate to obtain what he wanted, let who would have a hankering after the same article. It is in this way that pictures are so well sold at auctions; and Lord Dumbello regarded Miss Grantly as being now subject to the auctioneer's hammer, and conceived that Lord Lufton was bidding against him. There was, therefore, an air of triumph about him as he put his arm round Griselda's waist and whirled her up and down the room in obedience to the music.

Lady Lufton and her son were left together looking at each other. Of course, he had intended to ask Griselda to dance, but it cannot be said that he very much regretted his disappointment. Of course also Lady Lufton had expected that her son and Griselda would stand up together, and she was a little inclined to be angry with her *protégée.*

"I think she might have waited a minute," said Lady Lufton.

"But why, mother? There are certain things for which no one ever waits: to give a friend, for instance, the first passage through a gate out hunting, and such like. Miss Grantly was quite right to take the first that offered."

Lady Lufton had determined to learn what was to be the end of this scheme of hers. She could not have Griselda always with her, and if anything were to be arranged it must be arranged now, while both of them were in London. At the close of the season Griselda would return to Plumstead, and Lord Lufton would go — nobody as yet knew where. It would be useless to look forward to further opportunities. If they did not contrive to love each other now, they would never do so. Lady Lufton was beginning to fear that her plan would not work, but she made up her mind that she would learn the truth then and there, — at least, as far as her son was concerned.

"Oh, yes; quite so; — if it is equal to her with which she dances," said Lady Lufton.

"Quite equal, I should think — unless it be that Dumbello is longer-winded than I am."

"I am sorry to hear you speak of her in that way, Ludovic."

"Why sorry, mother?"

"Because I had hoped — that you and she would have liked each other."

This she said in a serious tone of voice, tender and sad, looking up into his face with a plaintive gaze, as though she knew that she were asking of him some great favour.

"Yes, mother, I have known that you have wished that."

"You have known it, Ludovic!"

"Oh, dear, yes; you are not at all sharp at keeping your secrets from me. And, mother, at one time, for a day or so, I thought that I could oblige you. You have been so good to me, that I would almost do anything for you."

"Oh, no, no, no," she said, deprecating his praise, and the sacrifice which he seemed to offer of his own hopes and aspirations. "I would not for worlds have you do so for my sake. No mother ever had a better son, and my only ambition is for your happiness."

"But, mother, she would not make me happy. I was mad enough for a moment to think that she could do so — for a moment I did think so. There was one occasion on which I would have asked her to take me, but —"

"But what, Ludovic?"

"Never mind; it passed away; and now I shall never ask her. Indeed I do not think she would have me. She is ambitious, and flying at higher game than

I am. And I must say this for her, that she knows well what she is doing, and plays her cards as though she had been born with them in her hand."

"You will never ask her?"

"No, mother; had I done so, it would have been for love of you — only for love of you."

"I would not for worlds that you should do that."

"Let her have Dumbello; she will make an excellent wife for him, just the wife that he will want. And you, you will have been so good to her in assisting her to such a matter."

"But, Ludovic, I am so anxious to see you settled."

"All in good time, mother!"

"Ah, but the good time is passing away. Years run so very quickly. I hope you think about marrying, Ludovic."

"But, mother, what if I brought you a wife that you did not approve?"

"I will approve of any one that you love; that is —"

"That is, if you love her also; eh, mother?"

"But I rely with such confidence on your taste. I know that you can like no one that is not ladylike and good."

"Lady-like and good! Will that suffice?" said he, thinking of Lucy Robarts.

"Yes; it will suffice, if you love her. I don't want you to care for money. Griselda will have a fortune that would have been convenient; but I do not wish you to care for that." And thus, as they stood together in Miss Dunstable's crowded room, the mother and son settled between themselves that the Lufton-Grantly alliance treaty was not to be ratified. "I suppose I must let Mrs. Grantly know," said Lady Lufton to herself, as Griselda returned to her side. There had not been above a dozen words spoken between Lord Dumbello and his partner, but that young lady also had now fully made up her mind that the treaty above mentioned should never be brought into operation.

We must go back to our hostess, whom we should not have left for so long a time, seeing that this chapter is written to show how well she could conduct herself in great emergencies. She had declared that after awhile she would be able to leave her position near the entrance door, and find out her own peculiar friends among the crowd; but the opportunity for doing so did not come till very late in the evening. There was a continuation of arrivals; she was wearied to death with making little speeches, and had more than once declared that she must depute Mrs. Harold Smith to take her place.

That lady stuck to her through all her labours with admirable constancy, and made the work bearable. Without some such constancy on a friend's part, it would have been unbearable. And it must be acknowledged that this was much to the credit of Mrs. Harold Smith. Her own hopes with reference to the great heiress had all been shattered, and her answer had been given to her in very plain language. But, nevertheless, she was true to her friendship, and was almost as willing to endure fatigue on the occasion as though she had a sister-in-law's right in the house.

At about one o'clock her brother came. He had not yet seen Miss Dunstable since the offer had been made, and had now with difficulty been persuaded by his sister to show himself.

"What can be the use?" said he. "The game is up with me now;" — meaning, poor, ruined ne'er-do-well, not only that that game with Miss Dunstable was up, but that the great game of his whole life was being brought to an uncomfortable termination.

"Nonsense," said his sister. "Do you mean to despair because a man like the Duke of Omnium wants his money? What has been good security for him will be good security for another;" and then Mrs. Harold Smith made herself more agreeable than ever to Miss Dunstable.

When Miss Dunstable was nearly worn out, but was still endeavouring to buoy herself up by a hope of the still-expected great arrival — for she knew that the hero would show himself only at a very late hour if it were to be her good fortune that he showed himself at all — Mr. Sowerby walked up the stairs. He had schooled himself to go through this ordeal with all the cool effrontery which was at his command; but it was clearly to be seen that all his effrontery did not stand him in sufficient stead, and that the interview would have been embarrassing had it not been for the genuine good-humour of the lady.

"Here is my brother," said Mrs. Harold Smith, showing by the tremulousness of the whisper that she looked forward to the meeting with some amount of apprehension.

"How do you do, Mr. Sowerby?" said Miss Dunstable, walking almost into the doorway to welcome him. "Better late than never."

"I have only just got away from the House," said he, as he gave her his hand.

"Oh, I know well that you are *sans reproche* among

senators; — as Mr. Harold Smith is *sans peur;* — eh, my dear?"

"I must confess that you have contrived to be uncommonly severe upon them both," said Mrs. Harold, laughing; "and as regards poor Harold, most undeservedly so: Nathaniel is here, and may defend himself."

"And no one is better able to do so on all occasions. But, my dear Mr. Sowerby, I am dying of despair. Do you think he'll come?"

"He? who?"

"You stupid man — as if there were more than one he! There were two, but the other has been."

"Upon my word, I don't understand," said Mr. Sowerby, now again at his ease. "But can I do anything? shall I go and fetch any one? Oh, Tom Towers; I fear I can't help you. But here he is at the foot of the stairs!" And then Mr. Sowerby stood back with his sister to make way for the great representative man of the age.

"Angels and ministers of grace, assist me!" said Miss Dunstable. "How on earth am I to behave myself? Mr. Sowerby, do you think that I ought to kneel down? My dear, will he have a reporter at his back in the royal livery?" And then Miss Dunstable advanced two or three steps, — not into the doorway, as she had done for Mr. Sowerby — put out her hand, and smiled her sweetest on Mr. Towers, of the *Jupiter*.

"Mr. Towers," she said, "I am delighted to have this opportunity of seeing you in my own house."

"Miss Dunstable, I am immensely honoured by the privilege of being here," said he.

"The honour done is all conferred on me," and she bowed and curtseyed with very stately grace. Each thoroughly understood the badinage of the other; and then, in a few moments, they were engaged in very easy conversation.

"By-the-by, Sowerby, what do you think of this threatened dissolution?" said Tom Towers.

"We are all in the hands of Providence," said Mr. Sowerby, striving to take the matter without any outward show of emotion. But the question was one of terrible import to him, and up to this time he had heard of no such threat. Nor had Mrs. Harold Smith, nor Miss Dunstable, nor had a hundred others who now either listened to the vaticinations of Mr. Towers, or to the immediate report made of them. But it is given to some men to originate such tidings, and the performance of the prophecy is often brought about by the authority of the prophet. On the following morning the rumour that there would be a dissolution was current in all high circles. "They have no conscience in such matters; no conscience whatever," said a small god, speaking of the giants, — a small god, whose constituency was expensive.

Mr. Towers stood there chatting for about twenty minutes, and then took his departure without making his way into the room. He had answered the purpose for which he had been invited, and left Miss Dunstable in a happy frame of mind.

"I am very glad that he came," said Mrs. Harold Smith, with an air of triumph.

"Yes, I am glad," said Miss Dunstable, "though I am thoroughly ashamed that I should be so. After all, what good has he done to me or to any one?" And having uttered this moral reflection, she made her way into the rooms, and soon discovered Dr. Thorne standing by himself against the wall.

"Well, doctor," she said, "where are Mary and Frank? You do not look at all comfortable, standing here by yourself."

"I am quite as comfortable as I expected, thank you," said he. "They are in the room somewhere, and, as I believe, equally happy."

"That's spiteful in you, doctor, to speak in that way. What would you say if you were called on to endure all that I have gone through this evening?"

"There is no accounting for tastes, but I presume you like it."

"I am not so sure of that. Give me your arm and let me get some supper. One always likes the idea of having done hard work, and one always likes to have been successful."

"We all know that virtue is its own reward," said the doctor.

"Well, that is something hard upon me," said Miss Dunstable, as she sat down to table. "And you really think that no good of any sort can come from my giving such a party as this?"

"Oh, yes; some people, no doubt, have been amused."

"It is all vanity in your estimation," said Miss Dunstable; "vanity and vexation of spirit. Well; there is a good deal of the latter, certainly. Sherry, if you please. I would give anything for a glass of beer, but that is out of the question. Vanity and vexation of spirit! And yet I meant to do good."

"Pray, do not suppose that I am condemning you, Miss Dunstable."

"Ah, but I do suppose it. Not only you, but another also, whose judgment I care for perhaps more than yours; and that, let me tell you, is saying a great deal. You do condemn me, Dr. Thorne, and I also condemn myself. It is not that I have done wrong, but the game is not worth the candle."

"Ah; that's the question."

"The game is not worth the candle. And yet it was a triumph to have both the duke and Tom Towers. You must confess that I have not managed badly."

Soon after that the Greshams went away, and in an hour's time or so, Miss Dunstable was allowed to drag herself to her own bed.

That is the great question to be asked on all such occasions, "Is the game worth the candle?"

CHAPTER VI.

The Grantly Triumph.

It has been mentioned cursorily — the reader no doubt, will have forgotten it — that Mrs. Grantly was not specially invited by her husband to go up to town with a view of being present at Miss Dunstable's party. Mrs. Grantly said nothing on the subject, but she was somewhat chagrined; not on account of the loss she sustained with reference to that celebrated assembly, but because she felt that her daughter's affairs required the supervision of a mother's eye. She also doubted the final ratification of that Lufton-Grantly treaty, and, doubting it, she did not feel quite satisfied that her daughter should be left in Lady Lufton's hands. She had said a word or two to the archdeacon before he went up, but only a word or two, for she hesitated to trust him in so delicate a matter. She was, therefore, not a little surprised at receiving, on the second morning after her husband's departure, a letter from him desiring her immediate presence in London. She was surprised; but her heart was filled rather with hope than dismay, for she had full confidence in her daughter's discretion.

On the morning after the party, Lady Lufton and Griselda had breakfasted together as usual, but each felt that the manner of the other was altered. Lady Lufton thought that her young friend was somewhat less attentive, and perhaps less meek in her demeanour, than usual; and Griselda felt that Lady Lufton was less affectionate. Very little, however, was said between them, and Lady Lufton expressed no surprise when Griselda begged to be left alone at home, instead of accompanying her ladyship when the carriage came to the door.

Nobody called in Bruton-street that afternoon — no one, at least, was let in — except the archdeacon. He came there late in the day, and remained with his daughter till Lady Lufton returned. Then he took his leave, with more abruptness than was usual with him, and without saying anything special to account for the duration of his visit. Neither did Griselda say anything special; and so the evening wore away, each feeling in some unconscious manner that she was on less intimate terms with the other than had previously been the case.

On the next day also Griselda would not go out,

but at four o'clock a servant brought a letter to her from Mount-street. Her mother had arrived in London and wished to see her at once. Mrs. Grantly sent her love to Lady Lufton, and would call at halfpast five, or at any later hour at which it might be convenient for Lady Lufton to see her. Griselda was to stay and dine in Mount-street; so said the letter. Lady Lufton declared that she would be very happy to see Mrs. Grantly at the hour named; and then, armed with this message, Griselda started for her mother's lodgings.

"I'll send the carriage for you," said Lady Lufton. "I suppose about ten will do."

"Thank you," said Griselda, "that will do very nicely;" and then she went.

Exactly at half-past five Mrs. Grantly was shown into Lady Lufton's drawing-room. Her daughter did not come with her, and Lady Lufton could see by the expression of her friend's face that business was to be discussed. Indeed, it was necessary that she herself should discuss business, for Mrs. Grantly must now be told that the family treaty could not be ratified. The gentleman declined the alliance, and poor Lady Lufton was uneasy in her mind at the nature of the task before her.

"Your coming up has been rather unexpected," said Lady Lufton, as soon as her friend was seated on the sofa.

"Yes, indeed; I got a letter from the archdeacon only this morning, which made it absolutely necessary that I should come."

"No bad news, I hope?" said Lady Lufton.

"No; I can't call it bad news. But, dear Lady

Lufton, things won't always turn out exactly as one would have them."

"No, indeed," said her ladyship, remembering that it was incumbent on her to explain to Mrs. Grantly now at this present interview the tidings with which her mind was fraught. She would, however, let Mrs. Grantly first tell her own story, feeling, perhaps, that the one might possibly bear upon the other.

"Poor dear Griselda!" said Mrs. Grantly, almost with a sigh. "I need not tell you, Lady Lufton, what my hopes were regarding her."

"Has she told you anything — anything that —"

"She would have spoken to you at once — and it was due to you that she should have done so — but she was timid; and not unnaturally so. And then it was right that she should see her father and me before she quite made up her own mind. But I may say that it is settled now."

"What is settled?" asked Lady Lufton.

"Of course it is impossible for any one to tell beforehand how these things will turn out," continued Mrs. Grantly, beating about the bush rather more than was necessary. "The dearest wish of my heart was to see her married to Lord Lufton. I should so much have wished to have her in the same county with me, and such a match as that would have fully satisfied my ambition."

"Well; I should rather think it might!" Lady Lufton did not say this out loud, but she thought it. Mrs. Grantly was absolutely speaking of a match between her daughter and Lord Lufton as though she would have displayed some amount of Christian moderation in putting up with it! Griselda Grantly might be a very nice girl; but even she — so thought Lady Lufton at the moment — might possibly be priced too highly.

"Dear Mrs. Grantly," she said, "I have foreseen for the last few days that our mutual hopes in this respect would not be gratified. Lord Lufton, I think; — but perhaps it is not necessary to explain — Had you not come up to town I should have written to you, — probably to-day. Whatever may be dear Griselda's fate in life, I sincerely hope that she may be happy."

"I think she will," said Mrs. Grantly, in a tone that expressed much satisfaction.

"Has — has anything —"

"Lord Dumbello proposed to Griselda the other night, at Miss Dunstable's party," said Mrs. Grantly, with her eyes fixed upon the floor, and assuming on the sudden much meekness in her manner; "and his lordship was with the archdeacon yesterday, and again this morning. I fancy he is in Mount-street at the present moment."

"Oh, indeed!" said Lady Lufton. She would have given worlds to have possessed at the moment sufficient self-command to have enabled her to express in her tone and manner unqualified satisfaction at the tidings. But she had not such self-command, and was painfully aware of her own deficiency.

"Yes," said Mrs. Grantly. "And as it is all so far settled, and as I know you are so kindly anxious about dear Griselda, I thought it right to let you know at once. Nothing can be more upright, honourable, and generous, than Lord Dumbello's conduct; and, on the whole, the match is one with which I and the archdeacon cannot but be contented."

"It is certainly a great match," said Lady Lufton. "Have you seen Lady Hartletop yet?"

Now Lady Hartletop could not be regarded as an agreeable connection, but this was the only word which escaped from Lady Lufton that could be considered in any way disparaging, and, on the whole, I think that she behaved well.

"Lord Dumbello is so completely his own master that that has not been necessary," said Mrs. Grantly. "The marquis has been told, and the archdeacon will see him either to-morrow or the day after."

There was nothing left for Lady Lufton but to congratulate her friend, and this she did in words perhaps not very sincere, but which, on the whole, were not badly chosen.

"I am sure I hope she will be very happy," said Lady Lufton, "and I trust that the alliance" — the word was very agreeable to Mrs. Grantly's ear — "will give unalloyed gratification to you and to her father. The position which she is called to fill is a very splendid one, but I do not think that it is above her merits."

This was very generous, and so Mrs. Grantly felt it. She had expected that her news would be received with the coldest shade of civility, and she was quite prepared to do battle if there were occasion. But she had no wish for war, and was almost grateful to Lady Lufton for her cordiality.

"Dear Lady Lufton," she said, "it is so kind of you to say so. I have told no one else, and of course would tell no one till you knew it. No one has known her and understood her so well as you have done. And I can assure you of this: that there is no one to whose friendship she looks forward in her new sphere of life with half so much pleasure as she does to yours."

Lady Lufton did not say much further. She could not declare that she expected much gratification from an intimacy with the future marchioness of Hartletop. The Hartletops and Luftons must, at any rate for her generation, live in a world apart, and she had now said all that her old friendship with Mrs. Grantly required. Mrs. Grantly understood all this quite as well as did Lady Lufton; but then Mrs. Grantly was much the better woman of the world.

It was arranged that Griselda should come back to Bruton Street for the night, and that her visit should then be brought to a close.

"The archdeacon thinks that for the present I had better remain up in town," said Mrs. Grantly, "and under the very peculiar circumstances Griselda will be — perhaps more comfortable with me."

To this Lady Lufton entirely agreed; and so they parted, excellent friends, embracing each other in a most affectionate manner.

That evening Griselda did return to Bruton Street, and Lady Lufton had to go through the further task of congratulating her. This was the more disagreeable of the two, especially so as it had to be thought over beforehand. But the young lady's excellent good sense and sterling qualities made the task comparatively an easy one. She neither cried, nor was impassioned, nor went into hysterics, nor showed any emotion. She did not even talk of her noble Dumbello — her generous Dumbello. She took Lady Lufton's kisses almost in silence, thanked her gently for her kindness, and made no allusion to her own future grandeur.

"I think I should like to go to bed early," she said, "as I must see to my packing-up."

"Richards will do all that for you, my dear."

"Oh, yes, thank you, nothing can be kinder than Richards. But I'll just see to my own dresses."

And so she went to bed early.

Lady Lufton did not see her son for the next two days, but when she did, of course she said a word or two about Griselda.

"You have heard the news, Ludovic?" she asked.

"Oh, yes; it's at all the clubs. I have been overwhelmed with presents of willow branches."

"You, at any rate, have got nothing to regret," she said.

"Nor you either, mother. I am sure that you do not think you have. Say that you do not regret it. Dearest mother, say so for my sake. Do you not know in your heart of hearts that she was not suited to be happy as my wife, — or to make me happy?"

"Perhaps not," said Lady Lufton, sighing. And then she kissed her son, and declared to herself that no girl in England could be good enough for him.

CHAPTER VII.

Salmon Fishing in Norway.

LORD DUMBELLO'S engagement with Griselda Grantly was the talk of the town for the next ten days. It formed, at least, one of two subjects which monopolized attention, the other being that dreadful rumour, first put in motion by Tom Towers at Miss Dunstable's party, as to a threatened dissolution of Parliament.

"Perhaps, after all, it will be the best thing for us," said Mr. Green Walker, who felt himself to be tolerably safe at Crewe Junction.

"I regard it as a most wicked attempt," said Harold Smith, who was not equally secure in his own borough, and to whom the expense of an election was disagreeable. "It is done in order that they may get time to tide over the autumn. They won't gain ten votes by a dissolution, and less than forty would hardly give them a majority. But they have no sense of public duty — none whatever. Indeed, I don't know who has."

"No, by Jove; that's just it. That's what my aunt Lady Hartletop says; there is no sense of duty left in the world. By-the-by, what an uncommon fool Dumbello is making himself!" And then the conversation went off to that other topic.

Lord Lufton's joke against himself about the willow branches was all very well, and nobody dreamed that his heart was sore in that matter. The world was laughing at Lord Dumbello for what it chose to call a foolish match, and Lord Lufton's friends talked to him about it as though they had never suspected that he could have made an ass of himself in the same direction; but, nevertheless, he was not altogether contented. He by no means wished to marry Griselda; he had declared to himself a dozen times since he had first suspected his mother's manœuvres, that no consideration on earth should induce him to do so; he had pronounced her to be cold, insipid, and unattractive in spite of her beauty; and yet he felt almost angry that Lord Dumbello should have been successful. And this, too, was the more inexcusable, seeing that he had never forgotten Lucy Robarts, had never ceased to love her, and that, in holding those various conversations within his own bosom, he was as loud in Lucy's favour as he was in dispraise of Griselda.

"Your hero, then," I hear some well-balanced critic say, "is not worth very much."

In the first place Lord Lufton is not my hero; and in the next place, a man may be very imperfect and yet worth a great deal. A man may be as imperfect as Lord Lufton, and yet worthy of a good mother and a good wife. If not, how many of us are unworthy of the mothers and wives we have! It is my belief that few young men settle themselves down to the work of the world, to the begetting of children, and carving and paying and struggling and fretting for the same, without having first been in love with four or five possible mothers for them, and probably with two or three at the same time. And yet these men are, as a rule, worthy of the excellent wives that ultimately fall to their lot. In this way Lord Lufton had, to a certain extent, been in love with Griselda. There had been one moment in his life in which he would have offered her his hand, had not her discretion been so excellent; and though that moment never returned, still he suffered from some feeling akin to disappointment, when he learned that Griselda had been won and was to be worn. He was, then, a dog in the manger, you will say. Well; and are we not all dogs in the manger, more or less actively? Is not that manger-doggishness one of the most common phases of the human heart?

But not the less was Lord Lufton truly in love with Lucy Robarts. Had he fancied that any Dumbello was carrying on a siege before that fortress, his vexation would have manifested itself in a very different manner. He could joke about Griselda Grantly with a frank face and a happy tone of voice; but had he heard of any tidings of a similar import with reference to Lucy, he would have been past all joking, and I much doubt whether it would not even have affected his appetite.

"Mother," he said to Lady Lufton, a day or two after the declaration of Griselda's engagement, "I am going to Norway to fish."

"To Norway, — to fish!"

"Yes. We've got rather a nice party. Clontarf is going, and Culpepper —"

"What, that horrid man!"

"He's an excellent hand at fishing; and Haddington Peebles, and — and — there'll be six of us altogether; and we start this day week."

"That's rather sudden, Ludovic."

"Yes, it is sudden; but we're sick of London. I should not care to go so soon myself, but Clontarf and Culpepper say that the season is early this year. I must go down to Framley before I start — about my horses; and therefore I came to tell you that I shall be there to-morrow."

"At Framley to-morrow! If you could put it off for three days I should be going myself."

But Lord Lufton could not put it off for three days. It may be that on this occasion he did not wish for his mother's presence at Framley while he was there; that he conceived that he should be more at his ease in giving orders about his stable if he were alone while so employed. At any rate he declined her company, and on the following morning did go down to Framley by himself.

"Mark," said Mrs. Robarts, hurrying into her husband's book-room about the middle of the day, "Lord Lufton is at home. Have you heard it?"

"What; here at Framley?"

"He is over at Framley Court; so the servants say. Carson saw him in the paddock with some of the horses. Won't you go and see him?"

"Of course I will," said Mark, shutting up his papers. "Lady Lufton can't be here, and if he is alone he will probably come and dine."

"I don't know about that," said Mrs. Robarts, thinking of poor Lucy.

"He is not in the least particular. What does for us will do for him. I shall ask him, at any rate." And without further parley the clergyman took up his hat and went off in search of his friend.

Lucy Robarts had been present when the gardener brought in tidings of Lord Lufton's arrival at Framley, and was aware that Fanny had gone to tell her husband.

"He won't come here, will he?" she said, as soon as Mrs. Robarts returned.

"I can't say," said Fanny. "I hope not. He ought not to do so, and I don't think he will. But Mark says that he will ask him to dinner."

"Then, Fanny, I must be taken ill. There is nothing else for it."

"I don't think he will come. I don't think he can be so cruel. Indeed, I feel sure that he won't; but I thought it right to tell you."

Lucy also conceived that it was improbable that Lord Lufton should come to the parsonage under the present circumstances; and she declared to herself that it would not be possible that she should appear at table if he did do so; but, nevertheless, the idea of his being at Framley was, perhaps, not altogether painful to her. She did not recognize any pleasure as coming to her from his arrival, but still there was something in his presence which was, unconsciously to herself, soothing to her feelings. But that terrible question remained; — how was she to act if it should turn out that he was coming to dinner?

"If he does come, Fanny," she said, solemnly, after a pause, "I must keep to my own room, and leave Mark to think what he pleases. It will be better for me to make a fool of myself there, than in his presence in the drawing-room."

Mark Robarts took his hat and stick and went over at once to the home paddock, in which he knew that Lord Lufton was engaged with the horses and grooms. He also was in no supremely happy frame of mind, for his correspondence with Mr. Tozer was on the increase. He had received notice from that indefatigable gentleman that certain "overdue bills" were now lying at the bank in Barchester, and were very desirous of his, Mr. Robarts's, notice. A concatenation of certain peculiarly unfortunate circumstances made it indispensably necessary that Mr. Tozer should be repaid, without further loss of time, the various sums of money which he had advanced on the credit of Mr. Robarts's name, &c. &c. &c. No absolute threat was put forth, and, singular to say, no actual amount was named. Mr. Robarts, however, could not but observe, with a most painfully accurate attention, that mention was made, not of an overdue bill, but of overdue bills. What if Mr. Tozer were to demand from him the instant repayment of nine hundred pounds? Hitherto he had merely written to Mr. Sowerby, and he might have had an answer from that gentleman this morning, but no such answer had as yet reached him. Consequently he was not, at the present moment, in a very happy frame of mind.

He soon found himself with Lord Lufton and the horses. Four or five of them were being walked slowly about the paddock, in the care of as many men or boys, and the sheets were being taken off them — off one after another, so that their master might look at them with the more accuracy and satisfaction. But though Lord Lufton was thus doing his duty, and going through his work, he was not doing it with his whole heart, — as the head groom perceived very well. He was fretful about the nags, and seemed anxious to get them out of his sight, as soon as he had made a decent pretext of looking at them.

"How are you, Lufton?" said Robarts, coming forward. "They told me that you were down, and so I came across at once."

"Yes; I only got here this morning, and should have been over with you directly. I am going to Norway for six weeks or so, and it seems that the fish are so early this year, that we must start at once. I have a matter on which I want to speak to you before

I leave; and, indeed, it was that which brought me down more than anything else."

There was something hurried and not altogether easy about his manner as he spoke, which struck Robarts, and made him think that this promised matter to be spoken of would not be agreeable in discussion. He did not know whether Lord Lufton might not again be mixed up with Tozer and the bills.

"You will dine with us to-day," he said, "if, as I suppose, you are all alone."

"Yes, I am all alone."

"Then, you'll come?"

"Well; I don't quite know. No, I don't think I can go over to dinner. Don't look so disgusted. I'll explain it all to you just now."

What could there be in the wind; and how was it possible that Tozer's bill should make it inexpedient for Lord Lufton to dine at the parsonage? Robarts, however, said nothing further about it at the moment, but turned off to look at the horses.

"They are an uncommonly nice set of animals," said he.

"Well, yes; I don't know. When a man has four or five horses to look at, somehow or other he never has one fit to go. That chesnut mare is a picture, now that nobody wants her; but she wasn't able to carry me well to hounds a single day last winter. Take them in, Pounce; that'll do."

"Won't your lordship run your eye over the old black 'oss?" said Pounce, the head groom, in a melancholy tone; "he's as fine, sir — as fine as a stag."

"To tell you the truth, I think they're too fine;

but that'll do; take them in. And now, Mark, if you're at leisure, we'll take a turn round the place."

Mark, of course, was at leisure, and so they started on their walk.

"You're too difficult to please about your stable," Robarts began.

"Never mind the stable now," said Lord Lufton. "The truth is, I am not thinking about it. Mark," he then said, very abruptly, "I want you to be frank with me. Has your sister ever spoken to you about me?"

"My sister; Lucy?"

"Yes; your sister Lucy."

"No, never; at least nothing especial; nothing that I can remember at this moment."

"Nor your wife?"

"Spoken about you! — Fanny? Of course she has, in an ordinary way. It would be impossible that she should not. But what do you mean?"

"Have either of them told you that I made an offer to your sister?"

"That you made an offer to Lucy?"

"Yes, that I made an offer to Lucy."

"No; nobody has told me so. I have never dreamed of such a thing; nor, as far as I believe, have they. If anybody has spread such a report, or said that either of them have hinted at such a thing, it is a base lie. Good heavens! Lufton, for what do you take them?"

"But I did," said his lordship.

"Did what?" said the parson.

"I did make your sister an offer."

"You made Lucy an offer of marriage!"

"Yes, I did; — in as plain language as a gentleman could use to a lady."

"And what answer did she make?"

"She refused me. And now, Mark, I have come down here with the express purpose of making that offer again. Nothing could be more decided than your sister's answer. It struck me as being almost uncourteously decided. But still it is possible that circumstances may have weighed with her, which ought not to weigh with her. If her love be not given to any one else, I may still have a chance of it. It's the old story of faint heart, you know: at any rate, I mean to try my luck again; and thinking over it with deliberate purpose, I have come to the conclusion that I ought to tell you before I see her."

Lord Lufton in love with Lucy! As these words repeated themselves over and over again within Mark Robarts's mind, his mind added to them notes of surprise without end. How had it possibly come about, — and why? In his estimation his sister Lucy was a very simple girl — not plain indeed, but by no means beautiful; certainly not stupid, but by no means brilliant. And then, he would have said, that of all men whom he knew, Lord Lufton would have been the last to fall in love with such a girl as his sister. And now, what was he to say or do? What views was he bound to hold? In what direction should he act? There was Lady Lufton on the one side, to whom he owed everything. How would life be possible to him in that parsonage — within a few yards of her elbow — if he consented to receive Lord Lufton as the acknowledged suitor of his sister? It would be a great match for Lucy, doubtless; but — Indeed, he could not bring himself to believe that Lucy could in truth become the absolute reigning queen of Framley Court.

"Do you think that Fanny knows anything of all this?" he said, after a moment or two.

"I cannot possibly tell. If she does, it is not with my knowledge. I should have thought that you could best answer that."

"I cannot answer it at all," said Mark. "I, at least, have had no remotest idea of such a thing."

"Your ideas of it now need not be at all remote," said Lord Lufton, with a faint smile; "and you may know it as a fact. I did make her an offer of marriage; I was refused; I am going to repeat it; and I am now taking you into my confidence, in order that, as her brother, and as my friend, you may give me such assistance as you can." They then walked on in silence for some yards, after which Lord Lufton added: "And now I'll dine with you to-day if you wish it."

Mr. Robarts did not know what to say; he could not bethink himself what answer duty required of him. He had no right to interfere between his sister and such a marriage, if she herself should wish it; but still there was something terrible in the thought of it! He had a vague conception that it must come to evil; that the project was a dangerous one; and that it could not finally result happily for any of them. What would Lady Lufton say? That undoubtedly was the chief source of his dismay.

"Have you spoken to your mother about this?" he said.

"My mother? no; why speak to her till I know my fate? A man does not like to speak much of such matters if there be a probability of his being rejected. I tell you because I do not like to make my way into your house under a false pretence."

"But what would Lady Lufton say?"

"I think it probable that she would be displeased on the first hearing it; that in four-and-twenty hours she would be reconciled; and that after a week or so Lucy would be her dearest favourite and the prime minister of all her machinations. You don't know my mother as well as I do. She would give her head off her shoulders to do me a pleasure."

"And for that reason," said Mark Robarts, "you ought, if possible, to do her pleasure."

"I cannot absolutely marry a wife of her choosing, if you mean that," said Lord Lufton.

They went on walking about the garden for an hour, but they hardly got any farther than the point to which we have now brought them. Mark Robarts could not make up his mind on the spur of the moment; nor, as he said more than once to Lord Lufton, could he be at all sure that Lucy would in any way be guided by him. It was, therefore, at last settled between them that Lord Lufton should come to the parsonage immediately after breakfast on the following morning. It was agreed also that the dinner had better not come off, and Robarts promised that he would, if possible, have determined by the morning as to what advice he would give his sister.

He went direct home to the parsonage from Framley Court, feeling that he was altogether in the dark till he should have consulted his wife. How would he feel if Lucy were to become Lady Lufton? and how would he look Lady Lufton in the face in telling her that such was to be his sister's destiny? On returning home he immediately found his wife, and had not been closeted with her five minutes before he knew, at any rate, all that she knew.

"And you mean to say that she does love him?" said Mark.

"Indeed she does; and is it not natural that she should? When I saw them so much together I feared that she would. But I never thought that he would care for her."

Even Fanny did not as yet give Lucy credit for half her attractiveness. After an hour's talking the interview between the husband and wife ended in a message to Lucy, begging her to join them both in the book-room.

"Aunt Lucy," said a chubby little darling, who was taken up into his aunt's arms as he spoke, "papa and mama 'ant 'oo in te tuddy, and I musn't go wis 'oo."

Lucy, as she kissed the boy and pressed his face against her own, felt that her blood was running quick to her heart.

"Musn't oo' go wis me, my own one?" she said as she put her playfellow down; but she played with the child only because she did not wish to betray even to him that she was hardly mistress of herself. She knew that Lord Lufton was at Framley; she knew that her brother had been to him; she knew that a proposal had been made that he should come there that day to dinner. Must it not therefore be the case that this call to a meeting in the study had arisen out of Lord Lufton's arrival at Framley? and yet, how could it have done so? Had Fanny betrayed her in order to prevent the dinner invitation? It could not be possible that Lord Lufton himself should have spoken on the subject! And then she again stooped to kiss the child, rubbed her hands across her forehead to smooth her hair, and erase, if that might be possible, the look of care which she wore, and then descended slowly to her brother's sitting-room.

Her hand paused for a second on the door ere she opened it, but she had resolved that, come what might, she would be brave. She pushed it open and walked in with a bold front, with eyes wide open, and a slow step.

"Frank says that you want me," she said.

Mr. Robarts and Fanny were both standing up by the fireplace, and each waited a second for the other to speak when Lucy entered the room, and then Fanny began, —

"Lord Lufton is here, Lucy."

"Here! Where? At the parsonage?"

"No, not at the parsonage; but over at Framley Court," said Mark.

"And he promises to call here after breakfast to-morrow," said Fanny. And then again there was a pause. Mrs. Robarts hardly dared to look Lucy in the face. She had not betrayed her trust, seeing that the secret had been told to Mark, not by her, but by Lord Lufton; but she could not but feel that Lucy would think that she had betrayed it.

"Very well," said Lucy, trying to smile; "I have no objection in life."

"But, Lucy, dear," — and now Mrs. Robarts put her arm round her sister-in-law's waist, — "he is coming here especially to see you."

"Oh; that makes a difference. I am afraid that I shall be — engaged."

"He has told everything to Mark," said Mrs. Robarts.

Lucy now felt that her bravery was almost deserting her. She hardly knew which way to look or how to stand. Had Fanny told everything also? There was so much that Fanny knew that Lord Lufton could not have known. But, in truth, Fanny had told all — the whole story of Lucy's love, and had described the reasons which had induced her to reject her suitor; and had done so in words which, had Lord Lufton heard them, would have made him twice as passionate in his love.

And then it certainly did occur to Lucy to think why Lord Lufton should have come to Framley and told all this history to her brother. She attempted for a moment to make herself believe that she was angry with him for doing so. But she was not angry. She had not time to argue much about it, but there came upon her a gratified sensation of having been remembered, and thought of, and — loved. Must it not be so? Could it be possible that he himself would have told this tale to her brother, if he did not still love her? Fifty times she had said to herself that his offer had been an affair of the moment, and fifty times she had been unhappy in so saying. But this new coming of his could not be an affair of the moment. She had been the dupe, she had thought, of an absurd passion on her own part; but now — how was it now? She did not bring herself to think that she should ever be Lady Lufton. She had still, in some perversely obstinate manner, made up her mind against that result. But yet, nevertheless, it did in some unaccountable manner satisfy her to feel that Lord Lufton had himself come down to Framley and himself told this story.

"He has told everything to Mark," said Mrs. Robarts; and then again there was a pause for a moment, during which these thoughts passed through Lucy's mind.

"Yes," said Mark, "he has told me all, and he is coming here to-morrow morning that he may receive an answer from yourself."

"What answer?" said Lucy, trembling.

"Nay, dearest; who can say that but yourself?" and her sister-in-law, as she spoke, pressed close against her. "You must say that yourself."

Mrs. Robarts in her long conversation with her husband had pleaded strongly on Lucy's behalf, taking, as it were, a part against Lady Lufton. She had said that if Lord Lufton persevered in his suit, they at the parsonage could not be justified in robbing Lucy of all that she had won for herself, in order to do Lady Lufton's pleasure.

"But she will think," said Mark, "that we have plotted and intrigued for this. She will call us ungrateful, and will make Lucy's life wretched." To which the wife had answered, that all that must be left in God's hands. They had not plotted or intrigued. Lucy, though loving the man in her heart of hearts, had already once refused him, because she would not be thought to have snatched at so great a prize. But if Lord Lufton loved her so warmly that he had come down there in this manner, on purpose, as he himself had put it, that he might learn his fate, then — so argued Mrs. Robarts — they two, let their loyalty to Lady Lufton be ever so strong, could not justify it to their consciences to stand between Lucy and her lover. Mark had still somewhat demurred to this, suggesting how terrible would be their plight if they should now encourage Lord Lufton, and if he, after such encouragement, when they should have quarrelled with Lady Lufton, should allow himself to be led away from his engagement by his mother. To which Fanny had announced that justice was justice, and that right was right. Everything must be told to Lucy, and she must judge for herself.

"But I do not know what Lord Lufton wants," said Lucy, with her eyes fixed upon the ground, and now trembling more than ever. "He did come to me, and I did give him an answer."

"And is that answer to be final?" said Mark, — somewhat cruelly, for Lucy had not yet been told that her lover had made any repetition of his proposal. Fanny, however, determined that no injustice should be done, and therefore she at last continued the story.

"We know that you did give him an answer, dearest; but gentlemen sometimes will not put up with one answer on such a subject. Lord Lufton has declared to Mark that he means to ask again. He has come down here on purpose to do so."

"And Lady Lufton —" said Lucy, speaking hardly above a whisper, and still hiding her face as she leaned against her sister's shoulder.

"Lord Lufton has not spoken to his mother about it," said Mark; and it immediately became clear to Lucy from the tone of her brother's voice, that he, at least, would not be pleased, should she accept her lover's vow.

"You must decide out of your own heart, dear," said Fanny, generously. "Mark and I know how well you have behaved, for I have told him everything." Lucy shuddered and leaned closer against her sister as this was said to her. "I had no alternative, dearest, but to tell him. It was best so; was it not? But nothing has been told to Lord Lufton. Mark would not let him come here to-day, because it would have flurried you, and he wished to give you time to think. But you can see him to-morrow morning, — can you not? and then answer him."

Lucy now stood perfectly silent, feeling that she dearly loved her sister-in-law for her sisterly kindness — for that sisterly wish to promote a sister's love, but still there was in her mind a strong resolve not to allow Lord Lufton to come there under the idea that he would be received as a favoured lover. Her love was powerful, but so also was her pride; and she could not bring herself to bear the scorn which would lay in Lady Lufton's eyes. "His mother will despise me, and then he will despise me too," she said to herself; and with a strong gulp of disappointed love and ambition she determined to persist.

"Shall we leave you now, dear; and speak of it again to-morrow morning, before he comes?" said Fanny.

"That will be the best" said Mark. "Turn it in your mind every way to-night. Think of it when you have said your prayers — and, Lucy, come here to me;" — then, taking her in his arms, he kissed her with a tenderness that was not customary with him towards her. "It is fair," said he, "that I should tell you this: that I have perfect confidence in your judgment and feeling; and that I will stand by you as your brother in whatever decision you may come to. Fanny and I both think that you have behaved excellently, and are both of us sure that you will do what is best. Whatever you do I will stick to you; — and so will Fanny."

"Dearest, dearest Mark!"

"And now we will say nothing more about it till to-morrow morning," said Fanny.

But Lucy felt that this saying nothing more about it till to-morrow morning would be tantamount to an acceptance on her part of Lord Lufton's offer. Mrs. Robarts knew, and Mr. Robarts also now knew, the secret of her heart; and if, such being the case, she allowed Lord Lufton to come there with the acknowledged purpose of pleading his own suit, it would be impossible for her not to yield. If she were resolved that she would not yield, now was the time for her to stand her ground and make her fight.

"Do not go, Fanny; at least not quite yet," she said.

"Well, dear?"

"I want you to stay while I tell Mark. He must not let Lord Lufton come here to-morrow."

"Not let him!" said Mrs. Robarts.

Mr. Robarts said nothing, but he felt that his sister was rising in his esteem from minute to minute.

"No; Mark must bid him not come. He will not wish to pain me when it can do no good. Look here, Mark;" and she walked over to her brother, and put both her hands upon his arm. "I do love Lord Lufton. I had no such meaning or thought when I first knew him. But I do love him — I love him dearly; almost as well as Fanny loves you, I suppose. You may tell him so if you think proper — nay, you must tell him so, or he will not understand me. But tell him this, as coming from me: that I will never marry him, unless his mother asks me."

"She will not do that, I fear," said Mark, sorrowfully.

"No; I suppose not," said Lucy, now regaining all her courage. "If I thought it probable that she should wish me to be her daughter-in-law, it would not be necessary that I should make such a stipulation. It is because she will not wish it; because she would regard me as unfit to — to — to mate with her son. She would hate me, and scorn me; and then he would begin to scorn me, and perhaps would cease to love me. I could not bear her eye upon me, if she thought that I had injured her son. Mark, you will go to him now; will you not? and explain this to him; — as much of it as is necessary. Tell him, that if his mother asks me I will — consent. But that as I know that she never will, he is to look upon all that he has said as forgotten. With me it shall be the same as though it were forgotten."

Such was her verdict, and so confident were they both of her firmness — of her obstinacy Mark would have called it on any other occasion, — that they, neither of them, sought to make her alter it.

"You will go to him now, — this afternoon; will you not?" she said; and Mark promised that he would. He could not but feel that he himself was greatly relieved. Lady Lufton might probably hear that her son had been fool enough to fall in love with the parson's sister, but under existing circumstances she could not consider herself aggrieved either by the parson or by his sister. Lucy was behaving well, and Mark was proud of her. Lucy was behaving with fierce spirit, and Fanny was grieving for her.

"I'd rather be by myself till dinner-time," said Lucy, as Mrs. Robarts prepared to go with her out of the room. "Dear Fanny, don't look unhappy; there's nothing to make us unhappy. I told you I should want goats' milk, and that will be all."

Robarts, after sitting for an hour with his wife, did return again to Framley Court; and, after a considerable search, found Lord Lufton returning home to a late dinner.

"Unless my mother asks her," said he, when the story had been told him. "That is nonsense. Surely you told her that such is not the way of the world."

Robarts endeavoured to explain to him that Lucy could not endure to think that her husband's mother should look on her with disfavour.

"Does she think that my mother dislikes her — her specially?" asked Lord Lufton.

No; Robarts could not suppose that that was the case; but Lady Lufton might probably think that a marriage with a clergyman's sister would be a mésalliance.

"That is out of the question," said Lord Lufton; "as she has especially wanted me to marry a clergyman's daughter for some time past. But, Mark, it is absurd talking about my mother. A man in these days is not to marry as his mother bids him."

Mark could only assure him, in answer to all this, that Lucy was very firm in what she was doing, that she had quite made up her mind, and that she altogether absolved Lord Lufton from any necessity to speak to his mother, if he did not think well of doing so. But all this was to very little purpose.

"She does love me then?" said Lord Lufton.

"Well," said Mark, "I will not say whether she does or does not. I can only repeat her own message. She cannot accept you, unless she does so at your mother's request." And having said that again, he took his leave, and went back to the parsonage.

Poor Lucy, having finished her interview with so much dignity, having fully satisfied her brother, and declined any immediate consolation from her sister-in-law, betook herself to her own bed-room. She had to think over what she had said and done, and it was necessary that she should be alone to do so. It might be that, when she came to reconsider the matter she would not be quite so well satisfied as was her brother. Her grandeur of demeanour and slow propriety of carriage lasted her till she was well into her own room. There are animals who, when they are ailing in any way, contrive to hide themselves, ashamed, as it were, that the weakness of their suffering should be witnessed. Indeed, I am not sure whether all dumb animals do not do so more or less; and in this respect Lucy was like a dumb animal. Even in her confidences with Fanny she made a joke of her own misfortunes, and spoke of her heart ailments with self-ridicule. But now, having walked up the staircase with no hurried step, and having deliberately locked the door, she turned herself round to suffer in silence and solitude — as do the beasts and birds.

She sat herself down on a low chair, which stood at the foot of her bed, and, throwing back her head, held her handkerchief across her eyes and forehead, holding it tight in both her hands; and then she began to think. She began to think and also to cry, for the tears came running down from beneath the handkerchief; and low sobs were to be heard, — only that the animal had taken itself off, to suffer in solitude.

Had she not thrown from her all her chances of happiness? Was it possible that he should come to her yet again, — a third time? No; it was not possible. The very mode and pride of this, her second rejection of him, made it impossible. In coming to her determination, and making her avowal, she had been actuated by the knowledge that Lady Lufton would regard such a marriage with abhorrence. Lady Lufton would not and could not ask her to condescend to be her son's bride. Her chance of happiness, of glory, of ambition, of love, was all gone. She had sacrificed everything, not to virtue, but to pride. And she had sacrificed not only herself, but him. When first he came there; when she had meditated over his first visit, she had hardly given him credit for deep love; but now, — there could be no doubt that he loved her now. After his season in London, his days and nights passed with all that was beautiful, he had returned there, to that little country parsonage, that he might again throw himself at her feet. And she — she had refused to see him, though she loved him with all her heart, she had refused to see him because she was so vile a coward that she could not bear the sour looks of an old woman!

"I will come down directly," she said, when Fanny at last knocked at the door, begging to be admitted. "I won't open it, love, but I will be with you in ten minutes; I will, indeed." And so she was; not, perhaps, without traces of tears, discernible by the experienced eye of Mrs. Robarts, but yet with a smooth brow, and voice under her own command.

"I wonder whether she really loves him," Mark said to his wife that night.

"Love him!" his wife had answered; "indeed she does; and, Mark, do not be led away by the stern quiet of her demeanour. To my thinking she is a girl who might almost die for love."

On the next day Lord Lufton left Framley; and started, according to his arrangements, for the Norway salmon fishing.

CHAPTER VIII.

The Goat and Compasses.

Harold Smith had been made unhappy by that rumour of a dissolution; but the misfortune to him would be as nothing compared to the severity with which it would fall on Mr. Sowerby. Harold Smith might or might not lose his borough, but Mr. Sowerby would undoubtedly lose his county; and, in losing that, he would lose everything. He felt very certain now that the duke would not support him again, let who would be master of Chaldicotes; and as he reflected on these things he found it very hard to keep up his spirits.

Tom Towers, it seems, had known all about it, as he always does. The little remark which had dropped from him at Miss Dunstable's, made, no doubt, after mature deliberation, and with profound political motives, was the forerunner, only by twelve hours, of a very general report that the giants were going to the country. It was manifest that the giants had not a majority in Parliament, generous as had been the promises of support disinterestedly made to them by the gods. This indeed was manifest, and therefore they were going to the country, although they had been deliberately warned by a very prominent scion of Olympus that if they did do so that disinterested support must be withdrawn. This threat did not seem to weigh much, and by two o'clock on the day following Miss Dunstable's party, the fiat was presumed to have gone forth. The rumour had begun with Tom Towers, but by that time it had reached Buggins at the Petty Bag Office.

"It won't make no difference to hus, sir; will it, Mr. Robarts?" said Buggins, as he leaned respectfully against the wall near the door, in the room of the private secretary at that establishment.

A good deal of conversation, miscellaneous, special, and political, went on between young Robarts and Buggins in the course of the day; as was natural, seeing that they were thrown in these evil times very much upon each other. The Lord Petty Bag of the present ministry was not such a one as Harold Smith. He was a giant indifferent to his private notes, and careless as to the duties even of patronage; he rarely visited the office, and as there were no other clerks in the establishment — owing to a root and branch reform carried out in the short reign of Harold Smith — to whom could young Robarts talk, if not to Buggins?

"No; I suppose not," said Robarts, as he completed on his blotting-paper an elaborate picture of a Turk seated on his divan.

"'Cause, you see, sir, we're in the Upper 'Ouse, now; — as I always thinks we hought to be. I don't think it ain't constitutional for the Petty Bag to be in the Commons, Mr. Robarts. Hany ways, it never usen't."

"They're changing all those sort of thing now-a-days, Buggins," said Robarts, giving the final touch to the Turk's smoke.

"Well; I'll tell you what it is, Mr. Robarts. I think I'll go. I can't stand all these changes. I'm turned of sixty now, and don't want any 'stifflicates. I think I'll take my pension and walk. The hoffice ain't the same place at all since it come down among the Commons." And then Buggins retired sighing, to console himself with a pot of porter behind a large open office ledger, set up on end on a small table in the little lobby outside the private secretary's room. Buggins sighed again as he saw that the date made visible in the open book was almost as old as his own appointment; for such a book as this lasted long in the Petty Bag Office. A peer of high degree had been Lord Petty Bag in those days; one whom a messenger's heart could respect with infinite veneration, as he made his unaccustomed visits to the office with much solemnity — perhaps four times during the season. The Lord Petty Bag then was highly regarded by his staff, and his coming among them was talked about for some hours previously and for some days afterwards; but Harold Smith had bustled in and out like the managing clerk in a Manchester house. "The service is going to the dogs," said Buggins to himself, as he put down the porter pot and looked up over the book at a gentleman who presented himself at the door.

"Mr. Robarts in his room?" said Buggins, repeating the gentleman's words. "Yes, Mr. Sowerby; you'll find him there; first door to the left." And then, remembering that the visitor was a county member, a position which Buggins regarded as next to that of a peer, he got up, and, opening the private secretary's door, ushered in the visitor.

Young Robarts and Mr. Sowerby had, of course, become acquainted in the days of Harold Smith's reign. During that short time the member for East Barset had on most days dropped in at the Petty Bag Office for a minute or two, finding out what the energetic cabinet minister was doing, chatting on semi-official subjects, and teaching the private secretary to laugh at his master. There was nothing, therefore, in his present visit which need appear to be singular, or which required any immediate special explanation. He sat himself down in his ordinary way, and began to speak of the subject of the day.

"We're all to go," said Sowerby.

"So I hear," said the private secretary. "It will give me no trouble, for, as the respectable Buggins says, we're in the Upper House now."

"What a delightful time those lucky dogs of lords do have!" said Sowerby. "No constituents, no turning out, no fighting, no necessity for political opinions, — and, as a rule, no such opinions at all!"

"I suppose you're tolerably safe in East Barsetshire?" said Robarts. "The duke has it pretty much his own way there."

"Yes; the duke does have it pretty much his own way. By-the-by, where is your brother?"

"At home," said Robarts; "at least I presume so."

"At Framley or at Barchester? I believe he was in residence at Barchester not long since."

"He's at Framley now, I know. I got a letter only yesterday, from his wife, with a commission. He was there, and Lord Lufton had just left."

"Yes; Lufton was down. He started for Norway this morning. I want to see your brother. You have not heard from him yourself, have you?"

"No; not lately. Mark is a bad correspondent. He would not do at all for a private secretary."

"At any rate, not to Harold Smith. But you are sure I should not catch him at Barchester?"

"Send down by telegraph, and he would meet you."

"I don't want to do that. A telegraph message makes such a fuss in the country, frightening people's wives, and setting all the horses about the place galloping."

"What is it about?"

"Nothing of any great consequence. I didn't know whether he might have told you. I'll write down by to-night's post, and then he can meet me at Barchester to-morrow. Or do you write. There's nothing I hate so much as letter-writing;—just tell him that I called, and that I shall be much obliged if he can meet me at the Dragon of Wantly — say at two to-morrow. I will go down by the express."

Mark Robarts, in talking over this coming money trouble with Sowerby, had once mentioned that if it were necessary to take up the bill for a short time he might be able to borrow the money from his brother. So much of the father's legacy still remained in the hands of the private secretary as would enable him to produce the amount of the latter bill, and there could be no doubt that he would lend it if asked. Mr. Sowerby's visit to the Petty Bag Office had been caused by a desire to learn whether any such request had been made, — and also by a half-formed resolution to make the request himself if he should find that the clergyman had not done so. It seemed to him to be a pity that such a sum should be lying about, as it were, within reach, and that he should not stoop to put his hands upon it. Such abstinence would be so contrary to all the practice of his life that it was as difficult to him as it is for a sportsman to let pass a cock-pheasant. But yet something like remorse touched his heart as he sat there balancing himself on his chair in the private secretary's room, and looking at the young man's open face.

"Yes; I'll write to him," said John Robarts; "but he hasn't said anything to me about anything particular."

"Hasn't he? It does not much signify. I only mentioned it because I thought I understood him to say that he would." And then Mr. Sowerby went on swinging himself. How was it that he felt so averse to mention that little sum of 500 *l.* to a young man like John Robarts, a fellow without wife or children or calls on him of any sort, who would not even be injured by the loss of the money, seeing that he had an ample salary on which to live? He wondered at his own weakness. The want of the money was urgent on him in the extreme. He had reasons for supposing that Mark would find it very difficult to renew the bills, but he, Sowerby, could stop their presentation if he could get this money at once into his own hands.

"Can I do anything for you?" said the innocent lamb, offering his throat to the butcher.

But some unwonted feeling numbed the butcher's fingers, and blunted his knife. He sat still for half a minute after the question, and then jumping from his seat, declined the offer. "No, no; nothing, thank you. Only write to Mark, and say that I shall be there to-morrow," and then, taking his hat, he hurried out of the office. "What an ass I am," he said to himself as he went: "as if it were of any use now to be particular!"

He then got into a cab and had himself driven half way up Portman Street towards the New Road, and walking from thence a few hundred yards down a cross-street he came to a public-house. It was called the "Goat and Compasses," — a very meaningless name, one would say; but the house boasted of being a place of public entertainment very long established on that site, having been a tavern out in the country in the days of Cromwell. At that time the pious landlord, putting up a pious legend for the benefit of his pious customers, had declared that — "God encompasseth us." The "Goat and Compasses" in these days does quite as well; and, considering the present character of the house, was perhaps less unsuitable than the old legend.

"Is Mr. Austen here?" asked Mr. Sowerby of the man at the bar.

"Which on 'em? Not Mr. John; he ain't here. Mr. Tom is in, — the little room on the left-hand side."

The man whom Mr. Sowerby would have preferred to see was the elder brother, John; but as he was not to be found, he did go into the little room. In that room he found — Mr. Austen, Junior, according to one arrangement of nomenclature, and Mr. Tom Tozer according to another. To gentlemen of the legal profession he generally chose to introduce himself as belonging to the respectable family of the Austens; but among his intimates, he had always been — Tozer.

Mr. Sowerby, though he was intimate with the family, did not love the Tozers: but he especially hated Tom Tozer. Tom Tozer was a bull-necked, beetle-browed fellow, the expression of whose face was eloquent with acknowledged roguery. "I am a rogue," it seemed to say. "I know it; all the world knows it: but you're another. All the world don't know that, but I do. Men are all rogues, pretty nigh. Some are soft rogues, and some are 'cute rogues. I am a 'cute one; so mind your eye." It was with such words that Tom Tozer's face spoke out; and though a thorough liar in his heart, he was not a liar in his face.

"Well, Tozer," said Mr. Sowerby, absolutely shaking hands with the dirty miscreant, "I wanted to see your brother."

"John ain't here, and ain't like; but it's all as one."

"Yes, yes; I suppose it is. I know you two hunt in couples."

"I don't know what you mean about hunting, Mr. Sowerby. You gents 'as all the hunting, and we poor folk 'as all the work. I hope you're going to make up this trifle of money we're out of so long."

"It's about that I've called. I don't know what you call long, Tozer; but the last bill was only dated in February."

"It's overdue; ain't it?"

"Oh, yes; it's overdue. There's no doubt about that."

"Well; when a bit of paper is come round, the next thing is to take it up. Them's my ideas. And to tell you the truth, Mr. Sowerby, we don't think as 'ow you've been treating us just on the square lately. In that matter of Lord Lufton's you was down on us uncommon."

"You know I couldn't help myself."

"Well; and we can't help ourselves now. That's where it is, Mr. Sowerby. Lord love you; we know what's what, we do. And so, the fact is we're uncommon low as to the ready just at present, and we must have them few hundred pounds. We must have them at once, or we must sell up that clerical gent. I'm dashed if it ain't as hard to get money from a parson as it is to take a bone from a dog. 'E's 'ad 'is account, no doubt, and why don't 'e pay?"

Mr. Sowerby had called with the intention of explaining that he was about to proceed to Barchester on the following day with the express view of "making arrangements" about this bill; and had he seen John Tozer, John would have been compelled to accord to him some little extension of time. Both Tom and John knew this; and, therefore, John — the soft-hearted one — kept out of the way. There was no danger that Tom would be weak; and, after some half-hour of parley, he was again left by Mr. Sowerby, without having evinced any symptom of weakness.

"It's the dibs as we want, Mr. Sowerby; that's all," were the last words which he spoke as the member of Parliament left the room.

Mr. Sowerby then got into another cab, and had himself driven to his sister's house. It is a remarkable thing with reference to men who are distressed for money — distressed as was now the case with Mr. Sowerby — that they never seem at a loss for small sums, or deny themselves those luxuries which small sums purchase. Cabs, dinners, wine, theatres, and new gloves are always at the command of men who are drowned in pecuniary embarrassments, whereas those who don't owe a shilling are so frequently obliged to go without them! It would seem that there is no gratification so costly as that of keeping out of debt. But then it is only fair that, if a man has a hobby, he should pay for it.

Any one else would have saved his shilling, as Mrs. Harold Smith's house was only just across Oxford Street, in the neighbourhood of Hanover Square; but Mr. Sowerby never thought of this. He had never saved a shilling in his life, and it did not occur to him to begin now. He had sent word to her to remain at home for him, and he now found her waiting.

"Harriet," said he, throwing himself back into an easy chair, "the game is pretty well up at last."

"Nonsense," said she. "The game is not up at all if you have the spirit to carry it on."

"I can only say that I got a formal notice this morning from the duke's lawyer, saying that he meant to foreclose at once; — not from Fothergill, but from those people in South Audley Street."

"You expected that," said his sister.

"I don't see how that makes it any better; besides, I am not quite sure that I did expect it; at any rate I did not feel certain. There is no doubt now."

"It is better that there should be no doubt. It is much better that you should know on what ground you have to stand."

"I shall soon have no ground to stand on, none at least of my own, — not an acre," said the unhappy man, with great bitterness in his tone.

"You can't in reality be poorer now than you were last year. You have not spent anything to speak of. There can be no doubt that Chaldicotes will be ample to pay all you owe the duke."

"It's as much as it will; and what am I to do then? I almost think more of the seat than I do of Chaldicotes."

"You know what I advise," said Mrs. Smith. "Ask Miss Dunstable to advance the money on the same security which the duke holds. She will be as safe then as he is now. And if you can arrange that, stand for the county against him; perhaps you may be beaten."

"I shouldn't have a chance."

"But it would show that you are not a creature in the duke's hands. That's my advice," said Mrs. Smith, with much spirit; "and if you wish, I'll broach it to Miss Dunstable, and ask her to get her lawyer to look into it."

"If I had done this before I had run my head into that other absurdity!"

"Don't fret yourself about that; she will lose nothing by such an investment, and therefore you are not asking any favour of her. Besides, did she not make the offer? and she is just the woman to do this for you now, because she refused to do that other thing for you yesterday. You understand most things, Nathaniel; but I am not sure that you understand women; not, at any rate, such a woman as her."

It went against the grain with Mr. Sowerby, this seeking of pecuniary assistance from the very woman whose hand he had attempted to gain about a fortnight since; but he allowed his sister to prevail. What could any man do in such straits that would not go against the grain? At the present moment he felt in his mind an infinite hatred against the duke, Mr. Fothergill, Gumption and Gagebee, and all the tribes of Gatherum Castle and South Audley Street; they wanted to rob him of that which had belonged to the Sowerbys before the name of Omnium had been heard of in the county, or in England! The great leviathan of the deep was anxious to swallow him up as a prey! He was to be swallowed up, and made away with, and put out of sight, without a pang of remorse! Any measure which could now present itself as the means of staving off so evil a day would be acceptable; and therefore he gave his sister the commission of making this second proposal to Miss Dunstable. In cursing the duke — for he did curse the duke lustily — it hardly occurred to him to think that, after all, the duke only asked for his own.

As for Mrs. Harold Smith, whatever may be the view taken of her general character as a wife and a member of society, it must be admitted that as a sister she had virtues.

CHAPTER IX.

Consolation.

On the next day at two o'clock punctually, Mark Robarts was at the "Dragon of Wantly," walking up and down the very room in which the party had breakfasted after Harold Smith's lecture, and waiting for the arrival of Mr. Sowerby. He had been very well able to divine what was the business on which his friend wished to see him, and he had been rather glad than otherwise to receive the summons. Judging of his friend's character by what he had hitherto seen, he thought that Mr. Sowerby would have kept out of the way, unless he had it in his power to make some provision for these terrible bills. So he walked up and down the dingy room, impatient for the expected arrival, and thought himself wickedly ill-used in that Mr. Sowerby was not there when the clock struck a quarter to three. But when the clock struck three, Mr. Sowerby was there, and Mark Robarts' hopes were nearly at an end.

"Do you mean that they will demand nine hundred pounds?" said Robarts, standing up and glaring angrily at the member of Parliament.

"I fear that they will," said Sowerby. "I think it is best to tell you the worst, in order that we may see what can be done."

"I can do nothing, and will do nothing," said Robarts. "They may do what they choose — what the law allows them."

And then he thought of Fanny and his nursery, and Lucy refusing in her pride Lord Lufton's offer, and he turned away his face that the hard man of the world before him might not see the tear gathering in his eye.

"But, Mark, my dear fellow ——" said Sowerby, trying to have recourse to the power of his cajoling voice.

Robarts, however, would not listen.

"Mr. Sowerby," said he, with an attempt at calmness which betrayed itself at every syllable, "it seems to me that you have robbed me. That I have been a fool, and worse than a fool, I know well; but — but — but I thought that your position in the world would guarantee me from such treatment as this."

Mr. Sowerby was by no means without feeling, and the words which he now heard cut him very deeply — the more so because it was impossible that he should answer them with an attempt at indignation. He had robbed his friend, and, with all his wit, knew no words at the present moment sufficiently witty to make it seem that he had not done so.

"Robarts," said he, "you may say what you like to me now; I shall not resent it."

"Who would care for your resentment?" said the clergyman, turning on him with ferocity. "The resentment of a gentleman is terrible to a gentleman; and the resentment of one just man is terrible to another. Your resentment!" and then he walked twice the length of the room, leaving Sowerby dumb in his seat. "I wonder whether you ever thought of my wife and children when you were plotting this ruin for me!" And then again he walked the room.

"I suppose you will be calm enough presently to speak of this with some attempt to make a settlement."

"No; I will make no such attempt. These friends of yours, you tell me, have a claim on me for nine hundred pounds, of which they demand immediate payment. You shall be asked in a court of law how much of that money I have handled. You know that I have never touched — have never wanted to touch — one shilling. I will make no attempt at any settlement. My person is here, and there is my house. Let them do their worst."

"But, Mark —"

"Call me by my name, sir, and drop that affectation of regard. What an ass I have been to be so cozened by a sharper!"

Sowerby had by no means expected this. He had always known that Robarts possessed, what he, Sowerby, would have called the spirit of a gentleman. He had regarded him as a bold, open, generous fellow, able to take his own part when called on to do so, and by no means disinclined to speak his own mind; but he had not expected from him such a torrent of indignation, or thought that he was capable of such a depth of anger.

"If you use such language as that, Robarts, I can only leave you."

"You are welcome. Go. You tell me that you are the messenger of these men who intend to work nine hundred pounds out of me. You have done your part in the plot, and have now brought their message. It seems to me that you had better go back to them. As for me, I want my time to prepare my wife for the destiny before her."

"Robarts, you will be sorry some day for the cruelty of your words."

"I wonder whether you will ever be sorry for the cruelty of your doings, or whether these things are really a joke to you."

"I am at this moment a ruined man," said Sowerby. "Everything is going from me, — my place in the world, the estate of my family, my father's house, my seat in Parliament, the power of living among my countrymen, or, indeed, of living anywhere; — but all this does not oppress me now so much as the misery which I have brought upon you." And then Sowerby also turned away his face, and wiped from his eyes tears which were not artificial.

Robarts was still walking up and down the room, but it was not possible for him to continue his reproaches after this. This is always the case. Let a man endure to heap contumely on his own head, and he will silence the contumely of others — for the moment. Sowerby, without meditating on the matter, had had some inkling of this, and immediately saw that there was at last an opening for conversation.

"You are unjust to me," said he, "in supposing that I have now no wish to save you. It is solely in the hope of doing so that I have come here."

"And what is your hope? That I should accept another brace of bills, I suppose."

"Not a brace; but one renewed bill for —"

"Look here, Mr. Sowerby. On no earthly consideration that can be put before me, will I again sign my name to any bill in the guise of an acceptance. I have been very weak, and am ashamed of my weakness; but so much strength as that, I hope, is left to me. I have been very wicked, and am ashamed of my wickedness; but so much right principle as that, I hope, remains. I will put my name to no other bill; not for you, not even for myself."

"But, Robarts, under your present circumstances that will be madness."

"Then I will be mad."

"Have you seen Forrest? If you will speak to him I think you will find that everything can be accommodated."

"I already owe Mr. Forrest a hundred and fifty pounds, which I obtained from him when you pressed me for the price of that horse, and I will not increase the debt. What a fool I was again there! Perhaps you do not remember that, when I agreed to buy the horse, the price was to be my contribution to the liquidation of these bills."

"I do remember it; but I will tell you how that was."

"It does not signify. It has been all of a piece."

"But listen to me. I think you would feel for me if you knew all that I have gone through. I pledge you my solemn word that I had no intention of asking you for the money when you took the horse; — indeed I had not. But you remember that affair of Lufton's, when he came to you at your hotel in London and was so angry about an outstanding bill."

"I know that he was very unreasonable as far as I was concerned."

"He was so; but that makes no difference. He was resolved, in his rage, to expose the whole affair; and I saw that, if he did so, it would be most injurious to you, seeing that you had just accepted your stall at Barchester." Here the poor prebendary winced terribly. "I moved heaven and earth to get up that bill. Those vultures stuck to their prey when they found the value which I attached to it, and I was forced to raise above a hundred pounds at the moment to obtain possession of it, although every shilling absolutely due on it had long since been paid. Never in my life did I wish to get money, as I did to raise that hundred and twenty pounds: and as I hope for mercy in my last moments, I did that for your sake. Lufton could not have injured me in that matter."

"But you told him that you got it for twenty-five pounds."

"Yes, I told him so. I was obliged to tell him that, or I should have apparently condemned myself by showing how anxious I was to get it. And you know I could not have explained all this before him and you. You would have thrown up the stall in disgust."

Would that he had! That was Mark's wish now,— his futile wish. In what a slough of despond had he come to wallow in consequence of his folly on that night at Gatherum Castle! He had then done a silly thing, and was he now to rue it by almost total ruin? He was sickened also with all these lies. His very soul was dismayed by the dirt through which he was forced to wade. He had become unconsciously connected with the lowest dregs of mankind, and would have to see his name mingled with theirs in the daily newspapers. And for what had he done this? Why had he thus filed his mind and made himself a disgrace to his cloth? In order that he might befriend such a one as Mr. Sowerby!

"Well," continued Sowerby; "I did get the money, but you would hardly believe the rigour of the pledge which was exacted from me for repayment. I got it from Harold Smith, and never, in my worst straits, will I again look to him for assistance. I borrowed it only for a fortnight; and in order that I might repay it, I was obliged to ask you for the price of the horse. Mark, it was on your behalf that I did all this, — indeed it was."

"And now I am to repay you for your kindness by the loss of all that I have in the world."

"If you will put the affairs into the hands of Mr. Forrest, nothing need be touched, — not a hair of a horse's back; no, not though you should be obliged to pay the whole amount yourself, gradually out of your income. You must execute a series of bills, falling due quarterly, and then —"

"I will execute no bill, I will put my name to no paper in the matter; as to that my mind is fully made up. They may come and do their worst."

Mr. Sowerby persevered for a long time, but he was quite unable to move the parson from this position. He would do nothing towards making what Mr. Sowerby called an arrangement, but persisted that he would remain at home at Framley, and that any one who had a claim upon him might take legal steps.

"I shall do nothing myself," he said; "but if proceedings against me be taken, I shall prove that I have never had a shilling of the money." And in this resolution he quitted the Dragon of Wantly.

Mr. Sowerby at one time said a word as to the expediency of borrowing that sum of money from John Robarts; but as to this Mark would say nothing. Mr. Sowerby was not the friend with whom he now intended to hold consultation in such matters. "I am not at present prepared," he said, "to declare what I may do;

I must first see what steps others take;" and then he took his hat and went off; and mounting his horse in the yard of the Dragon of Wantly — that horse which he had now so many reasons to dislike — he slowly rode back home.

Many thoughts passed through his mind during that ride, but only one resolution obtained for itself a fixture there. He must now tell his wife everything. He would not be so cruel as to let it remain untold until a bailiff were at the door, ready to walk him off to the county gaol, or until the bed on which they slept was to be sold from under them. Yes, he would tell her everything, — immediately, before his resolution could again have faded away. He got off his horse in the yard, and seeing his wife's maid at the kitchen door, desired her to beg her mistress to come to him in the book-room. He would not allow one half-hour to pass towards the waning of his purpose. If it be ordained that a man shall drown, had he not better drown and have done with it?

Mrs. Robarts came to him in his room, reaching him in time to touch his arm as he entered it.

"Mary says you want me. I have been gardening, and she caught me just as I came in."

"Yes, Fanny, I do want you. Sit down for a moment." And walking across the room, he placed his whip in its proper place.

"Oh, Mark, is there anything the matter?"

"Yes, dearest; yes. Sit down, Fanny; I can talk to you better if you will sit."

But she, poor lady, did not wish to sit. He had hinted at some misfortune, and therefore she felt a longing to stand by him and cling to him.

"Well, there; I will if I must; but, Mark, do not frighten me. Why is your face so very wretched?"

"Fanny, I have done very wrong," he said. "I have been very foolish. I fear that I have brought upon you great sorrow and trouble." And then he leaned his head upon his hand and turned his face away from her.

"Oh, Mark, dearest Mark, my own Mark! what is it?" and then she was quickly up from her chair, and went down on her knees before him. "Do not turn from me. Tell me, Mark! tell me, that we may share it."

"Yes, Fanny, I must tell you now; but I hardly know what you will think of me when you have heard it."

"I will think that you are my own husband, Mark; I will think that — that chiefly, whatever it may be." And then she caressed his knees, and looked up in his face, and, getting hold of one of his hands pressed it between her own. "Even if you have been foolish, who should forgive you if I cannot?"

And then he told it her all, beginning from that evening when Mr. Sowerby had got him into his bedroom, and going on gradually, now about the bills, and now about the horses, till his poor wife was utterly lost in the complexity of the accounts. She could by no means follow him in the details of his story; nor could she quite sympathize with him in his indignation against Mr. Sowerby, seeing that she did not comprehend at all the nature of the renewing of a bill. The only part to her of importance in the matter, was the amount of money which her husband would be called upon to pay; — that and her strong hope, which was already a conviction, that he would never again incur such debts.

"And how much is it, dearest, altogether?"

"These men claim nine hundred pounds of me."

"Oh, dear! that is a terrible sum."

"And then there is the hundred and fifty which I have borrowed from the bank — the price of the horse you know; and there are some other debts, — not a great deal, I think; but people will now look for every shilling that is due to them. If I have to pay it all, it will be twelve or thirteen hundred pounds."

"That will be as much as a year's income, Mark; even with the stall."

That was the only word of reproach she said, — if that could be called a reproach.

"Yes," he said; "and it is claimed by men who will have no pity in exacting it at any sacrifice, if they have the power. And to think that I should have incurred all this debt without having received anything for it. Oh, Fanny, what will you think of me!"

But she swore to him that she would think nothing of it, — that she would never bear it in her mind against him, — that it could have no effect in lessening her trust in him. Was he not her husband? She was so glad she knew it, that she might comfort him. And she did comfort him, making the weight seem lighter and lighter on his shoulders as he talked of it. And such weights do thus become lighter. A burden that will crush a single pair of shoulders, will, when equally divided — when shared by two, each of whom is willing to take the heavier part — become light as a feather. Is not that sharing of the mind's burdens one of the chief purposes for which man wants a wife?

For there is no folly so great as keeping one's sorrows hidden.

And this wife cheerfully, gladly, thankfully took her share. To endure with her lord all her lord's troubles was easy to her; it was the work to which she had pledged herself. But to have thought that her lord had troubles not communicated to her; — that would have been to her the one thing not to be borne.

And then they discussed their plans; — what mode of escape they might have out of this terrible money difficulty. Like a true woman, Mrs. Robarts proposed at once to abandon all superfluities. They would sell all their horses; they would not sell their cows, but would sell the butter that came from them; they would sell the pony-carriage, and get rid of the groom. That the footman must go was so much a matter of course, that it was hardly mentioned. But then, as to that house at Barchester, the dignified prebendal mansion in the close; might they not be allowed to leave it unoccupied for one year longer, — perhaps to let it? The world of course must know of their misfortune; but if that misfortune was faced bravely, the world would be less bitter in its condemnation. And then, above all things, everything must be told to Lady Lufton.

"You may, at any rate, believe this, Fanny," said he, "that for no consideration which can be offered to me, will I ever put my name to another bill."

The kiss with which she thanked him for this was as warm and generous as though he had brought to her that day news of the brightest; and when he sat, as he did that evening, discussing it all not only with his wife but with Lucy, he wondered how it was that his troubles were now so light.

Whether or no a man should have his own private pleasures, I will not now say; but it never can be worth his while to keep his sorrows private.

CHAPTER X.

Lady Lufton is Taken by Surprise.

LORD LUFTON, as he returned to town, found some difficulty in resolving what step he would next take. Sometimes, for a minute or two, he was half inclined to think — or rather to say to himself — that Lucy was perhaps not worth the trouble which she threw in his way. He loved her very dearly, and would willingly make her his wife, he thought or said at such moments; but—— Such moments, however, were only moments. A man in love seldom loves less because his love becomes difficult. And thus, when those moments were over, he would determine to tell his mother at once, and urge her to signify her consent to Miss Robarts. That she would not be quite pleased he knew; but if he were firm enough to show that he had a will of his own in this matter, she would probably not gainsay him. He would not ask this humbly, as a favour, but request her ladyship to go through the ceremony as though it were one of those motherly duties which she as a good mother could not hesitate to perform on behalf of her son. Such was the final resolve with which he reached his chambers in the Albany.

On the next day he did not see his mother. It would be well, he thought, to have his interview with her immediately before he started for Norway, so that there might be no repetition of it; and it was on the day before he did start that he made his communication, having invited himself to breakfast in Brook Street on the occasion.

"Mother," he said, quite abruptly, throwing himself into one of the dining-room arm-chairs, "I have a thing to tell you."

His mother at once knew that the thing was important, and with her own peculiar motherly instinct imagined that the question to be discussed had reference to matrimony. Had her son desired to speak to her about money, his tone and look would have been different; as would also have been the case — in a different way — had he entertained any thought of a pilgrimage to Pekin, or a prolonged fishing excursion to the Hudson Bay territories.

"A thing, Ludovic! well; I am quite at liberty."

"I want to know what you think of Lucy Robarts?"

Lady Lufton became pale and frightened, and the blood ran cold to her heart. She had feared more than rejoiced in conceiving that her son was about to talk of love, but she had feared nothing so bad as this.

"What do I think of Lucy Robarts?" she said repeating her son's words in a tone of evident dismay.

"Yes, mother; you have said once or twice lately that you thought I ought to marry, and I am beginning to think so too. You selected one clergyman's daughter for me, but that lady is going to do much better with herself" ——

"Indeed she is not," said Lady Lufton sharply.

"And therefore I rather think I shall select for myself another clergyman's sister. You don't dislike Miss Robarts, I hope?

"Oh, Ludovic!"

It was all that Lady Lufton could say at the spur of the moment.

"Is there any harm in her? Have you any objection to her? Is there anything about her that makes her unfit to be my wife?"

For a moment or two Lady Lufton sat silent, collecting her thoughts. She thought that there was very great objection to Lucy Robarts, regarding her as the possible future Lady Lufton. She could hardly have stated all her reasons, but they were very cogent. Lucy Robarts had, in her eyes, neither beauty, nor style, nor manner, nor even the education which was desirable. Lady Lufton was not herself a worldly woman. She was almost as far removed from being so as a woman could be in her position. But, nevertheless, there were certain worldly attributes which she regarded as essential to the character of any young lady who might be considered fit to take the place which she herself had so long filled. It was her desire in looking for a wife for her son to combine these with certain moral excellences which she regarded as equally essential. Lucy Robarts might have the moral excellences, or she might not; but as to the other attributes Lady Lufton regarded her as altogether deficient. She could never look like a Lady Lufton, or carry herself in the county as a Lady Lufton should do. She had not that quiet personal demeanour — that dignity of repose — which Lady Lufton loved to look upon in a young married woman of rank. Lucy, she would have said, could be nobody in a room except by dint of her tongue, whereas Griselda Grantly would have held her peace for a whole evening, and yet would have impressed everybody by the majesty of her presence. Then again Lucy had no money — and, again, Lucy was only the sister of her own parish clergyman. People are rarely prophets in their own country, and Lucy was no prophet at Framley; she was none, at least, in the eyes of Lady Lufton. Once before, as may be remembered, she had had fears on this subject — fears, not so much for her son, whom she could hardly bring herself to suspect of such a folly, but for Lucy, who might be foolish enough to fancy that the lord was in love with her. Alas! alas! her son's question fell upon the poor woman at the present moment with the weight of a terrible blow.

"Is there anything about her which makes her unfit to be my wife?"

Those were her son's last words.

"Dearest Ludovic, dearest Ludovic!" and she got up and came over to him, "I do think so; I do, indeed."

"Think what?" said he, in a tone that was almost angry.

"I do think that she is unfit to be your wife. She is not of that class from which I would wish to see you choose."

"She is of the same class as Griselda Grantly."

"No, dearest. I think you are in error there. The Grantlys have moved in a different sphere of life. I think you must feel that they are —"

"Upon my word, mother, I don't. One man is Rector of Plumstead, and the other is Vicar of Framley. But it is no good arguing that. I want you to take to Lucy Robarts. I have come to you on purpose to ask it of you as a favour."

"Do you mean as your wife, Ludovic?"

"Yes; as my wife."

"Am I to understand that you are — are engaged to her?"

"Well, I cannot say that I am — not actually engaged to her. But you may take this for granted, that, as far as it lies in my power, I intend to become so. My mind is made up, and I certainly shall not alter it."

"And the young lady knows all this?"

"Certainly."

"Horrid, sly, detestable, underhand girl," Lady Lufton said to herself, not being by any means brave enough to speak out such language before her son. What hope could there be if Lord Lufton had already committed himself by a positive offer? "And her brother, and Mrs. Robarts; are they aware of it?"

"Yes; both of them."

"And both approve of it?"

"Well, I cannot say that. I have not seen Mrs. Robarts, and do not know what may be her opinion. To speak my mind honestly about Mark, I do not think he does cordially approve. He is afraid of you, and would be desirous of knowing what you think."

"I am glad, at any rate, to hear that," said Lady Lufton, gravely. "Had he done anything to encourage this, it would have been very base." And then there was another short period of silence.

Lord Lufton had determined not to explain to his mother the whole state of the case. He would not tell her that everything depended on her word — that Lucy was ready to marry him only on condition that she, Lady Lufton, would desire her to do so. He would not let her know that everything depended on her — according to Lucy's present verdict. He had a strong disinclination to ask his mother's permission to get married; and he would have to ask it were he to tell her the whole truth. His object was to make her think well of Lucy, and to induce her to be kind, and generous, and affectionate down at Framley. Then things would all turn out comfortably when he again visited that place, as he intended to do on his return from Norway. So much he thought it possible he might effect, relying on his mother's probable calculation that it would be useless for her to oppose a measure which she had no power of stopping by authority. But were he to tell her that she was to be the final judge, that everything was to depend on her will, then, so thought Lord Lufton, that permission would in all probability be refused.

"Well, mother, what answer do you intend to give me?" he said. "My mind is positively made up. I should not have come to you had not that been the case. You will now be going down home, and I would wish you to treat Lucy as you yourself would wish to treat any girl to whom you knew that I was engaged."

"But you say that you are not engaged."

"No, I am not; but I have made my offer to her, and I have not been rejected. She has confessed that she — loves me, — not to myself, but to her brother. Under these circumstances, may I count upon your obliging me?"

There was something in his manner which almost frightened his mother, and made her think that there was more behind than was told to her. Generally speaking, his manner was open, gentle, and unguarded; but now he spoke as though he had prepared his words, and was resolved on being harsh as well as obstinate.

"I am so much taken by surprise, Ludovic, that I can hardly give you an answer. If you ask me whether I approve of such a marriage, I must say that I do not; I think that you would be throwing yourself away in marrying Miss Robarts."

"That is because you do not know her."

"May it not be possible that I know her better than you do, dear Ludovic? You have been flirting with her —"

"I hate that word; it always sounds to me to be vulgar."

"I will say making love to her, if you like it better; and gentlemen under these circumstances will sometimes become infatuated."

"You would not have a man marry a girl without making love to her. The fact is, mother, that your tastes and mine are not exactly the same; you like silent beauty, whereas I like talking beauty, and then —"

"Do you call Miss Robarts beautiful?"

"Yes, I do; very beautiful; she has the beauty that I admire. Good-bye now, mother, I shall not see you again before I start. It will be no use writing, as I shall be away so short a time, and I don't quite know where we shall be. I shall come down to Framley immediately I return, and shall learn from you how the land lies. I have told you my wishes, and you will consider how far you think it right to fall in with them." He then kissed her, and without waiting for her reply he took his leave.

Poor Lady Lufton, when she was left to herself, felt that her head was going round and round. Was this to be the end of all her ambition, — of all her love for her son? and was this to be the result of all her kindness to the Robarts's? She almost hated Mark Robarts as she reflected that she had been the means of bringing him and his sister to Framley. She thought over all his sins, his absences from the parish, his visit to Gatherum Castle, his dealings with reference to that farm which was to have been sold, his hunting, and then his acceptance of that stall given, as she had been told, through the Omnium interest. How could she love him at such a moment as this? And then she thought of his wife. Could it be possible that Fanny Robarts, her own friend Fanny, would be so untrue to her as to lend any assistance to such a marriage as this; as not to use all her power in preventing it? She had spoken to Fanny on this very subject, — not fearing for her son, but with a general idea of the impropriety of intimacies between such girls as Lucy and such men as Lord Lufton, and then Fanny had agreed with her. Could it be possible that even she must be regarded as an enemy?

And then by degrees Lady Lufton began to reflect what steps she had better take. In the first place, should she give in at once, and consent to the marriage? The only thing quite certain to her was this, that life would be not worth having if she were forced into a permanent quarrel with her son. Such an event would probably kill her. When she read of quarrels in other noble families — and the accounts of such quarrels will sometimes, unfortunately, force themselves upon the attention of unwilling readers — she would hug herself, with a spirit that was almost pharisaical, reflecting that her destiny was not like that of others. Such quarrels and hatreds between fathers and daughters, and mothers and sons, were in her eyes disreputable to all the persons concerned. She had lived happily with her husband, comfortably with her neighbours, respectably with the world, and, above all things, affectionately with her children. She spoke everywhere of Lord Lufton as though he were nearly perfect, — and in so speaking, she had not belied her convictions. Under these circumstances, would not any marriage be better than a quarrel?

But then, again, how much of the pride of her daily life would be destroyed by such a match as that! And might it not be within her power to prevent it without any quarrel? That her son would be sick of such a chit as Lucy before he had been married to her six months — of that Lady Lufton entertained no doubt, and therefore her conscience would not be disquieted in disturbing the consummation of an arrangement so pernicious. It was evident that the matter was not considered as settled even by her son; and also evident that he regarded the matter as being in some way dependent on his mother's consent. On the whole, might it not be better for her — better for them all — that she should think wholly of her duty, and not of the disagreeable results to which that duty might possibly lead? It could not be her duty to accede to such an alliance; and therefore she would do her best to prevent it. Such, at least, should be her attempt in the first instance.

Having so decided, she next resolved on her course of action. Immediately on her arrival at Framley, she would send for Lucy Robarts, and use all her eloquence — and perhaps also a little of that stern dignity for which she was so remarkable — in explaining to that young lady how very wicked it was on her part to think of forcing herself into such a family as that of the Luftons. She would explain to Lucy that no happiness could come of it, that people placed by misfortune above their sphere are always miserable; and, in short, make use of all those excellent moral lessons which are so customary on such occasions. The morality might, perhaps, be thrown away; but Lady Lufton depended much on her dignified sternness. And then, having so resolved, she prepared for her journey home.

Very little had been said at Framley Parsonage about Lord Lufton's offer after the departure of that gentleman; very little, at least, in Lucy's presence. That the parson and his wife should talk about it between themselves was a matter of course; but very few words were spoken on the matter either by or to Lucy. She was left to her own thoughts, and possibly to her own hopes.

And then other matters came up at Framley which turned the current of interest into other tracks. In the first place there was the visit made by Mr. Sowerby to the Dragon of Wantly, and the consequent revelation made by Mark Robarts to his wife. And while that latter subject was yet new, before Fanny and Lucy had as yet made up their minds as to all the little economies which might be practised in the household without serious detriment to the master's comfort, news reached them that Mrs. Crawley of Hogglestock had been stricken with fever. Nothing of the kind could well be more dreadful than this. To those who knew the family it seemed impossible that their most ordinary wants could be supplied if that courageous head were even for a day laid low; and then the poverty of poor Mr. Crawley was such that the sad necessities of a sick bed could hardly be supplied without assistance.

"I will go over at once," said Fanny.

"My dear!" said her husband. "It is typhus, and you must first think of the children. I will go."

"What on earth could you do, Mark?" said his wife. "Men on such occasions are almost worse than useless; and then they are so much more liable to infection."

"I have no children, nor am I a man," said Lucy, smiling; "for both of which exemptions I am thankful. I will go, and when I come back I will keep clear of the bairns."

So it was settled, and Lucy started in the pony-carriage, carrying with her such things from the parsonage storehouse as were thought to be suitable to the wants of the sick lady at Hogglestock. When she arrived there, she made her way into the house, finding the door open, and not being able to obtain the assistance of the servant girl in ushering her in. In the parlour she found Grace Crawley, the eldest child, sitting demurely in her mother's chair nursing an infant. She, Grace herself, was still a young child, but not the less, on this occasion of well-understood sorrow, did she go through her task not only with zeal but almost with solemnity. Her brother, a boy of six years old, was with her, and he had the care of another baby. There they sat in a cluster, quiet, grave, and silent, attending on themselves, because it had been willed by fate that no one else should attend on them.

"How is your mamma, dear Grace?" said Lucy, walking up to her, and holding out her hand.

"Poor mamma is very ill, indeed," said Grace.

"And papa is very unhappy," said Bobby, the boy.

"I can't get up because of baby," said Grace; "but Bobby can go and call papa out."

"I will knock at the door," said Lucy, and so saying she walked up to the bedroom door, and tapped against it lightly. She repeated this for the third time before she was summoned in by a low hoarse voice, and then on entering she saw Mr. Crawley standing by the bedside with a book in his hand. He looked at her uncomfortably, in a manner which seemed to show that he was annoyed by this intrusion, and Lucy was aware that she had disturbed him while at prayers by the bedside of his wife. He came across the room, however, and shook hands with her, and answered her inquiries in his ordinary grave and solemn voice.

"Mrs. Crawley is very ill," he said, "very ill. God has stricken us heavily, but His will be done. But you had better not go to her, Miss Robarts. It is typhus."

The caution, however, was too late; for Lucy was already by the bedside, and had taken the hand of the sick woman, which had been extended on the coverlid to greet her. "Dear Miss Robarts," said a weak voice. "This is very good of you; but it makes me unhappy to see you here."

Lucy lost no time in taking sundry matters into her own hands, and ascertaining what was most wanted in that wretched household. For it was wretched enough. Their only servant, a girl of sixteen, had been taken away by her mother as soon as it became known that Mrs. Crawley was ill with fever. The poor mother, to give her her due, had promised to come down morning and evening herself, to do such work as might be done in an hour or so; but she could not, she said, leave her child to catch the fever. And now, at the period of Lucy's visit, no step had been taken to procure a nurse, Mr. Crawley having resolved to take upon himself the duties of that position. In his absolute ignorance of all sanatory measures, he had thrown himself on his knees to pray; and if prayers — true prayers — might succour his poor wife, of such succour she might be confident. Lucy, however, thought that other aid also was wanting to her.

"If you can do anything for us," said Mrs. Crawley, "let it be for the poor children."

"I will have them all moved from this till you are better," said Lucy, boldly.

"Moved!" said Mr. Crawley, who even now, even in his present strait, felt a repugnance to the idea that any one should relieve him of any portion of his burden.

"Yes," said Lucy; "I am sure it will be better that you should lose them for a week or two, till Mrs. Crawley may be able to leave her room."

"But where are they to go?" said he, very gloomily.

As to this Lucy was not as yet able to say anything. Indeed when she left Framley Parsonage there had been no time for discussion. She would go back and talk it all over with Fanny, and find out in what way the children might be best put out of danger. Why should they not all be harboured at the parsonage, as soon as assurance could be felt that they were not tainted with the poison of the fever? An English lady of the right sort will do all things but one for a sick neighbour; but for no neighbour will she wittingly admit contagious sickness within the precincts of her own nursery.

Lucy unloaded her jellies and her febrifuges, Mr. Crawley frowning at her bitterly the while. It had come to this with him, that food had been brought into his house, as an act of charity, in his very presence, and in his heart of hearts he disliked Lucy Robarts in that she had brought it. He could not cause the jars and the pots to be replaced in the pony-carriage, as he would have done had the position of his wife been different. In her state it would have been barbarous to refuse them, and barbarous also to have created the *fracas* of a refusal; but each parcel that was introduced was an additional weight laid on the sore withers of his pride, till the total burden became almost intolerable. All this his wife saw and recognized even in her illness, and did make some slight ineffectual efforts to give him ease; but Lucy in her new power was ruthless, and the chicken to make the chicken-broth was taken out of the basket under his very nose.

But Lucy did not remain long. She had made up her mind what it behoved her to do herself, and she was soon ready to return to Framley. "I shall be back again, Mr. Crawley," she said, "probably this evening, and I shall stay with her till she is better."

"Nurses don't want rooms," she went on to say, when Mr. Crawley muttered something as to there being no bed-chamber. "I shall make up some sort of a litter near her; you'll see that I shall be very snug." And then she got into the pony-chaise, and drove herself home.

CHAPTER XI.

The Story of King Cophetua.

LUCY as she drove herself home had much as to which it was necessary that she should arouse her thoughts. That she would go back and nurse Mrs. Crawley through her fever she was resolved. She was free agent enough to take so much on herself, and to feel sure that she could carry it through. But how was she to redeem her promise about the children? Twenty plans ran through her mind, as to farm-houses in which they might be placed, or cottages which might be hired for them; but all these entailed the want of money; and at the present moment, were not all the inhabitants of the parsonage pledged to a dire economy? This use of the pony-carriage would have been illicit under any circumstances less pressing than the present, for it had been decided that the carriage, and even poor Puck himself, should be sold. She had, however, given her promise about the children, and though her own stock of money was very low, that promise should be redeemed.

When she reached the parsonage she was of course full of her schemes, but she found that another subject of interest had come up in her absence, which prevented her from obtaining the undivided attention of her sister-in-law to her present plans. Lady Lufton had returned that day, and immediately on her return had sent up a note addressed to Miss Lucy Robarts, which note was in Fanny's hands when Lucy stepped out of the pony-carriage. The servant who brought it had asked for an answer, and a verbal answer had been sent, saying that Miss Robarts was away from home, and would herself send a reply when she returned. It cannot be denied that the colour came to Lucy's face, and that her hand trembled when she took the note from Fanny in the drawing-room. Everything in the world to her might depend on what that note contained; and yet she did not open it at once, but stood with it in her hand, and when Fanny pressed her on the subject, still endeavoured to bring back the conversation to the subject of Mrs. Crawley.

But yet her mind was intent on the letter, and she had already augured ill from the handwriting and even from the words of the address. Had Lady Lufton intended to be propitious, she would have directed her letter to Miss Robarts, without the Christian name; so at least argued Lucy, — quite unconsciously, as one does argue in such matters. One forms half the conclusions of one's life without any distinct knowledge that the premises have even passed through one's mind.

They were now alone together, as Mark was out.

"Won't you open her letter?" said Mrs. Robarts.

"Yes, immediately; but, Fanny, I must speak to you about Mrs. Crawley first. I must go back there this evening, and stay there; I have promised to do so, and shall certainly keep my promise. I have promised also that the children shall be taken away, and we must arrange about that. It is dreadful, the state she is in. There is no one to see to her but Mr. Crawley, and the children are altogether left to themselves."

"Do you mean that you are going back to stay?"

"Yes, certainly; I have made a distinct promise that I would do so. And about the children; could not you manage for the children, Fanny, — not perhaps in the house; at least not at first perhaps?" And yet during all the time that she was thus speaking and pleading for the Crawleys, she was endeavouring to imagine what might be the contents of that letter which she held between her fingers.

"And is she so very ill?" asked Mrs. Robarts.

"I cannot say how ill she may be, except this, that she certainly has typhus fever. They have had some doctor or doctor's assistant from Silverbridge; but it seems to me that they are greatly in want of better advice."

"But, Lucy, will you not read your letter? It is astonishing to me that you should be so indifferent about it."

Lucy was anything but indifferent, and now did proceed to tear the envelope. The note was very short, and ran in these words, —

"MY DEAR MISS ROBARTS, — I am particularly anxious to see you, and shall feel much obliged to you if you can step over to me here, at Framley Court. I must apologize for taking this liberty with you, but you will probably feel that an interview here would suit us both better than one at the parsonage.

"Truly yours,

"M. LUFTON."

"There: I am in for it now," said Lucy, handing

the note over to Mrs. Robarts. "I shall have to be talked to as never poor girl was talked to before: and when one thinks of what I have done, it is hard."

"Yes; and of what you have not done."

"Exactly; and of what I have not done. But I suppose I must go," and she proceeded to re-tie the strings of her bonnet, which she had loosened.

"Do you mean that you are going over at once?"

"Yes; immediately. Why not? it will be better to have it over, and then I can go to the Crawleys. But, Fanny, the pity of it is that I know it all as well as though it had been already spoken; and what good can there be in my having to endure it? Can't you fancy the tone in which she will explain to me the conventional inconveniences which arose when King Cophetua would marry the beggar's daughter? how she will explain what Griselda went through; — not the archdeacon's daughter, but the other Griselda?"

"But it all came right with her."

"Yes; but then I am not Griselda, and she will explain how it would certainly all go wrong with me. But what's the good when I know it all beforehand? Have I not desired King Cophetua to take himself and sceptre elsewhere?"

And then she started, having first said another word or two about the Crawley children, and obtained a promise of Puck and the pony-carriage for the afternoon. It was also almost agreed that Puck on his return to Framley should bring back the four children with him; but on this subject it was necessary that Mark should be consulted. The present scheme was to prepare for them a room outside the house, once the dairy, at present occupied by the groom and his wife;

and to bring them into the house as soon as it was manifest that there was no danger from infection. But all this was to be matter for deliberation.

Fanny wanted her to send over a note, in reply to Lady Lufton's, as harbinger of her coming; but Lucy marched off, hardly answering this proposition.

"What's the use of such a deal of ceremony," she said. "I know she's at home; and if she is not, I shall only lose ten minutes in going." And so she went, and on reaching the door of Framley Court house found that her ladyship was at home. Her heart almost came to her mouth as she was told so, and then, in two minutes' time, she found herself in the little room upstairs. In that little room we found ourselves once before, — you, and I, O my reader; — but Lucy had never before visited that hallowed precinct. There was something in its air calculated to inspire awe in those who first saw Lady Lufton sitting bolt upright in the cane-bottomed arm-chair, which she always occupied when at work at her books and papers; and this she knew when she determined to receive Lucy in that apartment. But there was there another arm-chair, an easy, cozy chair, which stood by the fireside; and for those who had caught Lady Lufton napping in that chair of an afternoon, some of this awe had perhaps been dissipated.

"Miss Robarts," she said, not rising from her chair, but holding out her hand to her visitor; "I am much obliged to you for having come over to me here. You, no doubt, are aware of the subject on which I wish to speak to you, and will agree with me that it is better that we should meet here than over at the parsonage."

In answer to which Lucy merely bowed her head,

and took her seat on the chair which had been prepared for her.

"My son," continued her ladyship, "has spoken to me on the subject of —— I think I understand, Miss Robarts, that there has been no engagement between you and him?"

"None whatever," said Lucy. "He made me an offer and I refused him." This she said very sharply; — more so undoubtedly than the circumstances required; and with a brusqueness that was injudicious as well as uncourteous. But at the moment, she was thinking of her own position with reference to Lady Lufton — not to Lord Lufton; and of her feelings with reference to the lady — not to the gentleman.

"Oh," said Lady Lufton, a little startled by the manner of the communication. "Then I am to understand that there is nothing now going on between you and my son; — that the whole affair is over?"

"That depends entirely upon you."

"On me! does it?"

"I do not know what your son may have told you, Lady Lufton. For myself, I do not care to have any secrets from you in this matter; and as he has spoken to you about it, I suppose that such is his wish also. Am I right in presuming that he has spoken to you on the subject?"

"Yes, he has; and it is for that reason that I have taken the liberty of sending for you."

"And may I ask what he has told you? I mean, of course, as regards myself," said Lucy.

Lady Lufton, before she answered this question, began to reflect that the young lady was taking too much of the initiative in this conversation, and was, in fact, playing the game in her own fashion, which was not at all in accordance with those motives which had induced Lady Lufton to send for her.

"He has told me that he made you an offer of marriage," replied Lady Lufton; "a matter which, of course, is very serious to me, as his mother; and I have thought, therefore, that I had better see you, and appeal to your own good sense and judgment and high feeling. Of course you are aware —"

Now was coming the lecture to be illustrated by King Cophetua and Griselda, as Lucy had suggested to Mrs. Robarts; but she succeeded in stopping it for awhile.

"And did Lord Lufton tell you what was my answer?"

"Not in words. But you yourself now say that you refused him; and I must express my admiration for your good —"

"Wait half a moment, Lady Lufton. Your son did make me an offer. He made it to me in person, up at the parsonage, and I then refused him; — foolishly, as I now believe, for I dearly love him. But I did so from a mixture of feelings which I need not, perhaps, explain; that most prominent, no doubt, was a fear of your displeasure. And then he came again, not to me, but to my brother, and urged his suit to him. Nothing can have been kinder to me, more noble, more loving, more generous, than his conduct. At first I thought, when he was speaking to myself, that he was led on thoughtlessly to say all that he did say. I did not trust his love, though I saw that he did trust it himself. But I could not but trust it when he came again — to my brother, and made his proposal to him. I don't know whether you will understand me, Lady Lufton; but a girl placed as I am feels ten times more assurance in such a tender of affection as that, than in one made to herself, at the spur of the moment, perhaps. And then you must remember that I — I myself — I loved him from the first. I was foolish enough to think that I could know him and not love him."

"I saw all that going on," said Lady Lufton, with a certain assumption of wisdom about her; "and took steps which I hoped would have put a stop to it in time."

"Everybody saw it. It was a matter of course," said Lucy, destroying her ladyship's wisdom at a blow. "Well; I did learn to love him, not meaning to do so; and I do love him with all my heart. It is no use my striving to think that I do not; and I could stand with him at the altar to-morrow and give him my hand, feeling that I was doing my duty by him, as a woman should do. And now he has told you of his love, and I believe in that as I do in my own —" And then for a moment she paused.

"But, my dear Miss Robarts ——" began Lady Lufton.

Lucy, however, had now worked herself up into a condition of power, and would not allow her ladyship to interrupt her in her speech.

"I beg your pardon, Lady Lufton; I shall have done directly, and then I will hear you. And so my brother came to me, not urging this suit, expressing no wish for such a marriage, but allowing me to judge for myself, and proposing that I should see your son again on the following morning. Had I done so, I could not but have accepted him. Think of it, Lady

Lufton. How could I have done other than accept him, seeing that in my heart I had accepted his love already?"

"Well?" said Lady Lufton, not wishing now to put in any speech of her own.

"I did not see him — I refused to do so — because I was a coward. I could not endure to come into this house as your son's wife, and be coldly looked on by your son's mother. Much as I loved him, much as I do love him, dearly as I prize the generous offer which he came down here to repeat to me, I could not live with him to be made the object of your scorn. I sent him word, therefore, that I would have him when you would ask me, and not before."

And then, having thus pleaded her cause — and pleaded as she believed the cause of her lover also, — she ceased from speaking, and prepared herself to listen to the story of King Cophetua.

But Lady Lufton felt considerable difficulty in commencing her speech. In the first place she was by no means a hard-hearted or a selfish woman; and were it not that her own son was concerned, and all the glory which was reflected upon her from her son, her sympathies would have been given to Lucy Robarts. As it was, she did sympathize with her, and admire her, and to a certain extent like her. She began also to understand what it was that had brought about her son's love, and to feel that but for certain unfortunate concomitant circumstances the girl before her might have made a fitting Lady Lufton. Lucy had grown bigger in her eyes while sitting there and talking, and had lost much of that missish want of importance — that lack of social weight — which Lady Lufton in her own opinion had always imputed to her. A girl that could thus speak up and explain her own position now, would be able to speak up and explain her own, and perhaps some other positions at any future time.

But not for all or any of these reasons did Lady Lufton think of giving way. The power of making or marring this marriage was placed in her hands, as was very fitting, and that power it behoved her to use, as best she might use it, to her son's advantage. Much as she might admire Lucy, she could not sacrifice her son to that admiration. The unfortunate concomitant circumstances still remained, and were of sufficient force, as she thought, to make such a marriage inexpedient. Lucy was the sister of a gentleman, who by his peculiar position as parish clergyman of Framley was unfitted to be the brother-in-law of the owner of Framley. Nobody liked clergymen better than Lady Lufton, or was more willing to live with them on terms of affectionate intimacy, but she could not get over the feeling that the clergyman of her own parish, — or of her son's, — was a part of her own establishment, of her own appanage, — or of his, — and that it could not be well that Lord Lufton should marry among his own — dependants. Lady Lufton would not have used the word, but she did think it. And then, too, Lucy's education had been so deficient. She had had no one about her in early life accustomed to the ways of, — of what shall I say, without making Lady Lufton appear more worldly than she was? Lucy's wants in this respect, not to be defined in words, had been exemplified by the very way in which she had just now stated her case. She had shown talent, good temper, and sound judgment; but there had been no quiet, no repose about her. The species of power in young ladies which Lady Lufton most admired was the *vis inertiæ* belonging to beautiful and dignified reticence; of this poor Lucy had none. Then, too, she had no fortune, which, though a minor evil, was an evil; and she had no birth, in the high-life sense of the word, which was a greater evil. And then, though her eyes had sparkled when she confessed her love, Lady Lufton was not prepared to admit that she was possessed of positive beauty. Such were the unfortunate concomitant circumstances which still induced Lady Lufton to resolve that the match must be marred.

But the performance of her part in this play was much more difficult than she had imagined, and she found herself obliged to sit silent for a minute or two, during which, however, Miss Robarts made no attempt at further speech.

"I am greatly struck," Lady Lufton said at last, "by the excellent sense you have displayed in the whole of this affair; and you must allow me to say, Miss Robarts, that I now regard you with very different feelings from those which I entertained when I left London." Upon this Lucy bowed her head, slightly but very stiffly; acknowledging rather the former censure implied than the present eulogium expressed.

"But my feelings," continued Lady Lufton, "my strongest feelings in this matter must be those of a mother. What might be my conduct if such a marriage did take place, I need not now consider. But I must confess that I should think such a marriage very — very ill judged. A better-hearted young man than

Lord Lufton does not exist, nor one with better principles, or a deeper regard for his word; but he is exactly the man to be mistaken in any hurried outlook as to his future life. Were you and he to become man and wife, such a marriage would tend to the happiness neither of him nor of you."

It was clear that the whole lecture was now coming; and as Lucy had openly declared her own weakness, and thrown all the power of decision into the hands of Lady Lufton, she did not see why she should endure this.

"We need not argue about that, Lady Lufton," she said. "I have told you the only circumstances under which I would marry your son; and you, at any rate, are safe."

"No; I was not wishing to argue," answered Lady Lufton, almost humbly; "but I was desirous of excusing myself to you, so that you should not think me cruel in withholding my consent. I wished to make you believe that I was doing the best for my son."

"I am sure that you think you are, and therefore no excuse is necessary."

"No; exactly; of course it is a matter of opinion, and I do think so. I cannot believe that this marriage would make either of you happy, and therefore I should be very wrong to express my consent."

"Then, Lady Lufton," said Lucy, rising from her chair, "I suppose we have both now said what is necessary, and I will therefore wish you good-bye."

"Good-bye, Miss Robarts. I wish I could make you understand how very highly I regard your conduct in this matter. It has been above all praise, and so I shall not hesitate to say when speaking of it to your relatives." This was disagreeable enough to Lucy, who cared but little for any praise which Lady Lufton might express to her relatives in this matter. "And pray," continued Lady Lufton, "give my best love to Mrs. Robarts, and tell her that I shall hope to see her over here very soon, and Mr. Robarts also. I would name a day for you all to dine, but perhaps it will be better that I should have a little talk with Fanny first."

Lucy muttered something, which was intended to signify that any such dinner-party had better not be made up with the intention of including her, and then took her leave. She had decidedly had the best of the interview, and there was a consciousness of this in her heart as she allowed Lady Lufton to shake hands with her. She had stopped her antagonist short on each occasion on which an attempt had been made to produce the homily which had been prepared, and during the interview had spoken probably three words for every one which her ladyship had been able to utter. But, nevertheless, there was a bitter feeling of disappointment about her heart as she walked back home; and a feeling, also, that she herself had caused her own unhappiness. Why should she have been so romantic and chivalrous and self-sacrificing, seeing that her romance and chivalry had all been to his detriment as well as to hers, — seeing that she sacrificed him as well as herself? Why should she have been so anxious to play into Lady Lufton's hands? It was not because she thought it right, as a general social rule, that a lady should refuse a gentleman's hand, unless the gentleman's mother were a consenting party to the marriage. She would have held any such doctrine as absurd. The lady, she would have said, would have had to look to her own family and no further. It was not virtue but cowardice which had influenced her, and she had none of that solace which may come to us in misfortune from a consciousness that our own conduct has been blameless. Lady Lufton had inspired her with awe, and any such feeling on her part was mean, ignoble, and unbecoming the spirit with which she wished to think that she was endowed. That was the accusation which she brought against herself, and it forbade her to feel any triumph as to the result of her interview.

When she reached the parsonage, Mark was there, and they were of course expecting her.

"Well," said she, in her short, hurried manner, "is Puck ready again? I have no time to lose, and I must go and pack up a few things. Have you settled about the children, Fanny?"

"Yes; I will tell you directly; but you have seen Lady Lufton?"

"Seen her! Oh, yes, of course I have seen her. Did she not send for me? and in that case it was not on the cards that I should disobey her."

"And what did she say?"

"How green you are, Mark; and not only green, but impolite also, to make me repeat the story of my own disgrace. Of course she told me that she did not intend that I should marry my lord, her son; and of course I said that under those circumstances I should not think of doing such a thing."

"Lucy, I cannot understand you," said Fanny,

very gravely. "I am sometimes inclined to doubt whether you have any deep feeling in the matter or not. If you have, how can you bring yourself to joke about it?"

"Well, it is singular; and sometimes I doubt myself whether I have. I ought to be pale, ought I not? and very thin, and to go mad by degrees? I have not the least intention of doing anything of the kind, and, therefore, the matter is not worth any further notice."

"But was she civil to you, Lucy?" asked Mark; "civil in her manner, you know?"

"Oh, uncommonly so. You will hardly believe it, but she actually asked me to dine. She always does, you know, when she wants to show her good-humour. If you'd broken your leg, and she wished to commiserate you, she'd ask you to dinner."

"I suppose she meant to be kind," said Fanny, who was not disposed to give up her old friend, though she was quite ready to fight Lucy's battle, if there were any occasion for a battle to be fought.

"Lucy is so perverse," said Mark, "that it is impossible to learn from her what really has taken place."

"Upon my word, then, you know it all as well as I can tell you. She asked me if Lord Lufton had made me an offer. I said, yes. She asked next, if I meant to accept it. Not without her approval I said. And then she asked us all to dinner. That is exactly what took place, and I cannot see that I have been perverse at all." After that she threw herself into a chair, and Mark and Fanny stood looking at each other.

„Mark," she said, after a while, "don't be unkind to me. I make as little of it as I can, for all our sakes. It is better so, Fanny, than that I should go about moaning, like a sick cow;" and then they looked at her, and saw that the tears were already brimming over from her eyes.

"Dearest, dearest Lucy," said Fanny, immediately going down on her knees before her, "I won't be unkind to you again." And then they had a great cry together.

CHAPTER XII.

Kidnapping at Hogglestock.

THE great cry, however, did not take long, and Lucy was soon in the pony-carriage again. On this occasion her brother volunteered to drive her, and it was now understood that he was to bring back with him all the Crawley children. The whole thing had been arranged; the groom and his wife were to be taken into the house, and the big bedroom across the yard, usually occupied by them, was to be converted into a quarantine hospital until such time as it might be safe to pull down the yellow flag. They were about half way on their road to Hogglestock when they were overtaken by a man on horseback, whom, when he came up beside them, Mr. Robarts recognized as Dr. Arabin, Dean of Barchester, and head of the chapter to which he himself belonged. It immediately appeared that the dean also was going to Hogglestock, having heard of the misfortune that had befallen his friends there; he had, he said, started as soon as the news reached him, in order that he might ascertain how best he might render assistance. To effect this he had undertaken a ride of nearly forty miles, and explained that he did not expect to reach home again much before midnight.

"You pass by Framley?" said Robarts.

"Yes, I do," said the dean.

"Then of course you will dine with us as you go home; you and your horse also, which will be quite as important." This having been duly settled, and the proper ceremony of introduction having taken place between the dean and Lucy, they proceeded to discuss the character of Mr. Crawley.

"I have known him all my life," said the dean, "having been at school and college with him and for years since that I was not on terms of the closest intimacy with him; but in spite of that, I do not know how to help him in his need. A prouder-hearted man I never met, or one less willing to share his sorrows with his friends."

"I have often heard him speak of you," said Mark.

"One of the bitterest feelings I have is that a man so dear to me should live so near to me, and that I should see so little of him. But what can I do? He will not come to my house; and when I go to his he is angry with me because I wear a shovel hat and ride on horseback."

"I should leave my hat and my horse at the borders of the last parish," said Lucy timidly.

"Well; yes, certainly; one ought not to give offence even in such matters as that; but my coat and waistcoat would then be equally objectionable. I have changed, — in outward matters I mean, — and he has not. That irritates him, and unless I could be what I was in the old days, he will not look at me with the same eyes;" and then he rode on, in order, as he said, that the first pang of the interview might be over before Robarts and his sister came upon the scene.

Mr. Crawley was standing before his door, leaning over the little wooden railing, when the dean trotted up on his horse. He had come out after hours of close watching to get a few mouthfuls of the sweet summer air, and as he stood there he held the youngest of the children in his arms. The poor little baby sat there, quiet indeed, but hardly happy. This father, though he loved his offspring with an affection as intense as that which human nature can supply, was not gifted with the knack of making children fond of him; for it is hardly more than a knack, that aptitude which some men have of gaining the good graces of the young. Such men are not always the best fathers or the safest guardians; but they carry about with them a certain duc ad me which children recognize, and which in three minutes upsets all the barriers between five and five-and-forty. But Mr. Crawley was a stern man, thinking ever of the souls and minds of his bairns — as a father should do; and thinking also that every season was fitted for operating on these souls and minds — as, perhaps, he should not have done either as a father or as a teacher. And consequently his children avoided him when the choice was given them, thereby adding fresh wounds to his torn heart, but by no means quenching any of the great love with which he regarded them.

He was standing there thus with a placid little baby in his arms — a baby placid enough, but one that would not kiss him eagerly, and stroke his face with her soft little hands, as he would have had her do — when he saw the dean coming towards him. He was sharp-sighted as a lynx out in the open air, though now obliged to pore over his well-fingered books with spectacles on his nose; and thus he knew his friend from a long distance, and had time to meditate the mode of his greeting. He too doubtless had come, if not with jelly and chicken, then with money and advice; — with money and advice such as a thriving dean might offer to a poor brother clergyman; and Mr. Crawley, though no husband sould possibly be more anxious for a wife's safety than he was, immediately put his back up and began to bethink himself how these tenders might be rejected.

"How is she?" were the first words which the dean spoke as he pulled up his horse close to the little gate, and put out his hand to take that of his friend.

"How are you, Arabin?" said he. "It is very kind of you to come so far, seeing how much there is to keep you at Barchester. I cannot say that she is any better, but I do not know that she is worse. Sometimes I fancy that she is delirious, though I hardly know. At any rate her mind wanders, and then after that she sleeps."

"But is the fever less?"

"Sometimes less and sometimes more, I imagine."

"And the children?"

"Poor things; they are well as yet."

"They must be taken from this, Crawley, as a matter of course."

Mr. Crawley fancied that there was a tone of authority in the dean's advice, and immediately put himself into opposition.

"I do not know how that may be; I have not yet made up my mind."

"But, my dear Crawley —"

"Providence does not admit of such removals in all cases," said he. "Among the poorer classes the children must endure such perils."

"In many cases it is so," said the dean, by no means inclined to make an argument of it at the present moment; "but in this case they need not. You must allow me to make arrangements for sending for them, as of course your time is occupied here."

Miss Robarts, though she had mentioned her intention of staying with Mrs. Crawley, had said nothing of the Framley plan with reference to the children.

"What you mean is that you intend to take the burden off my shoulders — in fact, to pay for them. I cannot allow that, Arabin. They must take the lot of their father and their mother, as it is proper that they should do."

Again the dean had no inclination for arguing, and thought it might be well to let the question of the children drop for a little while.

"And is there no nurse with her?" said he.

"No, no; I am seeing to her myself at the present moment. A woman will be here just now."

"What woman?"

"Well; her name is Mrs. Stubbs; she lives in the

parish. She will put the younger children to bed, and — and — but it's no use troubling you with all that. There was a young lady talked of coming, but no doubt she has found it too inconvenient. It will be better as it is."

"You mean Miss Robarts; she will be here directly; I passed her as I came here;" and as Dr. Arabin was yet speaking, the noise of the carriage wheels was heard upon the road.

"I will go in now," said Mr. Crawley, "and see if she still sleeps; and then he entered the house, leaving the dean at the door still seated upon his horse. "He will be afraid of the infection, and I will not ask him to come in," said Mr. Crawley to himself.

"I shall seem to be prying into his poverty, if I enter unasked," said the dean to himself. And so he remained there till Puck, now acquainted with the locality, stopped at the door.

"Have you not been in?" said Robarts.

"No; Crawley has been at the door talking to me; he will be here directly, I suppose;" and then Mark Robarts also prepared himself to wait till the master of the house should reappear.

But Lucy had no such punctilious misgivings; she did not much care now whether she offended Mr. Crawley or no. Her idea was to place herself by the sick woman's bedside, and to send the four children away; — with their father's consent if it might be; but certainly without it if that consent were withheld. So she got down from the carriage, and taking certain packages in her hand made her way direct into the house.

"There's a big bundle under the seat, Mark," she said; "I'll come and fetch it directly, if you'll drag it out."

For some five minutes the two dignitaries of the Church remained at the door, one on his cob and the other in his low carriage, saying a few words to each other and waiting till some one should again appear from the house. It is all arranged, indeed it is," were the first words which reached their ears, and these came from Lucy. "There will be no trouble at all, and no expense, and they shall all come back as soon as Mrs. Crawley is able to get out of bed."

"But, Miss Robarts, I can assure —" That was Mr. Crawley's voice, heard from him as he followed Miss Robarts to the door; but one of the elder children had then called him into the sick room, and Lucy was left to do her worst.

"Are you going to take the children back with you?" said the dean.

"Yes; Mrs. Robarts has prepared for them."

"You can take greater liberties with my friend here than I can."

"It is all my sister's doing," said Robarts. "Women are always bolder in such matters than men." And then Lucy reappeared, bringing Bobby with her, and one of the younger children.

"Do not mind what he says," said she, "but drive away when you have got them all. Tell Fanny I have put into the basket what things I could find, but they are very few. She must borrow things for Grace from Mrs. Granger's little girl" — (Mrs. Granger was the wife of a Framley farmer); — "and, Mark, turn Puck's head round, so that you may be off in a moment. I'll have Grace and the other one here directly." And then, leaving her brother to pack Bobby and his little sister on the back part of the vehicle, she returned to her business in the house. She had just looked in at Mrs. Crawley's bed, and finding her awake, had smiled on her, and deposited her bundle in token of her intended stay, and then, without speaking a word, had gone on her errand about the children. She had called to Grace to show her where she might find such things as were to be taken to Framley, and having explained to the bairns, as well as she might, the destiny which immediately awaited them, prepared them for their departure without saying a word to Mr. Crawley on the subject. Bobby and the elder of the two infants were stowed away safely in the back part of the carriage, where they allowed themselves to be placed without saying a word. They opened their eyes and stared at the dean, who sat by on his horse, and assented to such orders as Mr. Robarts gave them, — no doubt with much surprise, but nevertheless in absolute silence.

"Now, Grace, be quick, there's a dear," said Lucy, returning with the infant in her arms. "And, Grace, mind you are very careful about baby; and bring the basket; I'll give it you when you are in." Grace and the other child were then packed on to the other seat, and a basket with children's clothes put in on the top of them. "That'll do, Mark; good-bye; tell Fanny to be sure and send the day after to-morrow, and not to forget —" and then she whispered into her brother's ear an injunction about certain dairy comforts which might not be spoken of in the hearing of Mr. Crawley. "Good-bye, dears; mind you are good children; you shall hear about mamma the day after to-morrow," said Lucy; and Puck, admonished by a sound from his master's voice, began to move just as Mr. Crawley reappeared at the house door.

"Oh, oh, stop!" he said. "Miss Robarts, you really had better not —"

"Go on, Mark," said Lucy, in a whisper, which, whether audible or not by Mr. Crawley, was heard very plainly by the dean. And Mark, who had slightly arrested Puck by the reins on the appearance of Mr. Crawley, now touched the impatient little beast with his whip; and the vehicle with its freight darted off rapidly, Puck shaking his head and going away with a tremendously quick short trot which soon separated Mr. Crawley from his family.

"Miss Robarts," he began, "this step has been taken altogether without —"

"Yes," said she, interrupting him. "My brother was obliged to return at once. The children, you know, will remain all together at the parsonage; and that, I think, is what Mrs. Crawley will best like. In a day or two they will be under Mrs. Robarts' own charge."

"But, my dear Miss Robarts, I had no intention whatever of putting the burden of my family on the shoulders of another person. They must return to their own home immediately — that is, as soon as they can be brought back."

"I really think Miss Robarts has managed very well," said the dean. "Mrs. Crawley must be so much more comfortable to think that they are out of danger."

"And they will be quite comfortable at the parsonage," said Lucy.

"I do not at all doubt that," said Mr. Crawley; "but too much of such comforts will unfit them for their home; and — and I could have wished that I had been consulted more at leisure before the proceeding had been taken."

"It was arranged, Mr. Crawley, when I was here before, that the children had better go away," pleaded Lucy.

"I do not remember agreeing to such a measure, Miss Robarts; however — I suppose they cannot be had back to-night?"

"No, not to-night," said Lucy. "And now I will go in to your wife." And then she returned to the house, leaving the two gentlemen at the door. At this moment a labourer's boy came sauntering by, and the dean, obtaining possession of his services for the custody of his horse, was able to dismount and put himself on a more equal footing for conversation with his friend.

"Crawley," said he, putting his hand affectionately on his friend's shoulder, as they both stood leaning on the little rail before the door; "that is a good girl — a very good girl."

"Yes," said he slowly; "she means well."

"Nay, but she does well; she does excellently. What can be better than her conduct now? While I was meditating how I might possibly assist your wife in this strait —"

"I want no assistance; none, at least, from man," said Crawley, bitterly.

"Oh, my friend, think of what you are saying!

Think of the wickedness which must accompany such a state of mind! Have you ever known any man able to walk alone, without assistance from his brother men?"

Mr. Crawley did not make any immediate answer, but putting his arms behind his back and closing his hands, as was his wont when he walked alone thinking of the general bitterness of his lot in life, began to move slowly along the road in front of his house. He did not invite the other to walk with him, but neither was there anything in his manner which seemed to indicate that he had intended to be left to himself. It was a beautiful summer afternoon, at that delicious period of the year when summer has just burst forth from the growth of spring; when the summer is yet but three days old, and all the various shades of green which nature can put forth are still in their unsoiled purity of freshness. The apple blossoms were on the trees, and the hedges were sweet with May. The cuckoo at five o'clock was still sounding his soft summer call with unabated energy, and even the common grasses of the hedgerows were sweet with the fragrance of their new growth. The foliage of the oaks was complete, so that every bough and twig was clothed; but the leaves did not yet hang heavy in masses, and the bend of every bough and the tapering curve of every twig were visible through their light green covering. There is no time of the year equal to beauty to the first week in summer; and no colour which nature gives, not even the gorgeous hues of autumn, which can equal the verdure produced by the first warm suns of May.

Hogglestock, as has been explained, has little to

offer in the way of landskip beauty, and the clergyman's house at Hogglestock was not placed on a green slopy bank of land, retired from the road, with its windows opening on to a lawn, surrounded by shrubs, with a view of the small church tower seen through them; it had none of that beauty which is so common to the cozy houses of our spiritual pastors in the agricultural parts of England. Hogglestock Parsonage stood bleak beside the road, with no pretty paling lined inside by hollies and laburnum, Portugal laurels and rose-trees. But, nevertheless, even Hogglestock was pretty now. There were apple-trees there covered with blossom, and the hedgerows were in full flower. There were thrushes singing, and here and there an oak-tree stood in the roadside, perfect in its solitary beauty.

"Let us walk on a little," said the dean. "Miss Robarts is with her now, and you will be better for leaving the room for a few minutes."

"No," said he; "I must go back; I cannot leave that young lady to do my work."

"Stop, Crawley!" And the dean, putting his hand upon him, stayed him in the road. "She is doing her own work, and if you were speaking of her with reference to any other household than your own, you would say so. Is it not a comfort to you to know that your wife has a woman near her at such a time as this; and a woman, too, who can speak to her as one lady does to another?"

"These are comforts which we have no right to expect. I could not have done much for poor Mary; but what a man could have done should not have been wanting."

"I am sure of it; I know it well. What any man could do by himself you would do — excepting one thing." And the dean as he spoke looked full into the other's face.

"And what is there I would not do?" said Crawley.

"Sacrifice your own pride."

"My pride?"

"Yes; your own pride."

"I have had but little pride this many a day. Arabin, you do not know what my life has been. How is a man to be proud who —" And then he stopped himself, not wishing to go through the catalogue of those grievances, which, as he thought, had killed the very germs of pride within him, or to insist by spoken words on his poverty, his wants, and the injustice of his position. "No; I wish I could be proud; but the world has been too heavy to me, and I have forgotten all that."

"How long have I known you, Crawley?"

"How long? Ah dear! a lifetime nearly, now."

"And we were like brothers once."

"Yes; we were equal as brothers then — in our fortunes, our tastes, and our modes of life."

"And yet you would begrudge me the pleasure of putting my hand in my pocket, and relieving the inconveniences which have been thrown on you, and those you love better than yourself, by the chances of your fate in life."

"I will live on no man's charity," said Crawley, with an abruptness which amounted almost to an expression of anger.

"And is not that pride?"

"No — yes; — it is a species of pride, but not

that pride of which you spoke. A man cannot be honest if he have not some pride. You yourself; — would you not rather starve than become a beggar?"

"I would rather beg than see my wife starve," said Arabin.

Crawley when he heard these words turned sharply round, and stood with his back to the dean, with his hands still behind him, and with his eyes fixed upon the ground.

"But in this case there is no question of begging," continued the dean. "I, out of those superfluities which it has pleased God to put at my disposal, am anxious to assist the needs of those whom I love."

"She is not starving," said Crawley, in a voice very bitter, but still intended to be exculpatory of himself.

"No, my dear friend; I know she is not, and do not you be angry with me because I have endeavoured to put the matter to you in the strongest language I could use."

"You look at it, Arabin, from one side only; I can only look at it from the other. It is very sweet to give; I do not doubt that. But the taking of what is given is very bitter. Gift bread chokes in a man's throat and poisons his blood, and sits like lead upon the heart. You have never tried it."

"But that is the very fault for which I blame you. That is the pride which I say you ought to sacrifice."

"And why should I be called on to do so? Is not the labourer worthy of his hire? Am I not able to work, and willing? Have I not always had my shoulder to the collar, and is it right that I should now be contented with the scraps from a rich man's kitchen?

Arabin, you and I were equal once and we were then friends, understanding each other's thoughts and sympathizing with each other's sorrows. But it cannot be so now."

"If there be such inability, it is all with you."

"It is all with me, — because in our connection the pain would all be on my side. It would not hurt you to see me at your table with worn shoes and a ragged shirt. I do not think so meanly of you as that. You would give me your feast to eat though I were not clad a tithe as well as the menial behind your chair. But it would hurt me to know that there were those looking at me who thought me unfit to sit in your rooms."

"That is the pride of which I speak; — false pride."

"Call it so if you will; but, Arabin, no preaching of yours can alter it. It is all that is left to me of my manliness. That poor broken reed who is lying there sick, — who has sacrificed all the world to her love for me, — who is the mother of my children, and the partner of my sorrows and the wife of my bosom, — even she cannot change me in this, though she pleads with the eloquence of all her wants. Not even for her can I hold out my hand for a dole."

They had now come back to the door of the house, and Mr. Crawley, hardly conscious of what he was doing, was preparing to enter.

"Will Mrs. Crawley be able to see me if I come in?" said the dean.

"Oh, stop; no; you had better not do so," said Mr. Crawley. "You, no doubt, might be subject to infection, and then Mrs. Arabin would be frightened."

"I do not care about it in the least," said the dean. "But it is of no use; you had better not. Her room, I fear, is quite unfit for you to see; and the whole house, you know, may be infected."

Dr. Arabin by this time was in the sitting-room; but seeing that his friend was really anxious that he should not go farther, he did not persist.

"It will be a comfort to us, at any rate, to know that Miss Robarts is with her."

"The young lady is very good — very good indeed," said Crawley; "but I trust she will return to her home to-morrow. It is impossible that she should remain in so poor a house as mine. There will be nothing here of all the things that she will want."

The dean thought that Lucy Robarts' wants during her present occupation of nursing would not be so numerous as to make her continued sojourn in Mrs. Crawley's sick room impossible, and therefore took his leave with a satisfied conviction that the poor lady would not be left wholly to the somewhat unskilful nursing of her husband.

CHAPTER XIII.

Mr. Sowerby without Company.

And now there were going to be wondrous doings in West Barsetshire, and men's minds were much disturbed. The fiat had gone forth from the high places, and the Queen had dissolved her faithful Commons. The giants, finding that they could effect little or nothing with the old House, had resolved to try what a new venture would do for them, and the hubbub of a general election was to pervade the country. This produced no inconsiderable irritation and annoyance, for the House was not as yet quite three years old; and members of parliament, though they naturally feel a constitutional pleasure in meeting their friends and in pressing the hands of their constituents, are, nevertheless, so far akin to the lower order of humanity that they appreciate the danger of losing their seats; and the certainty of a considerable outlay in their endeavours to retain them is not agreeable to the legislative mind.

Never did the old family fury between the gods and giants rage higher than at the present moment. The giants declared that every turn which they attempted to take in their country's service had been thwarted by faction, in spite of those benign promises of assistance made to them only a few weeks since by their opponents; and the gods answered by asserting that they were driven to this opposition by the Bœotian fatuity of the giants. They had no doubt promised their aid, and were ready to give it to measures that were decently prudent; but not to a bill enabling government at its will to pension aged bishops! No; there must be some limit to their tolerance, and when such attempts as these were made that limit had been clearly passed.

All this had taken place openly only a day or two after that casual whisper dropped by Tom Towers at Miss Dunstable's party — by Tom Towers, that most pleasant of all pleasant fellows. And how should he have known it, — he who flutters from one sweetest flower of the garden to another,

> "Adding sugar to the pink, and honey to the rose,
> So loved for what he gives, but taking nothing as he goes?"

But the whisper had grown into a rumour, and the rumour into a fact, and the political world was in a ferment. The giants, furious about their bishops' pension bill, threatened the House — most injudiciously; and then it was beautiful to see how indignant members got up, glowing with honesty, and declared that it was base to conceive that any gentleman in that House could be actuated in his vote by any hopes or fears with reference to his seat. And so matters grew from bad to worse, and these contending parties never hit at each other with such envenomed wrath as they did now; having entered the ring together so lately with such manifold promises of good-will, respect, and forbearance!

But going from the general to the particular, we may say that nowhere was a deeper consternation spread than in the electoral division of West Barsetshire. No sooner had the tidings of the dissolution reached the county than it was known that the duke intended to change his nominee. Mr. Sowerby had now sat for the division since the Reform Bill! He had become one of the county institutions, and by the dint of custom and long establishment had been borne with and even liked by the county gentlemen, in spite of his well-known pecuniary irregularities. Now all this was to be changed. No reason had as yet been publicly given, but it was understood that Lord Dumbello was to be returned, although he did not own an acre of land in the county. It is true that rumour went on to say that Lord Dumbello was about to form close connections with Barsetshire. He was on the eve of marrying a young lady, from the other division indeed, and was now engaged, so it was said, in completing arrangements with the government for the purchase of that noble crown property usually known as the Chase of Chaldicotes. It was also stated — this statement, however, had hitherto been only announced in confidential whispers — that Chaldicotes House itself would soon become the residence of the marquis. The duke was claiming it as his own — would very shortly have completed his claims and taken possession; — and then, by some arrangement between them, it was to be made over to Lord Dumbello.

But very contrary rumours to these got abroad also. Men said — such as dared to oppose the duke, and some few also who did not dare to oppose him when the day of battle came — that it was beyond his grace's power to turn Lord Dumbello into a Barsetshire magnate. The crown property — such men said — was to fall into the hands of young Mr. Gresham, of Boxall Hill, in the other division, and that the terms of purchase had been already settled. And as to Mr. Sowerby's property and the house of Chaldicotes — these opponents of the Omnium interest went on to explain — it was by no means as yet so certain that the duke would be able to enter it and take possession. The place was not to be given up to him quietly. A great fight would be made, and it was beginning to be believed that the enormous mortgages would be paid off by a lady of immense wealth. And then a dash of romance was not wanting to make these stories palatable. This lady of immense wealth had been courted by Mr. Sowerby, had acknowledged her love, — but had refused to marry him on account of his character. In testimony of her love, however, she was about to pay all his debts.

It was soon put beyond a rumour, and became manifest enough, that Mr. Sowerby did not intend to retire from the county in obedience to the duke's behests. A placard was posted through the whole division in which no allusion was made by name to the duke, but in which Mr. Sowerby warned his friends not to be led away by any report that he intended to retire from the representation of West Barsetshire. "He had sat," the placard said, "for the same county during the full period of a quarter of a century, and he would not lightly give up an honour that had been extended to him so often and which he prized so dearly. There were but few men now in the House whose connection with the same body of constituents had remained unbroken so long as had that which bound him to West Barsetshire; and he confidently hoped that that connection might be continued through another period of coming years till he might find himself in the glorious position of being the father of the county members of the House of Commons." The placard said much more than this, and hinted at sundry and various questions, all of great interest to the county; but it did not say one word of the Duke of Omnium, though every one knew what the duke was supposed to be doing in the matter. He was, as it were, a great Llama, shut up in a holy of holies, inscrutable, invisible, inexorable,—not to be seen by men's eyes or heard by their ears, hardly to be mentioned by ordinary men at such periods as these without an inward quaking. But, nevertheless, it was he who was supposed to rule them. Euphemism required that his name should be mentioned at no public meetings in connection with the coming election; but, nevertheless, most men in the county believed that he could send his dog up to the House of Commons as member for West Barsetshire if it so pleased him.

It was supposed, therefore, that our friend Sowerby would have no chance; but he was lucky in finding assistance in a quarter from which he certainly had not deserved it. He had been a staunch friend of the gods during the whole of his political life, — as, indeed, was to be expected, seeing that he had been the duke's nominee; but, nevertheless, on the present occasion, all the giants connected with the county came forward to his rescue. They did not do this with the acknowledged purpose of opposing the duke; they declared that they were actuated by a generous disinclination to see an old county member put from his seat, — but the world knew that the battle was to be waged against the great Llama. It was to be a contest between the powers of aristocracy and the powers of oligarchy, as those powers existed in West Barsetshire, — and, it may be added, that democracy would have very little to say to it, on one side or on the other. The lower order of voters, the small farmers and tradesmen, would no doubt range themselves on the side of the duke, and would endeavour to flatter themselves that they were thereby furthering the views of the liberal side; but they would in fact be led to the poll by an old-fashioned, time-honoured adherence to the will of their great Llama; and by an apprehension of evil if that Llama should arise and shake himself in his wrath. What might not come to the county if the Llama were to walk himself off, he with his satellites and armies and courtiers? There he was, a great Llama; and though he came among them but seldom, and was scarcely seen when he did come, nevertheless — and not the less but rather the more — was obedience to him considered as salutary and opposition regarded as dangerous. A great rural Llama is still sufficiently mighty in rural England.

But the priest of the temple, Mr. Fothergill, was frequent enough in men's eyes, and it was beautiful to hear with how varied a voice he alluded to the things around him and to the changes which were coming. To the small farmers, not only on the Gatherum property but on others also, he spoke of the duke as a beneficent influence, shedding prosperity on all around him, keeping up prices by his presence, and forbidding the poor rates to rise above one and fourpence in the pound by the general employment which he occasioned. Men must be mad, he thought, who would willingly fly in the duke's face. To the squires from a distance he declared that no one had a right to charge the duke with any interference; — as far, at least, as he knew the duke's mind. People would talk of things of which they understood nothing. Could any one say that he had traced a single request for a vote home to the duke? All this did not alter the settled conviction on men's minds; but it had its effect, and tended to increase the mystery in which the duke's doings were enveloped. But to his own familiars, to the gentry immediately around him, Mr. Fothergill merely winked his eye. They knew what was what, and so did he. The duke had never been bit yet in such matters, and Mr. Fothergill did not think that he would now submit himself to any such operation.

I never heard in what manner and at what rate Mr. Fothergill received remuneration for the various services performed by him with reference to the duke's property in Barsetshire; but I am very sure that, whatever might be the amount, he earned it thoroughly. Never was there a more faithful partisan, or one who, in his partisanship, was more discreet. In this matter of the coming election he declared that he himself, — personally, on his own hook, — did intend to bestir himself actively on behalf of Lord Dumbello. Mr. Sowerby was an old friend of his, and a very good fellow. That was true. But all the world must admit that Sowerby was not in the position which a county member ought to occupy. He was a ruined man, and it would not be for his own advantage that he should be maintained in a position which was fit only for a man of property. He knew — he, Fothergill — that Mr. Sowerby must abandon all right and claim to Chaldicotes; and if so, what would be more absurd than to acknowledge that he had a right and claim to the seat in Parliament. As to Lord Dumbello, it was probable that he would soon become one of the largest landowners in the county; and, as such, who could be more fit for the representation? Beyond this, Mr. Fothergill was not ashamed to confess — so he said — that he hoped to hold Lord Dumbello's agency. It would be compatible with his other duties, and therefore, as a matter of course, he intended to support Lord Dumbello; — he himself, that is. As to the duke's mind in the matter —! But I have already explained how Mr. Fothergill disposed of that.

In these days, Mr. Sowerby came down to his own house — for ostensibly it was still his own house: but he came very quietly, and his arrival was hardly known in his own village. Though his placard was stuck up so widely, he himself took no electioneering steps; none, at least, as yet. The protection against arrest which he derived from Parliament would soon be over, and those who were most bitter against the duke averred that steps would be taken to arrest him, should he give sufficient opportunity to the myrmidons of the law. That he would, in such case, be arrested was very likely; but it was not likely that this would be done in any way at the duke's instance. Mr. Fothergill declared indignantly that this insinuation made him very angry; but he was too prudent a man to be very angry at anything, and he knew how to make capital on his own side of charges such as these which overshot their own mark.

Mr. Sowerby came down very quietly to Chaldicotes, and there he remained for a couple of days, quite alone. The place bore a very different aspect now to that which we noticed when Mark Robarts drove up to it, in the early pages of this little narrative. There were no lights in the windows now, and no voices came from the stables; no dogs barked, and all was dead and silent as the grave. During the greater portion of those two days he sat alone within the house, almost unoccupied. He did not even open his letters, which lay piled on a crowded table in the small breakfast parlour in which he sat; for the letters of such men come in piles, and there are few of them which are pleasant in the reading. There he sat, troubled with thoughts which were sad enough, now and then moving to and fro the house, but for the most part occupied in thinking over the position to which he had brought himself. What would he be in the world's eye, if he ceased to be the owner of Chaldicotes, and ceased also to be the member for his county? He had lived ever before the world, and, though always harassed by encumbrances, had been sustained and comforted by the excitement of a prominent position. His debts and difficulties had hitherto been bearable, and he had borne them with ease so long that he had almost taught himself to think that they would never be unendurable. But now, —

The order for foreclosing had gone forth, and the harpies of the law, by their present speed in sticking their claws into the carcase of his property, were atoning to themselves for the delay with which they had hitherto been compelled to approach their prey. And the order as to his seat had gone forth also. That placard had been drawn up by the combined efforts of his sister, Miss Dunstable, and a certain well-known electioneering agent, named Closerstill, presumed to be in the interest of the giants. But poor Sowerby had but little confidence in the placard. No one knew better than he how great was the duke's power.

He was hopeless, therefore, as he walked about through those empty rooms, thinking of his past life and of that life which was to come. Would it not be well for him that he were dead, now that he was dying to all that had made the world pleasant. We see and hear of such men as Mr. Sowerby, and are apt to think that they enjoy all that the world can give, and that they enjoy that all without payment either in care or labour; but I doubt that, with even the most callous of them, their periods of wretchedness must be frequent, and that wretchedness very intense. Salmon and lamb in February and green pease and new potatoes in March can hardly make a man happy, even though nobody pays for them; and the feeling that one is an *antece-*

dentem scelestum after whom a sure, though lame, Nemesis is hobbling, must sometimes disturb one's slumbers. On the present occasion Scelestus felt that his Nemesis had overtaken him. Lame as she had been, and swift as he had run, she had mouthed him at last, and there was nothing left for him but to listen to the "whoop" set up at the sight of his own death-throes.

It was a melancholy, dreary place now, that big house of Chaldicotes; and though the woods were all green with their early leaves, and the garden thick with flowers, they also were melancholy and dreary. The lawns were untrimmed and weeds were growing through the gravel, and here and there a cracked Dryad, tumbled from her pedestal and sprawling in the grass, gave a look of disorder to the whole place. The wooden trellis-work was shattered here and bending there, the standard rose-trees were stooping to the ground, and the leaves of the winter still encumbered the borders. Late in the evening of the second day Mr. Sowerby strolled out, and went through the gardens into the wood. Of all the inanimate things of the world this wood of Chaldicotes was the dearest to him. He was not a man to whom his companions gave much credit for feelings or thoughts akin to poetry, but here, out in the Chase, his mind would be almost poetical. While wandering among the forest trees, he became susceptible of the tenderness of human nature: he would listen to the birds singing, and pick here and there a wild flower on his path. He would watch the decay of the old trees and the progress of the young, and make pictures in his eyes of every turn in the wood. He would mark the colour of a bit of road as it dipped into a dell, and then, passing through a water-course, rose brown, rough, irregular, and beautiful against the bank on the other side. And then he would sit and think of his old family: how they had roamed there time out of mind in those Caldicotes woods, father and son and grandson in regular succession, each giving them over, without blemish or decrease, to his successor. So he would sit; and so he did sit even now, and, thinking of these things, wished that he had never been born.

It was dark night when he returned to the house, and as he did so, he resolved that he would quit the place altogether, and give up the battle as lost. The duke should take it and do as he pleased with it; and as for the seat in Parliament, Lord Dumbello, or any other equally gifted young patrician, might hold it for him. He would vanish from the scene and betake himself to some land from whence he would be neither heard nor seen, and there — starve. Such were now his future outlooks into the world; and yet, as regards health and all physical capacities, he knew that he was still in the prime of his life. Yes; in the prime of his life! But what could he do with what remained to him of such prime? How could he turn either his mind or his strength to such account as might now be serviceable? How could he, in his sore need, earn for himself even the barest bread? Would it not be better for him that he should die? Let not any one covet the lot of a spendthrift, even though the days of his early pease and champagne seem to be unnumbered; for that lame Nemesis will surely be up before the game has been all played out.

When Mr. Sowerby reached his house he found that a message by telegraph had arrived for him in his absence. It was from his sister, and it informed him that she would be with him that night. She was coming down by the mail train, had telegraphed to Barchester for post-horses, and would be at Chaldicotes about two hours after midnight. It was therefore manifest enough that her business was of importance.

Exactly at two the Barchester post-chaise did arrive, and Mrs. Harold Smith, before she retired to her bed, was closeted for about an hour with her brother.

"Well," she said, the following morning, as they sat together at the breakfast-table, "what do you say to it now? If you accept her offer you should be with her lawyer this afternoon."

"I suppose I must accept it," said he.

"Certainly, I think so. No doubt it will take the property out of your own hands as completely as though the duke had it, but it will leave you the house, at any rate for your life."

"What good will the house be, when I can't keep it up?"

"But I am not so sure of that. She will not want more than her fair interest; and as it will be thoroughly well managed, I should think that there would be something over — something enough to keep up the house. And then, you know, we must have some place in the country."

"I tell you fairly, Harriet, that I will have nothing further to do with Harold in the way of money."

"Ah! that was because you would go to him. Why did you not come to me? And then, Nathaniel, it is the only way in which you can have a chance of keeping the seat. She is the queerest woman I ever met, but she seems resolved on beating the duke."

"I do not quite understand it, but I have not the slightest objection."

"She thinks that he is interfering with young Gresham about the Crown property. I had no idea that she had so much business at her fingers' ends. When I first proposed the matter she took it up quite as a lawyer might, and seemed to have forgotten altogether what occurred about that other matter."

"I wish I could forget it also," said Mr. Sowerby.

"I really think that she does. When I was obliged to make some allusion to it — at least, I felt myself obliged, and was sorry afterwards that I did — she merely laughed — a great loud laugh as she always does, and then went on about the business. However, she was clear about this, that all the expenses of the election should be added to the sum to be advanced by her, and that the house should be left to you without any rent. If you choose to take the land round the house you must pay for it, by the acre, as the tenants do. She was as clear about it all as though she had passed her life in a lawyer's office."

My readers will now pretty well understand what last step that excellent sister, Mrs. Harold Smith, had taken on her brother's behalf, nor will they be surprised to learn that in the course of the day Mr. Sowerby hurried back to town and put himself into communication with Miss Dunstable's lawyer.

CHAPTER XIV.

Is there Cause or Just Impediment?

I NOW purpose to visit another country house in Barsetshire, but on this occasion our sojourn shall be in the eastern division, in which, as in every other county in England, electioneering matters are paramount at the present moment. It has been mentioned that Mr. Gresham, junior, young Frank Gresham as he was always called, lived at a place called Boxall Hill. This property had come to his wife by will, and he was now settled there, — seeing that his father still held the family seat of the Greshams at Greshamsbury.

At the present moment Miss Dunstable was staying at Boxall Hill with Mrs. Frank Gresham. They had left London, — as, indeed, all the world had done, to the terrible dismay of the London tradesmen. This dissolution of parliament was ruining everybody except the country publicans, and had of course destroyed the London season among other things.

Mrs. Harold Smith had only just managed to catch Miss Dunstable before she left London; but she did do so, and the great heiress had at once seen her lawyers, and instructed them how to act with reference to the mortgages on the Chaldicotes property. Miss Dunstable was in the habit of speaking of herself and her own pecuniary concerns as though she herself were rarely allowed to meddle in their management; but this was one of those small jokes which she ordinarily perpetrated; for in truth few ladies, and perhaps not many gentlemen, have a more thorough knowledge of their own concerns or a more potent voice in their own affairs, than was possessed by Miss Dunstable. Circumstances had lately brought her much into Barsetshire, and she had there contracted very intimate friendships. She was now disposed to become, if possible, a Barsetshire proprietor, and with this view had lately agreed with young Mr. Gresham that she would become the purchaser of the Crown property. As, however, the purchase had been commenced in his name, it was so to be continued; but now, as we are aware, it was rumoured that, after all, the duke, or, if not the duke, then the Marquis of Dumbello, was to be the future owner of the Chase. Miss Dunstable, however, was not a person to give up her object if she could attain it, nor, under the circumstances, was she at all displeased at finding herself endowed with the power of rescuing the Sowerby portion of the Chaldicotes property from the duke's clutches. Why had the duke meddled with her, or with her friend, as to the other property? Therefore it was arranged that the full amount due to the duke on mortgage should be ready for immediate payment; but it was arranged also that the security as held by Miss Dunstable should be very valid.

Miss Dunstable, at Boxall Hill or at Greshamsbury, was a very different person from Miss Dunstable in London; and it was this difference which so much vexed Mrs. Gresham; not that her friend omitted to bring with her into the country her London wit and aptitude for fun, but that she did not take with her up to town the genuine goodness and love of honesty which made her loveable in the country. She was, as it were, two persons, and Mrs. Gresham could not understand that any lady should permit herself to be more worldly at one time of the year than at another — or in one place than in any other.

"Well, my dear, I am heartily glad we've done with that," Miss Dunstable said to her, as she sat herself down to her desk in the drawing-room on the first morning after her arrival at Boxall Hill.

"What does 'that' mean?" said Mrs. Gresham.

"Why, London and smoke and late hours, and standing on one's legs for four hours at a stretch on the top of one's own staircase, to be bowed at by any one who chooses to come. That's all done — for one year, at any rate."

"You know you like it."

"No, Mary; that's just what I don't know. I don't know whether I like it or not. Sometimes, when the spirit of that dearest of all women, Mrs. Harold Smith, is upon me, I think that I do like it; but then again, when other spirits are on me, I think that I don't."

"And who are the owners of the other spirits?"

"Oh, you are one, of course. But you are a weak little thing, by no means able to contend with such a Samson as Mrs. Harold. And then you are a little given to wickedness yourself, you know. You've learned to like London well enough since you sat down to the table of Dives. Your uncle, — he's the real impracticable, unapproachable Lazarus who declares that he can't come down because of the big gulf. I wonder how he'd behave, if somebody left him ten thousand a year?"

"Uncommonly well, I am sure."

"Oh, yes; he is a Lazarus now, so of course we

are bound to speak well of him; but I should like to see him tried. I don't doubt but what he'd have a house in Belgrave Square, and become noted for his little dinners before the first year of his trial was over."

"Well, and why not? You would not wish him to be an anchorite?"

"I am told that he is going to try his luck, — not with ten thousand a year, but with one or two."

"What do you mean?"

"Jane tells me that they all say at Greshamsbury that he is going to marry Lady Scatcherd." Now Lady Scatcherd was a widow living in those parts; an excellent woman, but one not formed by nature to grace society of the highest order.

"What!" exclaimed Mrs. Gresham, rising up from her chair while her eyes flashed with anger at such a rumour.

"Well, my dear, don't eat me. I don't say it is so; I only say that Jane said so."

"Then you ought to send Jane out of the house."

"You may be sure of this, my dear: Jane would not have told me if somebody had not told her."

"And you believed it?"

"I have said nothing about that."

"But you look as if you had believed it."

"Do I? Let us see what sort of a look it is, this look of faith." And Miss Dunstable got up and went to the glass over the fire-place. "But Mary, my dear, ain't you old enough to know that you should not credit people's looks? You should believe nothing now-a-days; and I did not believe the story about poor

Lady Scatcherd, I know the doctor well enough to be sure that he is not a marrying man."

"What a nasty, hackneyed, false phrase that is — that of a marrying man! It sounds as though some men were in the habit of getting married three or four times a month."

"It means a great deal all the same. One can tell very soon whether a man is likely to marry or no."

"And can one tell the same of a woman?"

"The thing is so different. All unmarried women are necessarily in the market; but if they behave themselves properly they make no signs. Now there was Griselda Grantly; of course she intended to get herself a husband, and a very grand one she has got; but she always looked as though butter would not melt in her mouth. It would have been very wrong to call her a marrying girl."

"Oh, of course she was," says Mrs. Gresham, with that sort of acrimony which one pretty young woman so frequently expresses with reference to another. "But if one could always tell of a woman, as you say you can of a man, I should be able to tell of you. Now, I wonder whether you are a marrying woman. I have never been able to make up my mind yet."

Miss Dunstable remained silent for a few moments, as though she were at first minded to take the question as being, in some sort, one made in earnest; but then she attempted to laugh it off. "Well, I wonder at that," said she, "as it was only the other day I told you how many offers I had refused."

"Yes; but you did not tell me whether any had been made that you meant to accept."

"None such was ever made to me. Talking of that, I shall never forget your cousin, the Honourable George."

"He is not my cousin."

"Well, your husband's. It would not be fair to show a man's letters; but I should like to show you his."

"You are determined, then, to remain single?"

"I didn't say that. But why do you cross-question me so?"

"Because I think so much about you. I am afraid that you will become so afraid of men's motives as to doubt that any one can be honest. And yet sometimes I think you would be a happier woman and a better woman, if you were married."

"To such an one as the Honourable George, for instance?"

"No, not to such an one as him; you have probably picked out the worst."

"Or to Mr. Sowerby?"

"Well, no; not to Mr. Sowerby, either. I would not have you marry any man that looked to you for your money principally."

"And how is it possible that I should expect any one to look to me principally for anything else? You don't see my difficulty, my dear? If I had only five hundred a year, I might come across some decent middle-aged personage, like myself, who would like me, myself, pretty well, and would like my little income — pretty well also. He would not tell me any violent lie, and perhaps no lie at all. I should take to him in the same sort of way, and we might do very well. But, as it is, how is it possible that any disinterested person should learn to like me? How could such a man set about it? If a sheep have two heads, is not the fact of the two heads the first and, indeed, only thing which the world regards in that sheep? Must it not be so as a matter of course? I am a sheep with two heads. All this money which my father put together, and which has been growing since like grass under May showers, has turned me into an abortion. I am not the giantess eight feet high, or the dwarf that stands in the man's hand, —"

"Or the two-headed sheep —"

"But I am the unmarried woman with — half a dozen millions of money — as I believe some people think. Under such circumstances have I a fair chance of getting my own sweet bit of grass to nibble, like any ordinary animal with one head? I never was very beautiful, and I am not more so now than I was fifteen years ago."

"I am quite sure it is not that which hinders it. You would not call yourself plain; and even plain women are married every day, and are loved too, as well as pretty women."

"Are they? Well, we won't say more about that; but I don't expect a great many lovers on account of my beauty. If ever you hear of such an one, mind you tell me."

It was almost on Mrs. Gresham's tongue to say that she did know of such — meaning her uncle. But in truth, she did not know any such thing; nor could she boast to herself that she had good grounds for feeling that it was so — certainly none sufficient to justify her in speaking of it. Her uncle had said no word to her on the matter, and had been confused and embarrassed when the idea of such a marriage was hinted to him. But, nevertheless, Mrs. Gresham did think that each of these two was well inclined to love the other, and that they would be happier together than they would be single. The difficulty, however, was very great, for the doctor would be terribly afraid of being thought covetous in regard to Miss Dunstable's money; and it would hardly be expected that she should be induced to make the first overture to the doctor.

"My uncle would be the only man that I can think of that would be at all fit for you," said Mrs. Gresham, boldly.

"What, and rob poor Lady Scatcherd!" said Miss Dunstable.

"Oh, very well. If you choose to make a joke of his name in that way, I have done."

"Why, God bless the girl, what does she want me to say? And as for joking, surely that is innocent enough. You're as tender about the doctor as though he were a girl of seventeen."

"It's not about him; but it's such a shame to laugh at poor dear Lady Scatcherd. If she were to hear it she'd lose all comfort in having my uncle near her."

"And I'm to marry him, so that she may be safe with her friend!"

"Very well; I have done." And Mrs. Gresham, who had already got up from her seat, employed herself very sedulously in arranging flowers which had been brought in for the drawing-room tables. Thus they remained silent for a minute or two, during which she began to reflect that, after all, it might probably be thought that she also was endeavouring to catch the great heiress for her uncle.

"And now you are angry with me," said Miss Dunstable.

"No, I am not."

"Oh, but you are. Do you think I'm such a fool as not to see when a person's vexed? You wouldn't have twitched that geranium's head off if you'd been in a proper frame of mind."

"I don't like that joke about Lady Scatcherd."

"And is that all, Mary? Now do try and be true, if you can. You remember the bishop? *Magna est veritas.*"

"The fact is you've got into such a way of being sharp, and saying sharp things among your friends up in London, that you can hardly answer a person without it."

"Can't I! Dear, dear, what a Mentor you are, Mary! No poor lad that ever ran up from Oxford for a spree in town got so lectured for his dissipation and iniquities as I do. Well, I beg Dr. Thorne's pardon, and Lady Scatcherd's, and I won't be sharp any more; and I will — let me see, what was it I was to do? Marry him myself, I believe; was not that it?"

"No; you're not half good enough for him."

"I know that. I'm quite sure of that. Though I am so sharp, I'm very humble. You can't accuse me of putting any very great value on myself."

"Perhaps not as much as you ought to do — on yourself.'

"Now what do you mean, Mary? I won't be bullied and teased, and have innuendos thrown out at me, because you've got something on your mind, and don't quite dare to speak it out. If you have got anything to say, say it."

But Mrs. Gresham did not choose to say it at that moment. She held her peace, and went on arranging her flowers — now with a more satisfied air, and without destruction to the geraniums. And when she had grouped her bunches properly she carried the jar from one part of the room to another, backwards and forwards, trying the effect of the colours, as though her mind was quite intent upon her flowers, and was for the moment wholly unoccupied with any other subject.

But Miss Dunstable was not the woman to put up with this. She sat silent in her place, while her friend made one or two turns about the room; and then she got up from her seat also. "Mary," she said, "give over about those wretched bits of green branches, and leave the jars where they are. You're trying to fidget me into a passion."

"Am I?" said Mrs. Gresham, standing opposite to a big bowl, and putting her head a little on one side, as though she could better look at her handiwork in that position.

"You know you are; and it's all because you lack courage to speak out. You didn't begin at me in this way for nothing."

"I do lack courage. That's just it," said Mrs. Gresham, still giving a twist here and a set there to some of the small sprigs which constituted the background of her bouquet. "I do lack courage — to have ill motives imputed to me. I was thinking of saying something, and I am afraid, and therefore I will not say it. And now, if you like, I will be ready to take you out in ten minutes."

But Miss Dunstable was not going to be put off in this way. And to tell the truth, I must admit that her friend Mrs. Gresham was not using her altogether well. She should either have held her peace on the matter altogether, — which would probably have been her wiser course, — or she should have declared her own ideas boldly, feeling secure in her own conscience as to her own motives. "I shall not stir from this room," said Miss Dunstable, "till I have had this matter out with you. And as for imputations, — my imputing bad motives to you, — I don't know how far you may be joking, and saying what you call sharp things to me; but you have no right to think that I should think evil of you. If you really do think so, it is treason to the love I have for you. If I thought that you thought so, I could not remain in the house with you. What, you are not able to know the difference which one makes between one's real friends and one's mock friends! I don't believe it of you, and I know you are only striving to bully me." And Miss Dunstable now took her turn of walking up and down the room.

"Well, she shan't be bullied," said Mrs. Gresham, leaving her flowers, and putting her arm round her friend's waist; — "at least, not here, in this house, although she is sometimes such a bully herself."

"Mary, you have gone too far about this to go back. Tell me what it was that was on your mind, and as far as it concerns me, I will answer you honestly."

Mrs. Gresham now began to repent that she had

made her little attempt. That uttering of hints in a half-joking way was all very well, and might possibly bring about the desired result, without the necessity of any formal suggestion on her part; but now she was so brought to book that she must say something formal. She must commit herself to the expression of her own wishes, and to an expression also of an opinion as to what had been the wishes of her friend; and this she must do without being able to say anything as to the wishes of that third person.

"Well," she said, "I suppose you know what I meant."

"I suppose I did," said Miss Dunstable; "but it is not at all the less necessary that you should say it out. I am not to commit myself by my interpretation of your thoughts, while you remain perfectly secure in having only hinted your own. I hate hints, as I do — the mischief. I go in for the bishop's doctrine. *Magna est veritas.*"

"Well, I don't know," said Mrs. Gresham.

"Ah! but I do," said Miss Dunstable. "And therefore go on, or for ever hold your peace."

"That's just it," said Mrs. Gresham.

"What's just it?" said Miss Dunstable.

"The quotation out of the Prayer Book which you finished just now. 'If any of you know cause or just impediment why these two persons should not be joined together in holy matrimony, ye are to declare it. This is the first time of asking.' Do you know any cause, Miss Dunstable?"

"Do you know any, Mrs. Gresham?"

"None, on my honour!" said the younger lady, putting her hand upon her breast.

"Ah! but do you not?" and Miss Dunstable caught hold of her arm, and spoke almost abruptly in her energy.

"No, certainly not. What impediment? If I did, I should not have broached the subject. I declare I think you would both be very happy together. Of course, there is one impediment; we all know that. That must be your look out."

"What do you mean? What impediment?"

"Your own money."

"Psha! Did you find that an impediment in marrying Frank Gresham?"

"Ah! the matter was so different there. He had much more to give than I had, when all was counted. And I had no money when we — when we were first engaged." And the tears came into her eyes as she thought of the circumstances of her early love; — all of which have been narrated in the county chronicles of Barsetshire, and may now be read by men and women interested therein.

"Yes; yours was a love match. I declare, Mary, I often think that you are the happiest woman of whom I ever heard; to have it all to give, when you were so sure that you were loved while you yet had nothing."

"Yes; I was sure," and she wiped the sweet tears from her eyes, as she remembered a certain day when a certain youth had come to her, claiming all kinds of privileges in a very determined manner. She had been no heiress then. "Yes; I was sure. But now with you, dear, you can't make yourself poor again. If you can trust no one —"

"I can. I can trust him. As regards that I do

trust him altogether. But how can I tell that he would care for me?"

"Do you not know that he likes you?"

"Ah, yes; and so he does Lady Scatcherd."

"Miss Dunstable!"

"And why not Lady Scatcherd, as well as me? We are of the same kind — come from the same class."

"Not quite that, I think."

"Yes, from the same class; only I have managed to poke myself up among dukes and duchesses, whereas she has been content to remain where God placed her. Where I beat her in art, she beats me in nature."

"You know you are talking nonsense."

"I think that we are both doing that — absolute nonsense; such as schoolgirls of eighteen talk to each other. But there is a relief in it; is there not? It would be a terrible curse to have to talk sense always. Well, that's done; and now let us go out."

Mrs. Gresham was sure after this that Miss Dunstable would be a consenting party to the little arrangement which she contemplated. But of that she had felt but little doubt for some considerable time past. The difficulty lay on the other side, and all that she had as yet done was to convince herself that she would be safe in assuring her uncle of success if he could be induced to take the enterprise in hand. He was to come to Boxall Hill that evening, and to remain there for a day or two. If anything could be done in the matter, now would be the time for doing it. So at least thought Mrs. Gresham.

The doctor did come, and did remain for the

allotted time at Boxall Hill; but when he left, Mrs. Gresham had not been successful. Indeed, he did not seem to enjoy his visit as was usual with him; and there was very little of that pleasant friendly intercourse which for some time past had been customary between him and Miss Dunstable. There were no passages of arms between them; no abuse from the doctor against the lady's London gaiety; no raillery from the lady as to the doctor's country habits. They were very courteous to each other, and, as Mrs. Gresham thought, too civil by half; nor, as far as she could see, did they ever remain alone in each other's company for five minutes at a time during the whole period of the doctor's visit. What, thought Mrs. Gresham to herself, — what if she had set these two friends at variance with each other, instead of binding them together in the closest and most durable friendship!

But still she had an idea that, as she had begun to play this game, she must play it out. She felt conscious that what she had done must do evil, unless she could so carry it on as to make it result in good. Indeed, unless she could so manage, she would have done a manifest injury to Miss Dunstable in forcing her to declare her thoughts and feelings. She had already spoken to her uncle in London, and though he had said nothing to show that he approved of her plan, neither had he said anything to show that he disapproved it. Therefore she had hoped through the whole of those three days that he would make some sign, — at any rate to her; that he would in some way declare what were his own thoughts on this matter. But the morning of his departure came, and he had declared nothing.

"Uncle," she said, in the last five minutes of his sojourn there, after he had already taken leave of Miss Dunstable and shaken hands with Mrs. Gresham, "have you ever thought of what I said to you up in London?"

"Yes, Mary; of course I have thought about it. Such an idea as that, when put into a man's head, will make itself thought about."

"Well; and what next? Do talk to me about it. Do not be so hard and unlike yourself."

"I have very little to say about it."

"I can tell you this for certain, you may if you like."

"Mary! Mary!"

"I would not say so if I were not sure that I should not lead you into trouble."

"You are foolish in wishing this, my dear; foolish in trying to tempt an old man into a folly."

"Not foolish if I know that it will make you both happier."

He made her no further reply, but stooping down that she might kiss him, as was his wont, went his way, leaving her almost miserable in the thought that she had troubled all these waters to no purpose. What would Miss Dunstable think of her? But on that afternoon Miss Dunstable seemed to be as happy and even-tempered as ever.

CHAPTER XV.

How to write a Love Letter.

DR. THORNE, in the few words which he spoke to his niece before he left Boxall Hill, had called himself an old man; but he was as yet on the right side of sixty by five good years, and bore about with him less of the marks of age than most men of fifty-five do bear. One would have said in looking at him that there was no reason why he should not marry if he found that such a step seemed good to him; and, looking at the age of the proposed bride, there was nothing unsuitable in that respect.

But nevertheless he felt almost ashamed of himself, in that he allowed himself even to think of the proposition which his niece had made. He mounted his horse that day at Boxall Hill — for he made all his journeys about the county on horseback — and rode slowly home to Greshamsbury, thinking not so much of the suggested marriage as of his own folly in thinking of it. How could he be such an ass at his time of life as to allow the even course of his way to be disturbed by any such idea? Of course he could not propose to himself such a wife as Miss Dunstable without having some thoughts as to her wealth; and it had been the pride of his life so to live that the world might know that he was indifferent about money. His profession was all in all to him, — the air which he breathed as well as the bread which he ate; and how could he follow his profession if he made such a marriage as this? She would expect him to go to London with her; and what would he become, dangling at her heels there, known only to the world as the husband of the richest woman in the town? The kind of life was one which would be unsuitable to him; — and yet, as he rode home, he could not resolve to rid himself of the idea. He went on thinking of it, though he still continued to condemn himself for keeping it in his thoughts. That night at home he would make up his mind, so he declared to himself; and would then write to his niece begging her to drop the subject. Having so far come to a resolution he went on meditating what course of life it might be well for him to pursue if he and Miss Dunstable should, after all, become man and wife.

There were two ladies whom it behoved him to see on the day of his arrival—whom, indeed, he generally saw every day except when absent from Greshamsbury. The first of these — first in the general consideration of the people of the place—was the wife of the squire, Lady Arabella Gresham, a very old patient of the doctor's. Her it was his custom to visit early in the afternoon; and then, if he were able to escape the squire's daily invitation to dinner, he customarily went to the other, Lady Scatcherd, when the rapid meal in his own house was over. Such, at least, was his summer practice.

"Well, doctor, how are they at Boxall Hill?" said the squire, waylaying him on the gravel sweep before the door. The squire was very hard set for occupation in these summer months.

"Quite well, I believe."

"I don't know what's come to Frank. I think he hates this place now. He's full of the election, I suppose."

"Oh, yes; he told me to say he should be over

here soon. Of course there'll be no contest, so he need not trouble himself."

"Happy dog; isn't he, doctor? to have it all before him instead of behind him. Well, well; he's as good a lad as ever lived, — as ever lived. And let me see; Mary's time — —" And then there were a few very important words spoken on that subject.

"I'll just step up to Lady Arabella now," said the doctor.

"She's as fretful as possible," said the squire. "I've just left her."

"Nothing special the matter, I hope?"

"No, I think not; nothing in your way, that is; only specially cross, which always comes in my way. You'll stop and dine to-day, of course?"

"Not to-day, squire."

"Nonsense; you will. I have been quite counting on you. I have a particular reason for wanting to have you to-day, — a most particular reason."

But the squire always had his particular reasons.

"I'm very sorry, but it is impossible to-day. I shall have a letter to write that I must sit down to seriously. Shall I see you when I come down from her ladyship?"

The squire turned away sulkily, almost without answering him, for he now had no prospect of any alleviation to the tedium of the evening; and the doctor went upstairs to his patient.

For Lady Arabella, though it cannot be said that she was ill, was always a patient. It must not be supposed that she kept her bed and swallowed daily doses, or was prevented from taking her share in such prosy gaieties as came from time to time in the way of her prosy life; but it suited her turn of mind to be an invalid and to have a doctor; and as the doctor whom her good fates had placed at her elbow thoroughly understood her case, no great harm was done.

"It frets me dreadfully that I cannot get to see Mary," Lady Arabella said, as soon as the first ordinary question as to her ailments had been asked and answered.

"She's quite well, and will be over to see you before long."

"Now I beg that she won't. She never thinks of coming when there can be no possible objection, and travelling, at the present moment, would be — —" Whereupon the Lady Arabella shook her head very gravely. "Only think of the importance of it, doctor," she said. "Remember the enormous stake there is to be considered."

"It would not do her a ha'porth of harm if the stake were twice as large."

"Nonsense, doctor, don't tell me; as if I didn't know myself. I was very much against her going to London this spring, but of course what I said was overruled. It always is. I do believe Mr. Gresham went over to Boxall Hill, on purpose to induce her to go. But what does he care? He's fond of Frank; but he never thinks of looking beyond the present day. He never did, as you know well enough, doctor."

"The trip did her all the good in the world," said Dr. Thorne, preferring anything to a conversation respecting the squire's sins.

"I very well remember that when I was in that way it wasn't thought that such trips would do me any good. But, perhaps, things are altered since then."

"Yes, they are," said the doctor. "We don't interfere so much now-a-days."

"I know I never asked for such amusements when so much depended on quietness. I remember before Frank was born — and, indeed, when all of them were born — But, as you say, things were different then; and I can easily believe that Mary is a person quite determined to have her own way."

"Why, Lady Arabella, she would have stayed at home without wishing to stir if Frank had done so much as hold up his little finger."

"So did I always. If Mr. Gresham made the slightest hint I gave way. But I really don't see what one gets in return for such implicit obedience. Now this year, doctor, of course I should have liked to have been up in London for a week or two. You seemed to think yourself that I might as well see Sir Omicron."

"There could be no possible objection, I said."

"Well; no; exactly; and as Mr. Gresham knew I wished it, I think he might as well have offered it. I suppose there can be no reason now about money."

"But I understood that Mary specially asked you and Augusta?"

"Yes; Mary was very good. She did ask me. But I know very well that Mary wants all the room she has got in London. The house is not at all too large for herself. And, for the matter of that, my sister, the countess, was very anxious that I should be with her. But one does like to be independent if one can, and for one fortnight I do think that Mr. Gresham might have managed it. When I knew that he was so dreadfully out at elbows I never troubled him about it,—though, goodness knows, all that was never my fault."

"The squire hates London. A fortnight there in warm weather would nearly be the death of him."

"He might at any rate have paid me the compliment of asking me. The chances are ten to one I should not have gone. It is that indifference that cuts me so. He was here just now, and, would you believe it? ——"

But the doctor was determined to avoid further complaint for the present day.

"I wonder what you would feel, Lady Arabella, if the squire were to take it into his head to go away and amuse himself, leaving you at home. There are worse men than Mr. Gresham, if you will believe me."

All this was an allusion to Earl de Courcy, her ladyship's brother, as Lady Arabella very well understood; and the argument was one which was very often used to silence her.

"Upon my word, then, I should like it better than his hanging about here doing nothing but attend to those nasty dogs. I really sometimes think that he has no spirit left."

"You are mistaken there, Lady Arabella," said the doctor, rising with his hat in his hand, and making his escape without further parley.

As he went home he could not but think that that phase of married life was not a very pleasant one. Mr. Gresham and his wife were supposed by the world to live on the best of terms. They always inhabited the same house, went out together when they did go out, always sat in their respective corners in the family pew, and in their wildest dreams after the happiness of novelty never thought of Sir Cresswell Cresswell. In some respects — with regard, for instance, to the continued duration of their joint domesticity at the family mansion of Greshamsbury — they might have been taken for a pattern couple. But yet, as far as the doctor could see, they did not seem to add much to the happiness of each other. They loved each other, doubtless, and had either of them been in real danger, that danger would have made the other miserable; but yet it might well be a question whether either would not be more comfortable without the other.

The doctor, as was his custom, dined at five, and at seven he went up to the cottage of his old friend Lady Scatcherd. Lady Scatcherd was not a refined woman, having in her early days been a labourer's daughter, and having then married a labourer. But her husband had risen in the world — as has been told in those chronicles before mentioned, — and his widow was now Lady Scatcherd with a pretty cottage and a good jointure. She was in all things the very opposite to Lady Arabella Gresham; nevertheless, under the doctor's auspices, the two ladies were in some measure acquainted with each other. Of her married life, also, Dr. Thorne had seen something, and it may be questioned whether the memory of that was more alluring than the reality now existing at Greshamsbury.

Of the two women Dr. Thorne much preferred his humbler friend, and to her he made his visits not in the guise of a doctor, but as a neighbour. "Well, my lady," he said, as he sat down by her on a broad garden seat — all the world called Lady Scatcherd "my lady," — "and how do these long summer days agree with you? Your roses are twice better out than any I see up at the big house."

"You may well call them long, doctor. They're long enough surely."

"But not too long. Come, now, I won't have you complaining. You don't mean to tell me that you have anything to make you wretched? You had better not, for I won't believe you."

"Eh; well; wretched! I don't know as I'm wretched. It'd be wicked to say that, and I with such comforts about me."

"I think it would, almost." The doctor did not say this harshly, but in a soft, friendly tone, and pressing her hand gently as he spoke.

"And I didn't mean to be wicked. I'm very thankful for everything — leastways, I always try to be. But, doctor, it is so lonely like."

"Lonely! not more lonely than I am."

"Oh, yes; you're different. You can go everywheres. But what can a lone woman do? I'll tell you what, doctor; I'd give it all up to have Roger back with his apron on and his pick in his hand. How well I mind his look when he'd come home o' nights!"

"And yet it was a hard life you had then, eh, old woman? It would be better for you to be thankful for what you've got."

"I am thankful. Didn't I tell you so before?" said she, somewhat crossly. "But it's a sad life, this living alone. I declares I envy Hannah, 'cause she's got Jemima to sit in the kitchen with her. I want her to sit with me sometimes, but she won't."

"Ah! but you shouldn't ask her. It's letting yourself down."

"What do I care about down or up? It makes no difference, as he's gone. If he had lived one might have cared about being up, as you call it. Eh, deary; I'll be going after him before long, and it will be no matter then."

"We shall all be going after him, sooner or later; that's sure enough."

"Eh, dear, that's true surely. It's only a span long, as Parson Oriel tells us, when he gets romantic in his sermons. But it's a hard thing, doctor, when two is married, as they can't have their span, as he calls it, out together. Well, I must only put up with it, I suppose, as others does. Now, you're not going, doctor? You'll stop and have a dish of tea with me. You never see such cream as Hannah has from the Alderney cow. Do'ey now, doctor."

But the doctor had his letter to write, and would not allow himself to be tempted even by the promise of Hannah's cream. So he went his way, angering Lady Scatcherd by his departure as he had before angered the squire, and thinking as he went which was most unreasonable in her wretchedness, his friend Lady Arabella, or his friend Lady Scatcherd. The former was always complaining of an existing husband who never refused her any moderate request; and the other passed her days in murmuring at the loss of a dead husband, who in his life had ever been to her imperious and harsh, and had sometimes been cruel and unjust.

The doctor had his letter to write, but even yet he had not quite made up his mind what he would put into it; indeed, he had not hitherto resolved to whom it should be written. Looking at the matter as he had endeavoured to look at it, his niece, Mrs. Gresham, would be his correspondent; but if he brought himself to take this jump in the dark, in that case he would address himself direct to Miss Dunstable.

He walked home, not by the straightest road, but taking a considerable curve, round by narrow lanes, and through thick flower-laden hedges, — very thoughtful. He was told that she wished to marry him; and was he to think only of himself? And as to that pride of his about money, was it in truth a hearty, manly feeling; or was it a false pride, of which it behoved him to be ashamed as it did of many cognate feelings? If he acted rightly in this matter, why should he be afraid of the thoughts of any one? A life of solitude was bitter enough, as poor Lady Scatcherd had complained. But then, looking at Lady Scatcherd, and looking also at his other near neighbour, his friend the squire, there was little thereabouts to lead him on to matrimony. So he walked home slowly through the lanes, very meditative, with his hands behind his back.

Nor when he got home was he much more inclined to any resolute line of action. He might have drunk his tea with Lady Scatcherd, as well as have sat there in his own drawing-room, drinking it alone; for he got no pen and paper, and he dawdled over his teacup with the utmost dilatoriness, putting off, as it were, the evil day. To only one thing was he fixed — to this, namely, that that letter should be written before he went to bed.

Having finished his tea, which did not take place till near eleven, he went downstairs to an untidy little room which lay behind his depôt of medicines, and in which he was wont to do his writing; and herein he did at last set himself down to his work. Even at that moment he was in doubt. But he would write his letter to Miss Dunstable and see how it looked. He was almost determined not to send it; so, at least, he said to himself: but he could do no harm by writing it. So he did write it, as follows: —

"Greshamsbury, — June, 185—.

"My dear Miss Dunstable, —"

When he had got so far, he leaned back in his chair and looked at the paper. How on earth was he to find words to say that which he now wished to have said? He had never written such a letter in his life, or anything approaching to it, and now found himself overwhelmed with a difficulty of which he had not previously thought. He spent another half-hour in looking at the paper, and was at last nearly deterred by this new difficulty. He would use the simplest, plainest language, he said to himself over and over again; but it is not always easy to use simple, plain language, — by no means so easy as to mount on stilts, and to march along with sesquipedalian words, with pathos, spasms, and notes of interjection. But the letter did at last get itself written, and there was not a note of interjection in it.

"My dear Miss Dunstable, — I think it right to confess that I should not be now writing this letter to you, had I not been led to believe by other judgment than my own that the proposition which I am going to make would be regarded by you with favour. Without such other judgment I should, I own, have feared that the great disparity between you and me in regard to money would have given to such a proposition an appearance of being false and mercenary. All I ask of you now, with confidence, is to acquit me of such fault as that.

"When you have read so far you will understand what I mean. We have known each other now somewhat intimately, though indeed not very long, and I have sometimes fancied that you were almost as well pleased to be with me as I have been to be with you. If I have been wrong in this, tell me so simply, and I will endeavour to let our friendship run on as though this letter had not been written. But if I have been right, and if it be possiblo that you can think that a union between us will make us both happier than we are single, I will plight you my word and troth with good faith, and will do what an old man may do to make the burden of the world lie light upon your shoulders. Looking at my age I can hardly keep myself from thinking that I am an old fool: but I try to reconcile myself to that by remembering that you yourself are no longer a girl. You see that I pay you no compliments, and that you need expect none from me.

"I do not know that I could add anything to the truth of this, if I were to write three times as much. All that is necessary is, that you should know what I mean. If you do not believe me to be true and honest already nothing that I can write will make you believe it.

"God bless you. I know you will not keep me long in suspense for an answer.

"Affectionately your friend,

"THOMAS THORNE."

When he had finished he meditated again for another half-hour whether it would not be right that he should add something about her money. Would it not be well for him to tell her — it might be said in a postscript — that with regard to all her wealth she would be free to do what she chose? At any rate he owed no debts for her to pay, and would still have his own income, sufficient for his own purposes. But about one o'clock he came to the conclusion that it would be better to leave the matter alone. If she cared for him, and could trust him, and was worthy also that he should trust her, no omission of such a statement would deter her from coming to him: and if there were no such trust, it would not be created by any such assurance on his part. So he read the letter over twice, sealed it, and took it up, together with his bed candle, into his bedroom. Now that the letter was written it seemed to be a thing fixed by fate that it must go. He had written it that he might see how it looked when written; but now that it was written, there remained no doubt but that it must be sent. So he went to bed, with the letter on the toilette-table beside him; and early in the morning — so early as to make it seem that the importance of the letter had disturbed his rest — he sent it off by a special messenger to Boxall Hill.

"I'se wait for an answer?" said the boy.

"No," said the doctor: "leave the letter, and come away."

The breakfast hour was not very early at Boxall Hill in these summer months. Frank Gresham, no doubt, went round his farm before he came in for prayers, and his wife was probably looking to the butter in the dairy. At any rate, they did not meet till near ten, and therefore, though the ride from Greshamsbury to Boxall Hill was nearly two hours' work, Miss Dunstable had her letter in her own room before she came down.

She read it in silence as she was dressing, while the maid was with her in the room; but she made no sign which could induce her Abigail to think that the epistle was more than ordinarily important. She read it, and then quietly refolding it and placing it in the envelope, she put it down on the table at which she was sitting. It was full fifteen minutes afterwards that she begged her servant to see if Mrs. Gresham were still in her own room. "Because I want to see her for five minutes, alone, before breakfast," said Miss Dunstable.

"You traitor; you false, black traitor!" were the

first words which Miss Dunstable spoke when she found herself alone with her friend.

"Why, what's the matter?"

"I did not think there was so much mischief in you, nor so keen and commonplace a desire for match-making. Look here. Read the first four lines; not more, if you please; the rest is private. Whose is the other judgment of whom your uncle speaks in his letter?"

"Oh, Miss Dunstable! I must read it all."

"Indeed you'll do no such thing. You think it's a love-letter, I daresay; but indeed there's not a word about love in it."

"I know he has offered. I shall be so glad, for I know you like him."

"He tells me that I am an old woman, and insinuates that I may probably be an old fool."

"I am sure he does not say that."

"Ah! but I'm sure that he does. The former is true enough, and I never complain of the truth. But as to the latter, I am by no means so certain that it is true — not in the sense that he means it."

"Dear, dearest woman, don't go on in that way now. Do speak out to me, and speak without jesting."

"Whose was the other judgment to whom he trusts so implicitly? Tell me that."

"Mine, mine, of course. No one else can have spoken to him about it. Of course I talked to him."

"And what did you tell him?"

"I told him —"

"Well, out with it. Let me have the real facts. Mind, I tell you fairly that you had no right to tell him anything. What passed between us, passed in confidence. But let us hear what you did say."

"I told him that you would have him if he offered." And Mrs. Gresham, as she spoke, looked into her friend's face doubtingly, not knowing whether in very truth Miss Dunstable were pleased with her or displeased. If she were displeased, then how had her uncle been deceived!

"You told him that as a fact?"

"I told him that I thought so."

"Then I suppose I am bound to have him," said Miss Dunstable, dropping the letter on to the floor in mock despair.

"My dear, dear, dearest woman!" said Mrs. Gresham, bursting into tears, and throwing herself on to her friend's neck.

"Mind you are a dutiful niece," said Miss Dunstable. "And now let me go and finish dressing."

In the course of the afternoon, an answer was sent back to Greshamsbury, in these words: —

"DEAR DR. THORNE, — I do and will trust you in everything; and it shall be as you would have it. Mary writes to you; but do not believe a word she says. I never will again, for she has behaved so bad in this matter.

"Yours affectionately and very truly,
"MARTHA DUNSTABLE."

"And so I am going to marry the richest woman in England," said Dr. Thorne to himself, as he sat down that day to his mutton-chop.

CHAPTER XVI.

Internecine.

It must be conceived that there was some feeling of triumph at Plumstead Episcopi, when the wife of the rector returned home with her daughter, the bride elect of the Lord Dumbello. The heir of the Marquis of Hartletop was, in wealth, the most considerable unmarried young nobleman of the day; he was noted, too, as a man difficult to be pleased, as one who was very fine and who gave himself airs, — and to have been selected as the wife of such a man as this was a great thing for the daughter of a parish clergyman. We have seen in what manner the happy girl's mother communicated the fact to Lady Lufton, hiding, as it were, her pride under a veil; and we have seen also how meekly the happy girl bore her own great fortune, applying herself humbly to the packing of her clothes, as though she ignored her own glory.

But nevertheless there was triumph at Plumstead Episcopi. The mother, when she returned home, began to feel that she had been thoroughly successful in the great object of her life. While she was yet in London she had hardly realized her satisfaction, and there were doubts then whether the cup might not be dashed from her lips before it was tasted. It might be that even the son of the Marquis of Hartletop was subject to parental authority, and that barriers should spring up between Griselda and her coronet; but there had been nothing of the kind. The archdeacon had been closeted with the marquis, and Mrs. Grantly had been closeted with the marchioness; and though neither of those noble persons had expressed themselves gratified by their son's proposed marriage, so also neither of them had made any attempt to prevent it. Lord Dumbello was a man who had a will of his own, — as the Grantlys boasted amongst themselves. Poor Griselda! the day may perhaps come when this fact of her lord's masterful will may not to her be matter of much boasting. But in London, as I was saying, there had been no time for an appreciation of the family joy. The work to be done was nervous in its nature, and self-glorification might have been fatal; but now, when they were safe at Plumstead, the great truth burst upon them in all its splendour.

Mrs. Grantly had but one daughter, and the formation of that child's character and her establishment in the world had been the one main object of the mother's life. Of Griselda's great beauty the Plumstead household had long been conscious; of her discretion also, of her conduct, and of her demeanour there had been no doubt. But the father had sometimes hinted to the mother that he did not think that Grizzy was quite so clever as her brothers. "I don't agree with you at all," Mrs. Grantly had answered. "Besides, what you call cleverness is not at all necessary in a girl; she is perfectly lady-like; even you won't deny that." The archdeacon had never wished to deny it, and was now fain to admit that what he had called cleverness was not necessary in a young lady.

At this period of the family glory the archdeacon himself was kept a little in abeyance, and was hardly allowed free intercourse with his own magnificent child. Indeed, to give him his due, it must be said of him that he would not consent to walk in the triumphal procession which moved with stately step, to and fro, through the

Barchester regions. He kissed his daughter and blessed her, and bade her love her husband and be a good wife; but such injunctions as these, seeing how splendidly she had done her duty in securing to herself a marquis, seemed out of place and almost vulgar. Girls about to marry curates or sucking barristers should be told to do their duty in that station of life to which God might be calling them; but it seemed to be almost an impertinence in a father to give such an injunction to a future marchioness.

"I do not think that you have any ground for fear on her behalf," said Mrs. Grantly, "seeing in what way she has hitherto conducted herself."

"She has been a good girl," said the archdeacon, "but she is about to be placed in a position of great temptation."

"She has a strength of mind suited for any position," replied Mrs. Grantly, vain-gloriously.

But nevertheless even the archdeacon moved about through the close at Barchester with a somewhat prouder step since the tidings of this alliance had become known there. The time had been — in the latter days of his father's lifetime — when he was the greatest man of the close. The dean had been old and infirm, and Dr. Grantly had wielded the bishop's authority. But since that things had altered. A new bishop had come there, absolutely hostile to him. A new dean had also come, who was not only his friend, but the brother-in-law of his wife; but even this advent had lessened the authority of the archdeacon. The vicars choral did not hang upon his words as they had been wont to do, and the minor canons smiled in return to his smile less obsequiously when they met him in the clerical circles of

Barchester. But now it seemed that his old supremacy was restored to him. In the minds of many men an archdeacon, who was the father-in-law of a marquis, was himself as good as any bishop. He did not say much of his new connection to others beside the dean, but he was conscious of the fact, and conscious also of the reflected glory which shone around his own head.

But as regards Mrs. Grantly it may be said that she moved in an unending procession of stately ovation. It must not be supposed that she continually talked to her friends and neighbours of Lord Dumbello and the marchioness. She was by far too wise for such folly as that. The coming alliance having been once announced, the name of Hartletop was hardly mentioned by her out of her own domestic circle. But she assumed, with an ease that was surprising even to herself, the airs and graces of a mighty woman. She went through her work of morning calls as though it were her business to be affable to the country gentry. She astonished her sister, the dean's wife, by the simplicity of her grandeur; and condescended to Mrs. Proudie in a manner which nearly broke that lady's heart. "I shall be even with her yet," said Mrs. Proudie to herself, who had contrived to learn various very deleterious circumstances respecting the Hartletop family since the news about Lord Dumbello and Griselda had become known to her.

Griselda herself was carried about in the procession, taking but little part in it of her own, like an Eastern god. She suffered her mother's caresses and smiled in her mother's face as she listened to her own praises, but her triumph was apparently within. To no one did she say much on the subject, and greatly disgusted the old family housekeeper by declining altogether to discuss the future Dumbello *ménage.* To her aunt, Mrs. Arabin, who strove hard to lead her into some open-hearted speech as to her future aspirations, she was perfectly impassive. "Oh, yes, aunt, of course," and "I'll think about it, aunt Eleanor," or "Of course I shall do that if Lord Dumbello wishes it." Nothing beyond this could be got from her; and so, after half-a-dozen ineffectual attempts, Mrs. Arabin abandoned the matter.

But then there arose the subject of clothes — of the wedding *trousseau!* Sarcastic people are wont to say that the tailor makes the man. Were I such a one, I might certainly assert that the milliner makes the bride. As regarding her bridehood, in distinction either to her girlhood or her wifehood — as being a line of plain demarcation between those two periods of a woman's life — the milliner does do much to make her. She would be hardly a bride if the *trousseau* were not there. A girl married without some such appendage would seem to pass into the condition of a wife without any such line of demarcation. In that moment in which she finds herself in the first fruition of her marriage finery she becomes a bride; and in that other moment when she begins to act upon the finest of these things as clothes to be packed up, she becomes a wife.

When this subject was discussed Griselda displayed no lack of a becoming interest. She went to work steadily, slowly, and almost with solemnity, as though the business in hand were one which it would be wicked to treat with impatience. She even struck her mother with awe by the grandeur of her ideas and the depth of her theories. Nor let it be supposed that she rushed away at once to the consideration of the great fabric which was to be the ultimate sign and mark of her status, the quintessence of ber briding, the outer veil, as it were, of the tabernacle — namely, her wedding-dress. As a great poet works himself up by degrees to that inspiration which is necessary for the grand turning point of his epic, so did she slowly approach the hallowed ground on which she would sit, with her ministers around her, when about to discuss the nature, the extent, the design, the colouring, the structure, and the ornamentation of that momentous piece of apparel. No; there was much indeed to be done before she came to this; and as the poet, to whom I have already alluded, first invokes his muse, and then brings his smaller events gradually out upon his stage, so did Miss Grantly with sacred fervour ask her mother's aid, and then prepare her list of all those articles of under-clothing which must be the substratum for the visible magnificence of her *trousseau.*

Money was no object. We all know what that means; and frequently understand, when the words are used, that a blaze of splendour is to be attained at the cheapest possible price. But, in this instance, money was no object; — such an amount of money, at least, as could by any possibility be spent on a lady's clothes, independently of her jewels. With reference to diamonds and such like, the archdeacon at once declared his intention of taking the matter into his own hands — except in so far as Lord Dumbello, or the Hartletop interest, might be pleased to participate in the selection. Nor was Mrs. Grantly sorry for such a decision. She was not an imprudent woman, and would have dreaded the responsibility of trusting herself on such an occasion among the dangerous temptations of a jeweller's shop. But as far as silks and satins went — in the matter of French bonnets, muslins, velvets, hats, riding-habits, artificial flowers, head-gilding, curious nettings, enamelled buckles, golden tagged bobbins, and mechanical petticoats — as regarded shoes, and gloves, and corsets, and stockings, and linen, and flannel, and calico — money, I may conscientiously assert, was no object. And, under these circumstances, Griselda Grantly went to work with a solemn industry and a steady perseverance that was beyond all praise.

"I hope she will be happy," Mrs. Arabin said to her sister, as the two were sitting together in the dean's drawing-room.

"Oh, yes; I think she will. Why should she not?" said the mother.

"Oh, no; I know of no reason. But she is going up into a station so much above her own in the eyes of the world that one cannot but feel anxious for her."

"I should feel much more anxious if she were going to marry a poor man," said Mrs. Grantly. "It has always seemed to me that Griselda was fitted for a high position; that nature intended her for rank and state. You see that she is not a bit elated. She takes it all as if it were her own by right. I do not think that there is any danger that her head will be turned, if you mean that."

"I was thinking rather of her heart," said Mrs. Arabin.

"She never would have taken Lord Dumbello

without loving him," said Mrs. Grantiy, speaking rather quickly.

"That is not quite what I mean either, Susan. I am sure she would not have accepted him had she not loved him. But it is so hard to keep the heart fresh among all the grandeurs of high rank; and it is harder for a girl to do so who has not been born to it, than for one who has enjoyed it as her birthright."

"I don't quite understand about fresh hearts," said Mrs. Grantly, pettishly. "If she does her duty, and loves her husband, and fills the position in which God has placed her with propriety, I don't know that we need look for anything more. I don't at all approve of the plan of frightening a young girl when she is making her first outset into the world."

"No; I would not frighten her. I think it would be almost difficult to frighten Griselda."

"I hope it would. The great matter with a girl is whether she has been brought up with proper notions as to a woman's duty. Of course it is not for me to boast on this subject. Such as she is, I, of course, am responsible. But I must own that I do not see occasion to wish for any change." And then the subject was allowed to drop.

Among those of her relations who wondered much at the girl's fortune, but allowed themselves to say but little, was her grandfather, Mr. Harding. He was an old clergyman, plain and simple in his manners, and not occupying a very prominent position, seeing that he was only precentor to the chapter. He was loved by his daughter, Mrs. Grantly, and was treated by the archdeacon, if not invariably with the highest respect, at least always with consideration and regard. But, old and plain as he was, the young people at Plumstead did not hold him in any great reverence. He was poorer than their other relatives, and made no attempt to hold his head high in Barsetshire circles. Moreover, in these latter days, the home of his heart had been at the deanery. He had, indeed, a lodging of his own in the city, but was gradually allowing himself to be weaned away from it. He had his own bedroom in the dean's house, his own arm-chair in the dean's library, and his own corner on a sofa in Mrs. Dean's drawing-room. It was not, therefore, necessary that he should interfere greatly in this coming marriage; but still it became his duty to say a word of congratulation to his granddaughter, — and perhaps to say a word of advice.

"Grizzy, my dear," he said to her — he always called her Grizzy, but the endearment of the appellation had never been appreciated by the young lady — "come and kiss me, and let me congratulate you on your great promotion. I do so very heartily."

"Thank you, grandpapa," she said, touching his forehead with her lips, thus being, as it were, very sparing with her kiss. But those lips now were august and reserved for nobler foreheads than that of an old cathedral hack. For Mr. Harding still chanted the Litany from Sunday to Sunday, unceasingly, standing at that well-known desk in the cathedral choir; and Griselda had a thought in her mind that when the Hartletop people should hear of the practice they would not be delighted. Dean and archdeacon might be very well, and if her grandfather had even been a prebendary, she might have put up with him; but he had, she thought, almost disgraced his family in being, at his age, one of the working menial clergy of the cathedral. She kissed him, therefore, sparingly, and resolved that her words with him should be few.

"You are going to be a great lady, Grizzy," said he.

"Umph!" said she.

What was she to say when so addressed?

"And I hope you will be happy, — and make others happy."

"I hope I shall," said she.

"But always think most about the latter, my dear. Think about the happiness of those around you, and your own will come without thinking. You understand that, do you not?"

"Oh, yes, I understand," she said.

As they were speaking Mr. Harding still held her hand, but Griselda left it with him unwillingly, and therefore ungraciously, looking as though she were dragging it from him.

"And Grizzy — I believe it is quite as easy for a rich countess to be happy, as for a dairymaid —"

Griselda gave her head a little chuck which was produced by two different operations of her mind. The first was a reflection that her grandpapa was robbing her of her rank. She was to be a rich marchioness. And the second was a feeling of anger at the old man for comparing her lot to that of a dairymaid.

"Quite as easy, I believe," continued he; "though others will tell you that it is not so. But with the countess as with the dairymaid, it must depend on the woman herself. Being a countess — that fact alone won't make you happy."

"Lord Dumbello at present is only a viscount," said Griselda. "There is no earl's title in the family."

"Oh! I did not know," said Mr. Harding, relinquishing his granddaughter's hand; and, after that, he troubled her with no further advice.

Both Mrs. Proudie and the bishop had called at Plumstead since Mrs. Grantly had come back from London, and the ladies from Plumstead, of course, returned the visit. It was natural that the Grantlys and Proudies should hate each other. They were essentially church people, and their views on all church matters were antagonistic. They had been compelled to fight for supremacy in the diocese, and neither family had so conquered the other as to have become capable of magnanimity and good-humour. They did hate each other, and this hatred had, at one time, almost produced an absolute disseverance of even the courtesies which are so necessary between a bishop and his clergy. But the bitterness of this rancour had been overcome, and the ladies of the families had continued on visiting terms.

But now this match was almost more than Mrs. Proudie could bear. The great disappointment which, as she well knew, the Grantlys had encountered in that matter of the proposed new bishopric had for the moment mollified her. She had been able to talk of poor dear Mrs. Grantly! "She is heartbroken, you know, in this matter, and the repetition of such misfortunes is hard to bear," she had been heard to say, with a complacency which had been quite becoming to her. But now that complacency was at an end. Olivia Proudie had just accepted a widowed preacher at a district church in Bethnal Green, — a man with three children, who was dependent on pew-rents; and Griselda Grantly was engaged to the eldest son of the Marquis of Hartletop! When women are enjoined to forgive their enemies it cannot be intended that such wrongs as these should be included.

But Mrs. Proudie's courage was nothing daunted. It may be boasted of her that nothing could daunt her courage. Soon after her return to Barchester, she and Olivia — Olivia being very unwilling — had driven over to Plumstead, and, not finding the Grantlys at home, had left their cards; and now, at a proper interval, Mrs. Grantly and Griselda returned the visit. It was the first time that Miss Grantly had been seen by the Proudie ladies since the fact of her engagement had become known.

The first bevy of compliments that passed might be likened to a crowd of flowers on a hedge rosebush. They were beautiful to the eye, but were so closely environed by thorns that they could not be plucked without great danger. As long as the compliments were allowed to remain on the hedge — while no attempt was made to garner them and realize their fruits for enjoyment — they did no mischief; but the first finger that was put forth for such a purpose was soon drawn back, marked with spots of blood.

"Of course it is a great match for Griselda," said Mrs. Grantly, in a whisper the meekness of which would have disarmed an enemy whose weapons were less firmly clutched than those of Mrs. Proudie; "but, independently of that, the connection is one which is gratifying in many ways."

"Oh, no doubt," said Mrs. Proudie.

"Lord Dumbello is so completely his own master," continued Mrs. Grantly, and a slight, unintended semitone of triumph mingled itself with the meekness of that whisper.

"And is likely to remain so, from all I hear," said Mrs. Proudie, and the scratched hand was at once drawn back.

"Of course the estab—," and then Mrs. Proudie, who was blandly continuing her list of congratulations, whispered her sentence close into the ear of Mrs. Grantly, so that not a word of what she said might be audible by the young people.

"I never heard a word of it,' said Mrs. Grantly, gathering herself up, "and I don't believe it."

"Oh, I may be wrong; and I'm sure I hope so. But young men will be young men, you know; — and children will take after their parents. I suppose you will see a great deal of the Duke of Omnium now."

But Mrs. Grantly was not a woman to be knocked down and trampled on without resistance; and though she had been lacerated by the rosebush she was not as yet placed altogether *hors de combat.* She said some word about the Duke of Omnium very tranquilly, speaking of him merely as a Barsetshire proprietor, and then, smiling with her sweetest smile, expressed a hope that she might soon have the pleasure of becoming acquainted with Mr. Tickler; and as she spoke she made a pretty little bow towards Olivia Proudie. Now Mr. Tickler was the worthy clergyman attached to the district church at Bethnal Green.

"He'll be down here in August," said Olivia, boldly, determined not to be shamefaced about her love affairs.

"You'll be starring it about the Continènt by that time, my dear," said Mrs. Proudie to Griselda. "Lord Dumbello is well known at Homburg and Ems, and places of that sort; so you will find yourself quite at home."

"We are going to Rome," said Griselda, majestically.

"I suppose Mr. Tickler will come into the diocese soon," said Mrs. Grantly. "I remember hearing him very favourably spoken of by Mr. Slope, who was a friend of his."

Nothing short of a fixed resolve on the part of Mrs. Grantly that the time had now come in which she must throw away her shield and stand behind her sword, declare war to the knife and neither give nor take quarter, could have justified such a speech as this. Any allusion to Mr. Slope acted on Mrs. Proudie as a red cloth is supposed to act on a bull; but when that allusion connected the name of Mr. Slope in a friendly bracket with that of Mrs. Proudie's future son-in-law it might be certain that the effect would be terrific. And there was more than this: for that very Mr. Slope had once entertained audacious hopes — hopes not thought to be audacious by the young lady herself — with reference to Miss Olivia Proudie. All this Mrs. Grantly knew, and, knowing it, still dared to mention his name.

The countenance of Mrs. Proudie became darkened with black anger, and the polished smile of her company manners gave place before the outraged feelings of her nature.

"The man you speak of, Mrs. Grantly," said she, "was never known as a friend by Mr. Tickler."

"Oh, indeed," said Mrs. Grantly. "Perhaps I have made a mistake. I am sure I have heard Mr. Slope mention him."

"When Mr. Slope was running after your sister, Mrs. Grantly, and was encouraged by her as he was, you perhaps saw more of him than I did."

"Mrs. Proudie, that was never the case."

"I have reason to know that the archdeacon conceived it to be so, and that he was very unhappy about it." Now this, unfortunately, was a fact which Mrs. Grantly could not deny.

"The archdeacon may have been mistaken about Mr. Slope," she said, "as were some other people at Barchester. But it was you, I think, Mrs. Proudie, who were responsible for bringing him here."

Mrs. Grantly, at this period of the engagement, might have inflicted a fatal wound by referring to poor Olivia's former love affairs, but she was not destitute of generosity. Even in the extremest heat of the battle she knew how to spare the young and tender.

"When I came here, Mrs. Grantly, I little dreamed what a depth of wickedness might be found in the very close of a cathedral city," said Mrs. Proudie.

"Then, for dear Olivia's sake, pray do not bring poor Mr. Tickler to Barchester."

"Mr. Tickler, Mrs. Grantly, is a man of assured morals and of a highly religious tone of thinking. I wish every one could be so safe as regards their daughters' future prospects as I am."

"Yes, I know he has the advantage of being a family man," said Mrs. Grantly, getting up. "Good morning, Mrs. Proudie; good day, Olivia."

"A great deal better that than —" But the blow

fell upon the empty air; for Mrs. Grantly had already escaped on to the staircase while Olivia was ringing the bell for the servant to attend the front-door.

Mrs. Grantly, as she got into her carriage, smiled slightly, thinking of the battle, and as she sat down she gently pressed her daughter's hand. But Mrs. Proudie's face was still dark as Acheron when her enemy withdrew, and with angry tone she sent her daughter to her work. "Mr. Tickler will have great reason to complain if, in your position, you indulge such habits of idleness," she said. Therefore I conceive that I am justified in saying that in that encounter Mrs. Grantly was the conqueror.

CHAPTER XVII.

Don Quixote.

On the day on which Lucy had her interview with Lady Lufton the dean dined at Framley Parsonage. He and Robarts had known each other since the latter had been in the diocese, and now, owing to Mark's preferment in the chapter, had become almost intimate. The dean was greatly pleased with the manner in which poor Mr. Crawley's children had been conveyed away from Hogglestock, and was inclined to open his heart to the whole Framley household. As he still had to ride home he could only allow himself to remain half an hour after dinner, but in that half-hour he said a great deal about Crawley, complimented Robarts on the manner in which he was playing the part of the Good Samaritan, and then by degrees informed him that it had come to his, the dean's ears, before he left

Barchester, that a writ was in the hands of certain persons in the city, enabling them to seize — he did not know whether it was the person or the property of the vicar of Framley.

The fact was that these tidings had been conveyed to the dean with the express intent that he might put Robarts on his guard; but the task of speaking on such a subject to a brother clergyman had been so unpleasant to him that he had been unable to introduce it till the last five minutes before his departure.

"I hope you will not put it down as an impertinent interference," said the dean, apologizing.

"No," said Mark; "no, I do not think that." He was so sad at heart that he hardly knew how to speak of it.

"I do not understand much about such matters," said the dean; "but I think, if I were you, I should go to a lawyer. I should imagine that anything so terribly disagreeable as an arrest might be avoided."

"It is a hard case," said Mark, pleading his own cause. "Though these men have this claim against me I have never received a shilling either in money or money's worth."

"And yet your name is to the bills!" said the dean.

"Yes, my name is to the bills, certainly, but it was to oblige a friend."

And then the dean, having given his advice, rode away. He could not understand how a clergyman, situated as was Mr. Robarts, could find himself called upon by friendship to attach his name to accommodation bills which he had not the power of liquidating when due!

On that evening they were both wretched enough at the parsonage. Hitherto Mark had hoped that perhaps, after all, no absolutely hostile steps would be taken against him with reference to these bills. Some unforeseen chance might occur in his favour, or the persons holding them might consent to take small instalments of payment from time to time; but now it seemed that the evil day was actually coming upon him at a blow. He had no longer any secrets from his wife. Should he go to a lawyer? and if so, to what lawyer? And when he had found his lawyer, what should he say to him? Mrs. Robarts at one time suggested that everything should be told to Lady Lufton. Mark, however, could not bring himself to do that. "It would seem," he said, "as though I wanted her to lend me the money."

On the following morning Mark did ride into Barchester, dreading, however, lest he should be arrested on his journey, and he did see a lawyer. During his absence two calls were made at the parsonage — one by a very rough-looking individual, who left a suspicious document in the hands of the servant, purporting to be an invitation — not to dinner — from one of the judges of the land; and the other call was made by Lady Lufton in person.

Mrs. Robarts had determined to go down to Framley Court on that day. In accordance with her usual custom she would have been there within an hour or two of Lady Lufton's return from London, but things between them were not now as they usually had been. This affair of Lucy's must make a difference, let them both resolve to the contrary as they might. And, indeed, Mrs. Robarts had found that the closeness of her intimacy with Framley Court had been diminishing from day to day since Lucy had first begun to be on friendly terms with Lord Lufton. Since that she had been less at Framley Court than usual; she had heard from Lady Lufton less frequently by letter during her absence than she had done in former years, and was aware that she was less implicitly trusted with all the affairs of the parish. This had not made her angry, for she was in a manner conscious that it must be so. It made her unhappy, but what could she do? She could not blame Lucy, nor could she blame Lady Lufton. Lord Lufton she did blame, but she did so in the hearing of no one but her husband.

Her mind, however, was made up to go over and bear the first brunt of her ladyship's arguments, when she was stopped by her ladyship's arrival. If it were not for this terrible matter of Lucy's love — a matter on which they could not now be silent when they met — there would be twenty subjects of pleasant, or, at any rate, not unpleasant conversation. But even then there would be those terrible bills hanging over her conscience, and almost crushing her by their weight. At the moment in which Lady Lufton walked up to the drawing-room window, Mrs. Robarts held in her hand that ominous invitation from the judge. Would it not be well that she should make a clean breast of it all, disregarding what her husband had said? It might be well: only this — she had never yet done anything in opposition to her husband's wishes. So she hid the slip within her desk, and left the matter open to consideration.

The interview commenced with an affectionate embrace, as was a matter of course. "Dear Fanny," and

"Dear Lady Lufton," was said between them with all the usual warmth. And then the first inquiry was made about the children, and the second about the school. For a minute or two Mrs. Robarts thought that, perhaps, nothing was to be said about Lucy. If it pleased Lady Lufton to be silent, she, at least, would not commence the subject.

Then there was a word or two spoken about Mrs. Podgens' baby, after which Lady Lufton asked whether Fanny were alone.

"Yes," said Mrs. Robarts. "Mark has gone over to Barchester."

"I hope he will not be long before he lets me see him. Perhaps he can call to-morrow. Would you both come and dine to-morrow?"

"Not to-morrow, I think, Lady Lufton; but Mark, I am sure, will go over and call."

"And why not come to dinner? I hope there is to be no change among us, eh, Fanny?" and Lady Lufton as she spoke looked into the other's face in a manner which almost made Mrs. Robarts get up and throw herself on her old friend's neck. Where was she to find a friend who would give her such constant love as she had received from Lady Lufton? And who was kinder, better, more honest than she?

"Change! no I hope not, Lady Lufton;" and as she spoke the tears stood in her eyes.

"Ah, but I shall think there is if you will not come to me as you used to do. You always used to come and dine with me the day I came home, as a matter of course."

What could she say, poor woman, to this?

"We were all in confusion yesterday about poor

Mrs. Crawley, and the dean dined here; he had been over at Hogglestock to see his friend."

"I have heard of her illness, and will go over and see what ought to be done. Don't you go, do you hear, Fanny? You with your young children! I should never forgive you if you did."

And then Mrs. Robarts explained how Lucy had gone there, had sent the four children back to Framley, and was herself now staying at Hogglestock with the object of nursing Mrs. Crawley. In telling the story she abstained from praising Lucy with all the strong language which she would have used had not Lucy's name and character been at the present moment of peculiar import to Lady Lufton; but nevertheless she could not tell it without dwelling much on Lucy's kindness. It would have been ungenerous to Lady Lufton to make much of Lucy's virtue at this present moment, but unjust to Lucy to make nothing of it.

"And she is actually with Mrs. Crawley now?" asked Lady Lufton.

"Oh, yes; Mark left her there yesterday afternoon."

"And the four children are all here in the house?"

"Not exactly in the house — that is, not as yet. We have arranged a sort of quarantine hospital over the coach-house."

"What, where Stubbs lives?'

"Yes; Stubbs and his wife have come into the house, and the children are to remain up there till the doctor says that there is no danger of infection. I have not even seen my visitors myself as yet," said Mrs. Robarts with a slight laugh.

"Dear me!" said Lady Lufton. "I declare you have been very prompt. And so Miss Robarts is over there! I should have thought Mr. Crawley would have made a difficulty about the children."

"Well, he did; but they kidnapped them, — that is, Lucy and Mark did. The dean gave me such an account of it. Lucy brought them out by two's and packed them in the pony-carriage, and then Mark drove off at a gallop while Mr. Crawley stood calling to them in the road. The dean was there at the time and saw it all."

"That Miss Lucy of yours seems to be a very determined young lady when she takes a thing into her head," said Lady Lufton, now sitting down for the first time.

"Yes, she is," said Mrs. Robarts, having laid aside all her pleasant animation, for the discussion which she dreaded was now at hand.

"A very determined young lady," continued Lady Lufton. "Of course, my dear Fanny, you know all this about Ludovic and your sister-in-law?"

"Yes, she has told me about it."

"It is very unfortunate — very."

"I do not think Lucy has been to blame," said Mrs. Robarts; and as she spoke the blood was already mounting to her cheeks.

"Do not be too anxious to defend her, my dear, before any one accuses her. Whenever a person does that it looks as though their cause were weak."

"But my cause is not weak as far as Lucy is concerned; I feel quite sure that she has not been to blame."

"I know how obstinate you can be, Fanny, when you think it necessary to dub yourself any one's champion. Don Quixote was not a better knight-errant than you are. But is it not a pity to take up your lance and shield before an enemy is within sight or hearing? But that was ever the way with your Don Quixotes."

"Perhaps there may be an enemy in ambush." That was Mrs. Robarts' thought to herself, but she did not dare to express it, so she remained silent.

"My only hope is," continued Lady Lufton, "that when my back is turned you fight as gallantly for me."

"Ah, you are never under a cloud, like poor Lucy."

"Am I not? But, Fanny, you do not see all the clouds. The sun does not always shine for any of us, and the down-pouring rain and the heavy wind scatter also my fairest flowers, — as they have done hers, poor girl. Dear Fanny, I hope it may be long before any cloud comes across the brightness of your heaven. Of all the creatures I know you are the one most fitted for quiet continued sunshine."

And then Mrs. Robarts did get up and embrace her friend, thus hiding the tears which were running down her face. Continued sunshine indeed! A dark spot had already gathered on her horizon which was likely to fall in a very waterspout of rain. What was to come of that terrible notice which was now lying in the desk under Lady Lufton's very arm?

"But I am not come here to croak like an old raven," continued Lady Lufton, when she had brought this embrace to an end. "It is probable that we all may have our sorrows; but I am quite sure of this, — that if we endeavour to do our duties honestly, we shall all find our consolation and all have our joys also. And now, my dear, let you and I say a few words about this unfortunate affair. It would not be natural if we were to hold our tongues to each other; would it?"

"I suppose not," said Mrs. Robarts.

"We should always be conceiving worse than the truth, — each as to the other's thoughts. Now, some time ago, when I spoke to you about your sister-in-law and Ludovic — I daresay you remember —"

"Oh, yes, I remember."

"We both thought then that there would really be no danger. To tell you the plain truth I fancied, and indeed hoped, that his affections were engaged elsewhere; but I was altogether wrong then; wrong in thinking it, and wrong in hoping it."

Mrs. Robarts knew well that Lady Lufton was alluding to Griselda Grantly, but she conceived that it would be discreet to say nothing herself on that subject at present. She remembered, however, Lucy's flashing eye when the possibility of Lord Lufton making such a marriage was spoken of in the pony-carriage, and could not but feel glad that Lady Lufton had been disappointed.

"I do not at all impute any blame to Miss Robarts for what has occurred since," continued her ladyship. "I wish you distinctly to understand that."

"I do not see how any one could blame her. She has behaved so nobly."

"It is of no use inquiring whether any one can. It is sufficient that I do not."

"But I think that is hardly sufficient," said Mrs. Robarts, pertinaciously.

"Is it not?" asked her ladyship, raising her eyebrows.

"No. Only think what Lucy has done and is doing. If she had chosen to say that she would accept your son I really do not know how you could have justly blamed her. I do not by any means say that I would have advised such a thing."

"I am glad of that, Fanny."

"I have not given any advice; nor is it needed. I know no one more able than Lucy to see clearly, by her own judgment, what course she ought to pursue. I should be afraid to advise one whose mind is so strong, and who, of her own nature, is so self-denying as she is. She is sacrificing herself now, because she will not be the means of bringing trouble and dissension between you and your son. If you ask me, Lady Lufton, I think you owe her a deep debt of gratitude. I do indeed. And as for blaming her — what has she done that you possibly could blame?"

"Don Quixote on horseback!" said Lady Lufton. "Fanny, I shall always call you Don Quixote, and some day or other I will get somebody to write your adventures. But the truth is this, my dear: there has been imprudence. You may call it mine, if you will — though I really hardly see how I am to take the blame. I could not do other than ask Miss Robarts to my house, and I could not very well turn my son out of it. In point of fact, it has been the old story."

"Exactly; the story that is as old as the world, and which will continue as long as people are born into it. It is a story of God's own telling!"

"But, my dear child, you do not mean that every young gentleman and every young lady should fall in love with each other directly they meet! Such a doctrine would be very inconvenient."

"No, I do not mean that. Lord Lufton and Miss Grantly did not fall in love with each other, though you meant them to do so. But was it not quite as natural that Lord Lufton and Lucy should do so instead?"

"It is generally thought, Fanny, that young ladies should not give loose to their affections until they have been certified of their friends' approval."

"And that young gentlemen of fortune may amuse themselves as they please! I know that is what the world teaches, but I cannot agree to the justice of it. The terrible suffering which Lucy has to endure makes me cry out against it. She did not seek your son. The moment she began to suspect that there might be danger she avoided him scrupulously. She would not go down to Framley Court, though her not doing so was remarked by yourself. She would hardly go out about the place lest she should meet him. She was contented to put herself altogether in the background till he should have pleased to leave the place. But he — he came to her here, and insisted on seeing her. He found her when I was out, and declared himself determined to speak to her. What was she to do? She did try to escape, but he stopped her at the door. Was it her fault that he made her an offer?"

"My dear, no one has said so."

"Yes, but you do say so when you tell me that young ladies should not give play to their affections without permission. He persisted in saying to her, here, all that it pleased him, though she implored him to be silent. I cannot tell the words she used, but she did implore him."

"I do not doubt that she behaved well."

"But he — he persisted, and begged her to accept his hand. She refused him then, Lady Lufton — not as some girls do, with a mock reserve, not intending to be taken at their words — but steadily, and, God forgive her, untruly. Knowing what your feelings would be, and knowing what the world would say, she declared to him that he was indifferent to her. What more could she do in your behalf?" And then Mrs. Robarts paused.

"I shall wait till you have done, Fanny."

"You spoke of girls giving loose to their affections. She did not do so. She went about her work exactly as she had done before. She did not even speak to me of what had passed — not then, at least. She determined that it should all be as though it had never been. She had learned to love your son; but that was her misfortune, and she would get over it as she might. Tidings came to us here that he was engaged, or about to engage himself, to Miss Grantly."

"Those tidings were untrue."

"Yes, we know that now; but she did not know it then. Of course she could not but suffer; but she suffered within herself." Mrs. Robarts, as she said this, remembered the pony-carriage and how Puck had been beaten. "She made no complaint that he had ill-treated her — not even to herself. She had thought it right to reject his offer; and there, as far as he was concerned, was to be an end of it."

"That would be a matter of course, I should suppose."

"But it was not a matter of course, Lady Lufton. He returned from London to Framley on purpose to repeat his offer. He sent for her brother — You talk of a young lady waiting for her friends' approval. In this matter who would be Lucy's friends?"

"You and Mr. Robarts of course."

"Exactly; her only friends. Well, Lord Lufton sent for Mark and repeated his offer to him. Mind you, Mark had never heard a word of this before, and you may guess whether or no he was surprised. Lord Lufton repeated his offer in the most formal manner and claimed permission to see Lucy. She refused to see him. She has never seen him since that day when, in opposition to all her efforts, he made his way into this room. Mark, — as I think very properly, — would have allowed Lord Lufton to come up here. Looking at both their ages and position he could have had no right to forbid it. But Lucy positively refused to see your son, and sent him a message instead, of the purport of which you are now aware — that she would never accept him unless she did so at your request."

"It was a very proper message."

"I say nothing about that. Had she accepted him I would not have blamed her: — and so I told her, Lady Lufton."

"I cannot understand your saying that, Fanny."

"Well; I did say so. I don't want to argue now about myself, — whether I was right or wrong, but I did say so. Whatever sanction I could give she would have had. But she again chose to sacrifice herself, although I believe she regards him with as true a love as ever a girl felt for a man. Upon my word I don't know that she is right. Those considerations for the world may perhaps be carried too far."

"I think that she was perfectly right."

"Very well, Lady Lufton; I can understand that. But after such sacrifice on her part — a sacrifice made entirely to you — how can you talk of 'not blaming her?' Is that the language in which you speak of those whose conduct from first to last has been superlatively excellent? If she is open to blame at all, it is — it is —"

But here Mrs. Robarts stopped herself. In defending her sister she had worked herself almost into a passion; but such a state of feeling was not customary to her, and now that she had spoken her mind she sank suddenly into silence.

"It seems to me, Fanny, that you almost regret Miss Robarts' decision," said Lady Lufton.

"My wish in this matter is for her happiness, and I regret anything that may mar it."

"You think nothing then of our welfare, and yet I do not know to whom I might have looked for hearty friendship and for sympathy in difficulties, if not to you?"

Poor Mrs. Robarts was almost upset by this. A few months ago, before Lucy's arrival, she would have declared that the interests of Lady Lufton's family would have been paramount with her, after and next to those of her own husband. And even now, it seemed to argue so black an ingratitude on her part — this accusation that she was indifferent to them! From her childhood upwards she had revered and loved Lady Lufton, and for years had taught herself to regard her as an epitome of all that was good and gracious in woman. Lady Lufton's theories of life had been accepted by her as the right theories, and those whom Lady Lufton had liked she had liked. But now it seemed that all these ideas which it had taken a life to build up were to be thrown to the ground, because she was bound to defend a sister-in-law whom she had only known for the last eight months. It was not that she regretted a word that she had spoken on Lucy's behalf. Chance had thrown her and Lucy together, and, as Lucy was her sister, she should receive from her a sister's treatment. But she did not the less feel how terrible would be the effect of any disseverance from Lady Lufton.

"O Lady Lufton," she said, "do not say that."

"But, Fanny, dear, I must speak as I find. You were talking about clouds just now, and do you think that all this is not a cloud in my sky? Ludovic tells me that he is attached to Miss Robarts, and you tell me that she is attached to him; and I am called upon to decide between them. Her very act obliges me to do so."

"Dear Lady Lufton," said Mrs. Robarts, springing from her seat. It seemed to her at the moment as though the whole difficulty were to be solved by an act of grace on the part of her old friend.

"And yet I cannot approve of such a marriage," said Lady Lufton.

Mrs. Robarts returned to her seat, saying nothing further.

"Is not that a cloud on one's horizon?" continued her ladyship. "Do you think that I can be basking in the sunshine while I have such a weight upon my heart as that? Ludovic will soon be home, but instead of looking to his return with pleasure I dread it. I would prefer that he should remain in Norway. I would wish that he should stay away for months.

And, Fanny, it is a great addition to my misfortune to feel that you do not sympathize with me."

Having said this, in a slow, sorrowful, and severe tone, Lady Lufton got up and took her departure. Of course Mrs. Robarts did not let her go without assuring her that she did sympathize with her, — did love her as she ever had loved her. But wounds cannot be cured as easily as they may be inflicted, and Lady Lufton went her way with much real sorrow at her heart. She was proud and masterful, fond of her own way, and much too careful of the worldly dignities to which her lot had called her: but she was a woman who could cause no sorrow to those she loved without deep sorrow to herself.

CHAPTER XVIII.

Touching Pitch.

In these hot midsummer days, the end of June and the beginning of July, Mr. Sowerby had but an uneasy time of it. At his sister's instance, he had hurried up to London, and there had remained for days in attendance on the lawyers. He had to see new lawyers, Miss Dunstable's men of business, quiet old cautious gentlemen whose place of business was in a dark alley behind the Bank, Messrs. Slow and Bideawhile by name, who had no scruple in detaining him for hours while they or their clerks talked to him about anything or about nothing. It was of vital consequence to Mr. Sowerby that this business of his should be settled without delay, and yet these men, to whose care this settling was now confided, went on as though law processes were a sunny bank on which it delighted men to bask easily. And then, too, he had to go more than once to South Audley Street, which was a worse infliction; for the men in South Audley Street were less civil now than had been their wont. It was well understood there that Mr. Sowerby was no longer a client of the duke's, but his opponent; no longer his nominee and dependent, but his enemy in the county. "Chaldicotes," as old Mr. Gumption remarked to young Mr. Gagebee; "Chaldicotes, Gagebee, is a cooked goose, as far as Sowerby is concerned. And what difference could it make to him whether the duke is to own it or Miss Dunstable? For my part I cannot understand how a gentleman like Sowerby can like to see his property go into the hands of a gallipot wench whose money still smells of bad drugs. And nothing can be more ungrateful," he said, "than Sowerby's conduct. He has held the county for five-and-twenty years without expense; and now that the time for payment has come, he begrudges the price." He called it no better than cheating, he did not — he, Mr. Gumption. According to his ideas Sowerby was attempting to cheat the duke. It may be imagined, therefore, that Mr. Sowerby did not feel any very great delight in attending at South Audley Street.

And then rumour was spread about among all the bill-discounting leeches that blood was once more to be sucked from the Sowerby carcase. The rich Miss Dunstable had taken up his affairs; so much as that became known in the purlieus of the Goat and Compasses. Tom Tozer's brother declared that she and Sowerby were going to make a match of it, and that any scrap of paper with Sowerby's name on it would become worth its weight in bank-notes; but Tom Tozer himself — Tom, who was the real hero of the family — pooh-poohed at this, screwing up his nose, and alluding in most contemptuous terms to his brother's softness. He knew better — as was indeed the fact. Miss Dunstable was buying up the squire, and by jingo she should buy them up — them, the Tozers, as well as others! They knew their value, the Tozers did; — whereupon they became more than ordinarily active.

From them and all their brethren Mr. Sowerby at this time endeavoured to keep his distance, but his endeavours were not altogether effectual. Whenever he could escape for a day or two from the lawyers he ran down to Chaldicotes; but Tom Tozer in his perseverance followed him there, and boldly sent in his name by the servant at the front-door.

"Mr. Sowerby is not just at home at the present moment," said the well-trained domestic.

"I'll wait about then," said Tom, seating himself on an heraldic stone griffin which flanked the big stone steps before the house. And in this way Mr. Tozer gained his purpose.

Sowerby was still contesting the county, and it behoved him not to let his enemies say that he was hiding himself. It had been a part of his bargain with Miss Dunstable that he should contest the county. She had taken it into her head that the duke had behaved badly, and she had resolved that he should be made to pay for it. "The duke," she said, "had meddled long enough;" she would now see whether the Chaldicotes interest would not suffice of itself to return a member for the county, even in opposition to the duke. Mr. Sowerby himself was so harassed at the time, that he would have given way on this point if he had had the power; but Miss Dunstable was determined, and he was obliged to yield to her. In this manner Mr. Tom Tozer succeeded and did make his way into Mr. Sowerby's presence — of which intrusion one effect was the following letter from Mr. Sowerby to his friend Mark Robarts: —

"MY DEAR ROBARTS, — "Chaldicotes, July, 185—.

"I AM so harassed at the present moment by an infinity of troubles of my own that I am almost callous to those of other people. They say that prosperity makes a man selfish. I have never tried that, but I am quite sure that adversity does so. Nevertheless I am anxious about those bills of yours" —

"Bills of mine!" said Robarts to himself, as he walked up and down the shrubbery-path at the parsonage, reading this letter. This happened a day or two after his visit to the lawyer at Barchester.

"—— and would rejoice greatly if I thought that I could save you from any further annoyance about them. That kite, Tom Tozer, has just been with me, and insists that both of them shall be paid. He knows — no one better — that no consideration was given for the latter. But he knows also that the dealing was not with him, nor even with his brother, and he will be prepared to swear that he gave value for both. He would swear anything for five hundred pounds — or for half the money, for that matter. I do not think that the father of mischief ever let loose upon the world a greater rascal than Tom Tozer.

"He declares that nothing shall induce him to take one shilling less than the whole sum of nine hundred pounds. He has been brought to this by hearing that my debts are about to be paid. Heaven help me! The meaning of that is that these wretched acres, which are now mortgaged to one millionnaire, are to change hands and be mortgaged to another instead. By this exchange I may possibly obtain the benefit of having a house to live in for the next twelve months, but no other. Tozer, however, is altogether wrong in his scent; and the worst of it is that his malice will fall on you rather than on me.

"What I want you to do is this: let us pay him one hundred pounds between us. Though I sell the last sorry jade of a horse I have, I will make up fifty; and I know you can, at any rate, do as much as that. Then do you accept a bill, conjointly with me, for eight hundred. It shall be done in Forrest's presence, and handed to him; and you shall receive back the two old bills into your own hands at the same time. This new bill should be timed to run ninety days; and I will move heaven and earth during that time to have it included in the general schedule of my debts which are to be secured on the Chaldicotes property."

The meaning of which was that Miss Dunstable was to be cozened into paying the money under an idea that it was part of the sum covered by the existing mortgage.

"What you said the other day at Barchester, as to never executing another bill, is very well as regards future transactions. Nothing can be wiser than such a resolution. But it would be folly — worse than folly — if you were to allow your furniture to be seized when the means of preventing it are so ready to your hand. By leaving the new bill in Forrest's hands you may be sure that you are safe from the claws of such birds of prey as these Tozers. Even if I cannot get it settled when the three months are over, Forrest will enable you to make any arrangement that may be most convenient.

"For Heaven's sake, my dear fellow, do not refuse this. You can hardly conceive how it weighs upon me, this fear that bailiffs should make their way into your wife's drawing-room. I know you think ill of me, and I do not wonder at it. But you would be less inclined to do so if you knew how terribly I am punished. Pray let me hear that you will do as I counsel you.

"Yours always faithfully,
"N. SOWERBY."

In answer to which the parson wrote a very short reply: —

"MY DEAR SOWERBY, — "Framley, July, 185—.

"I WILL sign no more bills on any consideration.

"Yours truly,
"MARK ROBARTS."

And then having written this, and having shown it to his wife, he returned to the shrubbery walk and paced it up and down, looking every now and then to Sowerby's letter as he thought over all the past circumstances of his friendship with that gentleman.

That the man who had written this letter should be his friend — that very fact was a disgrace to him. Sowerby so well knew himself and his own reputation, that he did not dare to suppose that his own word would be taken for anything, — not even when the thing promised was an act of the commonest honesty. "The old bills shall be given back into your own hands," he had declared with energy, knowing that his friend and correspondent would not feel himself secure against further fraud under any less stringent guarantee. This gentleman, this county member, the owner of Chaldicotes, with whom Mark Robarts had been so anxious to be on terms of intimacy, had now come to such a phase of life that he had given over speaking of himself as an honest man. He had become so used to suspicion that he argued of it as of a thing of course. He knew that no one could trust either his spoken or his written word, and he was content to speak and to write without attempt to hide this conviction.

And this was the man whom he had been so glad to call his friend; for whose sake he had been willing to quarrel with Lady Lufton, and at whose instance he had unconsciously abandoned so many of the best resolutions of his life. He looked back now, as he walked there slowly, still holding the letter in his hand, to the day when he had stopped at the school-house and written his letter to Mr. Sowerby, promising to join the party at Chaldicotes. He had been so eager then to have his own way, that he would not permit himself to go home and talk the matter over with his wife. He thought also of the manner in which he had been tempted to the house of the Duke of Omnium, and the conviction on his mind at the time that his giving way to that temptation would surely bring him to evil. And then he remembered the evening in Sowerby's bedroom, when the bill had been brought out, and he had allowed himself to be persuaded to put his name upon it; — not because he was willing in this way to assist his friend, but because he was unable to refuse. He had lacked the courage to say, "No," though he knew at the time how gross was the error which he was committing. He had lacked the courage to say, "No," and hence had come upon him and on his household all this misery and cause for bitter repentance.

I have written much of clergymen, but in doing so I have endeavoured to portray them as they bear on our social life rather than to describe the mode and working of their professional careers. Had I done the latter I could hardly have steered clear of subjects on which it has not been my intention to pronounce an opinion, and I should either have laden my fiction with sermons or I should have degraded my sermons into fiction. Therefore I have said but little in my narrative of this man's feelings or doings as a clergyman.

But I must protest against its being on this account considered that Mr. Robarts was indifferent to the duties of his clerical position. He had been fond of pleasure and had given way to temptation, — as is so customarily done by young men of six-and-twenty, who are placed beyond control and who have means at command. Had he remained as a curate till that age, subject in all his movements to the eye of a superior, he would, we may say, have put his name to no bills, have ridden after no hounds, have seen nothing of the iniquities of Gatherum Castle. There are men of twenty-six as fit to stand alone as ever they will be — fit to be prime ministers, heads of schools, judges on the bench — almost fit to be bishops; but Mark Robarts had not been one of them. He had within him many aptitudes for good, but not the strengthened courage of a man to act up to them. The stuff of which his manhood was to be formed had been slow of growth, as it is with many men; and consequently, when temptation was offered to him, he had fallen.

But he deeply grieved over his own stumbling, and from time to time, as his periods of penitence came upon him, he resolved that he would once more put his shoulder to the wheel as became one who fights upon earth that battle for which he had put on his armour. Over and over again did he think of those words of Mr. Crawley, and now as he walked up and down the path, crumpling Mr. Sowerby's letter in his hand, he thought of them again — "It is a terrible falling off, terrible in the fall, but doubly terrible through that difficulty of returning." Yes; that is a difficulty which multiplies itself in a fearful ratio as one goes on pleasantly running down the path — whitherward? Had it come to that with him that he could not return — that he could never again hold up his head with a safe conscience as the pastor of his parish! It was Sowerby who had led him into this misery, who had brought on him this ruin? But then had not Sowerby paid him? Had not that stall which he now held in Barchester been Sowerby's gift? He was a poor man now — a distressed, poverty-stricken man; but nevertheless he wished with all his heart that he had never become a sharer in the good things of the Barchester chapter.

"I shall resign the stall," he said to his wife that night. "I think I may say that I have made up my mind as to that."

"But, Mark, will not people say that it is odd?"

"I cannot help it — they must say it. Fanny, I fear that we shall have to bear the saying of harder words than that."

"Nobody can ever say that you have done anything that is unjust or dishonourable. If there are such men as Mr. Sowerby —"

"The blackness of his fault will not excuse mine." And then again he sat silent, hiding his eyes, while his wife, sitting by him, held his hand.

"Don't make yourself wretched, Mark. Matters will all come right yet. It cannot be that the loss of a few hundred pounds should ruin you."

"It is not the money — it is not the money!"

"But you have done nothing wrong, Mark."

"How am I to go into the church, and take my place before them all, when every one will know that bailiffs are in the house?" And then, dropping his head on to the table, he sobbed aloud.

Mark Robarts' mistake had been mainly this, — he had thought to touch pitch and not to be defiled. He, looking out from his pleasant parsonage into the pleasant upper ranks of the world around him, had seen that men and things in those quarters were very engaging. His own parsonage, with his sweet wife, were exceedingly dear to him, and Lady Lufton's affectionate friendship had its value; but were not these things rather dull for one who had lived in the best sets at Harrow and Oxford; — unless, indeed, he could supplement them with some occasional bursts of more lively life? Cakes and ale were as pleasant to his palate as to the palates of those with whom he had formerly lived at college. He had the same eye to look at a horse, and the same heart to make him go across a country, as they. And then, too, he found that men liked him, — men and women also; men and women who were high in worldly standing. His ass's ears were tickled, and he learned to fancy that he was intended by nature for the society of high people. It seemed as though he were following his appointed course in meeting men and women of the world at the houses of the fashionable and the rich. He was not the first clergyman that had so lived and had so prospered. Yes, clergymen had so lived, and had done their duties in their sphere of life altogether to the satisfaction of their countrymen — and of their sovereigns. Thus Mark Robarts had determined that he would touch pitch, and escape defilement if that were possible. With what result those who have read so far will have perceived.

Late on the following afternoon who should drive up to the parsonage door but Mr. Forrest, the bank manager from Barchester — Mr. Forrest, to whom Sowerby had always pointed as the *Deus ex machinâ* who, if duly invoked, could relieve them all from their present troubles, and dismiss the whole Tozer family — not howling into the wilderness, as one would have wished to do with that brood of Tozers, but so gorged with prey that from them no further annoyance need be dreaded? All this Mr. Forrest could do; nay, more, most willingly would do! Only let Mark Robarts put himself into the banker's hand, and blandly sign what documents the banker might desire.

"This is a very unpleasant affair," said Mr. Forrest as soon as they were closeted together in Mark's book-room. In answer to which observation the parson acknowledged that it was a very unpleasant affair.

"Mr. Sowerby has managed to put you into the hands of about the worst set of rogues now existing in their line of business in London."

"So I suppose; Curling told me the same." Curling was the Barchester attorney whose aid he had lately invoked.

"Curling has threatened them that he will expose their whole trade; but one of them who was down here, a man named Tozer, replied, that you had much more to lose by exposure than he had. He went further and declared that he would defy any jury in England to refuse him his money. He swore that he discounted both bills in the regular way of business; and, though this is of course false, I fear that it will be impossible to prove it so. He well knows that you are a clergyman, and that, therefore, he has a stronger hold on you than on other men."

"The disgrace shall fall on Sowerby," said Robarts, hardly actuated at the moment by any strong feeling of Christian forgiveness.

"I fear, Mr. Robarts, that he is somewhat in the condition of the Tozers. He will not feel it as you will do."

"I must bear it, Mr. Forrest, as best I may."

"Will you allow me, Mr. Robarts, to give you my advice. Perhaps I ought to apologize for intruding it upon you; but as the bills have been presented and dishonoured across my counter, I have, of necessity, become acquainted with the circumstances."

"I am sure I am very much obliged to you," said Mark.

"You must pay this money, or, at any rate, the most considerable portion of it; — the whole of it, indeed, with such deduction as a lawyer may be able to induce these hawks to make on the sight of the ready money. Perhaps 750 *l.* or 800 *l.* may see you clear of the whole affair."

"But I have not a quarter of that sum lying by me."

"No, I suppose not; but what I would recommend is this: that you should borrow the money from the bank, on your own responsibility, — with the joint security of some friend who may be willing to assist you with his name. Lord Lufton probably would do it."

"No, Mr. Forrest —"

"Listen to me first, before you make up your mind. If you took this step, of course you would do so with the fixed intention of paying the money yourself, — without any further reliance on Sowerby or on any one else."

"I shall not rely on Mr. Sowerby again; you may be sure of that."

"What I mean is that you must teach yourself to recognize the debt as your own. If you can do that, with your income you can surely pay it, with interest, in two years. If Lord Lufton will assist you with his name, I will so arrange the bills that the payments shall be made to fall equally over that period. In that way the world will know nothing about it, and in two years' time you will once more be a free man. Many men, Mr. Robarts, have bought their experience much dearer than that, I can assure you."

"Mr. Forrest, it is quite out of the question."

"You mean that Lord Lufton will not give you his name."

"I certainly shall not ask him, but that is not all. In the first place my income will not be what you think it, for I shall probably give up the prebend at Barchester."

"Give up the prebend! give up six hundred a year!"

"And, beyond this, I think I may say that nothing shall tempt me to put my name to another bill. I have learned a lesson which I hope I may never forget."

"Then what do you intend to do?"

"Nothing!"

"Then those men will sell every stick of furniture about the place. They know that your property here is enough to secure all that they claim."

"If they have the power, they must sell it."

"And all the world will know the fact."

"So it must be. Of the faults which a man commits he must bear the punishment. If it were only myself!"

"That's where it is, Mr. Robarts. Think what your wife will have to suffer in going through such misery as that! You had better take my advice. Lord Lufton, I am sure —"

But the very name of Lord Lufton, his sister's lover, again gave him courage. He thought, too, of the accusations which Lord Lufton had brought against him on that night, when he had come to him in the coffee-room of the hotel, and he felt that it was impossible that he should apply to him for such aid. It would be better to tell all to Lady Lufton! That she would relieve him, let the cost to herself be what it might, he was very sure. Only this; — that in looking to her for assistance he would be forced to bite the dust in very deed.

"Thank you, Mr. Forrest, but I have made up my mind. Do not think that I am the less obliged to you for your disinterested kindness, — for I know that it is disinterested; but this I think I may confidently say, that not even to avert so terrible a calamity will I again put my name to any bill. Even if you could take my own promise to pay without the addition of any second name, I would not do it."

There was nothing for Mr. Forrest to do under such circumstances but simply to drive back to Barchester. He had done the best for the young clergyman according to his lights, and perhaps, in a worldly view, his advice had not been bad. But Mark dreaded the very name of a bill. He was as a dog that had been terribly scorched, and nothing should again induce him to go near the fire.

"Was not that the man from the bank?" said Fanny, coming into the room when the sound of the wheels had died away.

"Yes; Mr. Forrest."

"Well, dearest?"

"We must prepare ourselves for the worst."

"You will not sign any more papers, eh, Mark?"

"No; I have just now positively refused to do so."

"Then I can bear anything. But, dearest, dearest Mark, will you not let me tell Lady Lufton?"

Let them look at the matter in any way the punishment was very heavy.

CHAPTER XIX.

Is she not Insignificant?

AND now a month went by at Framley without any increase of comfort to our friends there, and also without any absolute development of the ruin which had been daily expected at the parsonage. Sundry letters had reached Mr. Robarts from various personages acting in the Tozer interest, all of which he referred to Mr. Curling, of Barchester. Some of these letters contained prayers for the money, pointing out how an innocent widow lady had been induced to invest her all on the faith of Mr. Robarts' name, and was now starving in a garret, with her three children, because Mr. Robarts would not make good his own undertakings. But the majority of them were filled with threats; — only two days longer would be allowed and then the sheriff's officers would be enjoined to do their work; then one day of grace would be added, at the expiration of which the dogs of war would be unloosed. These, as fast as they came, were sent to Mr. Curling, who took no notice of them individually, but continued his endeavour to prevent the evil day. The second bill Mr. Robarts would take up — such was

Mr. Curling's proposition; and would pay by two instalments of 250*l.* each, the first in two months, and the second in four. If this were acceptable to the Tozer interest — well; if it were not, the sheriff's officers must do their worst and the Tozer interest must look for what it could get. The Tozer interest would not declare itself satisfied with these terms, and so the matter went on. During which the roses faded from day to day on the cheeks of Mrs. Robarts, as under such circumstances may easily be conceived.

In the meantime Lucy still remained at Hogglestock and had there become absolute mistress of the house. Poor Mrs. Crawley had been at death's door; for some days she was delirious, and afterwards remained so weak as to be almost unconscious; but now the worst was over and Mr. Crawley had been informed, that as far as human judgment might pronounce, his children would not become orphans nor would he become a widower. During these weeks Lucy had not once been home nor had she seen any of the Framley people. "Why should she incur the risk of conveying infection for so small an object?" as she herself argued, writing by letters, which were duly fumigated before they were opened at the parsonage. So she remained at Hogglestock, and the Crawley children, now admitted to all the honours of the nursery, were kept at Framley. They were kept at Framley, although it was expected from day to day that the beds on which they lay would be seized for the payment of Mr. Sowerby's debts.

Lucy, as I have said, became mistress of the house at Hogglestock and made herself absolutely ascendant over Mr. Crawley. Jellies, and broth, and fruit, and even butter, came from Lufton Court, which she displayed on the table, absolutely on the cloth before him, and yet he bore it. I cannot say that he partook of these delicacies with any freedom himself, but he did drink his tea when it was given to him although it contained Framley cream; — and, had he known it, Bohea itself from the Framley chest. In truth, in these days, he had given himself over to the dominion of this stranger; and he said nothing beyond, "Well, well," with two uplifted hands, when he came upon her as she was sewing the buttons on to his own shirts — sewing on the buttons and perhaps occasionally applying her needle elsewhere, — not without utility.

He said to her at this period very little in the way of thanks. Some protracted conversations they did have, now and again, during the long evenings; but even in these he did not utter many words as to their present state of life. It was on religion chiefly that he spoke, not lecturing her individually, but laying down his ideas as to what the life of a Christian should be, and especially what should be the life of a minister. "But though I can see this, Miss Robarts," he said, "I am bound to say that no one has fallen off so frequently as myself. I have renounced the devil and all his works; but it is by word of mouth only — by word of mouth only. How shall a man crucify the old Adam that is within him, unless he throw himself prostrate in the dust and acknowledge that all his strength is weaker than water?" To this, often as it might be repeated, she would listen patiently, comforting him by such words as her theology would supply; but then, when this was over, she would again resume her command and enforce from him a close obedience to her domestic behests.

At the end of the month Lord Lufton came back to Framley Court. His arrival there was quite unexpected; though, as he pointed out, when his mother expressed some surprise, he had returned exactly at the time named by him before he started.

"I need not say, Ludovic, how glad I am to have you," said she, looking to his face and pressing his arm; "the more so, indeed, seeing that I hardly expected it."

He said nothing to his mother about Lucy the first evening, although there was some conversation respecting the Robarts family.

"I am afraid Mr. Robarts has embarrassed himself," said Lady Lufton, looking very seriously. "Rumours reach me which are most distressing. I have said nothing to anybody as yet — not even to Fanny; but I can see in her face, and hear in the tones of her voice, that she is suffering some great sorrow."

"I know all about it," said Lord Lufton.

"You know all about it, Ludovic?"

"Yes; it is through that precious friend of mine, Mr. Sowerby, of Chaldicotes. He has accepted bills for Sowerby; indeed, he told me so."

"What business had he at Chaldicotes? What had he to do with such friends as that? I do not know how I am to forgive him."

"It was through me that he became acquainted with Sowerby. You must remember that, mother."

"I do not see that that is any excuse. Is he to consider that all your acquaintances must necessarily be his friends also? It is reasonable to suppose that you in your position must live occasionally with a great many people who are altogether unfit companions for him as a parish clergyman. He will not remember this, and he must be taught it. What business had he to go to Gatherum Castle?"

"He got his stall at Barchester by going there."

"He would be much better without his stall, and Fanny has the sense to know this. What does he want with two houses? Prebendal stalls are for older men than he — for men who have earned them, and who at the end of their lives want some ease. I wish with all my heart that he had never taken it."

"Six hundred a year has its charms all the same," said Lufton, getting up and strolling out of the room.

"If Mark really be in any difficulty," he said, later in the evening, "we must put him on his legs."

"You mean, pay his debts?"

"Yes; he has no debts except these acceptances of Sowerby's."

"How much will it be, Ludovic?"

"A thousand pounds, perhaps, more or less. I'll find the money, mother; only I shan't be able to pay you quite as soon as I intended." Whereupon his mother got up, and throwing her arms round his neck declared that she would never forgive him if he ever said a word more about her little present to him. I suppose there is no pleasure a mother can have more attractive than giving away her money to an only son.

Lucy's name was first mentioned at breakfast the next morning. Lord Lufton had made up his mind to attack his mother on the subject early in the morning — before he went up to the parsonage; but as matters turned out, Miss Robarts' doings were necessarily brought under discussion without reference to Lord Lufton's special aspirations regarding her. The fact of Mrs. Crawley's illness had been mentioned, and Lady Lufton had stated how it had come to pass that all the Crawleys' children were at the parsonage.

"I must say that Fanny has behaved excellently," said Lady Lufton. "It was just what might have been expected from her. And indeed," she added, speaking in an embarrassed tone, "so has Miss Robarts. Miss Robarts has remained at Hogglestock and nursed Mrs. Crawley through the whole."

"Remained at Hogglestock — through the fever!" exclaimed his lordship.

"Yes, indeed," said Lady Lufton.

"And is she there now?"

"Oh, yes; I am not aware that she thinks of leaving just yet."

"Then I say that it is a great shame — a scandalous shame!"

"But, Ludovic, it was her own doing."

"Oh, yes; I understand. But why should she be sacrificed? Were there no nurses in the country to be hired, but that she must go and remain there for a month at the bedside of a pestilent fever? There is no justice in it."

"Justice, Ludovic? I don't know about justice, but there was great Christian charity. Mrs. Crawley has probably owed her life to Miss Robarts."

"Has she been ill? Is she ill? I insist upon knowing whether she is ill. I shall go over to Hogglestock myself immediately after breakfast."

To this Lady Lufton made no reply. If Lord Lufton chose to go to Hogglestock she could not prevent him. She thought, however, that it would be much better that he should stay away. He would be quite as open to the infection as Lucy Robarts; and, moreover, Mrs. Crawley's bedside would be as inconvenient a place as might be selected for any interview between two lovers. Lady Lufton felt at the present moment that she was cruelly treated by circumstances with reference to Miss Robarts. Of course it would have been her part to lessen, if she could do so without injustice, that high idea which her son entertained of the beauty and worth of the young lady; but, unfortunately, she had been compelled to praise her and to load her name with all manner of eulogy. Lady Lufton was essentially a true woman, and not even with the object of carrying out her own views in so important a matter would she be guilty of such deception as she might have practised by simply holding her tongue; but nevertheless she could hardly reconcile herself to the necessity of singing Lucy's praises.

After breakfast Lady Lufton got up from her chair, but hung about the room without making any show of leaving. In accordance with her usual custom she would have asked her son what he was going to do; but she did not dare so to inquire now. Had he not declared, only a few minutes since, whither he would go? "I suppose I shall see you at lunch?" at last she said.

"At lunch? Well, I don't know. Look here, mother. What am I to say to Miss Robarts when I see her?" and he leaned with his back against the chimney-piece as he interrogated his mother.

"What are you to say to her, Ludovic?"

"Yes; what am I to say, — as coming from you?

Am I to tell her that you will receive her as your daughter-in-law?"

"Ludovic, I have explained all that to Miss Robarts herself."

"Explained what?"

"I have told her that I did not think that such a marriage would make either you or her happy."

"And why have you told her so? Why have you taken upon yourself to judge for me in such a matter, as though I were a child? Mother, you must unsay what you have said."

Lord Lufton, as he spoke, looked full into his mother's face; and he did so, not as though he were begging from her a favour, but issuing to her a command. She stood near him, with one hand on the breakfast-table, gazing at him almost furtively, not quite daring to meet the full view of his eye. There was only one thing on earth which Lady Lufton feared, and that was her son's displeasure. The sun of her earthly heaven shone upon her through the medium of his existence. If she were driven to quarrel with him, as some ladies of her acquaintance were driven to quarrel with their sons, the world to her would be over. Not but what facts might be so strong as to make it absolutely necessary that she should do this. As some people resolve that, under certain circumstances, they will commit suicide, so she could see that, under certain circumstances, she must consent even to be separated from him. She would not do wrong, — not that which she knew to be wrong, — even for his sake. If it were necessary that all her happiness should collapse and be crushed in ruin around her, she must endure it, and wait God's time to relieve her from so dark a world. The light of the sun was very dear to her, but even that might be purchased at too dear a cost.

"I told you before, mother, that my choice was made, and I asked you then to give your consent; you have now had time to think about it, and therefore I have come to ask you again. I have reason to know that there will be no impediment to my marriage if you will frankly hold out your hand to Lucy."

The matter was altogether in Lady Lufton's hands, but, fond as she was of power, she absolutely wished that it were not so. Had her son married without asking her and then brought Lucy home as his wife, she would undoubtedly have forgiven him; and much as she might have disliked the match, she would, ultimately, have embraced the bride. But now she was compelled to exercise her judgment. If he married imprudently, it would be her doing. How was she to give her expressed consent to that which she believed to be wrong?

"Do you know anything against her; any reason why she should not be my wife?" continued he.

"If you mean as regards her moral conduct certainly not," said Lady Lufton. "But I could say as much as that in favour of a great many young ladies whom I should regard as very ill suited for such a marriage."

"Yes; some might be vulgar, some might be ill-tempered, some might be ugly; others might be burdened with disagreeable connections. I can understand that you should object to a daughter-in-law under any of these circumstances. But none of these things can be said of Miss Robarts. I defy you to say that she is not in all respects what a lady should be."

But her father was a doctor of medicine, she is the sister of the parish clergyman, she is only five feet two in height, and is so uncommonly brown! Had Lady Lufton dared to give a catalogue of her objections, such would have been its extent and nature. But she did not dare to do this.

"I cannot say, Ludovic, that she is possessed of all that you should seek in a wife." Such was her answer.

"Do you mean that she has not got money?"

"No, not that; I should be very sorry to see you making money your chief object, or indeed any essential object. If it chanced that your wife did have money, no doubt you would find it a convenience. But pray understand me, Ludovic; I would not for a moment advise you to subject your happiness to such a necessity as that. It is not because she is without fortune —"

"Then why is it? At breakfast you were singing her praises, and saying how excellent she is."

"If I were forced to put my objection into one word, I should say —" and then she paused, hardly daring to encounter the frown which was already gathering itself on her son's brow.

"You would say what?" said Lord Lufton, almost roughly.

"Don't be angry with me, Ludovic; all that I think, and all that I say on this subject, I think and say with only one object — that of your happiness. What other motive can I have for anything in this world?" And then she came close to him and kissed him.

"But tell me, mother, what is this objection; what is this terrible word that is to sum up the list of all poor Lucy's sins, and prove that she is unfit for married life?"

"Ludovic, I did not say that. You know that I did not."

"What is the word, mother?"

And then at last Lady Lufton spoke it out. "She is — insignificant. I believe her to be a very good girl, but she is not qualified to fill the high position to which you would exalt her."

"Insignificant!"

"Yes, Ludovic, I think so."

"Then, mother, you do not know her. You must permit me to say that you are talking of a girl whom you do not know. Of all the epithets of opprobrium which the English language could give you, that would be nearly the last which she would deserve."

"I have not intended any opprobrium."

"Insignificant!"

"Perhaps you do not quite understand me, Ludovic."

"I know what insignificant means, mother."

"I think that she would not worthily fill the position which your wife should take in the world."

"I understand what you say."

"She would not do you honour at the head of your table."

"Ah, I understand. You want me to marry some bouncing amazon, some pink and white giantess of fashion who would frighten the little people into their proprieties."

"Oh, Ludovic! you are intending to laugh at me now."

"I was never less inclined to laugh in my life — never, I can assure you. And now I am more certain than ever that your objection to Miss Robarts arises from your not knowing her. You will find, I think, when you do know her, that she is as well able to hold her own as any lady of your acquaintance; — ay, and to maintain her husband's position, too. I can assure you that I shall have no fear of her on that score."

"I think, dearest, that perhaps you hardly —"

"I think this, mother, that in such a matter as this I must choose for myself. I have chosen; and I now ask you, as my mother, to go to her and bid her welcome. Dear mother, I will own this, that I should not be happy if I thought that you did not love my wife." These last words he said in a tone of affection that went to his mother's heart, and then he left the room.

Poor Lady Lufton, when she was alone, waited till she heard her son's steps retreating through the hall, and then betook herself up-stairs to her customary morning work. She sat down at last as though about so to occupy herself; but her mind was too full to allow of her taking up her pen. She had often said to herself, in days which to her were not as yet long gone by, that she would choose a bride for her son, and that then she would love the chosen one with all her heart. She would dethrone herself in favour of this new queen, sinking with joy into her dowager state, in order that her son's wife might shine with the greater splendour. The fondest day-dreams of her life had all had reference to the time when her son should bring home a new Lady Lufton, selected by herself from the female excellence of England, and in which she might be the first to worship her new idol. But could she dethrone herself for Lucy Robarts? Could she give up her chair of state in order to place thereon the little girl from the parsonage? Could she take to her heart, and treat with absolute loving confidence, with the confidence of an almost idolatrous mother, that little chit who, a few months since, had sat awkwardly in one corner of her drawing-room, afraid to speak to any one? And yet it seemed that it must come to this — to this: — or else those day-dreams of hers would in nowise come to pass.

She sat herself down, trying to think whether it were possible that Lucy might fill the throne; for she had begun to recognize it as probable that her son's will would be too strong for her; but her thoughts would fly away to Griselda Grantly. In her first and only matured attempt to realize her day-dreams, she had chosen Griselda for her queen. She had failed there, seeing that the Fates had destined Miss Grantly for another throne — for another and a higher one, as far as the world goes. She would have made Griselda the wife of a baron, but fate was about to make that young lady the wife of a marquis. Was there cause of grief in this? Did she really regret that Miss Grantly, with all her virtues, should be made over to the house of Hartletop? Lady Lufton was a woman who did not bear disappointment lightly; but nevertheless she did almost feel herself to have been relieved from a burden when she thought of the termination of the Lufton-Grantly marriage treaty. What if she had been successful, and, after all, the prize had been other than she had expected? She was sometimes prone to think that that prize was not exactly all that she had once hoped. Griselda looked the very thing that Lady Lufton wanted for a queen; — but how would a queen reign who trusted only to her looks? In that respect it was perhaps well for her that destiny had interposed. Griselda, she was driven to admit, was better suited to Lord Dumbello than to her son.

But still — such a queen as Lucy! Could it ever come to pass that the lieges of the kingdom would bow the knee in proper respect before so puny a sovereign? And then there was that feeling which, in still higher quarters, prevents the marriage of princes with the most noble of their people. Is it not a recognized rule of these realms that none of the blood royal shall raise to royal honours those of the subjects who are by birth un-royal! Lucy was a subject of the house of Lufton in that she was the sister of the parson and resident denizen of the parsonage. Presuming that Lucy herself might do for queen — granting that she might have some faculty to reign, the crown having been duly placed on her brow — how, then, about that clerical brother near the throne? Would it not come to this, that there would no longer be a queen at Framley?

And yet she knew that she must yield. She did not say so to herself. She did not as yet acknowledge that she must put out her hand to Lucy, calling her by name as her daughter. She did not absolutely say as much to her own heart; — not as yet. But she did begin to bethink herself of Lucy's high qualities, and to declare to herself that the girl, if not fit to be a queen, was at any rate fit to be a woman. That there was a spirit within that body, insignificant though the body might be, Lady Lufton was prepared to admit. That she had acquired the power — the chief of all powers in this world — of sacrificing herself for the sake of others; that, too, was evident enough. That she was a good girl, in the usual acceptation of the word good, Lady Lufton had never doubted. She was ready-witted too, prompt in action, gifted with a certain fire. It was that gift of fire which had won for her, so unfortunately, Lord Lufton's love. It was quite possible for her also to love Lucy Robarts; Lady Lufton admitted that to herself; — but then who could bow the knee before her, and serve her as a queen? Was it not a pity that she should be so insignificant?

But, nevertheless, we may say that as Lady Lufton sate that morning in her own room for two hours without employment, the star of Lucy Robarts was gradually rising in the firmament. After all, love was the food chiefly necessary for the nourishment of Lady Lufton, — the only food absolutely necessary. She was not aware of this herself, nor probably would those who knew her best have so spoken of her. They would have declared that family pride was her daily pabulum, and she herself would have said so too, calling it, however, by some less offensive name. Her son's honour, and the honour of her house! — of those she would have spoken as the things dearest to her in this world. And this was partly true, for had her son been dishonoured, she would have sunk with sorrow to the grave. But the one thing necessary to her daily life was the power of loving those who were near to her.

Lord Lufton, when he left the dining-room, intended at once to go up to the parsonage, but he first strolled round the garden in order that he might make up his mind what he would say there. He was angry with his mother, having not had the wit to see that she was about to give way and yield to him, and he was determined to make it understood that in this matter he would have his own way. He had learned that which it was necessary that he should know as to Lucy's heart, and such being the case he would not conceive it possible that he should be debarred by his mother's opposition. "There is no son in England loves his mother better than I do," he said to himself; "but there are some things which a man cannot stand. She would have married me to that block of stone if I would have let her; and now, because she is disappointed there — Insignificant! I never in my life heard anything so absurd, so untrue, so uncharitable, so — She'd like me to bring a dragon home, I suppose. It would serve her right if I did, — some creature that would make the house intolerable to her." "She must do it though," he said again, "or she and I will quarrel," and then he turned off towards the gate, preparing to go to the parsonage.

"My lord, have you heard what has happened?" said the gardener, coming to him at the gate. The man was out of breath and almost overwhelmed by the greatness of his own tidings.

"No; I have heard nothing. What is it?"

"The bailiffs have taken possession of everything at the parsonage."

CHAPTER XX.

The Philistines at the Parsonage.

It has been already told how things went on between the Tozers, Mr. Curling, and Mark Robarts during that month. Mr. Forrest had drifted out of the business altogether, as also had Mr. Sowerby, as far as any active participation in it went. Letters came frequently from Mr. Curling to the parsonage, and at last came a message by special mission to say that the evil day was at hand. As far as Mr. Curling's professional experience would enable him to anticipate or foretell the proceedings of such a man as Tom Tozer he thought that the sheriff's officers would be at Framley Parsonage on the following morning. Mr. Curling's experience did not mislead him in this respect.

"And what will you do, Mark?" said Fanny, speaking through her tears, after she had read the letter which her husband handed to her.

"Nothing. What can I do? They must come."

"Lord Lufton came to-day. Will you not go to him?"

"No. If I were to do so it would be the same as asking him for the money."

"Why not borrow it of him, dearest? Surely it would not be so much for him to lend."

"I could not do it. Think of Lucy, and how she stands with him. Besides I have already had words with Lufton about Sowerby and his money matters. He thinks that I am to blame, and he would tell me so; and then there would be sharp things said between us. He would advance me the money if I pressed for it, but he would do so in a way that would make it impossible that I should take it."

There was nothing more then to be said. If she had had her own way Mrs. Robarts would have gone at once to Lady Lufton, but she could not induce her husband to sanction such a proceeding. The objection to seeking assistance from her ladyship was as strong as that which prevailed as to her son. There had already been some little beginning of ill-feeling, and under such circumstances it was impossible to ask for pecuniary assistance. Fanny, however, had a prophetic assurance that assistance out of these difficulties must in the end come to them from that quarter, or not come at all; and she would fain, had she been allowed, make everything known at the big house.

On the following morning they breakfasted at the usual hour, but in great sadness. A maid-servant, whom Mrs. Robarts had brought with her when she married, told her that a rumour of what was to happen had reached the kitchen. Stubbs, the groom, had been in Barchester on the preceding day, and, according to his account — so said Mary — everybody in the city was talking about it. "Never mind, Mary," said Mrs. Robarts, and Mary replied, "Oh, no, of course not, ma'am."

In these days Mrs. Robarts was ordinarily very busy, seeing that there were six children in the house, four of whom had come to her but ill supplied with infantine belongings; and now, as usual, she went about her work immediately after breakfast. But she moved about the house very slowly, and was almost unable to give her orders to the servants, and spoke sadly to the children who hung about her wondering what was the matter. Her husband at the same time took himself to his book-room, but when there did not attempt any employment. He thrust his hands into his pockets, and, leaning against the fire-place, fixed his eyes upon the table before him without looking at anything that was on it; it was impossible for him to betake himself to his work. Remember what is the ordinary labour of a clergyman in his study, and think how fit he must have been for such employment! What would have been the nature of a sermon composed at such a moment, and with what satisfaction could he have used the sacred volume in referring to it for his arguments? He, in this respect, was worse off than his wife; she did employ herself, but he stood there without moving, doing nothing, with fixed eyes, thinking what men would say of him.

Luckily for him this state of suspense was not long, for within half an hour of his leaving the breakfast-table, the footman knocked at his door — that footman with whom, at the beginning of his difficulties, he had made up his mind to dispense, but who had been kept on because of the Barchester prebend.

"If you please, your reverence, there are two men outside," said the footman.

Two men! Mark knew well enough what men they were, but he could hardly take the coming of two such men to his quiet country parsonage quite as a matter of course.

"Who are they, John?" said he, not wishing any answer, but because the question was forced upor him.

"I'm afeard they're — bailiffs, sir."

"Very well, John; that will do; of course they must do what they please about the place."

And then, when the servant left him, he still stood without moving, exactly as he had stood before. There he remained for ten minutes, but the time went by very slowly. When about noon some circumstance told him what was the hour, he was astonished to find that the day had not nearly passed away.

And then another tap was struck on the door — a sound which he well recognized — and his wife crept silently into the room. She came close up to him before she spoke, and put her arm within his:

"Mark," she said, "the men are here; they are in the yard."

"I know it," he answered gruffly.

"Will it be better that you should see them, dearest?"

"See them; no; what good can I do by seeing them? But I shall see them soon enough; they will be here, I suppose, in a few minutes."

"They are taking an inventory, cook says; they are in the stable now."

"Very well; they must do as they please; I cannot help them."

"Cook says that if they are allowed their meals and some beer, and if nobody takes anything away, they will be quite civil."

"Civil! But what does it matter? Let them eat and drink what they please, as long as the food lasts. I don't suppose the butcher will send you more."

"But, Mark, there's nothing due to the butcher, — only the regular monthly bill."

"Very well; you'll see."

"Oh, Mark, don't look at me in that way. Do not turn away from me. What is to comfort us if we do not cling to each other now?"

"Comfort us! God help you! I wonder, Fanny, that you can bear to stay in the room with me."

"Mark, dearest Mark, my own dear, dearest husband! who is to be true to you, if I am not? You shall not turn from me. How can anything like this make a difference between you and me?" And then she threw her arms round his neck and embraced him.

It was a terrible morning to him, and one of which every incident will dwell on his memory to the last day of his life. He had been so proud in his position — had assumed to himself so prominent a standing — had contrived, by some trick which he had acquired, to carry his head so high above the heads of neighbouring parsons. It was this that had taken him among great people, had introduced him to the Duke of Omnium, had procured for him the stall at Barchester. But how was he to carry his head now? What would the Arabins and Grantlys say? How would the bishop sneer at him, and Mrs. Proudie and her daughters tell of him in all their quarters? How would Crawley look at him — Crawley, who had already once had him on the hip? The stern severity of Crawley's face loomed upon him now. Crawley, with his children half naked, and his wife a drudge, and himself half starved, had never had a bailiff in his house at Hogglestock! And then his own curate, Evans, whom he had patronized, and treated almost as a dependant — how was he to look his curate in the face and arrange with him for the sacred duties of the next Sunday?

His wife still stood by him, gazing into his face; and as he looked at her and thought of her misery, he could not control his heart with reference to the wrongs which Sowerby had heaped on him. It was Sowerby's falsehood and Sowerby's fraud which had brought upon him and his wife this terrible anguish.

"If there be justice on earth he will suffer for it yet," he said at last, not speaking intentionally to his wife, but unable to repress his feelings.

"Do not wish him evil, Mark; you may be sure he has his own sorrows."

"His own sorrows! No; he is callous to such misery as this. He has become so hardened in dishonesty that all this is mirth to him. If there be punishment in heaven for falsehood —"

"Oh, Mark, do not curse him!"

"How am I to keep myself from cursing when I see what he has brought upon you?"

"'Vengeance is mine, saith the Lord,'" answered the young wife, not with solemn, preaching accent, as though bent on reproof, but with the softest whisper into his ear. "Leave that to Him, Mark; and for us, let us pray that He may soften the hearts of us all; — of him who has caused us to suffer, and of our own."

Mark was not called upon to reply to this, for he was again disturbed by a servant at the door. It was the cook this time herself, who had come with a message from the men of the law. And she had come, be it remembered, not from any necessity that she as cook should do this line of work; for the footman, or Mrs. Robarts' maid, might have come as well as she. But when things are out of course servants are always out of course also. As a rule, nothing will induce a butler to go into a stable, or persuade a housemaid to put her hand to a frying-pan. But now that this new excitement had come upon the household — seeing that the bailiffs were in possession, and that the chattels were being entered in a catalogue, everybody was willing to do everything — everything but his or her own work. The gardener was looking after the dear children; the nurse was doing the rooms before the bailiffs should reach them; the groom had gone into the kitchen to get their lunch ready for them: and the cook was walking about with an inkstand, obeying all the orders of these great potentates. As far as the servants were concerned, it may be a question whether the coming of the bailiffs had not hitherto been regarded as a treat.

"If you please, ma'am," said Jemima cook, "they wishes to know in which room you'd be pleased to have the inmin-tory took fust. 'Cause, ma'am, they wouldn't disturb you nor master more than can be avoided. For their line of life, ma'am, they is very civil — very civil indeed."

"I suppose they may go into the drawing-room," said Mrs. Robarts, in a sad low voice. All nice women are proud of their drawing-rooms, and she was very proud of hers. It had been furnished when money was plenty with them, immediately after their marriage, and everything in it was pretty, good, and dear to her. O ladies, who have drawing-rooms in which the things are pretty, good, and dear to you, think of what it would be to have two bailiffs rummaging among them with pen and inkhorn, making a catalogue preparatory to a sheriff's auction; and all without fault or extravagance of your own! There were things there that had been given to her by Lady Lufton, by Lady Meredith, and other friends, and the idea did occur to her that it might be possible to save them from contamination; but she would not say a word, lest by so saying she might add to Mark's misery.

"And then the dining-room," said Jemima cook, in a tone almost of elation.

"Yes; if they please."

"And then master's book-room here; or perhaps the bedrooms, if you and master be still here."

"Any way they please, cook; it does not much signify," said Mrs. Robarts. But for some days after that Jemima was by no means a favourite with her.

The cook was hardly out of the room before a quick footstep was heard on the gravel before the window, and the hall door was immediately opened.

"Where is your master?" said the well-known voice of Lord Lufton; and then in half a minute he also was in the book-room.

"Mark, my dear fellow, what's all this?" said he, in a cheery tone and with a pleasant face. "Did not you know that I was here? I came down yesterday; landed from Hamburg only yesterday morning. How do you do, Mrs. Robarts? This is a terrible bore, isn't it?"

Robarts, at the first moment, hardly knew how to speak to his old friend. He was struck dumb by the disgrace of his position; the more so as his misfortune was one which it was partly in the power of Lord Lufton to remedy. He had never yet borrowed money since he had filled a man's position, but he had had words about money with the young peer, in which he knew that his friend had wronged him; and for this double reason he was now speechless.

"Mr. Sowerby has betrayed him," said Mrs. Robarts, wiping the tears from her eyes. Hitherto she had said no word against Sowerby, but now it was necessary to defend her husband.

"No doubt about it. I believe he has always betrayed every one who has ever trusted him. I told you what he was, some time since; did I not? But, Mark, why on earth have you let it go so far as this? Would not Forrest help you?"

"Mr. Forrest wanted him to sign more bills, and he would not do that," said Mrs. Robarts, sobbing.

"Bills are like dram-drinking," said the discreet young lord: "when one once begins, it is very hard to leave off. Is it true that the men are here now, Mark?"

"Yes, they are in the next room."

"What, in the drawing-room?"

"They are making out a list of the things," said Mrs. Robarts.

"We must stop that at any rate," said his lordship, walking off towards the scene of the operations; and as he left the room Mrs. Robarts followed him, leaving her husband by himself.

"Why did you not send down to my mother?" said he, speaking hardly above a whisper, as they stood together in the hall.

"He would not let me."

"But why not go yourself? or why not have written to me, — considering how intimate we are?"

Mrs. Robarts could not explain to him that the peculiar intimacy between him and Lucy must have hindered her from doing so, even if otherwise it might have been possible; but she felt such was the case.

"Well, my men, this is bad work you're doing here," said he, walking into the drawing-room. Whereupon the cook curtseyed low, and the bailiffs, knowing his lordship, stopped from their business and put their hands to their foreheads. "You must stop this, if you please, — at once. Come, let's go out into the kitchen, or some place outside. I don't like to see you here with your big boots and the pen and ink among the furniture."

"We ain't a-done no harm, my lord, so please your lordship, said Jemima cook.

"And we is only a-doing our bounden dooties," said one of the bailiffs.

"As we is sworn to do, so please your lordship," said the other.

"And is wery sorry to be unconwenient, my lord, to any gen'leman or lady as is a gen'lman or lady. But accidents will happen, and then what can the likes of us do?" said the first.

"Because we is sworn, my lord," said the second. But, nevertheless, in spite of their oaths, and in spite also of the stern necessity which they pleaded, they ceased their operations at the instance of the peer. For the name of a lord is still great in England.

"And now leave this, and let Mrs. Robarts go into her drawing-room."

"And, please your lordship, what is we to do? Who is we to look to?"

In satisfying them absolutely on this point Lord Lufton had to use more than his influence as a peer. It was necessary that he should have pen and paper. But with pen and paper he did satisfy them; — satisfy them so far that they agreed to return to Stubbs' room, the former hospital, due stipulation having been made for the meals and beer, and there await the order to evacuate the premises which would no doubt, under his lordship's influence, reach them on the following day. The meaning of all which was that Lord Lufton had undertaken to bear upon his own shoulder the whole debt due by Mr. Robarts.

And then he returned to the book-room where Mark was still standing almost on the spot in which he had placed himself immediately after breakfast. Mrs. Robarts did not return, but went up among the children to counterorder such directions as she had given for the preparation of the nursery for the Philistines. "Mark," he said, "do not trouble yourself about this more than you can help. The men have ceased doing anything, and they shall leave the place to-morrow morning."

"And how will the money — be paid?" said the poor clergyman.

"Do not bother yourself about that at present. It shall so be managed that the burden shall fall ultimately on yourself — not on any one else. But I am sure it must be a comfort to you to know that your wife need not be driven out of her drawing-room."

"But, Lufton, I cannot allow you — after what has passed — and at the present moment —"

"My dear fellow, I know all about it and I am coming to that just now. You have employed Curling, and he shall settle it; and upon my word, Mark, you shall pay the bill. But, for the present emergency, the money is at my banker's."

"But, Lufton —"

"And to deal honestly, about Curling's bill I mean, it ought to be as much my affair as your own. It was I that brought you into this mess with Sowerby, and I know now how unjust about it I was to you up in London. But the truth is that Sowerby's treachery had nearly driven me wild. It has done the same to you since, I have no doubt."

"He has ruined me," said Robarts.

"No, he has not done that. No thanks to him though; he would not have scrupled to do it had it come in his way. The fact is, Mark, that you and I cannot conceive the depth of fraud in such a man as that. He is always looking for money; I believe that in all his hours of most friendly intercourse, — when he is sitting with you over your wine, and riding beside you in the field, — he is still thinking how he can make use of you to tide him over some difficulty. He has lived in that way till he has a pleasure in cheating, and has become so clever in his line of life that if you or I were with him again to-morrow he would again get the better of us. He is a man that must be absolutely avoided; I, at any rate, have learned to know so much."

In the expression of which opinion Lord Lufton was too hard upon poor Sowerby; as indeed we are all apt to be too hard in forming an opinion upon the rogues of the world. That Mr. Sowerby had been a rogue, I cannot deny. It is roguish to lie, and he had been a great liar. It is roguish to make promises which the promiser knows he cannot perform, and such had been Mr. Sowerby's daily practice. It is roguish to live on other men's money, and Mr. Sowerby had long been doing so. It is roguish, at least so I would hold it, to deal willingly with rogues; and Mr. Sowerby had been constant in such dealings. I do not know whether he had not at times fallen even into more palpable roguery than is proved by such practices as those enumerated. Though I have for him some tender feeling, knowing that there was still a touch of gentle bearing round his heart, an abiding taste for better things within him, I cannot acquit him from the great accusation. But, for all that, in spite of his acknowledged roguery, Lord Lufton was too hard upon him in his judgment. There was yet within him the means of repentance, could a locus penitentiæ have been supplied to him. He grieved bitterly over his own ill doings, and knew well what changes gentlehood would have demanded from him. Whether or no he had gone too far for all changes — whether the locus penitentiæ was for him still a possibility — that was between him and a higher power.

"I have no one to blame but myself," said Mark, still speaking in the same heart-broken tone and with his face averted from his friend.

The debt would now be paid, and the bailiffs would be expelled; but that would not set him right before the world. It would be known to all men — to all clergymen in the diocese — that the sheriff's officers had been in charge of Framley Parsonage, and he could never again hold up his head in the close of Barchester.

"My dear fellow, if we were all to make ourselves miserable for such a trifle as this, —" said Lord

Lufton, putting his arm affectionately on his friend's shoulder.

"But we are not all clergymen," said Mark, and as he spoke he turned away to the window and Lord Lufton knew that the tears were on his cheek.

Nothing was then said between them for some moments, after which Lord Lufton again spoke, —

"Mark, my dear fellow!"

"Well," said Mark, with his face still turned towards the window.

"You must remember one thing; in helping you over this stile, which will be really a matter of no inconvenience to me, I have a better right than that even of an old friend; I look upon you now as my brother-in-law."

Marked turned slowly round, plainly showing the tears upon his face.

"Do you mean," said he, "that anything more has taken place?"

"I mean to make your sister my wife; she sent me word by you to say that she loved me, and I am not going to stand upon any nonsense after that. If she and I are both willing no one alive has a right to stand between us; and, by heavens, no one shall. I will do nothing secretly, so I tell you that, exactly as I have told her ladyship."

"But what does she say?"

"She says nothing; but it cannot go on like that. My mother and I cannot live here together if she opposes me in this way. I do not want to frighten your sister by going over to her at Hogglestock, but I expect you to tell her so much as I now tell you, as coming from me; otherwise she will think that I have forgotten her."

"She will not think that."

"She need not; good-bye, old fellow. I'll make it all right between you and her ladyship about this affair of Sowerby's."

And then he took his leave and walked off to settle about the payment of the money.

"Mother," said he to Lady Lufton that evening, "you must not bring this affair of the bailiffs up against Robarts. It has been more my fault than his."

Hitherto not a word had been spoken between Lady Lufton and her son on the subject. She had heard with terrible dismay of what had happened, and had heard also that Lord Lufton had immediately gone to the parsonage. It was impossible, therefore, that she should now interfere. That the necessary money would be forthcoming she was aware, but that would not wipe out the terrible disgrace attached to an execution in a clergyman's house. And then, too, he was her clergyman, — her own clergyman, selected, and appointed, and brought to Framley by herself, endowed with a wife of her own choosing, filled with good things by her own hand! It was a terrible misadventure, and she began to repent that she had ever heard the name of Robarts. She would not, however, have been slow to put forth the hand to lessen the evil by giving her own money, had this been either necessary or possible. But how could she interfere between Robarts and her son, especially when she remembered the proposed connection between Lucy and Lord Lufton?

"Your fault, Ludovic?"

"Yes, mother. It was I who introduced him to

Mr. Sowerby; and, to tell the truth, I do not think he would ever have been intimate with Sowerby if I had not given him some sort of a commission with reference to money matters then pending between Mr. Sowerby and me. They are all over now, — thanks to you, indeed."

"Mr. Robarts' character as a clergyman should have kept him from such troubles, if no other feeling did so."

"At any rate, mother, oblige me by letting it pass by."

"Oh, I shall say nothing to him."

"You had better say something to her, or otherwise it will be strange; and even to him I would say a word or two, — a word in kindness, as you so well know how. It will be easier to him in that way, than if you were to be altogether silent."

No further conversation took place between them at the time, but later in the evening she brushed her hand across her son's forehead, sweeping the long silken hairs into their place, as she was wont to do when moved by any special feeling of love. "Ludovic," she said, "no one, I think, has so good a heart as you. I will do exactly as you would have me about this affair of Mr. Robarts and the money." And then there was nothing more said about it.

CHAPTER XXI.

Palace Blessings.

AND now, at this period, terrible rumours found their way into Barchester, and flew about the cathedral towers and round the cathedral door; ay, and into the canons' houses and the humbler sitting-rooms of the vicars choral. Whether they made their way from thence up to the bishop's palace, or whether they descended from the palace to the close, I will not pretend to say. But they were shocking, unnatural, and no doubt grievous to all those excellent ecclesiastical hearts which cluster so thickly in those quarters.

The first of these had reference to the new prebendary, and to the disgrace which he had brought on the chapter; a disgrace, as some of them boasted, which Barchester had never known before. This, however, like most other boasts, was hardly true; for within but a very few years there had been an execution in the house of a late prebendary, old Dr. Stanhope; and on that occasion the doctor himself had been forced to fly away to Italy, starting in the night, lest he also should fall into the hands of the Philistines, as well as his chairs and tables.

"It is a scandalous shame," said Mrs. Proudie, speaking not of the old doctor, but of the new offender; "a scandalous shame: and it would only serve him right if the gown were stripped from his back."

"I suppose his living will be sequestrated," said a young minor canon who attended much to the ecclesiastical injunctions of the lady of the diocese, and was deservedly held in high favour. If Framley were sequestrated, why should not he, as well as another, undertake the duty — with such stipend as the bishop might award?

"I am told that he is over head and ears in debt," said the future Mrs. Tickler, "and chiefly for horses which he has bought and not paid for."

"I see him riding very splendid animals when he comes over for the cathedral duties," said the minor canon.

"The sheriff's officers are in the house at present, I am told," said Mrs. Proudie.

"And is not he in jail?" said Mrs. Tickler.

"If not, he ought to be," said Mrs. Tickler's mother.

"And no doubt soon will be," said the minor canon; "for I hear that he is linked up with a most discreditable gang of persons."

This was what was said in the palace on that heading; and though, no doubt, more spirit and poetry was displayed there than in the houses of the less gifted clergy, this shows the manner in which the misfortune of Mr. Robarts was generally discussed. Nor, indeed, had he deserved any better treatment at their hands. But his name did not run the gauntlet for the usual nine days; nor, indeed, did his fame endure at its height for more than two. This sudden fall was occasioned by other tidings of a still more distressing nature; by a rumour which so affected Mrs. Proudie that it caused, as she said, her blood to creep. And she was very careful that the blood of others should creep also, if the blood of others was equally sensitive. It was said that Lord Dumbello had jilted Miss Grantly.

From what adverse spot in the world these cruel tidings fell upon Barchester I have never been able to discover. We know how quickly rumour flies, making herself common through all the cities. That Mrs. Proudie should have known more of the facts connected with the Hartletop family than any one else in Barchester was not surprising, seeing that she was so much more conversant with the great world in which such people lived. She knew, and was therefore correct enough in declaring, that Lord Dumbello had already jilted one other young lady — the Lady Julia Mac Mull, to whom he had been engaged three seasons back, and that therefore his character in such matters was not to be trusted. That Lady Julia had been a terrible flirt and greatly given to waltzing with a certain German count with whom she had since gone off — that, I suppose, Mrs. Proudie did not know, much as she was conversant with the great world, — seeing that she said nothing about it to any of her ecclesiastical listeners on the present occasion.

"It will be a terrible warning, Mrs. Quiverful, to us all, a most useful warning to us — not to trust to the things of this world. I fear they made no inquiry about this young nobleman before they agreed that his name should be linked with that of their daughter." This she said to the wife of the present warden of Hiram's Hospital, a lady who had received favours from her, and was therefore bound to listen attentively to her voice.

"But I hope it may not be true," said Mrs. Quiverful, who, in spite of the allegiance due by her to Mrs. Proudie, had reasons of her own for wishing well to the Grantly family.

"I hope so, indeed," said Mrs. Proudie, with a slight tinge of anger in her voice; "but I fear that there is no doubt. And I must confess that it is no more than we had a right to expect. I hope that it may be taken by all of us as a lesson, and an ensample, and a teaching of the Lord's mercy. And I wish you would request your husband — from me, Mrs. Quiverful — to dwell on this subject in morning and evening lecture at the hospital on Sabbath next, showing how false is the trust which we put in the good things of this world;" which behest, to a certain extent, Mr. Quiverful did obey, feeling that a quiet life in Barchester was of great value to him; but he did not go so far as to caution his hearers, who consisted of the aged bedesmen of the hospital, against matrimonial projects of an ambitious nature.

In this case, as in all others of the kind, the report was known to all the chapter before it had been heard by the archdeacon or his wife. The dean heard it, and disregarded it; as did also the dean's wife — at first; and those who generally sided with the Grantlys in the diocesan battles pooh-poohed the tidings, saying to each other that both the archdeacon and Mrs. Grantly were very well able to take care of their own affairs. But dripping water hollows a stone; and at last it was admitted on all sides that there was ground for fear, — on all sides, except at Plumstead.

"I am sure there is nothing in it; I really am sure of it," said Mrs. Arabin, whispering to her sister; "but after turning it over in my mind, I thought it right to tell you. And yet I don't know now but I am wrong."

"Quite right, dearest Eleanor," said Mrs. Grantly. "And I am much obliged to you. But we understand it, you know. It comes, of course, like all other Christian blessings, from the palace." And then there was nothing more said about it between Mrs. Grantly and her sister.

But on the following morning there arrived a letter by post, addressed to Mrs. Grantly, bearing the post-mark of Littlebath. The letter ran: —

"MADAM,

"It is known to the writer that Lord Dumbello has arranged with certain friends how he may escape from his present engagement. I think, therefore, that it is my duty as a Christian to warn you of this.

"Yours truly,

"A WELLWISHER."

Now it had happened that the embryo Mrs. Tickler's most intimate bosom friend and confidante was known at Plumstead to live at Littlebath, and it had also happened — most unfortunately — that the embryo Mrs. Tickler, in the warmth of her neighbourly regard, had written a friendly line to her friend Griselda Grantly, congratulating her with all female sincerity on her splendid nuptials with the Lord Dumbello.

"It is not her natural hand," said Mrs. Grantly, talking the matter over with her husband, "but you may be sure it has come from her. It is a part of the new Christianity which we learn day by day from the palace teaching."

But these things had some effect on the arch-deacon's mind. He had learned lately the story of Lady Julia Mac Mull, and was not sure that his son-in-law — as ought to be about to be — had been entirely blameless in that matter. And then in these days Lord Dumbello made no great sign. Immediately on Griselda's return to Plumstead he had sent her a magnificent present of emeralds, which, however, had come to her direct from the jewellers, and might have been — and probably was — ordered by his man of business. Since that he had neither come, nor sent, nor written. Griselda did not seem to be in any way annoyed by this absence of the usual sign of love, and went on steadily with her great duties. "Nothing," as she told her mother, "had been said about writing and, therefore, she did not expect it." But the archdeacon was not quite at his ease. "Keep Dumbello up to his P's and Q's, you know," a friend of his had whispered to him at his club. By heavens, yes. The archdeacon was not a man to bear with indifference a wrong in such a quarter. In spite of his clerical profession, few men were more inclined to fight against personal wrongs — and few men more able.

"Can there be anything wrong, I wonder?" said he to his wife. "Is it worth while that I should go up to London?" But Mrs. Grantly attributed it all to the palace doctrine. What could be more natural, looking at all the circumstances of the Tickler engagement? She therefore gave her voice against any steps being taken by the archdeacon.

A day or two after that Mrs. Proudie met Mrs. Arabin in the close and condoled with her openly on the termination of the marriage treaty; — quite openly, for Mrs. Tickler — as she was to be — was with her mother, and Mrs. Arabin was accompanied by her sister-in-law, Mary Bold.

"It must be very grievous to Mrs. Grantly, very grievous indeed," said Mrs. Proudie, "and I sincerely feel for her. But, Mrs. Arabin, all these lessons are sent to us for our eternal welfare."

"Of course," said Mrs. Arabin. "But as to this special lesson, I am inclined to doubt that it —"

"Ah-h! I fear it is too true. I fear there is no room for doubt. Of course you are aware that Lord Dumbello is off for the Continent."

Mrs. Arabin was not aware of it, and she was obliged to admit as much.

"He started four days ago, by way of Boulogne," said Mrs. Tickler, who seemed to be very well up in the whole affair. "I am so sorry for poor dear Griselda. I am told she has got all her things. It is such a pity, you know."

"But why should not Lord Dumbello come back from the Continent?" said Miss Bold, very quietly.

"Why not indeed? I'm sure I hope he may," said Mrs. Proudie. "And no doubt he will, some day. But if he be such a man as they say he is, it is really well for Griselda that she should be relieved from such a marriage. For, after all, Mrs. Arabin, what are the things of this world? — dust beneath our feet, ashes between our teeth, grass cut for the oven, vanity, vexation, and nothing more!" — well pleased with which variety of Christian metaphors Mrs. Proudie walked on, still muttering, however, something about worms and grubs, by which she intended to signify her own species and the Dumbello and Grantly sects of it in particular.

This now had gone so far that Mrs. Arabin conceived herself bound in duty to see her sister, and it was then settled in consultation at Plumstead that the archdeacon should call officially at the palace and beg that the rumour might be contradicted. This he did early on the next morning and was shown into the bishop's study, in which he found both his lordship and Mrs. Proudie. The bishop rose to greet him with special civility, smiling his very sweetest on him, as though of all his clergy the archdeacon were the favourite; but Mrs. Proudie wore something of a gloomy aspect, as though she knew that such a visit at such an hour must have reference to some special business. The morning calls made by the archdeacon at the palace in the way of ordinary civility were not numerous.

On the present occasion he dashed at once into his subject. "I have called this morning, Mrs. Proudie," said he, "because I wish to ask a favour from you." Whereupon Mrs. Proudie bowed.

"Mrs. Proudie will be most happy, I am sure," said the bishop.

"I find that some foolish people have been talking in Barchester about my daughter," said the archdeacon; "and I wish to ask Mrs. Proudie —"

Most women under such circumstances would have felt the awkwardness of their situation, and would have prepared to eat their past words with wry faces. But not so Mrs. Proudie. Mrs. Grantly had had the imprudence to throw Mr. Slope in her face — there, in her own drawing-room, and she was resolved to be revenged. Mrs. Grantly, too, had ridiculed the Tickler match, and no too great great niceness should now prevent Mrs. Proudie from speaking her mind about the Dumbello match.

"A great many people are talking about her, I am sorry to say," said Mrs. Proudie; "but, poor dear, it is not her fault. It might have happened to any girl; only, perhaps, a little more care —; you'll excuse me, Dr. Grantly."

"I have come here to allude to a report which has been spread about in Barchester, that the match between Lord Dumbello and my daughter has been broken off; and —"

"Everybody in Barchester knows it, I believe," said Mrs. Proudie.

— — "and," continued the archdeacon, "to request that that report may be contradicted."

"Contradicted! Why, he has gone right away, — out of the country!"

"Never mind where he has gone to, Mrs. Proudie; I beg that the report may be contradicted."

"You'll have to go round to every house in Barchester," said she.

"By no means," replied the archdeacon. "And perhaps, it may be right that I should explain to the bishop that I came here because —"

"The bishop knows nothing about it," said Mrs. Proudie.

"Nothing in the world," said his lordship. "And I am sure I hope that the young lady may not be disappointed."

— "because the matter was so distinctly mentioned to Mrs. Arabin by yourself yesterday."

"Distinctly mentioned! Of course it was distinctly mentioned. There are some things which can't be kept under a bushel, Dr. Grantly; and this seems to be one of them. Your going about in this way won't make Lord Dumbello marry the young lady."

That was true; nor would it make Mrs. Proudie hold her tongue. Perhaps the archdeacon was wrong in his present errand, and so he now began to bethink himself. "At any rate," said he, "when I tell you that there is no ground whatever for such a report you will do me the kindness to say that, as far as you are concerned, it shall go no further. I think, my lord, I am not asking too much in asking that."

"The bishop knows nothing about it," said Mrs. Proudie again.

"Nothing at all," said the bishop.

"And as I must protest that I believe the information which has reached me on this head," said Mrs. Proudie, "I do not see how it is possible that I should contradict it. I can easily understand your feelings, Dr. Grantly. Considering your daughter's position the match was, as regards earthly wealth, a very great one. I do not wonder that you should be grieved at its being broken off; but I trust that this sorrow may eventuate in a blessing to you and to Miss Griselda. These worldly disappointments are precious balms, and I trust you know how to accept them as such."

The fact was that Dr. Grantly had done altogether wrong in coming to the palace. His wife might have some chance with Mrs. Proudie, but he had none. Since she had come to Barchester he had had only two or three encounters with her, and in all of these he had gone to the wall. His visits to the palace always resulted in his leaving the presence of the inhabitants in a frame of mind by no means desirable, and he now found that he had to do so once again. He could not compel Mrs. Proudie to say that the report was untrue; nor could he condescend to make counter hits at her about her own daughter, as his wife would have done. And thus, having utterly failed, he got up and took his leave.

But the worst of the matter was, that, in going home, he could not divest his mind of the idea that there might be some truth in the report. What if Lord

Dumbello had gone to the Continent resolved to send back from thence some reason why it was impossible that he should make Miss Grantly his wife? Such things had been done before now by men in his rank. Whether or no Mrs. Tickler had been the letter-writing wellwisher from Littlebath, or had induced her friend to be so, it did seem manifest to him, Dr. Grantly, that Mrs. Proudie absolutely believed the report which she promulgated so diligently. The wish might be father to the thought, no doubt; but that the thought was truly there, Dr. Grantly could not induce himself to disbelieve.

His wife was less credulous, and to a certain degree comforted him; but that evening he received a letter which greatly confirmed the suspicions set on foot by Mrs. Proudie, and even shook his wife's faith in Lord Dumbello. It was from a mere acquaintance, who in the ordinary course of things would not have written to him. And the bulk of the letter referred to ordinary things, as to which the gentleman in question would hardly have thought of giving himself the trouble to write a letter. But at the end of the note he said, —

"Of course you are aware that Dumbello is off to Paris; I have not heard whether the exact day of his return is fixed."

"It is true then," said the archdeacon, striking the library table with his hand, and becoming absolutely white about the mouth and jaws.

"It cannot be," said Mrs. Grantly; but even she was now trembling.

"If it be so I'll drag him back to England by the

collar of his coat, and disgrace him before the steps of his father's hall."

And the archdeacon as he uttered the threat looked his character as an irate British father much better than he did his other character as a clergyman of the Church of England. The archdeacon had been greatly worsted by Mrs. Proudie, but he was a man who knew how to fight his battles among men, — sometimes without too close a regard to his cloth.

"Had Lord Dumbello intended any such thing he would have written, or got some friend to write by this time," said Mrs. Grantly. "It is quite possible that he might wish to be off, but he would be too chary of his name not to endeavour to do so with decency."

Thus the matter was discussed, and it appeared to them both to be so serious that the archdeacon resolved to go at once to London. That Lord Dumbello had gone to France he did not doubt; but he would find some one in town acquainted with the young man's intentions, and he would, no doubt, be able to hear when his return was expected. If there were real reason for apprehension he would follow the runagate to the Continent, but he would not do this without absolute knowledge. According to Lord Dumbello's present engagements he was bound to present himself in August next at Plumstead Episcopi, with the view of then and there taking Griselda Grantly in marriage; but if he kept his word in this respect no one had a right to quarrel with him for going to Paris in the meantime. Most expectant bridegrooms would, no doubt, under such circumstances, have declared their intentions to their future brides; but if Lord Dumbello were different from others, who had a right on that account to be indignant with him? He was unlike other men in other things; and especially unlike other men in being the eldest son of the Marquis of Hartletop. It would be all very well for Tickler to proclaim his whereabouts from week to week; but the eldest son of a marquis might find it inconvenient to be so precise! Nevertheless the archdeacon thought it only prudent to go up to London.

"Susan," said the archdeacon to his wife, just as he was starting; — at this moment neither of them were in the happiest spirits, — "I think I would say a word of caution to Griselda."

"Do you feel so much doubt about it as that?" said Mrs. Grantly. But even she did not dare to put a direct negative to this proposal, so much had she been moved by what she had heard!

"I think I would do so, not frightening her more than I could help. It will lessen the blow if it be that the blow is to fall."

"It will kill me," said Mrs. Grantly; "but I think that she will be able to bear it."

On the next morning Mrs. Grantly, with much cunning preparation, went about the task which her husband had left her to perform. It took her long to do, for she was very cunning in the doing of it; but at last it dropped from her in words that there was a possibility — a bare possibility — that some disappointment might even yet be in store for them.

"Do you mean, mamma, that the marriage will be put off?"

"I don't mean to say that I think it will; God forbid! but it is just possible. I daresay that I am very wrong to tell you of this, but I know that you have sense enough to bear it. Papa has gone to London, and we shall hear from him soon."

"Then, mamma, I had better give them orders not to go on with the marking."

CHAPTER XXII.

Lady Lufton's Request.

THE bailiffs on that day had their meals regular, — and their beer, which state of things, together with an absence of all duty in the way of making inventories and the like, I take to be the earthly paradise of bailiffs; and on the next morning they walked off with civil speeches and many apologies as to their intrusion. "They was very sorry," they said, "to have troubled a gen'leman as were a gen'leman, but in their way of business what could they do?" To which one of them added a remark that, "business is business." This statement I am not prepared to contradict, but I would recommend all men in choosing a profession to avoid any that may require an apology at every turn; — either an apology or else a somewhat violent assertion of right. Each younger male reader may perhaps reply that he has no thought of becoming a sheriff's officer; but then are there not other cognate lines of life to which perhaps the attention of some such may be attracted?

On the evening of the day on which they went Mark received a note from Lady Lufton begging him to call early on the following morning, and immediately after breakfast he went across to Framley

Court. It may be imagined that he was not in a very happy frame of mind, but he felt the truth of his wife's remark that the first plunge into cold water was always the worst. Lady Lufton was not a woman who would continually throw his disgrace into his teeth, however terribly cold might be the first words with which she spoke of it. He strove hard as he entered her room to carry his usual look and bearing, and to put out his hand to greet her with his customary freedom, but he knew that he failed. And it may be said that no good man who has broken down in his goodness can carry the disgrace of his fall without some look of shame. When a man is able to do that, he ceases to be in any way good.

"This has been a distressing affair," said Lady Lufton after her first salutation.

"Yes, indeed," said he. "It has been very sad for poor Fanny."

"Well; we must all have our little periods of grief; and it may perhaps be fortunate if none of us have worse than this. She will not complain, herself, I am sure."

"She complain!"

"No, I am sure she will not. And now all I've got to say, Mr. Robarts, is this: I hope you and Lufton have had enough to do with black sheep to last you your lives; for I must protest that your late friend Mr. Sowerby is a black sheep."

In no possible way could Lady Lufton have alluded to the matter with greater kindness than in thus joining Mark's name with that of her son. It took away all the bitterness of the rebuke, and made the subject one on which even he might have spoken without difficulty. But now, seeing that she was so gentle to him, he could not but lean the more hardly on himself.

"I have been very foolish," said he, "very foolish, and very wrong, and very wicked."

"Very foolish, I believe, Mr. Robarts — to speak frankly and once for all; but, as I also believe, nothing worse. I thought it best for both of us that we should just have one word about it, and now I recommend that the matter be never mentioned between us again."

"God bless you, Lady Lufton," he said. "I think no man ever had such a friend as you are."

She had been very quiet during the interview, and almost subdued, not speaking with the animation that was usual to her; for this affair with Mr. Robarts was not the only one she had to complete that day, nor, perhaps, the one most difficult of completion. But she cheered up a little under the praise now bestowed on her, for it was the sort of praise she loved best. She did hope, and, perhaps, flatter herself, that she was a good friend.

"You must be good enough, then, to gratify my friendship by coming up to dinner this evening; and Fanny, too, of course. I cannot take any excuse, for the matter is completely arranged. I have a particular reason for wishing it." These last violent injunctions had been added because Lady Lufton had seen a refusal rising in the parson's face. Poor Lady Lufton! Her enemies — for even she had enemies — used to declare of her, that an invitation to dinner was the only method of showing itself of which her good-humour was cognizant. But let me ask of her enemies whether it is not as good a method as any other known to be extant?

Under such orders as these obedience was of course a necessity, and he promised that he, with his wife, would come across to dinner. And then, when he went away, Lady Lufton ordered her carriage.

During these doings at Framley Lucy Robarts still remained at Hogglestock, nursing Mrs. Crawley. Nothing occurred to take her back to Framley, for the same note from Fanny which gave her the first tidings of the arrival of the Philistines told her also of their departure — and also of the source from whence relief had reached them. "Don't come, therefore, for that reason," said the note, "but, nevertheless, do come as quickly as you can, for the whole house is sad without you."

On the morning after the receipt of this note Lucy was sitting, as was now usual with her, beside an old arm-chair to which her patient had lately been promoted. The fever had gone, and Mrs. Crawley was slowly regaining her strength — very slowly, and with frequent caution from the Silverbridge doctor that any attempt at being well too fast might again precipitate her into an abyss of illness and domestic inefficiency.

"I really think I can get about to-morrow," said she; "and then, dear Lucy, I need not keep you longer from your home."

"You are in a great hurry to get rid of me, I think. I suppose Mr. Crawley has been complaining again about the cream in his tea."

Mr. Crawley had on one occasion stated his assured conviction that surreptitious daily supplies were being brought into the house, because he had detected the presence of cream instead of milk in his own cup. As, however, the cream had been going for sundry days before this Miss Robarts had not thought much of his ingenuity in making the discovery.

"Ah, you do not know how he speaks of you when your back is turned."

"And how does he speak of me? I know you would not have the courage to tell me the whole."

"No, I have not; for you would think it absurd coming from one who looks like him. He says that if he were to write a poem about womanhood, he would make you the heroine."

"With a cream-jug in my hand, or else sewing buttons on to a shirt-collar. But he never forgave me about the mutton broth. He told me, in so many words, that I was a — storyteller. And for the matter of that, my dear, so I was."

"He told me that you were an angel."

"Goodness gracious!"

"A ministering angel. And so you have been. I can almost feel it in my heart to be glad that I have been ill, seeing that I have had you for my friend."

"But you might have had that good fortune without the fever."

"No, I should not. In my married life I have made no friends till my illness brought you to me; nor should I ever really have known you but for that. How should I get to know any one?"

"You will now, Mrs. Crawley; will you not? Promise that you will. You will come to us at Framley when you are well? You have promised already, you know."

"You made me do so when I was too weak to refuse."

"And I shall make you keep your promise too.

He shall come, also, if he likes; but you shall come whether he likes or no. And I won't hear a word about your old dresses. Old dresses will wear as well at Framley as at Hogglestock."

From all which it will appear that Mrs. Crawley and Lucy Robarts had become very intimate during this period of the nursing; as two women always will, or, at least, should do, when shut up for weeks together in the same sick room.

The conversation was still going on between them when the sound of wheels was heard upon the road. It was no highway that passed before the house, and carriages of any sort were not frequent there.

"It is Fanny, I am sure," said Lucy, rising from her chair.

"There are two horses," said Mrs. Crawley, distinguishing the noise with the accurate sense of hearing which is always attached to sickness; "and it is not the noise of the pony-carriage."

"It is a regular carriage," said Lucy, speaking from the window, "and stopping here. It is somebody from Framley Court, for I know the servant."

As she spoke a blush came to her forehead. Might it not be Lord Lufton, she thought to herself, — forgetting at the moment that Lord Lufton did not go about the country in a close chariot with a fat footman. Intimate as she had become with Mrs. Crawley she had said nothing to her new friend on the subject of her love affair.

The carriage stopped, and down came the footman, but nobody spoke to him from the inside.

"He has probably brought something from Framley," said Lucy, having cream and such like matters in her mind; for cream and such like matters had come from Framley Court more than once during her sojourn there. "And the carriage, probably, happened to be coming this way."

But the mystery soon elucidated itself partially, or, perhaps, became more mysterious in another way. The red-armed little girl who had been taken away by her frightened mother in the first burst of the fever had now returned to her place, and at the present moment entered the room, with awestruck face, declaring that Miss Robarts was to go at once to the big lady in the carriage.

"I suppose it's Lady Lufton," said Mrs. Crawley.

Lucy's heart was so absolutely in her mouth that any kind of speech was at the moment impossible to her. Why should Lady Lufton have come thither to Hogglestock, and why should she want to see her, Lucy Robarts, in the carriage? Had not everything between them been settled? And yet ——! Lucy, in the moment for thought that was allowed to her, could not determine what might be the probable upshot of such an interview. Her chief feeling was a desire to postpone it for the present instant. But the red-armed little girl would not allow that.

"You are to come at once," said she.

And then Lucy, without having spoken a word, got up and left the room. She walked downstairs, along the little passage, and out through the small garden, with firm steps, but hardly knowing whither she went or why. Her presence of mind and self-possession had all deserted her. She knew that she was unable to speak as she should do; she felt that she would have to regret her present behaviour, but yet she could not help herself. Why should Lady Lufton have come to her there? She went on, and the big footman stood with the carriage door open. She stepped up almost unconsciously, and, without knowing how she got there, she found herself seated by Lady Lufton.

To tell the truth her ladyship also was a little at a loss to know how she was to carry through her present plan of operations. The duty of beginning, however, was clearly with her, and therefore, having taken Lucy by the hand, she spoke.

"Miss Robarts," she said, "my son has come home. I don't know whether you are aware of it."

She spoke with a low, gentle voice, not quite like herself, but Lucy was much too confused to notice this.

"I was not aware of it," said Lucy.

She had, however, been so informed in Fanny's letter, but all that had gone out of her head.

"Yes; he has come back. He has been in Norway, you know, — fishing."

"Yes," said Lucy.

"I am sure you will remember all that took place when you came to me, not long ago, in my little room upstairs at Framley Court."

In answer to which, Lucy, quivering in every nerve, and wrongly thinking that she was visibly shaking in every limb, timidly answered that she did remember. Why was it that she had then been so bold, and now was so poor a coward?

"Well, my dear, all that I said to you then I said to you thinking that it was for the best. You, at any rate, will not be angry with me for loving my own son better than I love any one else."

"Oh, no," said Lucy.

"He is the best of sons, and the best of men, and I am sure that he will be the best of husbands."

Lucy had an idea, by instinct, however, rather than by sight, that Lady Lufton's eyes were full of tears as she spoke. As for herself she was altogether blinded and did not dare to lift her face or to turn her head. As for the utterance of any sound, that was quite out of the question.

"And now I have come here, Lucy, to ask you to be his wife."

She was quite sure that she heard the words. They came plainly to her ears, leaving on her brain their proper sense, but yet she could not move or make any sign that she had understood them. It seemed as though it would be ungenerous in her to take advantage of such conduct and to accept an offer made with so much self-sacrifice. She had not time at the first moment to think even of his happiness, let alone her own, but she thought only of the magnitude of the concession which had been made to her. When she had constituted Lady Lufton the arbiter of her destiny she had regarded the question of her love as decided against herself. She had found herself unable to endure the position of being Lady Lufton's daughter-in-law while Lady Lufton would be scorning her, and therefore she had given up the game. She had given up the game, sacrificing herself, and, as far as it might be a sacrifice, sacrificing him also. She had been resolute to stand to her word in this respect, but she had never allowed herself to think it possible that Lady Lufton should comply with the conditions which she, Lucy, had laid upon her. And yet such was the case, as she so plainly heard. "And now I have come here, Lucy, to ask you to be his wife."

How long they sat together silent, I cannot say; counted by minutes the time would not probably have amounted to many, but to each of them the duration seemed considerable. Lady Lufton, while she was speaking, had contrived to get hold of Lucy's hand, and she sat, still holding it, trying to look into Lucy's face, — which, however, she could hardly see, so much was it turned away. Neither, indeed, were Lady Lufton's eyes perfectly dry. No answer came to her question, and therefore, after a while, it was necessary that she should speak again.

"Must I go back to him, Lucy, and tell him that there is some other objection — something besides a stern old mother; some hindrance, perhaps, not so easily overcome."

"No," said Lucy, and it was all which at the moment she could say.

"What shall I tell him, then? Shall I say yes — simply yes."

"Simply yes," said Lucy.

"And as to the stern old mother who thought her only son too precious to be parted with at the first word — is nothing to be said to her?"

"Oh, Lady Lufton!"

"No forgiveness to be spoken, no sign of affection to be given? Is she always to be regarded as stern and cross, vexatious and disagreeable?"

Lucy slowly turned round her head and looked up into her companion's face. Though she had as yet no voice to speak of affection she could fill her eyes with love, and in that way make to her future mother all the promises that were needed.

"Lucy, dearest Lucy, you must be very dear to

me now." And then they were in each other's arms, kissing each other.

Lady Lufton now desired her coachman to drive up and down for some little space along the road while she completed her necessary conversation with Lucy. She wanted at first to carry her back to Framley that evening, promising to send her again to Mrs. Crawley on the following morning — "till some permanent arrangement could be made," by which Lady Lufton intended the substitution of a regular nurse for her future daughter-in-law, seeing that Lucy Robarts was now invested in her eyes with attributes which made it unbecoming that she should sit in attendance at Mrs. Crawley's bedside. But Lucy would not go back to Framley on that evening; no, nor on the next morning. She would be so glad if Fanny would come to her there, and then she would arrange about going home.

"But Lucy, dear, what am I to say to Ludovic? Perhaps you would feel it awkward if he were to come to see you here."

"Oh, yes, Lady Lufton; pray tell him not to do that."

"And is that all that I am to tell him?"

"Tell him — tell him — He won't want you to tell him anything; — only I should like to be quiet for a day, Lady Lufton."

"Well, dearest, you shall be quiet; the day after to-morrow then. — Mind, we must not spare you any longer, because it will be right that you should be at home now. He would think it very hard if you were to be so near, and he was not to be allowed to look at you. And there will be some one else who will want to see you. I shall want to have you very near to me, for I shall be wretched, Lucy, if I cannot teach you to love me." In answer to which Lucy did find voice enough to make sundry promises.

And then she was put out of the carriage at the little wicket gate, and Lady Lufton was driven back to Framley. I wonder whether the servant when he held the door for Miss Robarts was conscious that he was waiting on his future mistress. I fancy that he was, for these sort of people always know everything, and the peculiar courtesy of his demeanour as he let down the carriage steps was very observable.

Lucy felt almost beside herself as she returned upstairs, not knowing what to do, or how to look, and with what words to speak. It behoved her to go at once to Mrs. Crawley's room, and yet she longed to be alone. She knew that she was quite unable either to conceal her thoughts or express them; nor did she wish at the present moment to talk to any one about her happiness, — seeing that she could not at the present moment talk to Fanny Robarts. She went, however, without delay into Mrs. Crawley's room, and with that little eager way of speaking quickly which is so common with people who know that they are confused, said that she feared she had been a very long time away.

"And was it Lady Lufton?"

"Yes; it was Lady Lufton."

"Why, Lucy; I did not know that you and her ladyship were such friends."

"She had something particular she wanted to say," said Lucy, avoiding the question, and avoiding also Mrs. Crawley's eyes; and then she sat down in her usual chair.

"It was nothing unpleasant, I hope."

"No, nothing at all unpleasant; nothing of that kind. — Oh, Mrs. Crawley, I'll tell you some other time, but pray do not ask me now." And then she got up and escaped, for it was absolutely necessary that she should be alone.

When she reached her own room — that in which the children usually slept — she made a great effort to compose herself, but not altogether successfully. She got out her paper and blotting-book, intending, as she said to herself, to write to Fanny, knowing, however, that the letter when written would be destroyed; but she was not able even to form a word. Her hand was unsteady and her eyes were dim and her thoughts were incapable of being fixed. She could only sit, and think, and wonder and hope; occasionally wiping the tears from her eyes, and asking herself why her present frame of mind was so painful to her? During the last two or three months she had felt no fear of Lord Lufton, had always carried herself before him on equal terms, and had been signally capable of doing so when he made his declaration to her at the parsonage; but now she looked forward with an undefined dread to the first moment in which she should see him.

And then she thought of a certain evening she had passed at Framley Court, and acknowledged to herself that there was some pleasure in looking back to that. Griselda Grantly had been there, and all the constitutional powers of the two families had been at work to render easy a process of love-making between her and Lord Lufton. Lucy had seen and understood it all, without knowing that she understood it, and had, in a certain degree, suffered from beholding it. She had placed herself apart, not complaining — painfully conscious of some inferiority, but, at the same time, almost boasting to herself that in her own way she was the superior. And then he had come behind her chair, whispering to her, speaking to her his first words of kindness and good-nature, and she had resolved that she would be his friend — his friend, even though Griselda Grantly might be his wife. What those resolutions were worth had soon become manifest to her. She had soon confessed to herself the result of that friendship, and had determined to bear her punishment with courage. But now —

She sate so for about an hour, and would fain have so sat out the day. But as this could not be, she got up, and having washed her face and eyes returned to Mrs. Crawley's room. There she found Mr. Crawley also, to her great joy, for she knew that while he was there no questions would be asked of her. He was always very gentle to her, treating her with an old-fashioned, polished respect — except when compelled on that one occasion by his sense of duty to accuse her of mendacity respecting the purveying of victuals —, but he had never become absolutely familiar with her as his wife had done; and it was well for her now that he had not done so, for she could not have talked about Lady Lufton.

In the evening, when the three were present, she did manage to say that she expected Mrs. Robarts would come over on the following day.

"We shall part with you, Miss Robarts, with the deepest regret," said Mr. Crawley; "but we would not on any account keep you longer. Mrs. Crawley can do without you now. What she would have done, had you not come to us, I am at a loss to think."

"I did not say that I should go," said Lucy.

"But you will," said Mrs. Crawley. "Yes, dear, you will. I know that it is proper now that you should return. Nay, but we will not have you any longer. And the poor dear children, too, — they may return. How am I to thank Mrs. Robarts for what she has done for us?"

It was settled that if Mrs. Robarts came on the following day Lucy should go back with her; and then, during the long watches of the night — for on this last night Lucy would not leave the bed-side of her new friend till long after the dawn had broken, she did tell Mrs. Crawley what was to be her destiny in life. To herself there seemed nothing strange in her new position; but to Mrs. Crawley it was wonderful that she — she, poor as she was — should have an embryo peeress at her bedside, handing her her cup to drink, and smoothing her pillow that she might be at rest. It was strange, and she could hardly maintain her accustomed familiarity. Lucy felt this at the moment.

"It must make no difference, you know," said she, eagerly; "none at all, between you and me. Promise me that it shall make no difference."

The promise was, of course, exacted; but it was not possible that such a promise should be kept.

Very early on the following morning — so early that it woke her while still in her first sleep — there came a letter for her from the parsonage. Mrs. Robarts had written it, after her return home from Lady Lufton's dinner.

The letter said: —

"MY OWN OWN DARLING,

"How am I to congratulate you, and be eager enough in wishing you joy? I do wish you joy, and am so very happy. I write now chiefly to say that I shall be over with you about twelve to-morrow, and that I *must* bring you away with me. If I did not some one else, by no means so trustworthy, would insist on doing it."

But this, though it was thus stated to be the chief part of the letter, and though it might be so in matter, was by no means so in space. It was very long, for Mrs. Robarts had sat writing it till past midnight.

"I will not say anything about him," she went on to say, after two pages had been filled with his name, "but I must tell you how beautifully she has behaved. You will own that she is a dear woman; will you not?"

Lucy had already owned it many times since the visit of yesterday, and had declared to herself, as she has continued to declare ever since, that she had never doubted it.

"She took us by surprise when we got into the drawing-room before dinner, and she told us first of all that she had been to see you at Hogglestock. Lord Lufton, of course, could not keep the secret, but brought it out instantly. I can't tell you now how he told it all, but I am sure you will believe that he did it in the best possible manner. He took my hand and pressed it half a dozen times, and I thought he was going to do something else; but he did not, so you need not be jealous. And she was so nice to Mark, saying such things in praise of you, and paying all manner of compliments to your father. But Lord Lufton scolded her immensely for not bringing you. He said it was lackadaisical and nonsensical; but I could see how much he loved her for what she had done; and she could see it too, for I know her ways, and know that she was delighted with him. She could not keep her eyes off him all the evening, and certainly I never did see him look so well.

"And then while Lord Lufton and Mark were in the dining-room, where they remained a terribly long time, she would make me go through the house that she might show me your rooms, and explain how you were to be mistress there. She has got it all arranged to perfection, and I am sure she has been thinking about it for years. Her great fear at present is that you and he should go and live at Lufton. If you have any gratitude in you, either to her or me, you will not let him do this. I consoled her by saying that there are not two stones upon one another at Lufton as yet;

and I believe such is the case. Besides, everybody says that it is the ugliest spot in the world. She went on to declare, with tears in her eyes, that if you were content to remain at Framley, she would never interfere in anything. I do think that she is the best woman that ever lived."

So much as I have given of this letter formed but a small portion of it, but it comprises all that it is necessary that we should know. Exactly at twelve o'clock on that day Puck the Pony appeared, with Mrs. Robarts and Grace Crawley behind him, Grace having been brought back as being capable of some service in the house. Nothing that was confidential, and very little that was loving, could be said at the moment, because Mr. Crawley was there, waiting to bid Miss Robarts adieu; and he had not as yet been informed of what was to be the future fate of his visitor. So they could only press each other's hands and embrace, which to Lucy was almost a relief; for even to her sister-in-law she hardly as yet knew how to speak openly on this subject.

"May God Almighty bless you, Miss Robarts," said Mr. Crawley, as he stood in his dingy sitting-room ready to lead her out to the pony-carriage. "You have brought sunshine into this house, even in the time of sickness, when there was no sunshine; and He will bless you. You have been the Good Samaritan, binding up the wounds of the afflicted, pouring in oil and balm. To the mother of my children you have given life, and to me you have brought light, and comfort, and good words, — making my spirit glad within me, as it had not been gladdened before. All this hath come of charity, which vaunteth not itself and is not puffed up. Faith and hope are great and beautiful, but charity exceedeth them all." And having so spoken, instead of leading her out, he went away and hid himself.

How Puck behaved himself as Fanny drove him back to Framley, and how those two ladies in the carriage behaved themselves — of that, perhaps, nothing further need be said.

CHAPTER XXIII.

Nemesis.

But in spite of all these joyful tidings it must, alas! be remembered that Pœna, that just but Rhadamanthine goddess, whom we moderns ordinarily call Punishment, or Nemesis when we wish to speak of her goddess-ship, very seldom fails to catch a wicked man though she have sometimes a lame foot of her own, and though the wicked man may possibly get a start of her. In this instance the wicked man had been our unfortunate friend Mark Robarts; wicked in that he had wittingly touched pitch, gone to Gatherum Castle, ridden fast mares across the country to Cobbold's Ashes, and fallen very imprudently among the Tozers; and the instrument used by Nemesis was Mr. Tom Towers of the *Jupiter*, than whom, in these our days, there is no deadlier scourge in the hands of that goddess.

In the first instance, however, I must mention, though I will not relate, a little conversation which took place between Lady Lufton and Mr. Robarts. That gentleman thought it right to say a few words more to her ladyship respecting those money transactions. He could not but feel, he said, that he had received that prebendal stall from the hands of Mr. Sowerby; and under such circumstances, considering all that had happened, he could not be easy in his mind as long as he held it. What he was about to do would, he was aware, delay considerably his final settlement with Lord Lufton; but Lufton, he hoped, would pardon that, and agree with him as to the propriety of what he was about to do.

On the first blush of the thing Lady Lufton did not quite go along with him. Now that Lord Lufton was to marry the parson's sister it might be well that the parson should be a dignitary of the church; and it might be well, also, that one so nearly connected with her son should be comfortable in his money matters. There loomed also, in the future, some distant possibility of higher clerical honours for a peer's brother-in-law; and the top rung of the ladder is always more easily attained when a man has already ascended a step or two. But nevertheless, when the matter came to be fully explained to her, when she saw clearly the circumstances under which the stall had been conferred, she did agree that it had better be given up.

And well for both of them it was — well for them all at Framley — that this conclusion had been reached before the scourge of Nemesis had fallen. Nemesis, of course, declared that her scourge had produced the resignation; but it was generally understood that this was a false boast, for all clerical men at Barchester knew that the stall had been restored to the chapter, or, in other words, into the hands of the Government, before Tom Towers had twirled the fatal lash above his head. But the manner of the twirling was as follows: —

"It is with difficulty enough," said the article in the *Jupiter*, "that the Church of England maintains at the present moment that ascendancy among the religious sects of this country which it so loudly claims. And perhaps it is rather from an old-fashioned and time-honoured affection for its standing than from any intrinsic merits of its own that some such general acknowledgment of its ascendancy is still allowed to prevail. If, however, the patrons and clerical members of this Church are bold enough to disregard all general rules of decent behaviour, we think we may predict that this chivalrous feeling will be found to give way. From time to time we hear of instances of such imprudence, and are made to wonder at the folly of those who are supposed to hold the State Church in the greatest reverence.

"Among those positions of dignified ease to which fortunate clergymen may be promoted are the stalls of the canons or prebendaries in our cathedrals. Some of these, as is well known, carry little or no emolument with them, but some are rich in the good things of this world. Excellent family houses are attached to them, with we hardly know what domestic privileges, and clerical incomes, moreover, of an amount which, if divided, would make glad the hearts of many a hard-working clerical slave. Reform has been busy even among these stalls, attaching some amount of work to the pay, and paring off some superfluous wealth from such of them as were over full; but reform has been lenient with them, acknowledging that it was well to have some such places of comfortable and dignified retirement for those who have worn themselves ont in the hard work of their profession. There has of late prevailed a taste for the appointment of young bishops, produced no doubt by a feeling that bishops should be men fitted to get through really hard work; but we have never heard that young prebendaries were considered desirable. A clergyman selected for such a position should, we have always thought, have earned an evening of ease by a long day of work, and should, above all things, be one whose life has been, and therefore in human probability will be, so decorous as to be honourable to the cathedral of his adoption.

"We were, however, the other day given to understand that one of these luxurious benefices, belonging to the cathedral of Barchester had been bestowed on the Rev. Mark Robarts, the vicar of a neighbouring parish, on the nnderstanding that he should hold the living and the stall together; and on making further inquiry we were surprised to learn that this fortunate gentleman is as yet considerably under thirty years of age. We were desirous, however, of believing that his learning, his piety, and his conduct, might be of a nature to add peculiar grace to his chapter, and therefore, though almost unwillingly, we were silent. But now it has come to our ears, and, indeed, to the ears of all the world, that this piety and conduct are sadly wanting; and judging of Mr. Robarts by his life and associates, we are inclined to donbt even the learning. He has at this moment, or at any rate had but a few days since, an execution in his parsonage house at Framley, on the suit of certain most disreputable bill discounters in London; and probably would have another execution in his other house in Barchester close, but for the fact that he has never thought it necessary to go into residence."

Then followed some very stringent, and, no doubt, much-needed advice to those clerical members of the Church of England who are supposed to be mainly responsible for the conduct of their brethren; and the article ended as follows: —

"Many of these stalls are in the gift of the respective deans and chapters, and in such cases the dean and chapters are bound to see that proper persons are appointed; but in other instances the power of selection is vested in the Crown, and then an equal responsibility rests on the government of the day. Mr. Robarts, we learn, was appointed to the stall in Barchester by the late Prime Minister, and we really think that a grave censure rests on him for the manner in which his patronage has been exercised. It may be impossible that he should himself in all such cases satisfy himself by personal inquiry. But our government is altogether conducted on the footing of vicarial responsibility. *Quod facit per alium, facit per se,* is in a special manner true of our ministers, and any man who rises to high position among them must abide by the danger thereby incurred. In this peculiar case we are informed that the recommendation was made by a very recently admitted member of the Cabinet, to whose appointment we alluded at the time as a great mistake. The gentleman in question held no high individual office of his own; but evil such as this which has now been done at Barchester, is exactly the sort of mischief which follows the exaltation of unfit men to high positions, even though no great scope for executive failure may be placed within their reach.

"If Mr. Robarts will allow us to tender to him our advice he will lose no time in going through such ceremony as may be necessary again to place the stall at the disposal of the Crown!"

I may here observe that poor Harold Smith, when he read this, writhing in agony, declared it to be the handiwork of his hated enemy, Mr. Supplehouse. He knew the mark; so, at least, he said; but I myself am inclined to believe that his animosity misled him. I think that one greater than Mr. Supplehouse had taken upon himself the punishment of our poor vicar.

This was very dreadful to them all at Framley, and, when first read, seemed to crush them to atoms. Poor Mrs. Robarts, when she heard it, seemed to think that for them the world was over. An attempt had been made to keep it from her, but such attempts always fail, as did this. The article was copied into all the good-natured local newspapers, and she soon discovered that something was being hidden. At last it was shown to her by her husband, and then for a few hours she was annihilated; for a few days she was unwilling to show herself; and for a few weeks she was very sad. But after that the world seemed to go on much as it had done before, the sun shone upon them as warmly as though the article had not been written; and not only the sun of heaven, which as a rule, is not limited in his shining by any display of pagan thunder, but also the genial sun of their own sphere, the warmth and light of which were so essentially necessary to their happiness. Neighbouring rectors did not look glum, nor did the rectors' wives refuse to call. The people in the shops at Barchester did not regard her as though she were a disgraced woman, though it must be acknowledged that Mrs. Proudie passed her in the close with the coldest nod of recognition.

On Mrs. Proudie's mind alone did the article seem to have any enduring effect. In one respect it was, perhaps, beneficial; Lady Lufton was at once induced by it to make common cause with her own clergyman, and thus the remembrance of Mr. Robarts' sins passed away the quicker from the minds of the whole Framley Court household.

And, indeed, the county at large was not able to give to the matter that undivided attention which would have been considered its due at periods of no more than ordinary interest. At the present moment preparations were being made for a general election, and although no contest was to take place in the eastern division, a very violent fight was being carried on in the west; and the circumstances of that fight were so exciting that Mr. Robarts and his article were forgotten before their time. An edict had gone forth from Gatherum Castle directing that Mr. Sowerby should be turned out, and an answering note of defiance had been sounded from Chaldicotes, protesting on behalf of Mr. Sowerby, that the duke's behest would not be obeyed.

There are two classes of persons in this realm who are constitutionally inefficient to take any part in returning members to Parliament — peers, namely, and women; and yet it was soon known through the whole length and breadth of the county that the present electioneering fight was being carried on between a peer and a woman. Miss Dunstable had been declared the purchaser of the Chase of Chaldicotes, as it were just in the very nick of time; which purchase — so men in Barsetshire declared, not knowing anything of the facts — would have gone altogether the other way, had not the giants obtained temporary supremacy over the gods. The duke was a supporter of the gods, and therefore, so Mr. Fothergill hinted, his money had been refused. Miss Dunstable was prepared to beard this ducal friend of the gods in his own county, and therefore her money had been taken. I am inclined, however, to think that Mr. Fothergill knew nothing about it, and to opine that Miss Dunstable, in her eagerness for victory offered to the Crown more money than the property was worth in the duke's opinion, and that the Crown took advantage of her anxiety, to the manifest profit of the public at large.

And it soon became known also that Miss Dunstable was, in fact, the proprietor of the whole Chaldicotes estate, and that in promoting the success of Mr. Sowerby as a candidate for the county, she was standing by her own tenant. It also became known, in the course of the battle, that Miss Dunstable had herself at last succumbed, and that she was about to marry Dr. Thorne of Greshamsbury, or the "Greshamsbury apothecary," as the adverse party now delighted to call him. "He has been little better than a quack all his life," said Dr. Fillgrave, the eminent physician of Barchester, "and now he is going to marry a quack's daughter." By which, and the like to which, Dr. Thorne did not allow himself to be much annoyed.

But all this gave rise to a very pretty series of squibs arranged between Mr. Fothergill and Mr. Closerstill, the electioneering agent. Mr. Sowerby was named "the lady's pet," and descriptions were given of the lady who kept this pet, which were by no means flattering to Miss Dunstable's appearance, or manners, or age. And then the western division of the county was asked in a grave tone — as counties and boroughs are asked by means of advertisements stuck up on blind walls and barn doors — whether it was fitting and proper that it should be represented by a woman. Upon which the county was again asked whether it was fitting and proper that it should be represented by a duke. And then the question became more personal as against Miss Dunstable, and inquiry was urged whether the county would not be indelibly disgraced if it were not only handed over to a woman, but handed over to a woman who sold the oil of Lebanon. But little was got by this move, for an answering placard explained to the unfortunate county how deep would be its shame if it allowed itself to become the appanage of any peer, but more especially of a peer who was known to be the most immoral lord that ever disgraced the benches of the upper house.

And so the battle went on very prettily, and, as money was allowed to flow freely, the West Barsetshire world at large was not ill satisfied. It is wonderful how much disgrace of that kind a borough or county can endure without flinching; and wonderful, also, seeing how supreme is the value attached to the constitution by the realm at large, how very little the principles of that constitution are valued by the people in detail. The duke, of course, did not show himself. He rarely did on any occasion, and never on such occasions as this; but Mr. Fothergill was to be seen everywhere. Miss Dunstable, also, did not hide her light under a bushel; though I here declare, on the faith of an historian, that the rumour spread abroad of her having made a speech to the electors from the top of the porch over the hotel-door at Courcy was not founded on fact. No doubt she was at Courcy, and her carriage stopped at the hotel; but neither there nor elsewhere did she make any public exhibition. "They must have mistaken me for Mrs. Proudie," she said, when the rumour reached her ears.

But there was, alas! one great element of failure on Miss Dunstable's side of the battle. Mr. Sowerby himself could not be induced to fight it as became a man. Any positive injunctions that were laid upon him he did, in a sort, obey. It had been a part of the bargain that he should stand the contest, and from that bargain he could not well go back; but he had not the spirit left to him for any true fighting on his own part. He could not go up on the hustings, and there defy the duke. Early in the affair Mr. Fothergill challenged him to do so, and Mr. Sowerby never took up the gauntlet.

"We have heard," said Mr. Fothergill, in that great speech which he made at the Omnium Arms at Silverbridge — "we have heard much during this election of the Duke of Omnium, and of the injuries which he is supposed to have inflicted on one of the candidates. The duke's name is very frequent in the mouths of the gentlemen, — and of the lady, — who support Mr. Sowerby's claims. But I do not think that Mr. Sowerby himself has dared to say much about the duke. I defy Mr. Sowerby to mention the duke's name upon the hustings."

And it so happened that Mr. Sowerby never did mention the duke's name.

It is ill fighting when the spirit is gone, and Mr. Sowerby's spirit for such things was now well nigh broken. It is true that he had escaped from the net in which the duke, by Mr. Fothergill's aid, had entangled him; but he had only broken out of one captivity into another. Money is a serious thing; and when gone cannot be had back by a shuffle in the game, or a fortunate blow with the battledore, as may political power, or reputation, or fashion. One hundred thousand pounds gone, must remain as gone, let the person who claims to have had the honour of advancing it be Mrs. B. or my Lord C. No lucky dodge can erase such a claim from the things that be — unless, indeed, such dodge be possible as Mr. Sowerby tried with Miss Dunstable. It was better for him, undoubtedly, to have the lady for a creditor than the duke, seeing that it was possible for him to live as a tenant in his own old house under the lady's reign. But this he found to be a sad enough life, after all that was come and gone.

The election on Miss Dunstable's part was lost. She carried on the contest nobly, fighting it to the last moment, and sparing neither her own money nor that of her antagonist; but she carried it on unsuccessfully. Many gentlemen did support Mr. Sowerby because they were willing enough to emancipate their county from the duke's thraldom; but Mr. Sowerby was felt to be a black sheep, as Lady Lufton had called him, and at the close of the election he found himself banished from the representation of West Barchester; — banished for ever, after having held the county for five-and-twenty years.

Unfortunate Mr. Sowerby! I cannot take leave of him here without some feeling of regret, knowing that there was that within him which might, under better guidance, have produced better things. There are men even of high birth, who seem as though they were born to be rogues; but Mr. Sowerby was, to my thinking, born to be a gentleman. That he had not been a gentleman — that he had bolted from his appointed course, going terribly on the wrong side of the posts — let us all acknowledge. It is not a gentlemanlike deed, but a very blackguard action, to obtain a friend's acceptance to a bill in an unguarded hour of social intercourse. That and other similar doings have stamped his character too plainly. But, nevertheless, I claim a tear for Mr. Sowerby, and lament that he has failed to run his race discreetly, in accordance with the rules of the Jockey Club.

He attempted that plan of living as a tenant in his

old house at Chaldicotes and of making a living out of the land which he farmed; but he soon abandoned it. He had no aptitude for such industry, and could not endure his altered position in the county. He soon relinquished Chaldicotes of his own accord, and has vanished away, as such men do vanish — not altogether without necessary income; to which point in the final arrangement of their joint affairs, Mrs. Thorne's man of business — if I may be allowed so far to anticipate — paid special attention.

And thus Lord Dumbello, the duke's nominee, got in, as the duke's nominee had done for very many years past. There was no Nemesis here — none as yet. Nevertheless, she with the lame foot will assuredly catch him, the duke, if it be that he deserve to be caught. With us his grace's appearance has been so unfrequent that I think we may omit to make any further inquiry as to his concerns.

One point, however, is worthy of notice, as showing the good sense with which we manage our affairs here in England. In an early portion of this story the reader was introduced to the interior of Gatherum Castle, and there saw Miss Dunstable entertained by the duke in the most friendly manner. Since those days the lady has become the duke's neighbour, and has waged a war with him, which he probably felt to be very vexatious. But, nevertheless, on the next great occasion at Gatherum Castle Doctor and Mrs. Thorne were among the visitors, and to no one was the duke more personally courteous than to his opulent neighbour, the late Miss Dunstable.

CHAPTER XXIV.

How they were all Married, had Two Children, and lived Happy ever after.

DEAR, affectionate, sympathetic readers, we have four couple of sighing lovers with whom to deal in this our last chapter, and I, as leader of the chorus, disdain to press you further with doubts as to the happiness of any of that quadrille. They were all made happy, in spite of that little episode which so lately took place at Barchester; and in telling of their happiness — shortly, as is now necessary — we will take them chronologically, giving precedence to those who first appeared at the hymeneal altar.

In July, then, at the cathedral, by the father of the bride, assisted by his examining chaplain, Olivia Proudie, the eldest daughter of the Bishop of Barchester, was joined in marriage to the Rev. Tobias Tickler, incumbent of the Trinity district church in Bethnal Green. Of the bridegroom, in this instance, our acquaintance has been so short, that it is not, perhaps, necessary to say much. When coming to the wedding he proposed to bring his three darling children with him; but in this measure he was, I think prudently, stopped by advice, rather strongly worded, from his future valued mother-in-law. Mr. Tickler was not an opulent man, nor had he hitherto attained any great fame in his profession; but, at the age of forty-three he still had sufficient opportunity before him, and now that his merit has been properly viewed by high ecclesiastical eyes the refreshing dew of deserved promotion will no doubt fall upon him. The marriage was very smart, and Olivia carried herself through the trying ordeal with an excellent propriety of conduct.

Up to that time, and even for a few days longer, there was doubt at Barchester as to that strange journey which Lord Dumbello undoubtedly did take to France. When a man so circumstanced will suddenly go to Paris, without notice given even to his future bride, people must doubt; and grave were the apprehensions expressed on this occasion by Mrs. Proudie, even at her child's wedding-breakfast. "God bless you, my dear children," she said, standing up at the head of her table as she addressed Mr. Tickler and his wife; "when I see your perfect happiness — perfect, that is, as far as human happiness can be made perfect in this vale of tears — and think of the terrible calamity which has fallen on our unfortunate neighbours, I cannot but acknowledge His infinite mercy and goodness. The Lord giveth, and the Lord taketh away." By which she intended, no doubt, to signify that whereas Mr. Tickler had been given to her Olivia, Lord Dumbello had been taken away from the archdeacon's Griselda. The happy couple then went in Mrs. Proudie's carriage to the nearest railway station but one, and from thence proceeded to Malvern, and there spent the honeymoon.

And a great comfort it was, I am sure, to Mrs. Proudie when authenticated tidings reached Barchester that Lord Dumbello had returned from Paris, and that the Hartletop-Grantly alliance was to be carried to its completion. She still, however, held her opinion — whether correctly or not who shall say? — that the young lord had intended to escape. "The archdeacon has shown great firmness in the way in which he has done it," said Mrs. Proudie; "but whether he has consulted his child's best interests in forcing her into a marriage with an unwilling husband, I for one must take leave to doubt. But then, unfortunately, we all know how completely the archdeacon is devoted to worldly matters."

In this instance the archdeacon's devotion to worldly matters was rewarded by that success which he no doubt desired. He did go up to London, and did see one or two of Lord Dumbello's friends. This he did, not obtrusively, as though in fear of any falsehood or vacillation on the part of the viscount, but with that discretion and tact for which he has been so long noted. Mrs. Proudie declares that during the few days of his absence from Barsetshire he himself crossed to France and hunted down Lord Dumbello at Paris. As to this I am not prepared to say anything; but I am quite sure, as will be all those who knew the archdeacon, that he was not a man to see his daughter wronged as long as any measure remained by which such wrong might be avoided.

But, be that as it may — that mooted question as to the archdeacon's journey to Paris — Lord Dumbello was forthcoming at Plumstead on the 5th of August, and went through his work like a man. The Hartletop family, when the alliance was found to be unavoidable, endeavoured to arrange that the wedding should be held at Hartletop Priory, in order that the clerical dust and dinginess of Barchester Close might not soil the splendour of the marriage gala doings; for, to tell the truth, the Hartletopians, as a rule, were not proud of their new clerical connections. But on this subject Mrs. Grantly was very properly inexorable; nor, when an attempt was made on the bride to induce her to throw over her mamma at the last moment and pronounce for herself that she would be married at the priory, was it attended with any success. The Hartletopians knew nothing of the Grantly fibre and calibre, or they would have made no such attempt. The marriage took place at Plumstead, and on the morning of the day Lord Dumbello posted over from Barchester to the rectory. The ceremony was performed by the archdeacon, without assistance, although the dean, and the precentor, and two other clergymen, were at the ceremony. Griselda's propriety of conduct was quite equal to that of Olivia Proudie; indeed, nothing could exceed the statuesque grace and fine aristocratic bearing with which she carried herself on the occasion. The three or four words which the service required of her she said with ease and dignity; there was neither sobbing nor crying to disturb the work or embarrass her friends, and she signed her name in the church books as "Griselda Grantly" without a tremor — and without a regret.

Mrs. Grantly kissed her and blessed her in the hall as she was about to step forward to her travelling carriage, leaning on her father's arm, and the child put up her face to her mother for a last whisper. "Mamma," she said, "I suppose Jane can put her hand at once on the moire antique when we reach Dover?" Mrs. Grantly smiled and nodded, and again blessed her child. There was not a tear shed — at least, not then — nor a sign of sorrow to cloud for a moment the gay splendour of the day. But the mother did bethink herself, in the solitude of her own room, of those last words, and did acknowledge a lack of something for which her heart had sighed. She had boasted to her sister that she had nothing to regret as to her daughter's education; but now, when she was alone after her success, did she feel that she could still support herself with that boast? For, be it known, Mrs. Grantly had a heart within her bosom and a faith within her heart. The world, it is true, had pressed upon her sorely with all its weight of accumulated clerical wealth, but it had not utterly crushed her — not her, but only her child. For the sins of the father, are they not visited on the third and fourth generation?

But if any such feeling of remorse did for awhile mar the fulness of Mrs. Grantly's joy, it was soon dispelled by the perfect success of her daughter's married life. At the end of the autumn the bride and bridegroom returned from their tour, and it was evident to all the circle at Hartletop Priory that Lord Dumbello was by no means dissatisfied with his bargain. His wife had been admired everywhere to the top of his bent. All the world at Ems, and at Baden, and at Nice, had been stricken by the stately beauty of the young viscountess. And then, too, her manner, style, and high dignity of demeanour altogether supported the reverential feeling which her grace and form at first inspired. She never derogated from her husband's honour by the fictitious liveliness of gossip, or allowed any one to forget the peeress in the woman. Lord Dumbello soon found that his reputation for discretion was quite safe in her hands, and that there were no lessons as to conduct in which it was necessary that he should give instruction.

Before the winter was over she had equally won the hearts of all the circle at Hartletop Priory. The duke was there and declared to the marchioness that Dumbello could not possibly have done better. "Indeed, I do not think he could," said the happy mother. "She sees all that she ought to see, and nothing that she ought not."

And then, in London, when the season came, all men sang all manner of praises in her favour, and Lord Dumbello was made aware that he was reckoned among the wisest of his age. He had married a wife who managed everything for him, who never troubled him, whom no woman disliked, and whom every man admired. As for feast of reason and for flow of soul, is it not a question whether any such flows and feasts are necessary between a man and his wife? How many men can truly assert that they ever enjoy connubial flows of soul, or that connubial feasts of reason are in their nature enjoyable? But a handsome woman at the head of your table, who knows how to dress, and how to sit, and how to get in and out of her carriage — who will not disgrace her lord by her ignorance, or fret him by her coquetry, or disparage him by her talent — how beautiful a thing it is! For my own part I think that Griselda Grantly was born to be the wife of a great English peer.

"After all, then," said Miss Dunstable, speaking of Lady Dumbello — she was Mrs. Thorne at this time — "after all, there is some truth in what our quaint latter-day philosopher tells us — 'Great are thy powers, O Silence!'"

The marriage of our old friends Dr. Thorne and Miss Dunstable was the third on the list, but that did not take place till the latter end of September. The lawyers on such an occasion had no inconsiderable work to accomplish, and though the lady was not coy, nor the gentleman slow, it was not found practicable to arrange an earlier wedding. The ceremony was performed at St. George's, Hanover Square, and was not brilliant in any special degree. London at the time was empty, and the few persons whose presence was actually necessary were imported from the country for the occasion. The bride was given away by Dr. Easyman, and the two bridesmaids were ladies who had lived with Miss Dunstable as companions. Young Mr. Gresham and his wife were there, as was also Mrs. Harold Smith, who was not at all prepared to drop her old friend in her new sphere of life.

"We shall call her Mrs. Thorne instead of Miss Dunstable, and I really think that that will be all the difference," said Mrs. Harold Smith.

To Mrs. Harold Smith that probably was all the difference, but it was not so to the persons most concerned.

According to the plan of life arranged between the doctor and his wife she was still to keep up her house in London, remaining there during such period of the season as she might choose, and receiving him when it might appear good to him to visit her; but he was to be the master in the country. A mansion at the Chase was to be built, and till such time as that was completed, they would keep on the old house at Greshamsbury. Into this, small as it was, Mrs. Thorne, — in spite of her great wealth, — did not disdain to enter. But subsequent circumstances changed their plans. It was found that Mr. Sowerby could not or would not live at Chaldicotes; and, therefore, in the second year of their marriage, that place was prepared for them.

They are now well known to the whole county as Dr. and Mrs. Thorne of Chaldicotes, — of Chaldicotes, in distinction to the well-known Thornes of Ullathorne in the eastern division. Here they live respected by their neighbours, and on terms of alliance both with the Duke of Omnium and with Lady Lufton.

"Of course those dear old avenues will be very sad to me," said Mrs. Harold Smith, when at the end of a London season she was invited down to Chaldicotes; and as she spoke she put her handkerchief up to her eyes.

"Well, dear, what can I do?" said Mrs. Thorne. "I can't cut them down; the doctor would not let me."

"Oh, no," said Mrs. Harold Smith, sighing; and in spite of her feelings she did visit Chaldicotes.

But it was October before Lord Lufton was made a happy man; — that is, if the fruition of his happiness was a greater joy than the anticipation of it. I will not say that the happiness of marriage is like the Dead Sea fruit, — an apple which, when eaten, turns to bitter ashes in the mouth. Such pretended sarcasm would be very false. Nevertheless, is it not the fact that the sweetest morsel of love's feast has been eaten, that the freshest, fairest blush of the flower has been snatched and has passed away, when the ceremony at the altar has been performed, and legal possession has been given? There is an aroma of love, an undefinable delicacy of flavour, which escapes and is gone before the church portal is left, vanishing with the maiden name, and incompatible with the solid comfort appertaining to the rank of wife. To love one's own spouse, and to be loved by her, is the ordinary lot of man, and is a duty exacted under penalties. But to be allowed to love youth and beauty that is not one's own — to know that one is loved by a soft being who still hangs cowering from the eye of the world as though her love were all but illicit — can it be that a man is made happy when a state of anticipation such as this is brought to a close? No; when the husband walks back from the altar, he has already swallowed the choicest dainties of his banquet. The beef and pudding of married life are then in store for him; — or perhaps only the bread and cheese. Let him take care lest hardly a crust remain, — or perhaps not a crust.

But before we finish, let us go back for one moment to the dainties, — to the time before the beef and pudding were served, — while Lucy was still at the parsonage, and Lord Lufton still staying at Framley Court. He had come up one morning, as was now frequently his wont, and, after a few minutes' conversation, Mrs. Robarts had left the room, — as not unfrequently on such occasions was her wont. Lucy was working and continued her work, and Lord Lufton for a moment or two sat looking at her; then he got up abruptly, and, standing before her, thus questioned her: —

"Lucy," said he.

"Well, what of Lucy now? Any particular fault this morning?"

"Yes, a most particular fault. When I asked you, here, in this room, on this very spot, whether it was possible that you should love me — why did you say that it was impossible?"

Lucy, instead of answering at the moment, looked down upon the carpet, to see if his memory were as good as hers. Yes; he was standing on the exact spot where he had stood before. No spot in all the world was more frequently clear before her own eyes.

"Do you remember that day, Lucy?" he said again.

"Yes, I remember it," she said.

"Why did you say it was impossible?"

"Did I say impossible?"

She knew that she had said so. She remembered how she had waited till he had gone, and that then, going to her own room, she had reproached herself with the cowardice of the falsehood. She had lied to him then; and now — how was she punished for it?

"Well, I suppose it was possible," she said.

"But why did you say so when you knew it would make me so miserable?"

"Miserable! nay, but you went away happy enough! I thought I had never seen you look better satisfied."

"Lucy!"

"You had done your duty, and had had such a lucky escape! What astonishes me is that you should have ever come back again. But the pitcher may go to the well once too often, Lord Lufton."

"But will you tell me the truth now?"

"What truth?"

"That day, when I came to you, — did you love me at all then?"

"We'll let bygones be bygones, if you please."

"But I swear you shall tell me. It was such a cruel thing to answer me as you did, unless you meant it. And yet you never saw me again till after my mother had been over for you to Mrs. Crawley's."

"It was absence that made me — care for you."

"Lucy, I swear I believe you loved me then."

"Ludovic, some conjuror must have told you that."

She was standing as she spoke, and, laughing at him, she held up her hands and shook her head. But she was now in his power, and he had his revenge, — his revenge for her past falsehood and her present joke. How could he be more happy when he was made happy by having her all his own, than he was now?

And in these days there again came up that petition as to her riding — with very different result now than on that former occasion. There were ever so many objections, then. There was no habit, and Lucy was — or said that she was — afraid; and then, what would Lady Lufton say? But now Lady Lufton thought it would be quite right; only were they quite sure about the horse? Was Ludovic certain that the horse had been ridden by a lady? And Lady Meredith's habits were dragged out as a matter of course, and one of them chipped and snipped and altered, without any compunction. And as for fear, there could be no bolder horsewoman than Lucy Robarts. It was quite clear to all Framley that riding was the very thing for her. "But I never shall be happy, Ludovic, till you have got a horse properly suited for her," said Lady Lufton.

And then, also, came the affair of her wedding garments, of her *trousseau*, — as to which I cannot boast that she showed capacity or steadiness at all equal to that of Lady Dumbello. Lady Lufton, however, thought it a very serious matter; and as, in her opinion, Mrs. Robarts did not go about it with sufficient energy, she took the matter mainly into her own hands, striking Lucy dumb by her frowns and nods, deciding on everything herself, down to the very tags of the boot-ties.

"My dear, you really must allow me to know what I am about;" and Lady Lufton patted her on the arm as she spoke. "I did it all for Justinia, and she never had reason to regret a single thing that I bought. If you'll ask her, she'll tell you so."

Lucy did not ask her future sister-in-law, seeing that she had no doubt whatever as to her future mother-in-law's judgment on the articles in question. Only the money! And what could she want with six dozen pocket-handkerchiefs all at once? There was no question of Lord Lufton's going out as governor-general to India! But twelve dozen pocket-handkerchiefs had not been too many for Griselda's imagination.

And Lucy would sit alone in the drawing-room at Framley Court, filling her heart with thoughts of that evening when she had first sat there. She had then resolved, painfully, with inward tears, with groanings of her spirit, that she was wrongly placed in being in that company. Griselda Grantly had been there, quite at her ease, petted by Lady Lufton, admired by Lord Lufton; while she had retired out of sight, sore at heart, because she felt herself to be no fit companion to those around her. Then he had come to her, making matters almost worse by talking to her, bringing the tears into her eyes by his good-nature, but still wounding her by the feeling that she could not speak to him at her ease.

But things were at a different pass with her now. He had chosen her — her out of all the world, and brought her there to share with him his own home, his own honours, and all that he had to give. She was the apple of his eye, and the pride of his heart. And the stern mother, of whom she had stood so much in awe, who at first had passed her by as a thing not to be noticed, and had then sent out to her that she might be warned to keep herself aloof, now hardly knew in what way she might sufficiently show her love, regard, and solicitude.

I must not say that Lucy was not proud in these moments — that her heart was not elated at these thoughts. Success does beget pride, as failure begets shame. But her pride was of that sort which is in no way disgraceful to either man or woman, and was accompanied by pure true love, and a full resolution to do her duty in that state of life to which it had pleased her God to call her. She did rejoice greatly to think that she had been chosen, and not Griselda. Was it possible that having loved she should not so rejoice, or that, rejoicing, she should not be proud of her love?

They spent the whole winter abroad, leaving the dowager Lady Lufton to her plans and preparations for their reception at Framley Court; and in the following spring they appeared in London, and there set up their staff. Lucy had some inner tremblings of the spirit, and quiverings about the heart, at thus beginning her duty before the great world, but she said little or nothing to her husband on the matter. Other women had done as much before her time, and by courage had gone through with it. It would be dreadful enough, that position in her own house with lords and ladies bowing to her, and stiff members of Parliament for whom it would be necessary to make small talk; but, nevertheless, it was to be endured. The time came, and she did endure it. The time came, and before the first six weeks were over she found that it was easy enough. The lords and ladies got into their proper places and talked to her about ordinary matters in a way that made no effort necessary, and the members of Parliament were hardly more stiff than the clergymen she had known in the neighbourhood of Framley.

She had not been long in town before she met Lady Dumbello. At this interview also she had to overcome some little inward emotion. On the few occasions on which she had met Griselda Grantly at Framley they had not much progressed in friendship, and Lucy had felt that she had been despised by the rich beauty. She also in her turn had disliked, if she had not despised, her rival. But how would it be now? Lady Dumbello could hardly despise her, and yet it did not seem possible that they should meet as friends. They did meet, and Lucy came forward with a pretty eagerness to give her hand to Lady Lufton's late favourite. Lady Dumbello smiled slightly — the same old smile which had come across her face when they two had been first introduced in the Framley drawing-room; the same smile without the variation of a line, — took the offered hand, muttered a word or two, and then receded. It was exactly as she had done before. She had never despised Lucy Robarts. She had accorded to the parson's sister the amount of cordiality with which she usually received her acquaintance; and now she could do no more for the peer's wife. Lady Dumbello and Lady Lufton have known each other ever since, and have occasionally visited at each other's houses, but the intimacy between them has never gone beyond this.

The dowager came up to town for about a month, and while there was contented to fill a second place. She had no desire to be the great lady in London. But then came the trying period when they commenced their life together at Framley Court. The elder lady formally renounced her place at the top of the table, — formally persisted in renouncing it though Lucy with tears implored her to resume it. She said also, with equal formality — repeating her determination over and over again to Mrs. Robarts with great energy — that she would in no respect detract by interference of her own from the authority of the proper mistress of the house; but, nevertheless, it is well known to every one at Framley that old Lady Lufton still reigns paramount in the parish.

"Yes, my dear; the big room looking into the little garden to the south was always the nursery; and if you ask my advice, it will still remain so. But, of course, any room you please —"

And the big room looking into the little garden to the south is still the nursery at Framley Court.

THE END.